Simon Caley was born in Ceylon in the 1950s. He still lives in Wales and continues to keep a close eye on the activities of William Phalarope.

WILLIAM'S WAY TOO

SIMON CALEY

Copyright © 2014 Simon Caley

The moral right of the author has been asserted.

Apart from any fair dealing for the purposes of research or private study, or criticism or review, as permitted under the Copyright, Designs and Patents Act 1988, this publication may only be reproduced, stored or transmitted, in any form or by any means, with the prior permission in writing of the publishers, or in the case of reprographic reproduction in accordance with the terms of licences issued by the Copyright Licensing Agency. Enquiries concerning reproduction outside those terms should be sent to the publishers.

Matador
9 Priory Business Park,
Wistow Road, Kibworth Beauchamp,
Leicestershire. LE8 0RX
Tel: (+44) 116 279 2299
Fax: (+44) 116 279 2277
Email: books@troubador.co.uk
Web: www.troubador.co.uk/matador

ISBN 978 1783065 363

British Library Cataloguing in Publication Data.
A catalogue record for this book is available from the British Library.

Printed and bound in the UK by TJ International, Padstow, Cornwall
Typeset in 12pt Bembo by Troubador Publishing Ltd, Leicester, UK

Matador is an imprint of Troubador Publishing Ltd

Dedicated to Maxine, Ashley and Georgia.

My thanks to my daughter Ashley for all her help; and for not carrying out her threat if I ever bothered her again.

WILLIAM'S WAY TOO

Hello, and a very good day to you. Still sucking in air I hope, and still treating those two impostors both the same. Hats off to one and all for doing so, as Life has enough harbingers of gloom without adding to their rapidly swelling numbers.

Me? I'm still in the process of regaining my equilibrium after that sojourn to the city of San Francisco. What a place, eh! Uplifting, edifying, and full of surprises: and, as if pleased with the character-building effect that the experience had on yours truly, it seems that Providence hasn't quite finished singling me out for yet another slice of the blooming stuff. I really must remove the label on my back that reads 'Please Annoy'.

My latest *causa mali*? Have I ever mentioned my sibling? A sister by the name of Lynne? Yes, I'm sure I have. Well, the dear old thing has received a bit of bad news on the gynaecological front. Nothing too serious, I hasten to add; just a touch of whatever it is that can affect ladies of her age and cause certain inconveniences. I never like to delve too deeply into such matters; as I don't really want to know the details and I certainly wouldn't understand them even if I did. Matters of such a feminine nature are best left where they are, if you ask me.

I often think that Nature works – when you're considering the female construction arrangements that is – rather along the lines of an oil painting: you should only admire the *objet d'art* when it is finished. But you then have to choose the correct vantage point from which to appreciate the work. Stand too far away when observing and everything tends to be out of focus; stand too close and the brush-strokes can coarsen the image. However, if you find the correct distance you will seldom be disappointed.

I would, however, advise discretion if you try to employ this methodology when embarking on a new relationship. Using your fingers to make a square, then squinting through it and pulling faces can cause the object of your affection to feel a level of disquiet: especially if you are in the bedroom at the time. Women seem to take offence very easily.

But putting medical histories and inter-personal techniques to one side, I received a phone call from the afore-mentioned to say that she was going to be spending a few days between hospital sheets and would I care to have a small guest stay with me during that time.

"What!" I can recall exclaiming. You see, when a fellow has been on his own for a bit, he gets used to being able to do what he likes when he likes: and a guest, no matter what size, does tend to put the kibosh on that happy state of affairs.

"I want you to look after Mirabella whilst I have various bits and pieces sorted out."

"You want me to do *what*?"

"Look after Mirabella."

"............"

"William? Are you still there?"

"Yes. Just."

"Good. Now listen carefully. I am going to be out of commission for a while and I need someone to look after my daughter. I have decided that you are to be that someone."

"*Me*! Me? Oh. Well what about that carbuncle that I've seen wandering about your domicile?"

"Do you mean Geremy?"

"I believe that might well be the appellation ascribed."

"Utterly impossible. I can only rely on him with one of the issue; and as Mirabella made some noises about preferring to entrust her *bene esse* in your direction, I decided to ignore my better judgement. So I shall be bringing her down to you tomorrow."

"*Tomorrow!*"

"About midday."

"*Midday* tomorrow!"

"Is there a problem with that?"

"I… that is… if… er… well… in order to…"

"Oh do stop dithering, William. Your niece is coming to stay with you for a while, and that is all there is to it."

"But, um; shouldn't she be at school? Or somewhere else? Anywhere else?"

"For nine months of the year, it would most assuredly be at school. However, you will no doubt be delighted to discover, Mirabella is presently excused for the duration of her summer holiday."

"The *entire* holiday?"

"That is the usual arrangement."

"Isn't that... fortunate."

"Indeed it is."

And there it was: or rather *she* was – gone. Before I had replaced the receiver back on its cradle, I saw my *laisser-allez* walking off into the distance without so much as a backward glance. What was a fellow to do?

As I may have mentioned before, Mirabella is an individual upon whom the Gods of Mischief smiled the day she was born: and they almost certainly did the same for her twin brother. As blatant a pair of malingering miscreants as one could ever wish to set eyes upon: and now one of them was going to be spending some time with me.

Perhaps Byron was experiencing a similar incident with that child Harold when he wrote 'Let joy be unconfined'. Perhaps, however, he was simply flexing his irony muscles.

Anyway, the long and short of it all was that the result of some conjugal unpleasantness between said sister and her lawfully-wedded boil was going to be spending a while *chez moi*. A thousand and one visions of ecstasy did not immediately spring into view, I don't mind admitting. Actually, none made an appearance.

The next thought that came knocking on the door to my grey matter was how long is 'a while'? Was it going to be my sister's 'a while' or my 'a while'? Those two never seem to bear much relationship to one another. I mean to say, you only have to think about the occasions a man has asked a woman how long she is going to be, and on getting the answer 'A while', he never knows whether there is only enough time to have a glass of restorative or sufficient time to go and play a round of golf. It really is most bewildering.

I believe that it has something to with brain hemispheres. Those belonging to the male of the species happen to be larger and a jolly sight better organised when it comes to matters of time and space. The parking of cars illustrates this in a very satisfactory manner. Speaking of which, why do people describe parking their car between two others at the kerbside as being 'parallel parking'? If my memory of circuit diagrams is still functioning – bearing in mind that my cognitive powers used to trip over themselves in their haste to evade such eyesores – I thought that such an arrangement was known as being 'in series'. Wasn't being 'in parallel' used to describe items that were alongside one another? Rather like the lines in a barcode? Is there a clue in the word 'parallel' I wonder?

Women's brains, so I am led to believe, have the upper hand when it comes to matters of speech: which probably goes a long way to explain their proclivity for making the most use of it.

So was I to be burdened with a guest for a matter of hours or a matter of weeks? The thought of the latter option didn't bring much in the way of felicity, I have to say. However, I reminded myself of the adage about how a visit always brings pleasure – if not the arrival, then the departure. Small consolation I suppose.

The following noon arrived with undue haste, and before I knew it I was hearing the chimes inspired by a certain Johan E. Jonasson, and realised that it was probably a bit late for shouting through the letter-box that I had recently, and quite unexpectedly, contracted Lassa Fever.

I did try very hard not to let my dismay show when I opened the front door; but I do seem to have the sort of facial muscles that often want to display even my innermost thoughts. Did you know that it takes more muscles to smile than it does to frown? It's twelve as opposed to eleven: ammunition to use against people who try to cheer up those of us who enjoy a good scowl.

"Have you ever thought of using Botox?" my sister enquired as she breezed in.

"*Botox*? Why?" I replied.

"Because if your brow was any more furrowed you would be able to plant potatoes there."

"Oh."

"Do I take it that you are not wholly pleased to see us?"
"No."
"No!"
"Yes."
"What!"
"What?"

It is at this point that I have to admit that when it comes to the use of intentionally implied double-negatives I am often at a complete loss. So much of a loss in fact, that I can even end up being unsure what one is; but I seem to blunder into them with amazing frequency all the same.

I'm sure you know the sort of thing I mean. How would you answer (assuming that you possess an 'X' and a 'Y' chromosome and not 'XX') should someone ask you "Is it not true that you are a man?" What are you going to say? "Yes, it is not true that I am a man," or "No, it is not true that I am a man." All very confusing, and no mistake.

"Well?" my sister continued.
"Well what?"
"Are you pleased to see us?"
"Yes; of course I am. Absolutely delighted," I said, trying to work out if the look I got from the small person as she followed her mother had ever been definitively classified.

"I am not particularly impressed by your sense of enthusiasm, but it will have to do as I am in need of various pokes and prods whilst under an anaesthetic of the general variety: and Mirabella is in need of a *loco parentis* for the duration. You, dear William, were the first out of the bag of possibles."

"The *first?*"
"Well, maybe not the 'first': but close enough for my purposes."
"How gratifying."
"And you are as useless at disguising your displeasure with your voice as you are with your facial muscles. So perhaps you would be good enough to go to my car and fetch Mirabella's impedimenta. You surely cannot expect a woman with my current disposition to struggle."

I could, without fear of disappointment, easily expect anyone with my sister's disposition, current or otherwise, to hoist a packhorse on to her shoulders and gambol up a one-in-three slope with all the ease of an unencumbered ibex. But realising that to question her assertion would have been effort spent in vain, I trundled out to her voiture to collect the required luggage.

As you no doubt already know, I am a reasonable sort of fellow; and being such, I like to take a reasonable number of requisites whenever I go to stay anywhere reasonable. Furthermore, I always endeavour to keep the number of my valises down to a minimum; certainly three or fewer: so you will understand the pronounced jolt I received when I opened the boot of my sister's car.

There are several other relevant factors that I ought to bring to your attention. Firstly, my niece is in the region of fourteen years old; secondly, I was under the impression that her stay was only likely to be a couple of days; and thirdly, my sister's means of transport is an old Austin Healey Sprite – of the 'frog-eyed' variety – and I had always been of the opinion that the boot area in them was simply for show.

So, to return to the rather gasted nature in which my flabber currently found itself, I discovered sufficient belongings to suggest that a netball team was intending to play its next game in my back garden. How, I asked myself, can a young girl need all those things? Perhaps my database on females needs updating.

Anyway, with commendable stoicism, I manfully struggled on and brought all the items into the house.

"Is that the lot?" my sister asked when I had placed what could well have been the entire Samsonite Spring Collection in the middle of my lounge carpet.

"I sincerely hope so," I replied, scarcely able to disguise my facetious tone.

"Good."

"Quite."

"Now, listen here William; I have made a list of the comestibles that Mirabella likes and dislikes, and the times of day at which she is to be proffered same. I shall be most grateful if you stray from the designated path on as few occasions as possible. Mirabella is a growing child, and she must be nurtured as such."

I can only imagine – from the rather curious (or do I mean aggressive?) look that the aforementioned minor slung in my direction – that my eyeballs must have been very close to falling out of their sockets. They certainly felt that way.

"So I don't want to hear any tales of you trying to force-feed my little darling with all manner of fatty unsaturates. Do you comprehend?"

"Fatty unsaturates? I have no – "

"And we are still unsure if the wee thing might be developing a lactose intolerance."

"A *lactose* intolerance?" I could possibly have believed an *amicus humani generis* intolerance: but lactose? "Oh."

"And another thing; there is to be no watching of unsuitable television programmes: watershed or no watershed. I am justifiably sure that being a person of the male persuasion, and living on your own, you are quite likely to have developed a habit of watching entertainment of a less than wholesome nature. I do not wish for my daughter to be exposed to such influences. Is that clear?"

"Less than wholesome? I have absolutely no idea what – "

"I also wish to insist that Mirabella has a minimum of eight hours sleep each night."

"But that's about the same sort of – "

"Right; now that we have sorted out those details, I shall bid you both a fond farewell."

Said sibling of mine then embraced the fruit of her loins, dashed out to her car and roared off. Now don't get me wrong, I have little against women of a certain age cavorting around in cars of a sporting nature; but I cannot prevent images of Isadora Duncan from perambulating through my consciousness.

For the pedantic aficionados amongst you, yes, I know that Miss Duncan was in a red (Lynne's is green) Bugatti (Lynne's is an Austin-Healey), that both her children were born to different fathers and both out of wedlock (admittedly I have been known to describe my sister's progeny as falling within that latter category), and I have never heard Lynne bellow "Adieu, mes amis. Je vais à la gloire," before buzzing off anywhere: but the images keep pushing their way to the front all the same.

So there I was, left alone with a young female who had been foisted upon my hospitality for an unspecified period of time. Not a happy state of affairs, I don't mind saying.

"Uncle William…"

"Ye-es."

"Have you got wi-fi here?"

"Have I got what? Wi-fi?"

"Yes, wi-fi. You know, like, so I can use broadband on my smart phone."

At this point I feel obliged to confess to probably having been in another building when they were handing out enthusiasm towards and the understanding of modern technology; and only managing to join the party as they were tidying up. Yes, I had heard of Broadband and knew that it had something to do with the amount of information flowing per second. I believe an analogy is to be found, if you imagine data as being water, by thinking of the old 'dial-up' system as being a standard 1/2 garden hose that only allowed a gallon of data to arrive in thirty seconds. Broadband, apparently, would be the equivalent of a 4 pipe, and allow a gallon of data through in five seconds.

A nice description, but it doesn't really explain away the fact that the phone wire remains the same size. Perhaps it's my cognitive powers that need enlarging; or perhaps I should read up about sine waves, mixing signals with radio frequencies and something called time division multiplexing. Anyway, analogies notwithstanding, the answer was still the same.

"No."

"Then, like, how am I meant to keep in touch with my friends?"

Am I the only person to get irritated by the way that those born after 1985 seem unable to complete a sentence without using the word 'like'? Exempli gratia, "I like went there and it was like the most coolest thing ever". I shan't get started on tautological superlatives at this point, but merely ask if what they meant was that it (whatever 'it' was) wasn't actually the coolest thing ever, but only closely resembled it?

"You can always use the telephone," I replied, pointing at the item resting on the table next to my armchair. "I believe that speech is a very good way of communicating."

"Yeah, but I can't, like, access my facebook and stuff on it; can I?"

Whilst I may have a certain sympathy towards Ned Ludd and the activities of his followers, I do try to embrace as many of the modern-day appurtenances as I can. I am all for labour-saving devices; so long as they don't turn out to be imagination-saving devices as well. Teach a child to read, I say; instead of how to work the DVD machine.

I can muster no enthusiasm whatsoever for the likes of My-face and Whitter, or whatever they're called, where people feel compelled to let the world know all the fascinating details (or do I mean mind-numbing minutiae?) about such things as how many slices of toast they had for breakfast. Listen: I'm sure I can hear someone yelling "Get a Life" to all those who spend their days trawling through other people's insipid chronicles; or living vicariously through soap operas.

"So?"

"So, like, they're going to wonder if anything's the matter with me."

You'll be pleased to hear that I refrained from stating the obvious. It would seem that some of the interpersonal skills and refinements which I absorbed in San Francisco were still in working order; and that making a critical remark in the first two minutes of a social encounter had been put in my 'might do' rather than my 'must do' list.

"Didn't you tell your friends where you were going?"

"Yeah; and that's like why they'll be worried."

Have you ever wondered why human beings (well, some of them anyway) were imbued with a conscience, and generally tend to baulk when it comes to carrying out a justifiable act of homicide? What is it that they sometimes call a conscience? An inner voice that makes you wonder if someone's looking? A baffling state of affairs, and no mistake: I did, however, manage a clearly aggrieved 'harrumph'.

"I guess I'll have to use a 3G connection."

"I guess you will."

"What's the mobile phone signal like round here?"

"Practically non-existent." I would have said something about it varying with the time of day, the weather, and whether the sheep were standing up or lying down; but I had a feeling that I would have done little more than bring forth a look of unconcealed incredulity from my ward.

There then followed one of those silences that sound awfully loud; and which was finally broken by the question "Can I have a drink please?"

"Of...?"

"I don't know. What have you got?"

As much as I would have welcomed the chance of sedating the furuncle with a couple of stiff ones, I declined the opportunity. You see, I have read several theses on the subject of the damage that can be caused to young, and developing, minds by the overuse of alcoholic beverages; and I reasoned that any youngster already saddled with inheriting a range of genes from the merdivorous article who planted some motile male gametes within the uterine whereabouts of her mother could well do without any further impediments.

"Um... water."

"Water!"

"Yes. You know, that clear liquid that comes out of taps."

"I know what water is."

"Good. So, would you like some?"

I was going to point out that, because I don't trust the water suppliers with what they have to say about there being no possibility of heavy metal poisoning, I always filter the tap water and keep it in a jug in the fridge. But, as I had a feeling that it wouldn't have made a jot of difference, I decided not to.

"Haven't you got any, like, fizzy drinks?"

"*Like* fizzy drinks? What do you mean by 'like' fizzy drinks? Is that something that is similar *to* a fizzy drink?"

"I mean a fizzy drink."

"Well; I have soda water, dry ginger ale and some tonic water."

"No cola?"

"No."

A small discourse then took place during which it was unilaterally decided that a quick trip to a local store would rectify the shortfall in the cola department – and one or two other comestible imbalances that were sure to arise. I nearly embarked on a homily about the dangers I had read concerning the 'sugar-free' varieties. You know, the problems concerning a substance that goes by the name of Aspartame. Ghastly stuff, by all accounts; and not something you want to introduce into your body on a regular basis: or ever, if truth be told. So, after I quickly decided that then would not be a good time to begin discussing the matter, off we went.

I have to acknowledge that I am somewhat deficient in the 'shopping-with-a-fourteen-year-old-girl' line of experience; and I also have to say that I am the kind of purchaser who knows what he wants before he reaches the emporium. None of that browsing and impulse buying stuff for me: indeed not.

To my way of thinking, it does not matter one iota upon which shelf the proprietor decides to place his items; or whether he feels the need to pile all the heavy stuff near the entrance in order to convince me that I need a trolley; or how much 'baking bread' smell he wafts across the car park. Also, I object to the way that shops keep moving their goods around – presumably in the hope of exposing customers to other goods as they traipse round looking for what they want. In fact, all that particular tactic does for me is make me infuriated and cause me to forego half of what I went in for. I know what I want, and that is what I get: unless, of course, I happen to be with a fourteen year-old girl.

Now who on earth ever thought up that concept? And what mindset came up with the idea of placing capriciousness in one so young? Was there no way of making some kind of provision for the female of the species to go into hibernation from, say, the age of five to about the late-twenties? Maybe even introduce some sort of 'on appro' clause. You know, if the item under consideration isn't exactly what was required, you can send it back – either to keep in storage until a future date or, maybe, be allowed to exchange it for a different model. Do you know, I think that system might work. However, I also think that may well be sufficient griping from me: for the time being anyway.

So, my car having been parked in a sensible fashion (*id est* reversed into the space rather than – as is very popular with the ladies – going in front first) Mirabella and I entered the supermarket. As I may have mentioned previously, I am not an advocate of the trolley: neither in the principle of being seen pushing one, nor in my inability to do so without knocking over every corner display that I happen to pass. So, a basket it was.

My mind then drifted back to the few occasions that I accompanied my mother on a trip to the shops. I don't seem to recall there being any of the present range of 'superstores' that so blight the modern landscape: there were just shops. In fact, if my memory is working correctly, the largest stores were the likes of Grants, Alders, and a place called Gorringes (where I had to go in order to get my prep-school uniform). I am sure that there were many other large purveyors of essentials, but they have chosen not to linger within my memory banks: apart from a place where you could exchange 'Green Shield Stamps' for goods.

I remember that Gorringes had a restaurant which allowed you – for the princely sum of ten shillings – to eat as much as you could shovel down your oesophagus during the luncheon interval. I also remember a certain school-boy, about eight years old, who once ate so much that he could hardly get up from the table; and then had to spend nearly half an hour in the 'washrooms' deciding whether or not he was going to be reacquainted with all the meat and roast potatoes that had recently slid over his epiglottis. Small wonder that his recently ordered school trousers didn't fit as well as they should have; and small wonder that his mother gave him a clip round the ear, adding that she would be sure to bring a trough along next time.

Anyway, off we trundled, basket in hand and, so I thought, eager to collect the list of requirements; but the little madam decided that it would be necessary to tarry awhile near the confectionery aisle: and tarry awhile she did. In my day the choice of sweets was a comparatively small one; and included the likes of spangles, pear drops, pineapple chunks, gob-stoppers, blackjacks, fruit-gums, and some chewy articles known as American hard-gums: all served from behind the counter of the school tuck-shop by a rather hard-faced woman known as Mrs Ackrington.

We were allowed up to a total of one shilling and sixpence worth of goodies every week, so we had to be able to accurately do mental arithmetic as we went along: and woe betide any boy who got his sums wrong, as he then forfeited all that he had chosen. Not quite sure how modern-day school children would fare under those conditions, but I expect that dental caries would be greatly reduced; and quite a lot of childhood obesity as well.

Speaking of which, why aren't those parents who allow their offspring to become 'inflated' reprimanded in some way? If a child in a parent's care is allowed to develop a deleterious, and easily avoided, health condition, then I would have thought that said parent should be charged with child abuse. At the very least they ought to be –

"Uncle William." My thoughts were then interrupted. "Can I have some of those please?"

"Those what?"

"Those."

"Those?"

"Yes."

"What are they?"

"Flying saucers. They're great."

"No doubt."

"You can have one if you like."

"Really? How very kind of you."

"So is it okay if I, like, put some in your basket?"

Being the soft touch that I usually am, in the basket they went: as did a CD by someone called Shall-I-Twang (or something very like that) and several bottles of a well-known cola. I bought myself a newspaper and, having paid for the sundries, was in the process of beating a pretty rapid retreat back to my car when that small voice piped up once again.

"Uncle William…"

"Yes…"

"Mummy asked me to tell you that I need a pair of jeans."

"Did she indeed."

"Yes."

"Your point being?"

"Can you take me to buy some? Please."

"Didn't they sell any back there?" I asked, pointing behind me.

"Yes; but only cheap and nasty ones. We need to like, go to a proper shop."

"Once again I feel the need to enquire about the use of that preposition. Do you mean that we don't actually need to go to a proper shop? That we simply give the impression of doing so?"

"What?"

"You said that we need to 'like' go to a proper shop. I just want your intentions clarified."

"When I say 'like', it's just the modern way kids speak."

"Really. So do you want to go to a shop or not?"

"Uh yair-air. Der-err."

Was something introduced into the drinking-water supplies around the 1990s? I know that there has been a disagreeable plan to contaminate our drinking water with a poison that is known as fluoride; on the pretext of strengthening the developing permanent teeth in children. But "Ha, ha!" I say to that; and thrice "Ha!"

To my knowledge, fluoride – in the exact quantity – might do a bit of good to the enamel in those teeth actually in the process of being formed: which is roughly between the ages of 1 and 16 years old. But I stress that it must be administered in the precise amount. This would probably be possible if your children lived under laboratory conditions and never, for example, swallowed toothpaste.

In the wrong, and continuous, amounts, apart from mottling the teeth (fluorosis) it can do untold damage to the rest of the body: brain included. Then apart from the fact that – Actually, I'm not going to bombard you with information about fluoride as you can always go and look it up on the Internet. Just prepare yourself for a shock!

"So how about that one?"

I looked in the direction that a small index finger was pointing, and saw a façade that looked remarkably similar to the one in which I had once met a certain Jocelyn Forsopition.

"Ah," I managed, as my mandible headed in a southerly direction.

"Can we?"

"Jeans, you say."

"Yes. Please."

After I had placed our supermarket purchases in my car, it was with a great deal of consternation and hesitancy that I followed my young charge into the requested establishment. Goodness me! Jeans indeed!

Obviously there must have been a change in the definition of the trousers made from material that originally came from Nimes (de Nimes), and whose name derived from the fact that they looked very similar to the trousers worn by Italian sailors in Genoa.

My first reaction was that whoever was responsible for devising the collection of clobber that assaulted my visual organs when we entered must have been suffering from Munchausen's syndrome by proxy. I had seen trousers on tramps that looked in better condition. Some of them even looked as though tramps had already been wearing them. They had worn patches, tears, and loose threads hanging out in several places: absolutely unbelievable. How the shop dared to put clothes in such a state of disrepair on display – never mind try to sell them – quite escaped me. I suppose it really underlines the power of suggestive advertisements and the fashion gullibility of many consumers.

My second reaction was that we had, unwittingly, stumbled into the wardrobe suppliers for a local drama group's production of the Rocky Horror Show. Whichever would prove to be correct, I instinctively knew that something was amiss and I tried to shepherd Mirabella away from the offending items.

"What are you doing?" she said. Actually 'yelled' might have been a better description, such was the cacophony going on in the background.

"Come away from there," I replied, anxious to protect her tender eyes.

"Don't do that."

"It's for your own good."

"No it isn't. Now leave me alone."

"I want you out of here."

"Well I don't want to leave here."

"Bad luck. You're coming with me."

"I don't want to."

"I want you to leave this shop, with me, now. If you do so, I shall… um… I shall buy you some more sweets."

It was right about then that I felt a hand the size, and weight, of a bag of cement land on my shoulder.

"Oi; what are you trying to do to that child?" asked a voice that seemed to emanate from a throat as deep as a mineshaft.

"What?"

"I said, what are you trying to do with that child?"

"That *child*? Oh, her. I'm trying to take her away from here."

"Is that right?"

"Yes."

"By offering 'er sweets?"

"Naturally."

"Are you 'er father?"

"Good lord no."

"No? Then where's 'er mother?"

"Her mother? At this very moment? I have no idea. Why?"

"And you say you're not this little girl's father."

"Perish the thought."

It was then that I happened to notice a rather strange metamorphosis occurring. My small companion had somehow – rather cleverly as it happens – managed to alter her appearance from the type of blighter you wouldn't trust on her own in a padded cell to a cherub in whose mouth you could confidently place a wafer-thin knob of New Zealand's finest for safe keeping.

"Really!"

"Yes." And then a couple of potential scenarios popped into my mind. "No… that is… I… oo-er…"

"Do you know this man?" asked the owner of the enormous hand.

"No sir."

"Right then, you: you'd better come along with me."

"I had better *what*! Mirabella, tell this Brobdingnagian here who I am."

"I don't know you: and I don't know what you're talking about."

"I beg your pardon!"

"Like I said, you had better come with me," the ogre growled.

"Now look here; this lump of detritus is my niece."

"This lump of what?"

"Detritus. From the Latin *detritus*; which is the perfect participle passive of the verb *detero*. Meaning to rub away."

"Eh?"

"I am simply trying to say that this child resembles that stuff left behind when you have been rubbing something."

"You've been rubbing something?"

"What?"

"Are you saying that you've been rubbing something? What? Against 'er?"

"What are you talking about?" Honestly, I think it would have been easier trying to explain to a goldfish what makes some irrational numbers transcendental. Well, apart from the obvious problem – the fact that I know a smaller than infinitesimal amount about fractions and finite equations. "Now listen to me, my man," I continued anyway. "I am trying to convey to you that this child is my niece."

"Is that true, miss?"

"No," was the plaintive reply.

"What! Just you wait until your mother hears about this."

"My mother is dead."

And then the little oik turned on the lachrymal glands with such aplomb that even I began to feel sorry for her. However, the Phalaropes are not known for anything if not for their ability to maintain their bearings when under the sternest of pressures; so I ploughed ahead in my best stentorian tones.

"Now, you Lilliputian larrikin; just tell this paid-up member of the Nephalim Society here that you know me and that – by the greatest of travesties – we happen to be related."

"But I don't know you. And you're scaring me."

"Scaring you! You little – "

"That's enough of that, feller. You're coming with me."

"What! No, you've got this all wrong. You've only got to – "

And so it came to pass that I was grabbed by the collar and frogmarched off to some office, whilst that confounded waste of good skin stood and smirked. It took nearly half an hour before my dear niece decided that perhaps she did know me after all. Coincidentally, just about the same amount of time it took her to work out that in the absence of Uncle William she would more than likely end up spending some time in the care of the social services; and not even someone with her twisted mind would have wanted that.

Whilst I'm on the subject of those certain 'services'; are they, after whatever the most recent bout of inexcusable errors happens to be, still bleating on about how 'lessons must be learned'? It does make me wonder how the people in charge ever got to be put there. Actually, it doesn't really. I think we all have a pretty good idea. Anyway.

"Look here," I said, as we wandered back to the car, "that was a bit of a nasty trick to play on me."

"I'm sorry, Uncle William. I'm not sure what happened. It must have been, like, the shock of that man grabbing you. He was well scary, wasn't he?"

"So why did you tell him that *I* was scaring you?"

"I just got confused. You know how it is; right?"

"Do I? Well... that is... I..."

Yes, I know I should have laid down the law and made it quite clear that gentlemen of my age and bearing have little truck with such juvenile shenanigans; but it is frightfully testing when you are looking into a pair of sparkling baby-blues. Really it is.

I don't know what sort of views you hold on the possibility of a life after this one; but should such an event occur, I know that I intend to go straight to the Main Man and try to elicit answers to certain questions.

For a start, "If You are inventing a species that is supposed to be in Your image and so forth, and You want them to reproduce with hybrid vigour (sexually, that is, rather than asexually) on a regular basis, why did You design them in such a way that they have so little in common?"

To a simple-minded fellow like me, it would be rather a good idea – at the blueprint stage – to have opted for compatible versions. You know, make them similar in tastes and outlooks: the type of individuals who would want to share an afternoon fishing or shopping, rather than spend the time chucking plates at each other. A great deal of trouble would have been avoided: or perhaps the Main Man is a bit of a divorce lawyer at heart.

I think my second question would be "Why, when You started with a blank sheet of paper, did You arrange things so that (to go back to the reproductive phases) the male of the species is at his most energetic about the age of nineteen whilst the female gets there around the age of forty?"

Thirdly, "Why did You decide that the female of the species would need about thirty minutes to realise 'satisfaction' during the reproduction activities, whilst the male only needs about thirty seconds?"

All very peculiar, I'm sure you will agree. Then my fourth enquiry would be "Can You please show me the way to the reference library?"

Now that's a place I would dearly like to visit. I can imagine many an hour spent sifting through articles on matters such as 'Who shot Kennedy?' 'What happened at Dyatlov Pass?' 'What was the Voynich Manuscript all about?' 'If the post-mortem showed that Mary Jo Copechnik suffocated rather than drowned, how did the driver who left her in the car get away without being prosecuted?' and 'Why did Rosalind (my first love, by the way) give me the elbow for a certain blister whose name escapes me?' All very weighty matters indeed.

So there you have it. One half of the species has – on the whole – got his head screwed on properly; and the other half has – on the whole – got the ability to change her mind with infuriating regularity. Makes me wonder how humans have lasted as long as we have.

Anyway, back to the matter of my wayward niece who was due to spend an indefinite amount of time with me; and the fact that I may well require psychiatric therapy by the end of it. What was my best course of action going to be? Especially as all thoughts of chastisement seem to dissolve when faced with a phizog that might well have inspired a certain M. Buonarroti to rustle up a female version to match his statue of David.

Mirabella meets Uncle Douglas.

By the third day of Mirabella's enforced billeting with me, I could feel that a sense of ennui was beginning to materialise. Not on my part, I hasten to add; as I was born with a psyche that allows me to sit still for prolonged periods without feeling the need to move any muscle that wasn't under the control of my autonomic nervous system. I might well have been playing hookey when I should have been attending lessons in understanding body language, but I generally know when someone is getting restless through inactivity.

Remarks such as "I'm bored" and "What are we going to do today?" seem to regularly crop up. I know that some people wouldn't spot such signals, but I seem to be rather sensitive to them. What to do about it, of course, is another matter entirely.

I can spend endless hours with my proboscis stuck in a good tome: not for me the flat line on an EEG when the day fails to provide external stimulation. Give me a book with a good storyline and a satisfactory denouement, and I'll happily spend a rainy Friday turning the pages, and going to all the places that the writer wanted me to visit. Splendid things, books; and reading them, I feel, should be made compulsory in all schools.

These days, unfortunately, the standard of teaching appears to fall a long way short of what it was in my day: and I don't think that is just my opinion either. I can recall a newspaper headline that told of how one third of school-leavers couldn't read, another third couldn't write, and the remaining half couldn't add up. This fact was then underlined when the paper printed a copy of an 1898 exam for 11-year-olds.

There were questions concerning Latin; there was an outline of the British Isles on which you had to mark the locations of places such as Worcester, Morecambe Bay and St Bees Head; History required giving accounts of William II, Robert Blake, and Lord Nelson; and Arithmetic meant multiplying 642035 by 24506. I have a feeling that present-day 11-year-olds would be well into their 30s by the time they managed to complete their answers.

I believe, also, that I may have mentioned my theory of why the British government decided that it would be a good thing to 'decimalise' the currency, and make it 100 pennies to the pound instead of 240. No more tanners, shillings, florins and half-crowns. Great shame, if you ask me.

Was it done for reasons of progress? No. Was it done in obedience to our EU masters? Possibly. But I believe the main reason it was done was because the standard of mathematics education had slumped so much that it would have taken hours for people to get their change at the shops. I can clearly see those with a larger selection of memories at their disposal having to wait for so long whilst the youngster at the till tried to work out how much change was owing – when, say, the customer had handed over a ten-bob note to pay for eight shillings and six-pence three farthings' worth of goods – that the items (in pre-preservative days) would probably have perished in the interim. I can also see that customers would be fighting to join the queue at check-outs operated by people in their sixties.

Anyway, there I was, book in hand, making my way through the part where the main character finds out that his wife has been indulging in a touch of the extra-maritals with some blaggard from Milton Keynes, when I felt a tug on my right sleeve.

"Uncle William…"

"Yes…"

"I'm bored."

"With what?"

"With doing nothing."

"Oh."

"So, like, what can we go and do?"

"How about going for a walk?"

"It's raining."

"Is it?"

"Not yet; but it might. Have you got any DVDs?"

I have a small selection of Digital Versatile Discs, so I replied "Yes, I have a small selection of DVDs."

"Which ones?"

"I've got 'A Tale of Two Cities'. The one with Ronald Colman playing the part of Sydney Carton."

"Who?"

"Ronald Colman."

"Never heard of him."

"He's the chap with one of the finest speaking voices of all time. Coincidentally, another actor with one of the other finest voices is also in the film. Basil Rathbone."

"I've never heard of him either."

I do pity those of Mirabella's inclinations, as they miss out on such a lot. Well, I think they do. And apart from the wonderful voices of the 'B&W' actors, you can actually hear every word they say. Why do so many of the modern films employ casts that either mumble or have to compete with a deafening soundtrack?

"That doesn't matter: you'll still enjoy the film," I continued. "As you probably know, it's from a novel by Charles Dickens; all about London and Paris, and an act of selfless bravery during the French Revolution."

"Yuk!"

"It's very good."

"Yeah right. Any others."

"Mario Lanza playing 'The Great Caruso'."

"What's that about?"

"What's that about! Have you ever heard of Enrico Caruso?"

"No."

"Don't they teach you anything at school?"

"Yeah. We've got like loads of subjects to do for GCSEs."

"GC whats?"

"GCSEs."

"And what are they?"

"Exams."

"Along the lines of O-levels?"

"What?"

"O-levels."

"Never heard of them."

"Oh. So what subjects are you doing?"

"When?"

"For your GCSEs?"

"I'm not doing any GCSEs."

"But I thought you said that you were."

"When I'm like sixteen."

"Then what subjects will you be doing when you are 'like' sixteen?"

"Two Sciences, French, Two in English, Food Tech, History, RE, IT and Maths."

"IT?"

"Information Technology."

"And that is…?"

"Stuff to do with computers. Obviously! Derr-err."

"And RE is… Religious Education?"

"Yes."

"Do you get taught by a priest?"

"Ha, ha… I don't think so!"

"So what does it involve?"

"All sorts."

"I'm listening."

"We live in a world where most people have like a personal faith; so it's important to know about religion and the effect that it like has on people's lives and stuff. From knowledge comes an understanding of world events and tolerance towards others."

For some strange reason, through my mind there then crashed an embarrassment of images concerning Hindus and Muslims, Catholics and Protestants, and virtually every conflict about which I had read. Regarding the promotion of tolerance… Which religion is it that purports to be peace-loving, but whose followers will kill you if you say it isn't?

As for their excuse that the violence is in retaliation for the way that the Crusades used violence! Excuse me? I don't think so. I was always under the impression that followers of that certain religion began invading other parts of the world – in an attempt to force everybody to adopt their beliefs and rules – around the seventh and eight centuries. Didn't parts of the Iberian Peninsula get a hammering from them around 710 AD?

I believe that Palestine, Syria and Egypt were also overrun as part of the subjugation process. In fact, it wasn't until Pope Urban II, in 1095, called upon the Knights of Christendom to push back the conquests, reclaim Jerusalem, and make a stand before Christianity was erased from the face of the earth that the Crusades got under way. So the argument that the current attitude is in response to Christian aggression is, to put it very mildly, somewhat spurious.

I suppose now that I have mentioned that piece of information I can expect some sort of fatwa to be arranged for me. Although I suppose these days it's more likely to be a morbidly obese-wa.

"And what is food technology?" I then asked.

"Cooking and stuff. What works with what and why."

"I have a feeling that used to be known as Home Economics. Probably not a whole lot of use in today's world."

"I could have chosen Drama; or Personal and Social Development!"

"Point taken."

My mind dashed away to a time when subjects were subjects – with the possible exception of Latin; but I suppose that was really meant as a form of mental exercise through which language construction could be understood – and getting more than seven or eight 'O' levels was something that simply didn't happen. Never mind the fourteen or so that seem so commonplace these days. Mind you, with the subjects on offer and pass-marks in the region of fifteen percent I shouldn't really be surprised.

"So what are we going to do?"

"How about a visit to see my Uncle Douglas?" I suggested.

"Who?"

"Uncle Douglas. Come to think of it, he would be your great uncle."

"Oh."

"So how about it?"

"Do we have to?"

"It'll get us out of the house. And there might be a cola in it for you: and a packet of crisps."

A non-committal shrug of small shoulders was followed by a languorous "Okay; I suppose."

When it comes right down to it, I believe that I have a way with children. I don't, to my knowledge that is, have any of my own; but then I appear to have a charmed life. I don't know where the talent to quickly make young people feel comfortable and relaxed comes from: something in my genes, I expect. Which is odd really, as young people tend not to be on my list of desirable companions.

Anyway, a few minutes and a quick bathroom visit later, and with no rain in evidence, Mirabella and I were on our way to meet Uncle Douglas. Before I go any further, perhaps I should explain a little bit about my uncle.

Douglas, like my father, is in his late eighties and, also like my father, used to be a captain in the Merchant Navy. Nothing particularly unusual so far. He is also a fellow who is rather keen on hydroxyl groups and had – or should that be *has?* – a tendency to overdo it on more than a few occasions and, as a result, is rather well known to the local constabulary. I am not sure what the national statistics are for octogenarians getting banned from public houses on account of confrontational behaviour, but Douglas has cornered the market in this part of the world.

Now what you don't want to witness is my father and Douglas getting together to sink a few and reminisce about their years in the fleet that flew the Red Duster: or perhaps you do. However, I had reasoned that at eleven o'clock in the morning there was a better than average chance of finding Douglas in an abstemious mode and, as such, he was usually a mine of interesting information. This meant that there was a good chance that Mirabella might find him fascinating enough to stop pestering me: even if only for half an hour or so.

We approached the low wall around his property, and as I reached for the latch on his gate I could hear his dulcet tones.

"Bloody dog."

"Ha!" I said to Mirabella, who gave me an expression similar to that employed by people who have just mistaken a nettle for a piece of lettuce.

"Useless mangy animal," continued Douglas.

It was then I perceived a largish rump, covered in a pair of trousers fashioned from heavy-duty corduroy. Douglas was kneeling down in his front garden.

"Douglas," I hailed, anxious to cut off the flow of expletives before it became a torrent of prose unsuitable for a teenager's ears.

"Who's that?"

"It is I, William."

"Who?"

"William. Your sister's son."

"And…?"

"And… my father's son as well."

"There's two of you?"

"Two of what?"

"Sons."

"No."

"Thank god for that."

"Quite. But there are two of us here: and one of us is not me."

"What the hell are you talking about?"

"What I mean to say is, that taking into account the fact that only one of us can be me, and I am the one doing the talking, I would say… Actually, I think I've forgotten what I was going to say."

Douglas got to his feet. "Oh it's you," he said. "I thought it sounded daft enough. I said what – " It was then that Douglas took a leap backwards as his eyes fell upon Mirabella.

Did I mention that, as her *mode de chevelure* for the day, Mirabella had chosen to construct strands in her hair that seemed to be comprised of small wooden balls and, as if that wasn't alarming enough, had (I believe the correct term is 'gelled') done something to her fringe and turned it into an arrangement that the average porcupine would have been proud to sport at an annual porcupine ball. The overall effect was to lead one to believe that a terrible accident with an electrically powered abacus had recently befallen her. I believe that was the overall effect the sight had on Douglas.

"Good god alive!" he continued, shaking his head from side to side. "What's happened here? Have you called for an ambulance? I didn't hear a crash."

"What's his problem?" asked my diminutive companion.

"Douglas thinks you have suffered some sort of a calamity."

"Why?"

"Because of the way… That is… What I mean to say…"

"Because of the way I look?"

"Um… that might be it."

"Well," Mirabella's attention focused back on Douglas, "you don't look so hot yourself. Crawling about on your hands and knees in the front garden, and poking around in little piles of dog poo. What's that all about?"

"That, young lady, is none of your… Hang on, who are you?"

"This, Douglas, is Mirabella. My niece."

"Eh?"

"My niece. You know, Lynne's daughter."

"Lynne?"

"My sister."

"You've got a sister?"

"Yes. Have had for a while, actually. Shortish type; stays with mum and dad from time to time. You may have seen her."

"Face like a prune?"

"Now and then."

"Hey; that's my mother you're talking about," interjected my houseguest.

"Well, that can't be helped," Douglas went on. "But what can be helped, is me looking for my lottery ticket."

"Where is it?" I asked.

"If I knew that I wouldn't be looking for it, would I?"

"So where's the last place you would think of looking for it?"

"No idea. Why?"

"Because that's always a good place to start. People are always telling me that things are often to be found in the last place they look."

"That's because," ventured the smallest of we merry three, "you don't have to look after you find it. So it like has to be in the last place. Der-err."

"Thank you Mirabella. If I need any more advice I'll be sure to come to you first."

"If you know where to look for me."

"I'll have you know that I am quite the orienteerer."

"The *what*?"

"Orienteerer. One of those chaps who is into orienteering. Why, many is the time that I have found my bearings by using just a wrist watch and an OS map."

"Ha! Using a sat-nav more like."

"As much as it may come as a shock to you, the generation before the one before yours managed to get by without the plethora of thought-saving devices without which your generation couldn't find its way to the bathroom. It was a generation that received its education before the standards of teaching entered their current downward spiral."

"Whatever."

"Exactly. So, Douglas, where did you last see it?"

"In the kitchen."

"Wouldn't that be a good place to be directing your attention? Rather than in the front garden?"

"No."

"Why not? I thought you said you last saw it there."

"I did… while it was in the dog's bowl."

"Ah."

"And then it was in the dog."

"Ah-ha."

"And that is why I am crawling about poking in all the deposits I can find."

"I see. Is the ticket worth anything?"

"No: I'm looking for it because I have decided to write a treatise on the durability of paper in canine digestive tracts. Of course it's worth something, you blooming idiot."

"Oh. Much?"

"Could be. I can remember that at least three of the numbers came up."

"You need like five or six for any *real* money."

"I know that, missy. But unless I find the ticket, I won't know if I had five or six. Will I?"

"Obviously."

"So…"

"So what?"

"So help me look for it."

"What!"

"Help me look for it."

"By prodding through dog's mess?"

"Yes."

"You must be joking."

Loathe as I am to admitting agreement with *ma petite bête noire*, I did see her point. There must be countless more appealing ways of spending a morning than on your hands and knees, sifting through piles of material that had recently been within the confines of a dog's intestines.

"Well don't expect any imbursement when I locate it."

"How many numbers did you say you had?" Mirabella asked, with one of those facial expressions that generally lead you to believe that several other things are going on inside the head of the questioner.

"As I said; at least three," Douglas replied, with one of those expressions that generally lead you to believe that several other things are going on inside the head of the respondent.

"But that's only worth a tenner."

"But it might well be four numbers. Or more."

"Hmm. So what's my cut if I help you find it."

"Five percent."

"Five! Uh-uh. No way."

"Ten."

"Twenty."

"Fifteen."

"Done."

And with that the two of them spat on the palms of their hands and shook to finalise the transaction.

"Where shall I start?" Mirabella then asked Douglas.

"With the piles that look undisturbed."

"Right."

Just then the telephone rang.

"Get that will you, William."

As a rule, I am a bit loath to answer the telephone in other people's houses. Actually, it is more than 'as a rule'; it features fairly prominently in the *Ius Phalaropicus*. You never know who might be calling. Double-glazing salesmen are fairly easy to parry away: you just have to say that you are the tenant of the property and the landlord is sailing round the world… single-handedly… the wrong way. But calls of a more personal nature can cause all manner of confusion.

My powers of recollection jogged back to the time I answered the telephone whilst staying in San Francisco; and the subsequent misunderstanding with a gentleman, named Ron, who thought I had encroached upon the area occupied by his close friend, named Sam. I expect you can work out my discomfort and hesitancy: but on this occasion I sallied forth.

"Hello," I said, applying my most amenable voice.

"Douglas, it's Eileen here."

"Ah. Actually this is – "

"When can I come round?"

"Come round? Where?"

"Your place, you big tup. I must see you."

"See *me*? Look here, I think you might have the wrong – "

"Don't be bashful, cariad."

"Now just a moment: I'm not the object of your – "

"I wish you wouldn't keep pushing me away all the time, bach. I'd be so good for you. We'd be so good together. I know that for a fact."

"I have no doubt that you – "

"Oh Douglas; my beloved."

"*Beloved?*"

"How I have waited to hear you agree with me."

"What! Listen up; I am trying to tell you that I am not he."

"None of us is really free, my lovely."

"I didn't say 'free'… I said *he*."

"What tree?"

"Tree?"

"You want me to have a look at a tree?"

"No, not *tree*. He."

"Okay. That gives me plenty of time. I'll see you then. Bye for now."

"What?"

It didn't take long for the mental acuities of the Phalarope brain to work out that Douglas had an admirer; albeit a somewhat thwarted one; and a bit deficient in the auricular department. The whys and wherefores of such a craving are not for me to speculate upon; but even if I did, I have a feeling that the suggestions box would remain empty for quite some time. Baffling in the extreme.

Now don't get me wrong, Douglas is a nice enough fellow – from a distance and over short, specified, periods of time – and in his heyday was, so I believe, quite the Don Juan: but these days, in his dotage, a lady would find better reasons for marrying an umbrella than casting her betrothals in his direction. However, as a bachelor of some duration myself, I don't suppose I am in any position to pass comment.

Have I ever entertained the prospect of marriage with a member of the fairer sex? On one or two occasions I am sure: but, fortunately, whilst waiting at a stop for prospective husbands, women have always managed to get on the bus that came along just before mine did. I suppose I must have some kind of a guardian angel.

I shall refrain from passing a comment about the possibility of marriage with a member of my own sex – other than to say I think my feelings on the subject were adequately expressed while I was in San Francisco: on top of which, marriage is meant to be between a man and a woman. If two gentlemen, or ladies, wish to exchange vows, I shall be more than grateful if they would please call it anything other than a 'marriage'. If such as they want to do something that is different to conventional practice, then please call it something different as well. Not too much to ask, surely.

Anyway, I went back outside to pass on the glad tidings.

"Who was it?" asked Douglas, continuing with his faecal rummaging.

"A lady called Eileen."

"Oh god. What did she want?"

"I'm not entirely sure; but I think the gist is that she is coming round here this afternoon to have a look at a tree."

"What?"

"Quite. Had me flummoxed as well, I can tell you."

"What tree?"

"I've no idea."

"This afternoon, you say?"

"Yes."

"I wonder where she got that idea from?"

"Is she a bit low in the ear functioning department?" I proffered.

"A *bit*! Like a bloody post she is."

"Ah."

"What time is it now?"

"Midday."

"Right. Well, that gives me enough time to get well hidden. Found the ticket yet, young 'un?"

"Of course not! Do you think I'm like still sifting through all this dog business because I think it's good fun?"

"Stranger things have happened."

"Not to me, they haven't."

"So that's a 'no' then?"

"Uh, yair-air. Der-err."

"William, is your niece prone to doing animal impressions?"

"Only at the dinner table."

"I heard that! And, FYI, I have very good table manners."

I am not a fan of the use of initials instead of words. Except, possibly, when the use of initials saves time. Obviously, 'FYI' has only three syllables, whilst 'For your information' has six. So yes, *ergo*, time saved; but I still put it in the same pigeon-hole as 'OMG'. Very trendy, I'm sure. But, if the use of letters is designed to cut down on the use of syllables, what happens when using the interweb and people say – as part of the web address – 'WWW'? That has nine syllables, and 'World Wide Web' only has three. Although I do believe that 'dub-dub-dub' has recently become the fashion: and so back to three syllables.

Speaking of letters, I do so dislike it when people, especially if talking about cars, refer to ABS, ESC and DPF as acronyms. To my mind – and I know that many think otherwise – ABS is not an acronym as it does not form a word: it is simply the first letters of the words Advanced Braking System. Surely an acronym is such as Quango (quasi autonomous non-governmental organisation) or Radar (radio, detection and ranging). One of my favourites has to be Patriot – as in those missiles they use. I had always assumed they were so named because they defended your country: but it's actually an acronym for Phased Array Tracking Radar to Intercept On Target.

Anyway, back to the subject of good table manners. I was once told that I would always stay ahead of the pack if I had good table manners, good handwriting and good grammar. Always kept me in good stead, I have to say. It's just a pity that so many of the younger generation don't receive similar advice these days, and are, effectively, consigned to a lifetime of unfulfilling mediocrity. Rather in the same way that I could never employ someone who pronounced 'H' as Haich, rather than Aitch. Ghastly.

Speaking of that generation, have you seen some of the hand-written job application 'letters' they submit? Block capitals throughout, no punctuation, sentence construction that looks as though the letter has been translated into English from Punjabi via Mandarin; and absolutely no concept of homonyms. I wonder why they seldom manage to get a good job.

I once visited Gretna Green and, whilst there, I read through a selection of letters that people had sent in their search for prospective spouses. An early 'lonely hearts' set up, I suppose. Most were penned more than one hundred years ago, and all were beautifully written – both as regards the handwriting and the use of English. I cannot decide whether that is a reflection on past or present standards of schooling.

"Well?"

My thoughts were brought back to my present environs. "Well what?"

"You were saying something about my table manners. Making out like they're bad."

"It was just a joke. Ha-ha."

I have a feeling that the resultant 'Huh' was designed to convey the esteem in which my jocundity was to be held. Fortunately any further ruminations were put on hold when a resonant "Gotcha" assailed my ears. Douglas had found the itinerant lottery ticket.

"There you are, you little bugger."

Up until that moment I would never have imagined that it was possible for a person to have their hands covered in a dog's waste products and smile broadly at the same time.

"How much has it won?" Mirabella asked, wiping her hands on the grass and keeping a safe distance; probably in case Douglas should suddenly feel the need to hug someone.

It took a few moments, while the excess stucco was wiped away from the ticket. Then, "I don't know. But it's four numbers."

"Whoo-hoo. Does that mean we're rich?"

"*We*? Oh, that's right. Um, I shouldn't think so. Well, I suppose we're richer than we were a few minutes ago."

After both parties had cleaned up, Mirabella went online and checked what the ticket was worth.

"It's £95," she proclaimed, after a few moments of 3g surfing. "So that's… £14.25 you owe me."

"As much as that?"

"It's 15 percent of 95. As near as makes no difference."

"Fair enough."

And with that, Douglas settled the contract and, sensing that he needed some time to relocate before the hard-of-hearing harridan arrived, Mirabella and I bade him farewell and set off to find a method of filling the rest of our day.

Trip to Snowdon.

Another day soon dawned in the Phalarope household. If you have similar inclinations to me, I expect that you enjoy starting the day with a mug of tea and a newspaper whilst sitting up in bed: but I have found that one of the drawbacks of living on your own is that you have to get up in order to procure said items.

I am sure that I can hear some of you saying "Well, why don't you get one of those automatic tea-making things?"

I shall answer that by saying that they – at least all the ones that I have tried, and if, in fact, they are still obtainable – make such a confounded noise, what with all their whooshing and hissing, that I am woken about twenty minutes before the desired time and then have to wait whilst said beverage is drawing away. Not that there aren't worse places to wait than supine in your own bed: but all the same, I like to have my tea within a couple of minutes of regaining consciousness.

Then there is the paper. I have managed, after much instruction to the paperboy, to make it clear that I prefer to have my newspaper neatly folded and then eased, in its entirety, through the letterbox in such a way that I am able to read it without resorting to the use of adhesive tape. The concept of which, I can assure you, was stretching the poor lad's acumen to near breaking-point; and I felt that it would be a little unfair of me to expect him to bring the paper up to my room. To say nothing of all the potential ramifications that would surely result if I requested such a thing.

My routine, therefore, has to be that when my alarm has penetrated the hazy murk of my slumber, I place my feet in my slippers and toddle off down to the kitchen to assemble my restorative, grab my broadsheet and toddle back up again. Say what you will, but there's nothing quite like tea and paper first thing in the morning to get your equilibrium back on course.

But will my niece listen to a word I say? No. Will she partake of same? No. I was more than willing to request delivery of whatever periodical took her fancy, and intimated as such; but all to no avail. Mind you, I suppose I can't really blame her for that. Have you seen the current magazines that are available for girls of her age? Correct me if I'm wrong, but I had always assumed that girls like Mirabella were still children. You know the sort of thing; enjoying a jape or two, playing with toys and what not, trips to the seaside and so forth: but apparently not.

It appears that these days girls (and boys for that matter) of the pubescent whereabouts are rather more likely to want information on contraception and how to roll a decent joint. How times have changed.

I'm sure that when I was of the same age, I was more interested in getting a copy of the 'Valiant' or the 'Hurricane', and whether or not I could get my hair to fall in the same way as Typhoon Tracy – the cheery 'soldier-of-fortune', in case any of you were in the process of raising an eyebrow or two.

I don't know how you feel about seeing girls – some as young as six, and who ought to be in a stage of life when pigtails and toy prams should be fairly prominent – walking along in short leather skirts, heels and make-up. Always makes me wonder what variety of brain surgery the parents have recently undergone: assuming, of course, that they had one on which to operate in the first place. But I am not here to comment upon the intellectual shortcomings of some of the modern-day parents.

So where was I? Oh yes… morning rituals. When I suggested the idea of Mirabella drinking a cup of tea whilst reading her chosen publication, I was subjected to a barrage of noises that sounded rather like 'Yeeuuww' and 'Yeerrhhh', and then reliably informed that madam would rather stick the handle of a garden spade up her nose.

Next came the matter of her choice of breakfast consumption. She told me that she would like to have a bowl of some ghastly concoction that contained material which wouldn't have looked out of place on the floor of a gerbil's cage. Absolutely revolting; but apparently she had to think about her figure.

"Eh?" I remember saying.
"My figure. I'm too fat and too heavy."
"What?"
"All the girls in my class are like on a diet."
"Oh. And do they all look the same as you?"
"Pretty much."
"Are lobotomy practicals on the school curriculum?"
"No. Why?"
"Never mind."

Honestly! The poor child was a mere waif of a girl – with the construction that would enable her to play a tune on her ribs if she breathed in – and there she was talking of diets. Speaking of dimensions, why are people so obsessed with their weight? A much wiser man than I once told me that weight shouldn't be the yardstick, and that I should always remember that muscle weighs more than fat.

"Take off all your clothes and stand in front of a mirror," he once told his wife. "Then, if it *looks* revolting, it *is* revolting."

Wise words indeed: caused his marriage to fall apart, all the same.

"What are we going to do today?" I was asked a bit later that morning.

"Ahm…" I replied.

"Where's that a picture of?" Mirabella continued, pointing at a photograph on the dining-room wall.

"That? Snowdon."

"A mountain?"

"Yes."

"Can we go there?"

"Why?"

"Because… Can we climb it?"

"What!"

"Can we climb it?"

"When?"

"Today."

"Oh… I… er…"

"Oh per-leeeze."

"I don't think we can manage it today."

"Why not?"

"Because it's about a four hour drive from here; and it would be well into the night by the time we got down again."

"Oh. So how about tomorrow?"

"Tomorrow?" Then, quickly thinking that if her current form was to be continued, the answer would surely be in the negative, I asked "Can you get up at half-past five in the morning?"

"Half past five in the morning?"

"Yes. And that's really early."

"Um; I guess so. Yeah."

"Oh."

Another ruse waylaid by the vagaries of the female brain.

Have any of you ever had a close encounter with Snowdon – the mountain in North Wales, rather than a particular member of the aristocracy? Rather spectacular, isn't it? For some reason beyond my ken, I have always felt a bit of a close affinity with the place. I know most people will say that's because we both have our heads in the clouds most of the time, and that we're a bit on the thick side; but I would prefer to cite other characteristics. And no, I don't mean we're both challenging.

Although I have been known to partake of the odd scramble, I cannot claim to be a climber. Not for me the bag of Karabiners, belay brakes and double-axled SLCDs. Oh no; just a rucksack full of sandwiches and a bottle of water, a cheery 'fol-de-ray', and away I go: and Snowdon seems to call to me on a fairly regular basis.

As I said, nothing too adventurous; and I tend to saunter along one of the well-known routes: usually up via the Pyg trail, and down via the Miner's track. With the exceptions of Christmas Day and my birthday, I stick to going up during the summer months – not just because the weather is usually friendlier, but also because the café thing at the top is open. I know the Prince of Wales once described the old place as the 'highest slum in Britain', but I can assure you that on a wet and windy day the place always seems like a palace to me. Plus, there is little to compare with a pie and a pint after three hours of exertion, I can tell you.

"But why on Christmas Day?" you ask. "That's a bit strange."

Well, possibly: but as I tend to spend Christmas Day on my own – something to do with not wanting to indulge in the oft-enacted family battles that are generally fought up and down the country – I like to spend it going up Snowdon. Apart from anything else, it does seem to me to be more of a spiritual experience than sitting in front of the television wishing you hadn't forced those last three mince pies down your throat.

About ten years ago I never saw more than twenty people making their way up. All with the same contented expression – brought about, no doubt, by the knowledge that they are unlikely to have to endure any relatives or washing-up.

Of late, however, weather depending, there have been as many as a hundred or more people. Not a problem with the number in itself, you understand; it's just that I would prefer the place, especially on a

Christian day, to have a Christian feel to it. I wonder if the powers that be could see their way to putting a cross on the summit; in the way they have done with many Alpine peaks.

I can now hear lots of liberalists bleating on about not wanting to upset those of other faiths; so let me make it plain. We are a Christian country, and we should be allowed – nay, encouraged – to reinforce the basis on which our way of life has been structured. We'll be sorry if we don't; as once a way of life and its religion have been lost it is nigh on impossible to restore them.

Anyway, when nine o'clock rolled around, I had parked my car in the Pen-y-pass car-park, and Mirabella and I were getting ourselves ready for the ascent.

"Do I really have to take all this stuff?" she asked, with an indolent aspect to her voice.

"Yes," I replied, trying to avoid any feelings of guilt about making the sprog carry most of her own things.

"Why?"

"Because it might get a bit hairy up there. The weather can change in an instant, don't you know."

"But it's heavy; and I'll look ridiculous if I have to wear all that waterproof gear you've given me."

There then followed a five minute discussion during which I stressed how it was always better to have three items of clothing too many than one too few; and a couple of sizes on the large side of things was better than a couple on the small side. Not sure if the info made it all the way into her grey matter or decided to take the straight route from one ear to the other, but Mirabella nodded at the right places; and then off we went.

I am one of those chaps who prefers to keep a steady pace when I walk. It might well be described as a slow pace; but it's what you would call 'steadily' slow. I was soon to realise that Mirabella had learned her technique from the school of walking that was founded by both the tortoise *and* the hare. Absolutely astonishing; and jolly disconcerting, I don't mind admitting.

One moment she was forty yards ahead of me and making

comments about how she would like to get to the top before the week was out; and the next moment she was forty yards behind me and wanting to know why I was in such a hurry and would I help her to tie up one of her bootlaces. I am sure that John Hunt never had to put up with that kind of nonsense when he was in the area preparing for his Everest expedition. I am also sure that should I ever decide to have a bash at something a bit more demanding, I would not be pencilling in the name of my current companion on my list of possible sherpas.

Plus, on top of all that, I was having to put up with an incessant barrage of questioning.

"Uncle William, why are there so many sheep here?" "Uncle William, how much longer is there?" and "Why is Snowdon so high?" But her most absurd enquiry was "Uncle William, are we there yet?"

"Are we still going in an upward direction?" I replied.

"Yes…"

"Then, quite obviously, we are not there yet."

It was enough to drive a fellow a touch doolally. Isn't that word derived from the name of a place called Deolali – about 100 miles from Bombay – where there used to be some kind of a military sanatorium? Anyway.

Then there were the multiple requests to stop for something to eat and drink. I realise, and am always the first to admit so (usually while standing near a long queue of people lining up and pointing at me), that I might not be the sharpest knife in the drawer; but I have always regarded it as pretty sensible to keep plenty of goodies in my rucksack in case of any unforeseen eventualities.

You know the things I mean – poor visibility, twisted ankle, and so forth – which might result in having to spend a bit longer than anticipated on the slopes. However, quite why Mirabella needed to top up her reserves with such frequency, especially after such a short way into the enterprise, I expect I shall never know. Should she ever decide to have a bash at a Himalayan undertaking, I imagine that half the porter population of Nepal would be needed to carry her provisions.

Speaking of unforeseen eventualities, I am under the impression that – as of late – the emergency services (mountain rescue and whatnot) have been inundated with people calling for help because they couldn't find their way back down, didn't think of packing waterproofs and were getting wet, felt a bit cold as they had thought that their shorts/t-shirt/gym shoes would have been okay, and – best of all – were under the impression that a mobile phone was more important than a compass and map. There really ought to be a vetting process before people are allowed to go more than 200 yards from the car parks.

Speaking of stupid people, I can recall – one Christmas Day – sitting at the side of Glaslyn (the lake at the eastern foot of Snowdon) to enjoy a small bar of chocolate whilst on my way back to the car park at Pen-y-pass, when I was approached by three young men who asked me if they were on the right path to take them up to the top of Snowdon. Now bearing in mind that it was just about the shortest day, that it was nearly 2.00 pm, and that they were dressed in less than I would have chosen to wear for a trip to the shops, even someone with a modicum of intelligence would have reached the opinion that the young men were asking for trouble.

I did start to explain that they would be best advised to take a few photographs from where they were and then head back to their car; but my words were clearly falling upon ears that may well have been affected by the dropping temperature or the fact that English was probably not their first language. The end result was that they spurned my advice and carried on up. I heard echoes of that passage from Proverbs which tells of the perils about advising fools: still, at least it didn't spoil my day.

Now, where was I? Oh yes, provisions. I also have a tendency to carry a good novel, a largish packet of cashew nuts, some of those wet-wipe things (I cannot bear to hold a book with sticky fingers), a head torch, and the ubiquitous mobile phone. Yes, I know I just made some fairly disparaging remarks about the damn things – and also when I was out and about in San Francisco – but I feel justified in saying that, second to having the proper equipment, a mobile phone can be very handy should a spot of unpredicted, and potentially life-threatening, bother befall you in mountain environs: as long as there happens to be a signal of course.

On top of which, you need to have a phone which has buttons that are larger than your iris on a sunny day. Small buttons are hard enough to press in the right order when in full command of your digits, and nigh on impossible when the temperature drops below freezing and you're wearing a pair of thick gloves. As to how you can manage if your phone has one of those touch-sensitive screens I dread to think. If, indeed, you can see what's on the screen should the sun be shining brightly. Fortunately, to date, I have not had to use a mobile phone for any clambering emergency.

Our progress continued and, try as the little madam did to make the climb a labour in every aspect she could think of, we made it to the top in about three hours. Where, much to her surprise, and although tired and having spent the last two hours wishing that she had opted for a couple of days in bed, I could tell that Mirabella was feeling rather pleased with herself.

Call me a touch antediluvian, if you must, but I do think that youngsters these days miss out on so many experiences that are good for them: in both a physical and psychological way. Let them have a dose of the rush that exertion and achievement bring, and then ask them how it compares to a video game. As for my views on the attitudes that many modern 'thinkers' (I use the term loosely) have on the subject… Yes, I do mean people who think that everybody should get a prize because nobody must ever feel that they didn't succeed at everything they do. I ask you! How daft is that?

"Ooh," they bleat. "We must wrap up all the children in cotton wool and give them good marks in all their exams. We must never let them think that anyone is better than they are; we must never let them take responsibility for anything; we must never let them know what failure feels like."

Absolutely pathetic. Mind you, the good news is that if you are one of those parents who is bringing up their children in the 'old ways', your children are going to stand head and shoulders above the others, and prospective employers will spot them approaching from several miles away.

Now where was I? Oh yes, going up Snowdon: and, joy of joys, the café was open and serving refreshments.

Speaking of the summit and the café, I wish to make one observation. The views from the top of Snowdon are – on a fine day, obviously – amongst the best available in the UK. They are simply splendid; and they make you feel good to be alive and grateful that the great architect involved with assembling the surrounding panorama must be the type who loves the outdoors.

Then why, I often ask myself, do so many of those who journey up on the train disembark and head straight for the cafeteria? Not so much as a pause to take in and marvel at the vista, nor even a moment to absorb the thrill of being at the top, as they scurry for their refreshments. Why don't they take the time to enjoy the view? They must know that they only have thirty minutes before their train goes back down again.

Admittedly the train journey to the summit is probably not the most comfortable one that they will have ever enjoyed; but, at around one hour's duration, it is also unlikely to have reduced them to quivering masses whose distress can only be placated by shovelling a tray-full of food down their throats. Especially as they almost certainly partook of one form of consumption or another at their point of embarkation. And, as it so often seems, many of their number look as though going a few days, never mind a few hours, without food may do them the world of good.

While I am on the subject of the cafeteria, and I have no idea of your thoughts on the matter, I think that those who have trudged up Snowdon on foot should be allowed some privileges, recognition even, when compared with those who have made the trip by train. Not sure what though: maybe a shorter queue at the checkout, maybe the better tables by the windows, or maybe the use of an executive washroom. I am sure the authorities could think of something suitable. I know I could: well, I just did.

So there we were; me with a pint of lubricant and something that described itself as a Cornish pasty, and Mirabella tucking into several chocolate delights and a can of something orange and carbonated.

"Ucle Illum, yam oh grie I ould eat a orse."

Perhaps it was the cloistered education I received during my formative years; perhaps it was a housemaster who delighted in whacking me across the back of the head whenever I committed any size of indiscretion; perhaps it could have been for a whole host of reasons that currently lie just outside my memory scan: but I have an aversion to bad table manners. Actually, I think it is to all types of bad manners; and bad table manners is right up there near the pole position.

What is it that makes some people imagine it is endearing to chew food with their mouth wide open; or to talk with a mouthful of food? I usually find the spectacle of human beings eating to be on the repugnant side of objectionable; but to have them compound it by indulging in either of the two aforementioned unpleasantries is quite unbearable. As for those football managers who chew gum as though they were being sponsored to produce saliva…

"I am so sorry," I said, "but I don't speak 'gobful'."

"Uh?"

"If you wish to converse with me, I shall be very grateful if you would first empty your oral cavity of all half-masticated comestibles."

"Eh?"

"Don't speak with your mouth full: especially as you recently took the trouble to extol the virtues of your table manners."

"Orry."

Several swallows later – none of which did anything to denote summer had arrived, by the way – Mirabella tried again.

"Sorry; I'm just so tired: and, I guess, excited, that I forgot. Anyway, I said that I was so hungry I could eat a horse."

"Be that as it may, I am fairly sure that nothing of an equine nature will be found on the menu."

"Can you be sure? Remember what happened with lots of those supermarket burgers."

"I'd like to think I can be sure. Well, in so much as I didn't actually find a hoof, or part of a saddle, inside my pasty."

Several moments of quiet contemplation followed – or as quiet as it could be with a table occupied by some people of a Teutonic nature in the vicinity. I expect that they were simply discussing how nice it was to be at the summit of Snowdon, how much they admired the Welsh and their quaint customs, and how rain and cricket did so much to improve one's complexion and understanding of the meaning of life. However, as I may have mentioned on a previous occasion, whenever I hear German being spoken it always sounds as if plans are being drawn up for an invasion of someone else's country: once again. And no, I am not going to get started on the French; even though I would very much like to.

"Are we going back now?"

"Have you had enough?"

"Yes."

However lackadaisical my outward demeanour may seem, I have been known, on occasion, to plonk down my plantar regions with a large slice of resolution: and this was one such occasion. "Well, hard lines," I said. "As I wish to spend a little bit longer absorbing the rarefied atmosphere."

"Why?"

"Because I like clean air, dear child. No pollutants to clog my bronchioles."

"In here?"

"No, outside: and I wish to feast my eyes for a while."

"On what?"

"The views."

"What views?"

"Those," I replied, turning to point out of the window.

My gesture, and intention, was somewhat thwarted by the fact that a mist as thick as someone whose family had been living in the same area for six generations had descended whilst my back was turned.

"Oo-er," I can recall voicing.

"Oo-er indeed," came the sardonic reply.

There is something very peculiar about the air in the immediate vicinity of Snowdon. You can be bathed in sunlight, a lovely cerulean sky, and experience an irresistible urge to sing a canzonet or two from the 'Sound of Music' one minute, and then fumbling about in near zero visibility the next. Maybe the mountain is not all that keen on the music of Rodgers and Hammerstein: or maybe it is just my singing.

Actually, come to think of it, it might well be my cantonations. Every year at my school, there used to be a 'House Song' competition. This was intended as a means of allowing the houses (subdivisions of the school population – seven in all) a means to compete against one another without causing any bones to be broken. I think it was really just an excuse to carry out communal humiliation. Perhaps some Human Rights lawyer has since managed to get the ritual stopped.

Anyway, I am reminded of the fact that I and two or three others in my 'house' would always be asked if we minded terribly not allowing any sounds to emanate from our vocal regions: or anywhere else for that matter. Apparently we gave the impression that we were unable to carry a tune; even in a bucket marked 'Tune'. I, naturally enough, begged to differ; but when faced with the choice of keeping mum or cleaning out the dormitories for a month I would always choose the former option.

Do you have any idea how difficult it is to keep a straight face when you – and two or three others around you – are having to look as if you are trilling along with the best of them when not a sound is passing your lips? Well, you can take it from someone who has tried; it is challenging in the extreme. Having said that, I expect it would be a lot easier if being paid the exorbitant sums of money that some performers get for... is it called 'lip-synching'? Anyway.

I also have memories of one particular year when we arranged for several of the boys in my row (which happened to be at the front of the school theatre on that occasion) to bend forward at the start of one of the renditions – I believe it may have been that belonging to 'Eagle' house – and insert a long, thin piece of green foam rubber into each nostril, and then sit back up again. The geography of the situation was that the master doing the conducting had his back to us and, as they were sitting at the back of the auditorium, the rest of the staff was unable to see what was going on: but the boys on the stage were able to see a row of fellow pupils who all seemed to be suffering from a particularly vehement, and phlegm-laden, cold.

The effect was as instant as it was spectacular. A wave of shudders was seen to pass along the rows of vocalists as, one by one, they all dissolved into uncontrollable sniggers. Naturally, by the time the conductor turned around to see what might have caused the disorder we had all removed the offending articles and were innocently smiling. Further, as protocol demanded that you did not tell tales on your fellow pupils, the explanation for the mayhem was never discovered.

As pranks went, that one was rated highly and is still, so I believe, spoken of in school folklore and held in great esteem.

So there we were, on top of a mountain and shrouded in mist. I expect many of you would have felt a trifle insecure, and possibly fretted about what to do next: but not I. Oh no; even allowing for the fact that I was going to have a juvenile delinquent to keep me company, my experience on the slopes allowed me to feel confident in my ability to negotiate our descent. Well, that and the fact that there was a train leaving every thirty minutes.

So did I choose the easy option? No, I do not mean throwing the aforementioned adolescent off one of the many precipitous edges – I mean taking the train: and no, I did not do that either. Primarily, as I said, because I felt I had the necessary wherewithal to find my way back down. However, a secondary consideration was that I did not have the necessary wherewithal to purchase a brace of tickets. Enough for me; but I felt that it would have been considered a pretty poor show if I trundled off and left the blood relative stranded at the top.

Although always ready with a convincing excuse to extricate myself from many a tricky situation, I felt that I would have been a bit short of choices when confronted with an anxious mother who was a touch concerned as to the whereabouts of her darling daughter: especially when she was last seen gadding about on a mist-covered mountain.

"Righty-ho," I said.
"Righty-ho what?"
"Time to up sticks."
"And do what?"
"Go back down."
"In this weather?"
"Yes."
"In this misty weather?"
"Yes ."
"In this thick, wet, way-losing, misty weather?"

"Yes; in all of those," I affirmed.

"But how will we know where we're going? The path wasn't all that clear on the way up; and that was in, like, good conditions. And you're the type that usually has trouble finding where you parked your car."

"Now just a minute, minor kin: I'll have you know that I am a bit of a past master at route finding... and such things."

"I don't want a *past* master; I want a *present* one; thank you very much."

"Well, as I am the only one who is present, you'll have to make do with me."

"Huh."

"I have a map, a compass, and one of those GSP things," I proudly declared.

"*GSP*? Don't you mean GPS?"

"Er... yes. Naturally."

"Do you know how to use it?"

"Of course I do!"

"So how many satellites does it latch on to?"

"Eh?"

"How... many... satellites... does... it... latch... on... to?"

"Enough."

"Enough? What do you mean *enough*? You haven't got a clue, have you?"

"Would you like another chocolate muffin?"

"Did you mark any, like, waypoints on the way up here?"

"More cola perhaps?"

"In other words, you bought a gadget and you don't know how to use it."

"I think that's a bit strong."

"But true."

"I... that is... Possibly."

"Give it to me."

There are many things that can happen to a fellow to undermine his self-confidence; I can certainly furnish you with a long list of such, if requested. And pretty near the top of that list is being shown up to be a bit of a nincompoop by someone (especially of the female gender) who is only about one quarter of your age: especially when the tone of her voice puts the sneerometer under considerable strain.

I am happy to admit that I have a slight problem when it comes to understanding things with an electronic flavour to them. Give me something mechanical, like a bicycle, and I'll be more than happy to take you on a conducted tour of how cogs, pedals and a chain all pull together in the propulsion department. Nothing too complicated, or requiring petrol, you understand: just straightforward mechanics. Unfortunately, when it comes to matters of circuitry, transistors, capacitors and so forth, the Phalarope brain goes a bit limp. Can't be helped I suppose; but there you have it.

"Oh, these ones are pretty good."

"They are?"

"Yeah. I've seen them advertised quite a lot in Outdoor magazines."

"You read Outdoor magazines?"

"Our neighbours are like into that stuff. I go to school with one of their children."

"Really."

"Yes. Anyway, this thing has masses of functions."

"Is that so?"

"Obviously it's not as neat as those satellite map thingies you can get; but it's still pretty cool all the same."

"Oh."

"Yeah. Look… it uses four satellites… and we are just about 3,530 feet above sea level. And, in case you're interested, our exact location is 53-4-08 N and 4-4-32 W. That's the location using the proper longitude and latitude readings: or at least to a good degree of accuracy. Not the OS grid references."

"Well, well."

"And it does like all sorts of other really neat things: time zones, sun rise times, bearing, routes and tracers, track logs and GOTOs. This is really up there."

I suppose that I must have had a 'bemused' expression showing, as madam then embarked upon several minutes of explanation as to how they all worked. It sounded very interesting, and really rather impressive; but I have to say that most of it passed over the top of my cranium with several inches to spare.

I have tried, on several occasions, to embrace all that modern technology has to offer; but have invariably fallen well short of the mark. I realise that all this GPS stuff is designed to make ascertaining one's whereabouts in the wilderness a jolly sight easier than it would have been not so long ago; but a chap such as me would rather have something even simpler: such as signposts every hundred yards or so, and a passer-by always willing to point a finger in the required direction.

Now that is a talent with which women will always have the advantage over men.

"What talent?" I hear you ask.

"The ability to summon help," I reply.

Although I haven't exactly spent many hours trying to perfect the technique, I just cannot get my face or posture to accept the mode known as 'coquettish'. My coquetry skills are, to put it mildly, lamentable. Women on the other hand, have the ability to do so at the drop of a hat.

Is it something taught while dandled on their mother's knee? Is it something passed on whilst reading bedtime stories to them? Perhaps it is genetic. There could, especially if a male of the species happens to be within earshot, even be an element of a form of idioglossia that can span two generations. Whatever the answer, it is most effective.

I once had the misfortune to have my motor car develop a handling problem whilst driving one day, and I noticed that one of the tyres was looking more than a little downcast. Actually, thoroughly depressed might have been more accurate. As you may have gathered by simple deduction, I am not the most digitally dextrous of individuals. You must know the type who usually is – dirty hands, sweating, and so on. Yes, I realise that the mechanics (if you'll pardon the pun) involved with changing a flat tyre are not exactly rocket science, but those wheels do weigh rather a lot, don't they? And the behemoth who tightened up the wheel-nuts the last time that tyre was changed must have been using one of those compressed-air contraptions, with the result that the wrench now needed a twelve-foot extension and the Pontypool front row to loosen said nuts.

So what was a chap to do to entice others to come forward and offer assistance? Difficult to figure out. A lady, on the other hand, as I mentioned, merely has to look coquettish. A slight tilt of the head, a flutter of the eyelashes, and gallants in their droves will spring into action. If, however, a fellow such as I were to adopt the same technique, the person most likely to step forward would be someone with a limp wrist and an extensive collection of ABBA CDs. On the one occasion I tried rolling up a trouser-leg in order to flash a shapely calf, the only passing vehicle that stopped was full of Freemasons.

I dread to think how I might have fared in those days of Yore, when so much of that which we take for granted hadn't even been dreamed of. Except, perhaps, by that chap Archimedes: and speaking of the son of Phidias, I could have done with that lever of his, and a place to stand, when struggling with those blasted wheel-nuts. But what a mind the chap had. One of the few that God created to have genius; and what an advert for the benefits of taking long baths. I bet he just wishes that his final words hadn't been *"Noli turbane circulos meos."* Still, I suppose it serves him right for messing about in that cornfield.

While I am on the subject of the days before we had access to all this electronic positional gadgetry; can you imagine setting sail with just a quadrant, a sandglass and a compass? I doubt very much if I would have had the courage to venture out of sight of land.

How those mariners managed with techniques such as 'Dead Reckoning' I shall never understand: but manage it, they did. I am sure that had I been in charge of navigation I would probably have wondered why there was a length of rope in the water and who had tied all the knots in it.

"Come on then," I continued, trying to regain the floor. "Onward and downward."

"How?"

"On foot, of course."

"But the train is like only half full."

"Even if it were completely empty and they were handing out triple 'train miles', we are still going back down on foot."

"Huh!"

Knowing that it is very easy to stray off the desired trail in misty conditions on Snowdon, we set off. The plan was to turn right at the first buttress stone, join the Pyg Trail, and then, having located the next buttress stone, make our way down to the lake and the start of the Miner's track. I had been expecting mist all the way, but fortunately it only lasted until we reached the second buttress stone, and the improved visibility allowed us to continue in relative safety.

But then something rather odd happened. I didn't recall seeing any amphetamine peddlers in the café, and I was pretty sure that Missy didn't down half a dozen bottles of 'energy' drink when I had my back turned; but there was the most amazing (and, subsequently, embarrassment causing) change in the small person's level of activity.

It was as if somebody had found a hidden switch. All the way up it had been a stream of procrastinations, scaturient in the extreme, with any excuse to tarry awhile; and yet now she was off as though she knew something that I had failed to notice: and that, I can assure you, was extremely disconcerting.

My mind was now working overtime, trying to figure out what had happened to the small person. I had felt justified in assuming the mantle of 'King of the Hill' on the way up, but I was most assuredly left in the umbra on the way down.

A fellow less magnanimous than I would bleat about being at a disadvantage in the senescence stakes, or maybe bring to the reader's attention that by standing a foot taller than the opposition I was encountering thicker cloud cover. But not I. Oh no; if there is one thing that you can say about this particular Phalarope, it is not that I omit to acknowledge talent in others.

The girl was like a springbok on performance enhancers. *Boing – boing – boing* she went; or at least that's the way it seemed: and that was one mystery. The other was the aggressive way that most of those making their way up were looking at me. As for their remarks…

'Someone that age should be ashamed of himself'.

'Young girls aren't safe anywhere these days'.

'He certainly looks the type'.

I think it was after the eighth – it may have been the ninth – comment I heard that I ventured to ask what the matter was: and that turned out to be a mistake. I had, as I may have mentioned before, the privilege of having received a large part of my formal education at one of England's public schools and – apart from the occasional colloquialism – most of my discourse is conducted in the old *langue maternelle,* as they say. Ventures into lands occupied by those conversant in the *langage de carrefour* have been few and far between.

So anyway, this fellow was blabbering on about all manner of inappropriate behaviour towards children, and how people who really ought to know better should be locked up. At least I think that was the gist of what he said: he had a most unfortunate London accent, and I was unable to decipher much that made any sense.

"I'm awfully sorry," I ventured. "Are you saying that there is a rapscallion loose upon these slopes?"

"Eh?"

"Is there a ne'er-do-well, a malefactor loose in our midst?"

"Look, mate, ah dunno 'ooh you are, an that; but I've a good mind to ring the old bill and tell'em wot you're up to."

"Yeah, you tell 'im, Wayne."

Did I mention that the man was accompanied by a woman? Well, he was; and it was she who spoke at that juncture: and a most peculiar-looking female she was too. I am fully aware that people do not choose their progenitors, or have any say in the allocation of looks and intelligence; so I am not usually in the habit of making acerbic remarks about the shortage of one or the other in some people. But in this case I feel obliged to make an exception.

I would have estimated her age to have been somewhere between twenty-five and sixty. Yes, I know that hardly narrows it down, but you must take into account that I have never been a great one for correctly assessing ages of women; and I feel little or no embarrassment in admitting such. After all, how is a fellow to reach a correct decision when faced with all manner of devices designed to confuse him?

Hair colourings, exfoliates and moisturisers to name but three; and I am not even going to begin on the subject of surgical intervention. Well, maybe just a quick mention. I was reading one of those magazines that lie strewn around waiting rooms, and I happened upon an article about those parts of the body that can be tucked, lifted, enhanced, augmented, reduced, or just emptied. Well!

I shall happily endorse procedures that are used for reconstruction purposes – such as those required post accident or major surgery – but what on earth is the thinking behind most of the others? I remember seeing a wedding photograph of some celebrity or other that showed the happy couple and their entourage of friends. It was like looking at the early stages of an alien invasion. Bizarre didn't even come close to describing it.

I often find myself watching a film and thinking 'Hey, doesn't he look like old so-and-so? Maybe it's his brother'. But then, when the credits roll, it turns out to have been 'old so-and-so' all the time. However, you're not convinced. 'Has he been in an accident?' you ask yourself. Then you remember the wrinkled skin on his neck and the back of his hands, and all becomes clear.

I also find myself sympathising with the fellow whose wife has been in for a selection of surgical procedures, and now has some parts that are newer than others: and then he gets blamed for forgetting her birthday. How on earth is the poor man supposed to remember it? So many bits of her might be new (or adjusted) that he loses track of when they first appeared. Maybe some enterprising manufacturer will produce a card that has boxes which can be ticked to correspond with whichever bits are celebrating an anniversary. I'm sure that such cards will prove to be very popular.

Apart from anything else, the human body has the capacity to renew most of itself as it goes along. You get a new liver about every five months, new skin and lungs every three to four weeks, new red blood cells every four months, and a new heart roughly every twenty years. Your brain (and most nerve cells) keeps going, as do your eyes (with the exception of the cornea), for your entire life; so you have to really look after those. Oh, and the enamel on your teeth cannot be replaced either.

The card manufacturers have got people buying them for Mothers' day, Fathers' day, Grannies' day; and second cousin's day for all I know. I'm sure some enterprising supplier could devise a way to sucker people into forking out for cards to celebrate body-part-days as well? How much should you have to drink to celebrate New Liver's Day?

Now where was I? Oh yes, the lady in question and her possible age. She had a relatively lithe figure; so that leans towards the lower end of the scale. She had hands that might have done sterling service on a building site; so that moved the pointer a bit higher. But it was her face that caused me the most confusion. I wouldn't describe it as ugly – although ugly would have been an ideal description – but it did look rather as though someone had been chopping wood on it: and when she spoke, it was to display an assortment of teeth that resembled a piano keyboard. Aging her would have proved very difficult indeed.

"Yeah, Sharon; that's roight."

Wayne and Sharon! Isn't it marvellous how Nature tries to make sure that defective genes are kept to as small a group as possible by ensuring that those harbouring said characteristics often find mutual attraction? Very thoughtful, I have to say. Well it would be if those same types didn't then go and have eight children: and I don't just mean simply keeping them all in that one family. What is it they say about the definition of 'confusion'? Father's Day on a council estate? As you can well imagine, I couldn't possibly endorse such a slur.

"Go on, Wayne; do it."

"Wot?"

"Tell 'im."

"Yeah. Roight."

"Bleedin' perv."

"Nonce."

If you are having a spot of bother understanding all that, then multiply it several times to get an idea of the difficulty I was having: and that was whilst facing a fellow of what can only be described as 'interesting' proportions.

"What?" I hear you murmur. "*Interesting?*"

Indeed. Well, that is what I would say if asked about someone who stood at least six and a half feet tall, had arms that reached down to his knees, walked with his palms facing backwards, and had supra-orbital ridges that looked as though he was halfway through being made up for a stage production of 'Planet of the Apes'. I am quite sure that there was at least another dozen similar remarks that sprang easily to mind; but even seeming to be a teensy bit acrimonious wasn't high on my agenda at the time. We Phalaropes have sometimes been described as being on an intellectual par with a pile of house-bricks; but wanting to end up with a nose that resembled one of them…? I don't think so.

Gradually, however, and after having persuaded the gentleman that I usually find it easier to speak without having my throat held tightly, I was able to work out the reason for his consternation. It transpired that the little abscess in my care had been telling others that she was being pursued by an elderly man, with a funny hat and two walking poles, who had been offering her inducements in order to get her to rub his legs with liniment as, so he said, he had fallen over and strained several muscles.

I wasn't sure which I found to be more offensive – that the pustule had pulled this little stunt, that she had described me as elderly, or that she had found my head covering to be a source of amusement.

I don't know if you favour a hat or not, but I have – ever since my sojourn to San Francisco – been a touch partial to sporting the rather natty Fedora that I purchased in a small shop on Pier 39. Not just plonked on the dome, you understand; but worn at a slightly rakish, maybe even jaunty, angle. And, though I say so myself, I think it is rather fetching: maybe a touch dashing, if you know what I mean.

"So?"

"Excuse me?"

"Are you the geezer?"

"What geezer?"

"The geezer wot's chasin' that lih-el girl?"

"I beg your pardon."

"Is yer or isn't yer 'im?"

I realise that areas designated as being National Parks are, quite rightly, open to all and sundry: but I do feel, as I mentioned earlier, that there ought to be a few pre-requisites and that those entering should, at the very least, be competent in the use of the English language. Not, I hasten to add, on account of harbouring any thoughts of exclusivity – even though that may be true – but merely to assist those engaged in acts of rescue and suchlike. How difficult must it be, when trying to establish the exact location of the individual who has summoned help, if said individual converses with an accent that is thick enough to use as a road surface? Or has a vocabulary that consists of little more than 'you know', 'like', 'sort of', and a selection of grunts that might be put to better use in the primate cage of a zoo. As for those who live in the UK and regard English as a second, or even third, language…? I hesitate to say, as my opinions may offend those of a delicate and politically correct nature.

Actually, I don't care if they do. As far as I'm concerned, if people come to live in the UK then they should learn our language and abide by our rules. If they don't, then I would be more than happy to get them an interpreter to tell them the location of the nearest airport: it's just a pity that our pusillanimous politicians don't hold the same view. I didn't know that they had even been letting people take their driving test in a language other than English. How can that be sensible? Whoever allowed it to happen should be made to stand in front of a car driven by someone who can't read English and hold up a sign that, of necessity, reads 'Slow down, Icy surface'.

Where was I? Oh yes, getting lost. I, it must be said, am a bit of a dimwit when it comes to detailing my exact whereabouts. I don't have too much trouble when armed with a street map, or standing right outside a hostelry: but ask me when I'm out in the wilderness and I might appear more than a little bit vague. And that, when you think about it, is hardly surprising. After all, how would you describe a tree or a pile of stones when the area is simply heaving with trees and piles of stones?

It's rather along the lines of those 'route books' you can purchase. There you are, making your way up towards a summit on an untried (as far as you're concerned) route, when the book tells you that upon reaching a 'cairn' you have to veer off in a Northerly direction.

"Which cairn?" I would want to ask. The place is positively dotted with the things. You see, a description such as 'cairn' or 'rocky crag' doesn't really help me in the slightest when there is a plethora of them from which to choose. Do they mean the small one a few yards behind me, or the larger one a few yards in front?

"Why does it matter?" I hear you say. "North is North."

Well, that is true of course. But when 'North from the first cairn' leads you on to a different path than 'North from the second cairn', you should begin to see the dilemma. I would rather have a guidebook that consists of photographs which show you what you should be looking at when standing in the designated position, and a series of small arrows that point out the direction in which you should be heading. In other words, a progressive sequence of 'You are here' and 'You head over there' photographs. Simple to understand, and simple to follow. Things that would suit me down to the ground: and along it as well.

Actually, if truth be known, and you don't mind the sound of a self-blown trumpet, I did once approach a publisher with such an idea. I suggested having the different routes made into a few pages of laminated photographs (so they wouldn't fall to pieces in the rain) which would fit into a 6" by 4" ring-binder. That way – so my thinking went – you wouldn't have to lug a whole book around: just one series of photographs for your chosen route up, and another one for the chosen route down. I even spoke of enclosing an opaque page that could be placed over the photographs to show how it would look in the mist. Seed on stony ground I'm afraid; but there we are.

I believe that they have now brought out something that works on a mobile phone: handy, I've no doubt, and also, I've no doubt, expensive; and will use up the battery in next to no time. Well, certainly next to the time that you have to make that call for help. However, back to the two cerebrally-challenged individuals who had waylaid me.

"If by 'lih-el' girl," I said, keeping a distance of more than an arm's length away, "you mean the walking infection that passed this way a few minutes ago, then I have to say that I jolly well am not in the process of chasing her. If your enquiry is to ascertain whether or not I am he who has been entrusted – as *loco parentis* – to keep an eye on said sepsis, then I have to admit to my obligation."

"Wot?"

"What?"

"Wot did yer say?"

"What."

"Oi said, wot did yer say?"

"I know: and I said that I had said 'what'."

"Don't try and get clever wiv me, mate. I don't like being made to look silly."

"Then that is going to limit our communication somewhat."

"Eh?"

"I have always found it rather restricting to converse in monosyllabic terms."

"Now look 'ere... er..."

"My dear fellow, if your prowess with the English language is anything to go by, I fear that even our ovine friends would have difficulty allowing you to occupy the intellectual high-ground."

"Wot?"

What was it that Proverbs mentioned? Oh yes, 'He that increaseth knowledge increaseth sorrow'. Or something very similar: and I suppose it has a point. Ignorance is bliss type of thing: and my end of the Phalarope clan has always borne that in mind. There is certainly not much point in getting too clever if it's going to make you unhappy. But I did think that the chap blocking my path was taking the concept a bit too far: one must be careful not to over-egg the cake, I always say.

And speaking of concepts, I had a feeling that the exchange was going to rapidly go from verbal back to physical and that a quick change of tack was required.

"I feel I should mention that the bar at the top is open," I said.

"The *bar*?"

"Indeed. Lots of lovely, refreshing, cold lager."

"Yeah? Did yer 'ear that, Shaz?"

"Wot?"

"This bloke says they got lager at the top."

"Yeah?"

"Yeah. That's right, mate, innit?"

"Oh yes. Assuming, of course, that those people ahead of you don't drink it all before you get there."

"Bloody 'ell. They wouldn't do that, would they?"

"Well, they did look rather thirsty."

"Come on, Shaz, we gotta get movin'. Fanks mate."

"You are more than welcome."

And so it was that Shaz and Wayne dipped into and, thankfully, straight out of my life. Then, as if by magic, my legs found new vigour with which to continue my downward journey at a pace that would allow me to catch up with the source of my discomfort and give her a jolly good clip around the ear-hole.

Before all you social workers write in to complain, I didn't actually give her a jolly good clip round the ear-hole. She deserved one of course, and administering it would probably have shaved off many months of misconduct from her ensuing formative years: but I just couldn't be bothered to spend any time explaining, and then defending, my actions to some halfwit in a wig whose contact with the real world ceased the moment he simultaneously donned two pairs of tights at his work place.

No, I had to settle for venting some of my spleen with a few well-chosen words of admonishment. The drive back to my cottage was then accomplished in relative peace and quiet: so at least there was a silver lining of sorts.

I get talked into Internet Dating.

"Uncle William…"

A fellow instinctively knows that when a female starts a sentence which seems to tail off for no apparent reason, a leading question is just about to materialise.

"Yes…" I replied, bracing myself.

"You haven't got a girlfriend, have you?"

Even as braced as I was, you could have quite easily knocked me over with a good-sized shovel. I would have said "a feather", but I have never really held with that view: and a shovel is usually nearer to hand.

"I… er… that is… Not on me at the moment; no."

"When was the last time you had one?"

"That's a bit on the personal side, isn't it?" Especially when *had* can have so many salacious connotations.

"I wasn't being nosy."

"Well, it certainly sounded as though you were."

"I was just being curious."

"Is there a difference?"

"Oh yes. Like the one between inquisitive and meddlesome. So you can think of me as simply a concerned person."

"May I indeed?" I replied, unwilling to get into a semantic debate.

"Absolutely."

"And why, might I ask, this sudden interest in my societal endeavours?"

"It's because of Aunty Hortense."

"What about her?"

"I heard her ask mummy if you were gay."

"What!"

Before we go any further, I ought, perhaps, to tell you that Hortense is one of two sisters belonging to that ghastly smell which passes the time as my sister's husband. I have been wracking my grey matter to find a kind word to say about the woman, but the task is quite beyond my present capability.

There is no end of apt words to describe the chancre – amongst which are repellent, appalling, obnoxious, hideous: in fact, enough to fill several pages – but kind ones? I'm afraid not. I can only assume that Hortense's mother was exposed to too much alcohol, tobacco, and heavy lifting during her gestation; and had possibly even been roped into closely observing an A-bomb test as well. As an act of kindness, one should really not pour scorn upon the afflicted; but in her case I have always been prepared to countermand that rule.

So why does she not think kindly of me? Hard to tell, really. It is not as though I have ever lied to the woman: quite the opposite in fact.

On the rare occasions that she has ever asked for my opinion – be it regarding the suitability of an article of her clothing, or the manner in which my taste buds received a sample of her culinary skills – I have always striven to be as ingenuous as possible.

I can recall – I believe it was accompanying Hortense and Lynne, albeit very reluctantly (as I had been too slow to find an excuse to sidestep it, and was the only person who had a car at the time) when they were choosing dresses for some dinner soirée they had to attend – finding myself being asked by Hortense if a particular dress was flattering on her. Quite why I should have been singled out to pass comment was way outside my sphere of comprehension. The conversation, short as it was, went thus…

"William, do you think these stripes make me look a little overweight?"

"No, my dear," I replied, anxious to display my knowledge on matters of couture. "I think it is the colossal amount of food you eat which makes you look a little overweight: and, I have to say, I think it is actually more than just 'a little' overweight."

There then followed a very enthusiastic *pas-de-deux* whilst Hortense took it into her head to chase me around the store. The lack of any accompanying strains by Piotr Ilyitch Tchaikovsky was more than compensated for by the barrage of expletives that emanated from her. I had hitherto not known that she had such a wide range of vocabulary concerning matters of an earthy nature. I am constantly being surprised by the woman.

Why on earth Lynne should have chosen to go with Hortense, of the two sisters on offer, to look for a dress was – at that time – beyond me. I have since had an opportunity to meet the other sister: she doesn't exactly have six fingers and live in the attic, but you know what I mean.

"Aunty Hortense thinks you're gay."

"How utterly preposterous!"

I ought, also, to make it clear that William Phalarope has never played for the other team: the Phalarope shirt has always remained firmly tucked in. And, I might add, if I managed to spend nine years in a Public School without feeling any inclinations in that direction, I feel confident that thus it shall remain. At least it had jolly well better do so.

I recall making comments about such tendencies whilst I was in San Francisco; and I further recall commenting that, even though I had no such predispositions, I would paraphrase the maxim attributed to Voltaire (Francoise-Marie Arouet) but actually penned by Stephen G Tallentyre (Evelyn Beatrice Hall) and say that although I may disapprove of what they do or say, I will defend to the death their right to do or say it.

Well, maybe not to the death exactly; but you get the idea.

"Well she does."

I wondered why; and paused for a moment to reflect on whether I had a penchant to move about employing a gait that might be construed as 'mincing'. I pondered about whether I flicked my hair in a manner that some might interpret as being a touch too graceful to guarantee admission into the Royal Marines. I certainly did not consider that my wardrobe contained items of clothing with an excess, or indeed any, of pastel colours. So whence cometh this vituperative opinion?

A few minutes deliberation brought me to the conclusion that her malevolent thoughts might be due to the fact that Hortense perceived me to be a touch short of the macho traits which she deemed necessary to be considered a fully paid up member of the male side of the species. That opinion of hers, however, has never caused me undue concern and was soon dismissed as being of no significance: for two reasons. Firstly, I do not consider that my demeanour has ever even approached that area; and secondly, compared to Hortense, even a charging rhinoceros would look a trifle on the camp side.

"So what about a girlfriend then?"

"A girlfriend?"

"Yes."

"Yes…?"

"Well?"

"Well what?"

"I think you need one."

"Do you indeed."

"And I think I'll help you find one."

"Will you indeed."

"Yes. You know, like, before you get too old. Too old to catch one, that is. And too old to be able to turn on the style."

It was then that my thoughts flashed across the Atlantic, and a good section of the North American continent, to a certain Gabriella LaQuenta. Now I realise that for a good deal of my time in San Francisco I was probably being subjected to stimuli that I would not have ordinarily encountered on an excursion to get the paper and some milk, and that there was a goodish chance my cognitive processes might not have been operating to their full potential. But, regardless, I don't think I behaved in a manner that gave Gabriella cause to wonder just how long it would be before I became eligible for a pension. But you can never tell. I was, however, unable to fathom how the undersized stain before me had arrived at her judgement.

"I see," I said, with more than a hint of disdain. "And just how were you thinking of finding me a female companion?"

"On the Internet."

"What!"

"On the Internet. It's really easy."

"Is it? And how do you know?"

"I read about it in one of my magazines, right."

"Another of those 'outdoor' magazines I suppose."

"No. It was like a proper woman's magazine."

"Oh." I began considering if she meant a magazine for proper women, or that the magazine was a proper one. Then, if the former, could the vendor be prosecuted? Did Lynne know her issue was purchasing reading material likely to taint her young mind? Would there be any –

"Come on. It'll be like so much fun."

"For whom?"

"You; der-err."

It has often been my experience that whenever someone tries to assure me that a particular course of action will be 'fun' – especially when that someone is a fourteen-year-old girl with a genetic link to a bad smell

– that 'fun' is seldom a description I would feel happy choosing if veracity were paramount.

I have, I am pleased to say, partaken of the occasional venture with the Internet; so I am aware of what it is. I have, however, and I am not quite so pleased to say, little idea of how it works or under whose control it lies. I can boast a small working knowledge of the e-mail functions, and I even possess an e-mail address: but, once again, no real notion of how it all operates.

I have tried speaking to others in order to expand (actually, *start* might be nearer the mark) my knowledge on the subject; but have always found that most people who try to explain the matter do so at a speed that suits those who already have a pretty good grasp of the subject. I find the whole thing borders on a mixture of black magic and quantum physics; and most of what they say either goes over my head or takes the shortest route between those listening devices stuck to each side of it.

The thought of using the Internet to search for female company didn't exactly fill me with enthusiasm. In fact, I found myself bombarded with visions of a dozen desperate demimondaines assailing me with visions of what my life would be like in their company: and that is more than enough of a disincentive for any fellow.

Yes, I admit I have known the occasional lady (or do I mean 'the odd lady'? Actually 'odd' would probably be a very accurate description of some of them.): and yes, I shall also admit, some of those encounters lasted more than a matter of minutes.

I shall, however, further admit that whilst the more satisfactory of the trysts gave me a bit of a spring to my step, there always seemed to come a time when the 'pros' of being in a relationship became outweighed by the 'cons'.

Not always, I have to say, as a result of any shortcomings in the fair lady – more usually as a result of finding myself being less in control of my life than I want to be: and finding myself having to put up with social occasions that involved suffering people who I would willingly walk barefoot across hot coals to evade.

You must know what I mean – being required to go to see a play that could only prove entertaining if the stage caught fire; or having to go to dinner parties where most of the people present would, if their IQs were twenty points higher, be classified as potatoes.

Is it just me, or is the world filling up with people who, not to put too fine a point on it, appear to be a bit thick? More and more, when engaging in conversation with another, it is becoming increasingly difficult for me to find a topic with which the other person is even slightly conversant. I should, perhaps, point out that I am mostly referring to those whose formal school education began after the mid seventies.

Yes, I do have a peculiar habit of learning – and remembering – quotations and poems from various bards and philosophers; and whilst I do not necessarily expect others to be able to recite a selection of soliloquies from, say, Shakespeare's plays; I do expect them to recognise some. Well, at least *one* of them: and certainly to have *heard* of Shakespeare. These days, however, I am made to feel like a Pariah and should, perhaps, walk around with a small bell to warn others.

Speaking of which, I didn't realise that the reason lepers used to ring a bell wasn't as a warning to others to keep clear; but as a way of letting people know that they were there and would very much appreciate the receiving of alms. A fine example of how charity begins at home. None of that present-day nonsense where aid, especially that of a foreign nature, nearly always ends up in the wrong hands. What is it they say? Overseas aid is poor people in rich countries giving money to rich people in poor countries?

Where was I? Oh yes, standards of education. I have always felt that it would make more sense for a parent, when sending one of their children to their room for committing some misdemeanour, to say "Go to your room and don't come down until you have learned a sonnet," instead of saying "Go to your room and don't come down until you have learned how to behave."

I think the world would become a better place if that happened: but that's just my way of thinking.

"Right," I replied, trying to show an obvious degree of apathy.

"So come on then, let's get started."

"Now?" I cleverly upped the degree.

"Uh, yair-air."

Ten minutes later – having, I might add, had a stab at indifference and indolence – Mirabella and I were positioned in front of my laptop. I sat, slightly bemused I have to say, and watched as her small fingers tapped away and brought forth all manner of sounds and images.

"Right… here we are… Home-Dating."

"Which is…?"

"A website for lonely people… like you."

"Who said I was lonely?"

"I did."

"Have you ever heard of the Latin expression '*Nunquam minus solus, quam cum solus*'?" I asked.

"No."

"Well, it means 'Never less alone than when alone'."

"So?"

"So now do you understand?"

"Understand what?"

"That, although I might be on my own, I am not lonely."

"Whatever. Right… Male seeking female. Any preference for age?"

"No; you can tell them that I am quite happy with the one I've got."

"Not you! Your prospective girlfriend."

"Oh… er… well…"

"How old are you?"

"I don't think that's any of your business, is it?"

"It is for this exercise, yes."

"Does it have to be exact?"

"No. Roughly will do. I know you must be like about the same age as my mother."

"Younger, if you must know."

"So what is it?"

"Is there an 'in one's prime' category?"

"Not on this site; they only want numbers."

"Prime numbers?"

"Is that likely, Uncle William? Now come on, be serious."

"In that case… let's say…"

"Well, like how much older than you is my mother?"

"A few years. Or she used to be."

"*Used* to be? What do you mean by 'used' to be?"

"Ever since I was old enough to understand the concept of age, I had been under the impression that your mother was three years older than me. But recently I overheard her telling someone that she was an age which would have made her several years younger than me."

"That's weird."

"That's putting it mildly."

"Well I think she's fifty-something: so that would make you…?"

"Late forties?"

"By 'late forties' do you mean early fifties?"

"I might."

I have never really understood the hesitancy that a lot of people, me included you will have noticed, have with admitting their age. Or do I mean that I don't understand the way that people's attitude towards admitting their age changes with their age. At least I think that's what I mean. Well, I'm sure you know what I mean. Children will say that they are eight *and a half* – if indeed they are eight years and six months old: teenagers are always "I'm nearly sixteen, you know" – especially if they are fourteen: people (mainly women it has to be said) then keep very quiet about their ages between thirty and sixty; and then, for some reason, when they pass seventy (again, mainly women) they take every opportunity to let others know exactly how old they are. Especially when pushing their way to the front of any queue.

I, however, had never had a problem with my age.

"Wow! That is old."

Until just then.

"Thank you so much."

"So, I'll say you want a woman who is… what?"

"I hope you are not going to say 'desperate'."

"What *age*?"

I was able to detect a touch of impatience coming through from my attendant. Mind you, it may have been exasperation. I've always been rather good at spotting that: probably because it happens to me quite a lot.

"Mid forties will do nicely."

"Mid forties? *Mid forties*! What? You don't fancy a young partner?"

"No."

"Why not? I thought they were a 'must have' with men your age."

"Perhaps with some of my contemporaries: but not, however, with me."

What is it they call such younger ladies? I believe that the term for younger men is 'Toy Boy'; but I have a feeling that 'Toy Girl' might bring images of inflatable dolls to mind – so I shall refrain from using that. Oh yes… 'Trophy Wife'. No, I have to say, I have no real interest in acquiring myself a trophy wife.

Such an acquisition might look jolly nice on your arm when going out for an evening – maybe even inducing the occasional envious glance – but, I fear, the acquisition will become a bit too much trouble when matters such as money, spring-cleaning and existing grandchildren appear on the scene.

I seem to recall a pal of mine obtaining a consort who was several years younger than him – a couple of decades actually – and then taking every opportunity to swank around town with said nursling. I can also bring to mind how the smile on his face seemed broad enough in which to place a wide-screen television. However, I can further summon up a recollection of when – a year or so down the line – he confided in me how willing he was, of an evening, to simply settle down with a cup of tea and a good book; instead of booking appointments with a chiropractor to reset his back after another evening at a nightclub and bedroom gymnastics had taken their toll.

"So how old, then?"

"As I said, mid-forties."

"From any particular part of the country?"

"Er, not really; no. Well, not from Merseyside: obviously. Nor Middlesbrough. It might also be a good idea to give Birmingham a miss as well. Actually, perhaps the whole of the Midlands: and Essex: and quite a few parts of London."

"Scotland?"

"I'm not all that keen on Iron Brew."

"Northern England?"

"Do they know how to use computers up there?"

"Well where then?"

"How about around here."

"That's not casting the net very wide, is it?"

"Not to worry."

A few more minutes, a few more buttons pushed.

"Hobbies?" she asked.

"That would be nice. People with a hobby are usually more interesting than those without one."

"I mean what hobbies shall I say *you* enjoy? And I don't mean things like correcting other people's grammar."

"Oh. Ahm… How about listening to opera?"

"Oh that's really going to get women excited, isn't it? You man of action, you."

"Then what about doing the Alcatraz swim? That was action, wasn't it?"

"Yes; the action of a lunatic."

"Steady on."

"They'll want you to have 'interesting' hobbies: maybe even *mildly* adventurous ones. The daring hobbies are like best left to film heroes. Women want a man they know will be waiting for them, with flowers, and chocolates; and not stuck halfway up K2."

The brat was beginning to sound a bit too clued up for my liking; but even I could sense that she might have had a point. "Then what do you suggest?" I asked. "And please don't say origami and raising funds for an apiary."

"Can you think of any creative hobbies? You know: oil painting, or playing the piano."

My mind hopped back to my brief endeavour with the world of oil painting, and instantly decided that the unmitigated disaster it was would be best not mentioned.

"Not really, no," I said.

"Can you make up some?"

"Probably; but won't they want proof at some stage?"

"Good point. Then it will have to be something you could like master in the time available."

There was a brief hiatus, during which each of the participants soon remembered that dogs over a certain age aren't very likely to acquire the ability to perform new tricks; no matter how intensive the tuition.

"There must be something, Uncle William: surely."

Another lull: another selection of untrained curs.

"I guess we can come back to that. Next item. Physical characteristics?"

"Most definitely."

"I mean, how tall would you like her to be?"

"Um… somewhere between my shoulders and my eyes would be ideal."

"Which is…?"

I showed her. The resulting facial movements indicated that wasn't the answer she was looking for. "Between five three and five ten," I quantified.

"Body shape?"

"Human."

"No, I mean what size. Honestly, Uncle William; please try and help. Your choices are slim, average, a little extra weight, or large."

I had a feeling that those categories would be open to misinterpretation. After all, how much is 'a little extra' weight? A few pounds maybe; or a few stones? Then, to what is 'large' being compared? I also felt that 'average' was rather misleading, as average these days is quite large anyway. Slim, I decided, was the most prudent choice. "Slim."

"Children?"

"I've no idea. I haven't seen what the woman looks like yet. And anyway, I think I'm way past the age of considering becoming a father."

I am one of those fellows who feel that it is a tad on the selfish side fathering offspring when you have seen five decades pass by. Yes, it is possible – from a physical point of view – but I don't think it would be fair, or all that flattering, toasting the child's coming of age whilst needing to be supported on either side. Having said that, I have been to one or two twenty-first birthday celebrations where the father has required support when the time came to make the toast: but not, usually, because of the ravages of time.

"I meant do you mind if the woman has any children?"

My immediate response was going to be an unequivocal 'Yes'. I wasn't exactly having a barrel of laughs with my current compañero; and she came under the heading of kith and kin. The notion of having to endure an unrelated urchin being foisted on my *dolce vita* brought me over a bit faint. But then, needs must, I supposed.

"Depends on how many."

"Three or more?"

"Good grief, no. I might be accommodating for fewer than two."

"Do you mean one?"

"I believe that is the number I had in mind."

"That narrows it down somewhat."

"Good."

"Smoker?"

"Absolutely not."

I don't know how you feel regarding the vexed question of drawing smoke into your lungs, but I have always been of the opinion that it is a filthy habit which is undertaken by those who have personalities that are usually on the defective side of thoughtful. A sweeping generalisation, I must admit; but good enough for my purposes. Show me someone who smokes in company, and I can usually show you someone with a wealth of inconsideration for other people.

"And I don't want a drinker either," I added. "Is there a category for abstemious?"

"The choices are none, social, or heavy. Take your pick."

"I would prefer it to be none, as I think that 'social' usually hides a superfluity of amounts that range from a couple glasses of wine a day to a couple of bottles of the stuff. And 'heavy' doesn't even bear thinking about. But then I suppose that 'none' might mean someone who will try to stop me enjoying the occasional quaff. So I suppose 'Social' it will have to be."

"Religion?"

"C of E. But definitely not other than Christian."

I can't say that I am a religious man, but I do believe that there is a Creator involved somewhere along the line. I expect you know all about the Ontological, Teleological, Cosmological and Moral theories for the existence of a Deity; but I find what I call the Numerical theory to be the one that sways me the most.

"The *Numerical* theory?" I hear you pose. "Pray expand."

Okay then; but I shall be brief, as I don't think that thirty pages of the stuff would be welcomed at this juncture. Essentially, even though there are several, it all boils down to two main facets. The first involves the initial velocity of Big Bang and the rate at which the universe expanded. Too fast and the matter present would never coalesce into planets and suchlike, too slow and all the matter would quickly collapse back into itself. The initial velocity needed to be specified to a precision of 1 in 10^{60}, and that requirement would, so I believe, rule out the involvement of 'chance'.

The second is all about creating a typical, functional protein which would have 100 amino acids (from a choice of 4) arranged in a chain that will only work if those amino acids are in the right order. The probability of getting that from a primordial soup is about 1 in 10^{190}. Or to put it another way, if you took all the carbon in the universe and converted it into amino acids, allowed it to react at 10^{13} interactions per second for five billion years, the probability of making a single functioning protein is 1 in 10^{60}.

For those reasons, I surmise that some kind of 'guiding hand' must have been involved.

Where was I? Oh yes. As I said, I couldn't be described as religious, but I do hold with the precept that – providing it's not abused – it is worth having. But which one? One that makes you feel happy and kind to your neighbours, I guess. As long as they're nice neighbours! I also enjoy hearing carols at Christmas, and the feeling that is engendered at that time of year. Indeed, give me a cheerful religion with hymns that rouse your soul every time. Oh, and I definitely wouldn't choose one whose prophet married a six-year-old girl.

"Profession?" my small companion continued.

"Not fussed," I replied. Then, "But not a social worker; nor a compensation lawyer: and it might prove expeditious to remove prison officer, proctologist, politician, human resources manager, and media consultant from the list as well."

"Income?"

"Definitely: in fact, the larger the better."

Luckily, I am not one of those men who feel threatened or emasculated by a woman who earns more than him. After all, how insecure must a fellow be to judge his manliness on the comparative size of his pay packet? I shall resist the temptation to make a pun here; but I think you know what I mean!

"Okay then, let's see what comes up."

"I am verily on tenterhooks."

I have to point out that, despite my genial air, I really wasn't happy about the proceedings. You see, a chap like me, and of my age, becomes rather used to being on his own. Yes, I have to admit, I do have a liking for the ladies and the pleasures that they are able to provide. And by that – just in case those of you with a penchant for the smutty innuendo have conjured up all manner of licentious images – I mean their ability to round off many of the rough edges that can detract from one's corporeal journey along Life's ever-winding road.

However, despite all the advantages that female company may provide, I must add that I rather like the ability to carry on negotiating my trip through this vale of tears at pretty much the speed of my own choosing. As well as being able to rest easy in the knowledge that my clothes will be exactly where I left them the night before; and also to know that the sound of a vacuum-cleaner will not interrupt an afternoon nap.

Furthermore, what is it they say? A man joins up with the woman of his dreams; a woman joins up with a man she thinks she can change into the man of her dreams. Something like that; and probably why I'm still single.

I could also make reference to the probable assault upon my organs of hearing when I return from an evening's *ad libitum* with such as my good friend Duncan. Makes a fellow shudder even to think about it.

I am not going to invoke the German attitude of *Kinder, Kirche, und*

Kuche – even though there might be a lot of merit in it – but there really is a lot to be said for being able to do as I please without having to get permission or being subjected to several hours of threats (or should that be promises?) of going home to her mother.

"Here's one. She's a woman who only has one child. Do you want to hear about her?"

"Will she be telling the truth?"

"Why shouldn't she?"

"Well, for some fairly obvious reasons."

"Such as?"

"Such as she's hardly likely to write that she's vain, capricious, prone to starting arguments, and takes ninety minutes deciding which shoes to wear."

"Uncle William! That is like so sexist."

"And so true. Women are fickle. It's a stipulation within their genes."

"Like you're not?"

"My dear girl, a more affable cove you are unlikely to ever meet. Salt of the earth, that's me. *Honesta quam splendida*, if you don't mind me saying."

"I doubt very much if any of your potential ladies are going to even know what that means."

"Well they should. Reputable rather than showy. Nothing beats a classical education."

"Oh, really? Well, just don't expect too many others to share your passion for a dead language."

"More's the pity."

"Huh. So, do you want to hear about her?"

"I suppose I had better. But I have heard such awful tales of those who – how shall I put it? – have been a tad 'economical' with the truth. I just don't want to get all keen and then find out she's over seventy and one short in the leg department."

"You really shouldn't judge people by their appearance."

"I was thinking more along the lines of the Sale of Goods Act."

"Just listen."

And so it came to pass that I sat and paid attention while Mirabella rattled through a handful of descriptions of women who had placed their particulars – I believe those were referred to as 'Profiles' – on the website in question.

I have to admit to being slightly uneasy in the presence of women. Not all women, you understand; just the vast majority. There is something about their innate superiority – some might say smugness – that confounds me somewhat; and meeting with them usually makes me feel as if I have been called before my old headmaster. Not quite sure what it is, but I feel the need to admit to almost any wrongdoing I may have perpetrated, or even read about, within the last twelve months. Such an approach, I should imagine, is unlikely to hold much sway when participating in the dating game.

Then there was the question of my 'Profile'. What, I ask myself, is the possibility of members of the opposite sex finding attractive a fellow whose best attributes are that he has a pleasant accent, his own hair and teeth, and a tendency to appear a bit simple-minded? These days, women seem to want men who are tall, muscular, erudite, handsome, wealthy, humorous, and endowed with wedding-tackle that wouldn't look out of place on an adult donkey. Does rather narrow down the field somewhat; but there we are. Maybe I should be looking for a woman whose main attribute is that she has very low expectations.

"So," asked my diminutive companion, "what do we say about you?"
"Something flattering I should hope."
"We tell lies then?"
"I wouldn't go that far: a little embellishment, perhaps."
"Lies."
"Now look here, my petite packet of pestilence; I thought the object was to find me a companion."
"Yes…"
"Well, then I think that a dash of artistic licence should be allowed."
"Well, then isn't that being a dash hypocritical?"
"A dash is all I'm after."
"Okay; just a dash then."
"Right."
"Height?"

"Six feet three."

"What's that in centimetres?"

"I don't care. It's imperial or nothing."

"Build?"

"Would 'Like an Adonis' be acceptable?" I queried.

"I'll put 'average'."

"That sounds very ordinary, don't you think?"

"You're not slim, you're not overweight, and I somehow doubt that 'athletic' fits the bill."

"Are those the only other choices?"

"Yes. I don't think people are like going to want to tick a box marked skinny, fat or revolting, are they?"

"No, I suppose not," I ceded.

There then followed several minutes of questioning, by the end of which I felt as if I had put my soul on a shelf in a bric-a-brac store. As for the bit that needs to be tagged on at the end – you know, that part about why others would want to meet you – well, that made me feel awfully vulnerable: especially as I couldn't really think of any good reason why a woman would want to meet me.

"Have you got a recent photo?"

"How recent?"

"Within the last year."

"Probably."

"Good. As long as it doesn't show you in fancy-dress, bladdered or in a compromising pose."

"Bladdered?"

"You know… drunk."

"Oh. And what do you mean by 'compromising'?"

"Like getting out of a bath."

"That's not the sort of thing I have a habit of doing."

"What? Getting out of a bath?"

"Recording the event on celluloid."

But you'd be surprised how many people do. As well as being happy to have their photograph taken whilst wearing a dress – members of my sex, that is. I have never quite understood what possesses a man to even want to put on a dress in the first place: never mind then go out in public. Yes, I did meet several thus inclined while I was in San Francisco; and yes, I did empathise with those who felt as if they were occupying the wrong body: well, at least where they felt it was one of the wrong sex rather than one that wasn't as impressive as they would have liked.

But the fellow who makes a habit of going to parties dressed as a pupil of St. Trinian's always seems to me to be harbouring some very latent and, almost certainly, peculiar inclinations. Rather as the way that someone with a fondness for chucking Chablis down their throat is always on the lookout for an excuse to have a drink, so the chap under discussion is always on the lookout for an excuse to wear a frock and a pair of sling-backs. Nowt so queer as folk, and all that, I suppose.

I am not even going to get started on the sights that nearly detached my retinas when I was at the Folsom Street Fair! Other than to say that people never fail to surprise me. I have just made a mental note that when I get to meet my Creator I shall ask if perhaps he spilled some coffee on the plans while he was designing us: I can't think of another explanation as to why it all went so awry.

After several more minutes of IT wizardry from the open sore, I was up and running: and then it was simply a matter of sitting back and waiting. I did, however, have a quick gander through the selection of females who had ventured to hoist their particulars into view.

I suppose, when you think about it, the concept of looking for potential dates on the Internet is no more out of the ordinary than frequenting places where people have a tendency to gather. I refer to the most common – pubs and clubs – where you are quite likely to get a punch on the nose if you happen to be eying someone who is already spoken for. I am sure that the person who comes up with a method for letting others know whether or not someone is 'available' will make a mint. When I say 'a method', I mean (apart from the wearing of a ring on the third finger of the left hand of course) a discreet one. I understand that there are several systems already available; some of which could hardly be described as discreet, however. Could a drunken, sonorous "Yoo-hoo big boy," ever be described as discreet? I rather doubt it. Although, in some circles…

For myself, I am absolutely hopeless at reading what is commonly referred to as body language; so the method, as well as being discreet, would have to be foolproof. What I know about signs such as the crossing and uncrossing of legs, flicked hair and the adjustment of ties could be written in block capitals on the back of a postage stamp. I do not have a clue, I'm afraid: not a clue. Maybe I should read Alexandre Dumas's 'La Dame aux Camélias', or watch *La Traviata* a few more times!

Speaking of frequenting suitable venues for meeting members of the opposite sex, I did visit a local gymnasium once. I have always understood the plural of gymnasium to be gymnasia, but the modern trend is to refer to them as 'Tone Zones'.

Tone Zones! What on earth does that mean? Only those who have tone are allowed to use them? I hardly think so; especially if the number of large ladies with a weakness for wearing inappropriate clothing is anything to go by. I ask you; if you possessed the largest pair of thighs this side of the Euphrates, would you advertise that fact by wearing bright yellow lycra shorts? I rather doubt I would. As for combining that colour with a material that leaves little or nothing to the imagination… Well, the mind fair flinches at the invitation.

Perhaps the owners of such establishments mean 'Zones for those who would like to Tone'. Sounds a bit better – a bit more accurate, that is – but I suppose it would make the sign over the door rather wide. Maybe 'Hope Zone' would be more apposite: or how about 'Flounce and Bounce'?

Anyway, there I was, eager to dazzle all the women with my flexibility and strength. Perhaps this might be a good spot to point out that I am going back several years. I shan't elaborate on exactly how many, but it was at a time when my strength and flexibility were higher up the list of my attributes than they are now. Not prominent, you understand; but discernable nonetheless.

So it was, with a heady mixture of testosterone and poise, that I settled myself to do some of those sit-up things. I was feeling fairly confident that day – a mixture of youth and the fact that I was sure several pairs of eyes were swivelling in my direction – so I set myself a target of ten. I also recall that by about the fourth repetition I had attracted the attention of two pulchritudinous blondes and was feeling rather pleased with myself.

Unfortunately, I also have a vivid memory of what greeted me in the wall mirror when I sat up for the fifth time: and that, I fear, was what had produced the approbation in the young ladies. You see, I had foolishly chosen to wear a pair of shorts that day.

"Nothing untoward in that," I hear you comment. "Lots of gym-users do."

Absolutely: and it would have been 'toward' were it not for the fact that said shorts had probably been designed to be best worn whilst standing, with a modicum of perambulation, and not lying on your back with knees raised and slightly bent. I don't feel the need to provide any further details. Needless to say, the excursion as an exercise in meeting those of a female construction wasn't a roaring success, and did little to encourage me to try further.

But on through the photographs on the web site I went; and may I say how very attractive some of the women looked: and that, of course, made me wonder why on earth they felt the need to bung their details on the site in the first place. Well, at least up to the moment that Mirabella pointed out that a lot of the photographs were in the 'soft focus' format, probably not recent, and may not even be of the woman concerned. Pretty poor show if you ask me.

Anyway, into the ring went my hat.

Making an initial contact with other users of the aforementioned website was the next move. Which one – or ones – was I to choose? Perhaps it was just as well – or was it? – that Mirabella was close by to whisper in my shell-like that a certain amount of caution would, almost certainly, prove to be a sagacious course of action. I'm not sure that those were the exact words she used: perhaps it was something along the lines of 'don't jump in like a gormless geek'.

Whichever version it may have been, the point reached its intended target; and together we ambled through the selection available.

It is surprising how the same person can assume two contrasting lists of qualities when observed through two different pairs of eyes; especially if those two pairs first had occasion to focus on their respective environs over thirty-five years apart.

Someone, whom to me seemed to be in possession of a more than pleasant phizog would, to Mirabella, have eyes that looked shifty and who had used all manner of badly-chosen hair colourings. Which, incidentally, was arranged in a style that was, apparently, 'Like, that's so last year'.

Conversely, there were ladies whom Mirabella would have been more than happy to accept as a potential step-aunt (or whatever title the relevant position would assume), whilst I felt the need to point out that the lady in question seemed to possess a mouth into which I could effortlessly push a carriage clock.

I do not, you understand, wish to denigrate those who have the misfortune to own an oral orifice into which a dental surgeon would have no trouble fitting a bridge – say, for instance, Hammersmith. It's just that I have always felt a certain amount of perturbation when hearing an echo should I be talking to one of these poor individuals when they happen to yawn.

Eventually, after a certain amount of time spent perusing the advertised ladies, Mirabella and I were able to reach agreement – albeit tenuously – on six of them. Now six may seem quite a lot, but when you realise that there were about twenty women that fell within the list of criteria that Mirabella and I (mainly Mirabella it must be said) deemed essential, you will understand that six wasn't a display of avarice on my part.

I should perhaps mention another deciding factor in reaching the choice of six. Although Mirabella and I saw quite a few other women who either met, or came close to meeting, with my requirements – age, occupation, size etc – I didn't meet with theirs. It seemed that a lot of women who, even allowing for a small fib or two, hovered between the ages of 45 and 50 were after men who hovered between the ages of 35 and 40. Still, I suppose I can't blame them for being optimistic.

Anyway, and with more than sufficient anxiety, I thought it wise to wait until after Mirabella had gone back to her mother's before embarking upon my quest.

I get to meet my dates.

Mirabella had suggested that I make initial contact with all six at the same time. Not in the flesh, I was relieved to hear, but across the ether. This was the best way as, apparently, some might find another suitor before I had time to get round to meeting them. I was also to discover that exchanging missives was quite a good way of finding out if the ladies in question had had any formal education.

You see, even though computers have a facility known as 'Spell Check', they do tend to err rather a lot on the side of the American orthography. So, if the reply to my opening gambit arrived with a surplus of words such 'traveled', 'center' and 'theater', then it was a reasonable bet that the lady in question had either not adjusted her 'Spell Check' from English US to English UK, didn't know that there was a difference, or was American. None of which was exactly a good portent for sufficient intellect; but I was prepared to yield a few inches, on the grounds of magnanimity.

If, however, her reply was deluged with errors of a grammatical nature, I could be forgiven for raising an eyebrow and thinking that there was a possibility the lady in question had missed the occasional E. Lang. lesson. In which instance I could also be forgiven for refusing to yield even a hair's breadth.

As I may have mentioned, I am not a stickler for flawless grammar: after all, I have been known to split infinitives occasionally. And start a sentence with a conjunction. But I do like to see the requisite use of punctuation: and if the letter is handwritten, I expect that the letters of the same word are joined together and not written in block capitals. E-mail correspondence, unfortunately, bypasses the necessity for the latter, and so removes part of the vetting process. Anyway, off went my introductions.

Number 1 was a pleasant-sounding lady who had described herself as being of an arty disposition. Fair enough, I thought; as long as that didn't entail her turning up covered in dollops of kaolin or oil paint.

Fortunately neither of those possibilities came into play: but she was wearing a pair of dungarees that was covered in a wide array – probably her entire range – of earthenware badges.

Once again, I do not wish to lob aspersions around willy-nilly, but am I alone in feeling uncomfortable sharing a cup of Kenco's finest with someone who is festooned with all manner of slogans, as well as effigies of farmyard animals and wild flowers?

It really was awfully difficult trying to focus on impressing the lady whilst being visually assailed with labels suggesting – amongst other things – that I might like to adopt a giraffe. Speaking of which, I think the practice of adopting animals is cruel: after all, sooner or later you're going to have to tell them.

Anyway, although the evening ended cordially enough, the net result was that no arrangements were made, or even suggested, to meet again.

Number 2 was one of those women who believe that the more make-up you apply the prettier you become: and believe you me, she had intended being the prettiest woman on the planet. I can't say exactly how much foundation cream she had used; but to give you an idea, even if she had used a trowel to apply it, she would have taken the best part of an hour to do so. I could only assume that, in order to facilitate the later removal of the stuff, some kind of sandblaster must have been stored in her bathroom.

The taxi-driver who drove me home politely enquired if my skin condition was catching. I had, rather foolishly, accepted a 'mwah' goodnight from the lady; and, as a result of our cheeks touching, I now had several patches of matter hanging off the side of my face.

The silly thing was that she would almost certainly have been more than attractive enough without it all. Perhaps she worked on the cosmetics counter of one of the large stores and felt obliged to try out all the products. I just wish she hadn't tried them all at the same time.

Number 3 was an executive type. As you know, I have no problem with members of the opposite sex going out and earning a living: quite the contrary in fact, and all the better for it. But why oh why do some of them feel the need to dress in a way – I believe it's called 'power dressing' – that is designed to intimidate all those in the immediate vicinity; and give the impression that they spend rather too much of their spare time training their deltoid muscles?

There I was, trying to enjoy a ham salad with a lady whose clothes were sharp enough to cut through roofing felt; and despite my attempts to remind myself that I was on a blind date, I couldn't shake off the feeling that I was attending a hostile take-over bid in some high-level boardroom.

Then there were the many interruptions from her mobile phone. I thought that was rather rude; but perhaps I was simply missing the point. Were the constant calls all part of the ritual? Were they meant to impress me? Or were they simply prearranged to offer her the chance of a 'get-out' clause in case my company became unappealing and no longer merited any investment?

'Sorry, er, William. That was the office: major situation; must dash; ciao'. I'm sure you recognise the sort of thing I mean.

But I never got to find out; as her husband wandered in when we were halfway through the Pavlova. Bad enough on its own, but he had a rather vacant-looking article clinging to his arm to whom Number 3 took exception.

Whilst I have never encouraged the exchange of profanities between people, I have been known to listen attentively – and even jot down some of them – in case I happen upon an expletive that might prove useful should I ever find myself lost for one whilst spending an evening of excessive libation with members of Her Majesty's Armed Forces.

On this occasion, however, I would have had difficulty keeping up with the lady in question; even had I been proficient in shorthand. Honestly! I had never before heard someone deliver such a wide range of invective, and supply it at a rate that would have had tobacco auctioneers deciding on another career. It was as astonishing as it was unexpected: quite extraordinary.

Needless to say, I didn't get the opportunity to enquire if a second meeting was on the cards as the local constabulary declined my request to have a quick word with the object of my assignation before they carted her off in their Black Maria.

Number 4 was – how can I put it politely? – a bit intellectually challenged. Not that I am saying she was thick, you understand; but I have a feeling that someone else must have written her profile. I instinctively knew something was amiss when, upon meeting, I asked her if she would like an aperitif and she said that she was happy with the set she had.

I smiled, just in case it was a bit of a jape, and ordered her one anyway. But I was later to realise that it hadn't been a joke and, when she took a bite into a crusty roll, that she did indeed have a complete set of dentures.

Once again, I want to keep a tight grip on all my calumniations, and emphasise the fact that false teeth do not a virago make: but when said acrylic gnashers fall into a bowl of soup and are then repositioned with scarcely a by-your-leave, I do feel the stirrings of protestations from within.

I remember thinking that had I been my good friend Duncan Strewper (you remember, my pal the dentist) I may well have pointed out that although the teeth were of the L46 mould and in a very nice shade of A3, perhaps a shade of B2 might have been more suitable. Especially when considering the lady's overall complexion.

I, however, have little knowledge of such matters; except that the best way of making your teeth look whiter is to paint your face black. Not always socially acceptable, and invariably scorned by members of the PC Brigade; but highly effective nonetheless.

Anyway, by the time the coffee was on the table I found out that she had a brother enjoying a break at Her Majesty's expense – something to do with cut and shut – and decided that, despite the alluring way she kept wiping her mouth with the back of her hand, she probably wasn't the one for me.

Number 5 was a good deal older than she had led me to believe. Quite a good bit older, as it happens. I have nothing against women – or men for that matter – who say that they are a decade or two younger than that displayed on their birth certificate. Unless, of course, they expect me to believe them: I do draw the line at that point.

Assuming Providence decrees that I shall live long enough, I fully expect to show the occasional sign of tempus having fugited. That is, as a certain W. Shakespeare once put it, when 'In eternal lines to time I grow'st'.

I don't think I possess the specific genes which allow people to sidestep the normal ravages that accompany septuagenarians and above; but even if I do, I really doubt if I would ever have the brass neck to arrange a meeting with someone twenty years my junior and expect her to believe that she occupied the elder berth.

Honestly, the woman needed a bloody good ironing: and help getting to and from the bathroom. And then there was the rather embarrassing incident when, having successfully negotiated her way out of the ladies, she abruptly forgot at which table she had been sitting, and insisted that the *maitre d'* tell me to stop pestering her, and whether he would be kind enough to bring her horse and carriage round to the front.

Number 6 went by the name of Judy. In her correspondence, she wrote that, apart from bringing up a sixteen-year-old son, she owned – and worked – a smallholding: about 15 acres of pastoral land on which she kept several items of livestock. As I have never been one to advocate that those of the fairer sex should miss out on doing manual labour, especially if it meant that I could, I looked forward to meeting her.

I decided to defer any thoughts as to how I might fare with her offspring – if my accomplishments with that which came forth from my sister's loins were anything to go by, then pushing aside such thoughts was probably a very wise thing to do – and I sallied forth to our rendezvous.

When she approached I think I quickly realised that there was a lot of physical labour involved with her brand of husbandry, as she had a pair of shoulders that would not have looked out of place on a rugby second-row forward. Quite extraordinary, if not a little intimidating; and she seemed to have a desire to show them off by wearing a dress that had very narrow straps. I was also fairly certain what one variety of her livestock was.

Call me a bit of a martinet by all means, but I do prefer the smell given off by most brands of perfume to that given off by a Gloucester Long Back. I am all in favour of equality and women making their own way, and I am more than happy for said female to take a little while to shrug off any residue from her day's labour. Absolutely insistent would be an accurate description. You see, I found myself drawing a line when it came to the lady sitting down in a restaurant smelling like one of the main courses before it had been dispatched.

I did try, quite valiantly as it happens, to explain that the reason my eyes were watering so much was because my puree d'oignons was a bit too aux oignons for my liking; and not because of the porcine-laden breeze wafting in my direction from the other side of the table. I don't think I was all that convincing, as the lady left before the dessert was served: or perhaps it was because by that stage I had tied my serviette across my nose like a cowboy's bandana in a cattle drive. Hard to tell.

So, as you may have gathered, my foray into Internet Dating did not go according to plan.

"Then how about speed-dating?" was the next suggestion from Mirabella, when she telephoned to ask how things had gone.

To be perfectly honest, I rather felt that the Internet variety was, in one or two instances, over rather quicker than I had originally anticipated; and a format bearing the prefix 'Speed' might well prove to be far too swift for me. I know they say 'faint heart ne'er won fair maiden'; but as I was having more than enough problems with maidens of any hair colour, I did begin to wonder just how robust my constitution would have to prove before I won the fabled flaxen-haired female.

Against my better judgement, speed-dating came under scrutiny. I carried out an internet trawl, to try and find a venue that was both within reasonable travelling distance and catered for people of my age. Not an easy task, I have to say.

Upon inspection, it seemed that most of the 'events' were designed for those between the ages of 25 and 35; and that as I couldn't guarantee having a seat in a dark corner of the room, I felt that I would end up being mistaken for a parent of one of the participants.

As evenings for those between 45 and 55 didn't exist, the closest I could find that was taking place within the same calendar year and less than 200 miles away that is, was one for 35 to 45. My sense of propriety dictated that I contacted the organisers to ascertain if someone who was possibly five years outside the upper limit would still be able to attend.

Yes, was the answer. It seems that the demographics involved in the 'dating game' are such that between the ages of 25 and 35 there is an abundance of men who want a relationship, the numbers show parity between 35 and 45, but between the ages of 45 and 55 – and more strikingly the higher you go above that – there is a shortage of men. Well, at least men who could be described as being of a suitable nature. Men who are married, or of an inclination to want the available men, are not allowed; and are, by all accounts, to be actively hindered from attending.

My presence, as it turned out, was not merely going to be tolerated, but almost encouraged. Now whether such a patter was simply to obtain my sponduliks I shall never know; but 'Hey ho' I thought all the same, and made the necessary booking.

I expect a lot of you are conversant with the format of such occasions, so I shall spare you the minutiae; except to say that it was in a well-known, and much frequented, establishment in Cardiff: and no, I do not mean the middle of the pitch in the Millennium Stadium.

So it was, at the appointed time, along with a large slice of apprehension, I found myself standing, with a drink in hand, waiting for the proceedings to begin: and I also found all kinds of thoughts rampaging through my grey matter.

Was I dressed appropriately? Would the majority, if not all, of those attending be at the lower end of the age spectrum? Would I, almost inevitably, end up saying something that would lead the object of my attentions to start wondering if I was either on, or urgently required, continuous and strong medication? How was I going to get rid of Mirabella's corpse the following morning?

Before I had too long to dwell on the possible outcomes of the proceedings, I saw several people making their collective way up to the next floor.

"And how were you able to discern that you shared a common goal?" you ask. "After all, it might well have been the biennial meeting of a local branch of the Wheel-tappers and Shunters Association."

Well, yes, so it might well have. Were it not for the fact that there was a certain air of hope, possibly mixed with desperation, discernable amongst them; and apart from two of the ladies, none of them looked as though they had been anywhere near a railway yard.

I stood on the bottom step, preparing to follow them – as imperceptibly as possible, you understand – with all manner of images of Julius Caesar on the banks of the Rubicon going though my head. Then, once further images of Shackleton and Mallory came into view, I proceeded on up.

I don't know about you, but I quite often find that my cup of personal shyness has a tendency to overflow at times. Not in one of those spilling everywhere episodes, where you have an irresistible urge to crawl under the nearest table and pretend to be part of the carpet; but in a wobbly meniscus way, where your first urge is to find an empty corner and stand there facing the wall and hope that your jacket blends in nicely with the wall-paper. This was one such occasion.

The room was filled to the gunwales with people, and my initial estimate was that there were around eight hundred of them. However, once the part of my brain concerned with arithmetic worked out that having to meet 400 women would, if the advertised three minutes was enforced, take the best part of twenty hours; or, if the estimated time was to be equally divided, then I would have approximately 25 seconds with each lady. Hardly time enough to sit down; never mind indulge in a spot of verbal exchange: well, apart from "Hello" and "Cheerio."

As neither alternative seemed within the realms of common sense, I embarked upon a recount and, as the evening would later confirm, somewhere in the region of 34 people was nearer the mark.

We were instructed to 'sign in', collect a badge number (mine, for the fastidious among you, was 16) and listen while the lady in charge took us through the format that was to be used. I took my drink to a quiet part of the room, and listened attentively as the instructions were read out to one and all.

I could only assume, if the manner in which everybody else seemed to ignore what was being said was anything to go by, that I was the only newcomer to such an event: and that did little to boost my rapidly dwindling levels of confidence.

Anyway, in next to no time, the event was underway. Also in next to no time, the organiser realised that I didn't have a clue what I should be doing, and I was escorted to a table that bore the same number as that glued to my lapel. The object, it transpired, was to talk with the lady seated there until, upon hearing the sound of a whistle, I was to get up and move to the next, numerically ordered, table and repeat the procedure. Seemed fair enough: so, conveying a good deal more *savoir-faire* than I actually possessed, I began.

I shall not go into details of all seventeen of the ladies with whom I was meant to converse: firstly, because I think that your attention may waver; secondly, because I can't describe more than seven of them anyway; and thirdly, because I was asked to leave before I met the tenth lady.

The whole experience was, to put it mildly, rather bizarre. I am fairly sure that my concentration held firm to begin with: fairly sure, but not certain. It seemed that at whatever table my physical form was seated, my thought processes were lagging at least two tables behind. You see, three minutes is not a long time to find out about someone. That, for the mathematically challenged amongst you, is 90 seconds for each person to ask the other person questions that will reveal aspects of character that may, or may not, make you wish to see that person again.

Three minutes. Or do I mean – *Three minutes*! And what enquiries would help me reach my verdict? I had imagined that a reply of 'Yes' to the question 'Have you any unusual pastimes?', followed by a 'No' to the question 'Are you going to tell me about them?' would cause me to tread carefully. I could also imagine that being told their occupation was mortician might dampen my ardour somewhat.

I had, by the application of the smattering of common sense that lurks within me, already decided that the ladies might rapidly tire of being asked the same, predictable, questions – What do you do? Have you come far? etc.

– by each of the male participants as they sat down at their respective tables. So, I had further reasoned, that it might help the Phalarope cause if I asked questions that normally roamed about outside the average pathways. I tried…

> "Which three adjectives would friends use to describe you?"
> "What do you do on a typical Saturday?"
> "What is the craziest thing you have ever done?"
> "Do you have any phobias?"

A decent range of questions I thought; which were neither outlandish nor intrusive. Well, at least up until I received the answers from the lady at the third table I visited.

> "*Friends?*"
> "I spend the morning trying to recover from the rat-arsing I get on Friday night, and then go and play rugby for 'Holloway Old Girls' in the afternoon."
> "Robbed a Post Office."
> "Men who look like rozzers." Then, after taking a closer look at me, "Aarghhhh," before diving under the table.

Needless to say, at the next table I quickly reverted to 'What do you do?' and 'Have you come far?' I also added 'Are you enjoying this?'

It was at about the fifth – might have been the sixth – lady that something Mirabella said to me stumbled to the front of my thought processes. "They say you can tell if you like someone within six seconds of seeing them." Maybe the organisers should cater for that and allow people to get up before the bell goes: or maybe not.

Anyway, on I went, lurching from table to table. As it turned out, I needn't have worried about the quality of question diversity, as the first enquiry I received at each new table was 'Why are you doing this?'

Not wishing to state what must have been blindingly obvious – *videlicet* 'I don't meet many people in the normal course of things' – I thought that it might be a good idea to introduce a dash of levity into the proceedings at the next table.

"Because the police have been round all the telephone boxes in my area and removed the business cards," I said, hoping to elicit a jocular response.

'Oh good, here's a person of highly amusing intellect,' would have been my first thought, had I been on the receiving end. 'Well worth another probe,' would almost certainly have been a close second.

Alas, neither of those was to fashion itself within the cranial confines of the lady to whom I addressed my witticism. At least that was the impression I got when the aforementioned addressee got to her feet, gave me a look that could have burnt a hole in the wallpaper, and said, in stentorian tones "Get away from me, you filthy pervert."

No, the evening couldn't have been described as an unqualified success by any standards; nor was it one that I shall fondly remember in years to come. I did, however, stay downstairs for a swift half and spoke with a fellow who had been through it all on a previous occasion, and was made aware of something rather paradoxical. Apparently, so he told me, women get fussier as they get older. Now whether that is true, or just a combination of a defence mechanism by the women and sour grapes by the chap, I couldn't say.

It could well be an example of one of the other illogicalities that surfaces as people get older: that even though they have less life ahead of them, they take an age to do even the simplest of things.

Perhaps getting a dog might be the answer for me. You know where you are with a dog. As someone once said, a dog will always love you more than a woman. This can be proved by locking your wife and your dog in the garage for two hours, and then see which one is the happier to see you when you let them out.

I need to see a dentist.

Fortunately, as a rule, I tend not to get problems with my teeth. Unfortunately, as a rule, when I do tend to get one, I tend to get it at the most inconvenient moment. You must know the sort of thing – a bit of filling thinks that a jolly good time to drop out is just as you take your seat in the theatre: or that bit of gingiva (I believe it is referred to as an operculum) which has spent the last five years peacefully lying on top of one of your wisdom teeth decides that it would be a laugh to swell up just as you start chomping on a piece of steak at some expensive restaurant. Very painful and, as a result of you biting hard on to it, very noisy as well.

Yes indeed; and rather alarming for the poor waiter who happened to be passing your table at the time: and probably pretty much the same for the chap at the adjacent table over whose lap the tureen of hot soup that the waiter was carrying happened to finish.

So it was that a little piece of filling on the second tooth from the back on the lower left – a second molar I understand is the official term, and sometimes known as a 'seven' – thought that a good time to work loose was whilst that delightful child came to spend a few more days with me: on account of her mother having to go back for a follow-up appointment. Not exactly an apocalyptic event (the filling loosening, rather than Mirabella staying, that is) by any means, but one that was destined to cause quite a lot of exasperation.

However, using part of the vast initiative resources I possess, I decided to give my friend – the dentist, Duncan Strewper – a call, and book an appointment to remedy the malady. Have I mentioned Duncan before? I think I may have. He's the chap who pays the occasional visit to that Parkhurst place on the Isle of Wight; and, fortunately, he also has a practice of his own.

Yes, I am quite sure that there are plenty of capable dental surgeons in my own locality; but I am also equally sure that they would quite happily charge an arm and a leg and still not be able to see me for three or four months. On top of which, going to see Duncan would eat up the best part of a day of young Mirabella's company. So a phone call it was.

"Good afternoon, dental surgery. How may I help you?"

"Oh, hello… um… Is Duncan free at the moment?"

I used the name 'Duncan' as that should have given the receptionist an indication that he and I are on a first name basis. Little touches like that are designed to get you into the fast lane of making contact, and circumvent all those hard-nosed delaying tactics that so many receptionists enjoy using.

"Is *who* free?"

"Duncan."

"Do you mean Dr Strewper?"

"*Doctor* Strewper? No, I don't think so. I mean the dentist chappie."

"That is Dr Strewper."

"No, no, no; I'm sure he was a dentist the last time we spoke."

"Well, he *is* a dentist."

There was a short pause while I assimilated that concept.

"So *Dr* Duncan Strewper is a *dentist*?"

"Look, I don't know who you are or what institution doesn't yet know you're missing, but I really am very busy."

"Quite. Ah. Right. In that case… please may I speak with him?"

"No."

"No? But I am a personal friend of his."

"I don't care. You still can't speak with him."

"Why not?"

"Because he's at lunch."

"*At lunch*! But it's only a quarter past twelve."

"That's right. Dr Strewper goes for lunch at midday."

"Goodness. Until when?"

"His first appointment of the afternoon is at half-past two."

I am a *laissez-faire* sort of chap – well, most of the time – but two and a half hours for lunch did, initially at any rate, feel a bit extravagant to me. Ninety minutes has always seemed to be a fairly acceptable interval in which to enjoy a spot of sustenance; a hundred and twenty minutes has even been deemed worthy of consideration: but one hundred and fifty minutes?

"Would you like me to make you an appointment? It won't be for a month or so, though."

"A month… or so? Oh good heavens, no. It'll have to be a lot sooner than that."

"We're fully booked."

"So you said; but as I said, I am a *personal* friend of Duncan."

"In that case, you'll have to speak to him yourself."

"In that case, that is what I shall do. I'll give him a ring later. Um, do you have his mobile number? I appear to have mislaid it."

"We don't give out those phone numbers. It might invite all sorts of abuse."

"Er, quite. Okay. Ahm; then how about if I speak with him at the practice?"

"When?"

"When would be a good time?"

"His last appointment is at five."

"Would you please leave him a message to say that William Phalarope telephoned, and that I shall call again shortly after five o'clock?"

"I suppose so."

"Thank you."

I would be lying if I said I felt confident that my message would reach its intended destination. There was something about the attitude of the receptionist that made me think of a prison officer in charge of visiting times. Terse may have been a bit strong. Perhaps laconic? Possibly. However, quickly putting potential defamations to one side, I duly waited until five minutes past five before telephoning once again.

"Evenin'. Dr Strewper's surgery 'ere. Can oi 'elps you?"

I immediately felt my heart sink. Do you ever get the same sort of feeling when embarking on verbal interaction with someone who holds the key to your aspirations and at the same time sounds as if they might be missing more than a few brain cells? It may have been the West Country lilt to her voice; it may have been the endearing way she felt no need for certain consonants; it may have been the way she sniffed at the end of each sentence: it may well have been all three.

"It's me, William Phalarope; back again."

"Ooh?"

"William Phalarope. I telephoned earlier."

"Dids yer?"

"Yes."

"Oh. Well oi wasn't 'ere earlier, oi wasn't."

"Ah."

"Oi only works the shift after lunch."

"Oh."

"So what's it you be wannin'?"

"I... er..."

"Oh, come on now; spit it out."

"Ha-ha! Perhaps a dental receptionist in-joke? Yes? *Très amusant*."

"Whart?"

"Your little joke. Your *petit bon mot*."

"Moy whart?"

"*Bon mot*. I was just admiring your little quip."

"Whart! When 'ave you seen thart?"

"Seen what?"

"Moy little quip. Is this 'ere some kind of crank carl? 'Cos if it is, oi'll 'ave the police on you in no times oi will. Bloody perv. Oi knows your sort."

"I am quite sure that you do; but this, at the probable risk of causing you a lot of disappointment, is not a crank call. And I am not, as you say, a perv. My name is William Phalarope. I telephoned earlier today, and was asked to ring back in order to have a word with Dunc – *Dr* Strewper. The young lady with whom I spoke assured me that she would leave a message to that effect."

"Did she?"

"Yes."

"Well, oi 'aven't seen it."

"Have you looked?"

"If she leaves a note that oi'm s'posed to see then it's always – Oh! 'Ere it is. Let's see... da-de-da-de-da... 'Ere, is your name Phil Rope?"

"No, it is not. It's Phalarope. William Phalarope."

"Not Phil Rope?"

"No."

"Pity, cos there's a note 'ere bout someone carled Phil Rope."

"Does it say anything about a gentleman who would be telephoning back later this afternoon?"

"'Ang on... er... Yeah! Bloomin' 'eck. Ee'll 'af to 'urry up: doc Strewper's nearly finished, 'e is."

It really is awfully difficult to conduct a conversation with someone whose age almost certainly exceeds their IQ: someone who, even on a good day, would find opening a box of matches intellectually challenging. I found myself struggling to figure out why on earth Duncan would have employed someone of that calibre.

I could only assume that he must have been subjected to one of three influences when he decided to hire the plum duff presently using his telephone. Firstly, he might have had a fairly heavy night and wasn't thinking straight; secondly, the suet pudding with whom I was conversing possessed a chestal area of commendable magnitude; and thirdly, the other applicants had mistaken 'dental' for 'mental' in the advertisement for a required receptionist. Or perhaps Duncan was simply doing his bit to help the local 'Care in the Community'. All creditable reasons, I have no doubt; but not one of them was going to help me deal with the current circumstances. What was I to do?

Are you the sort of person who owns a mind that can assess a situation in an instant? An intellect that sifts through conundrums at a speed approaching that of light? If your answer is in the affirmative, then you may consider yourself to be very lucky: unless, of course, you didn't understand the question. For my own part, generally speaking, the Phalarope brain does grind a bit slowly. Admittedly it does grind finely; but the grain occasionally has had time to exceed its 'best by' date before reaching the desired texture. I decided to valiantly struggle on.

"Well, I am he," I said.

"Eee ooh?"

"He; Phil Rope."

"Oi thart you said your name was summart else."

"Ah... that is..."

"Well, is you Phil Rope or nart?"

I decided to strike while the iron was hot: or at least at a tepid malleability. "Yes," I said, trying to use a mixture of candour and firmness in my voice, in the hope that it might help.

"Yeah? Then what 'appened to that other geezer?"

"That... Oh, him. Ah, *he* was my alter ego."

"Walter who?"

"Not 'Walter'... 'alter'."

"So ooh wants to talk to doc Strewper then? You or 'im?"

"I do: and now; if you please."

There then followed a short pause; during which I was sure that I could hear a faint whirring sound.

"Roight. 'Ang arn. Oi'll see if ee's free."

Another moment or two passed. Then...

"Hello..."

"Duncan?"

"Yes..."

"It's William. William Phalarope."

"William! Good heavens. How the devil are you? Long time no... something."

"Quite. Now listen up, old nash-bash artiste; I appear to have unsaddled a small piece of filling from a tooth in the lower left region."

"One of mine?"

"I doubt it: it had been there for quite some time."

"Ha ha! Just as well I remembered to wear my incontinence pants today."

"And if they are also air-tight then I expect that all your patients will have been very grateful as well. However, I am phoning to discuss the state of my teeth, rather than the looseness or otherwise of certain of your sphincter muscles. And speaking of sphincter muscles, who on earth is working the telephone on your reception desk?"

"I'll explain later," Duncan replied, almost whispering. "So," his voice having assumed its original register, "Do I detect the requisition for a certain favour about to appear?"

"More than likely. Although, if you prefer, you may consider this to be an opportunity to honour your obligation."

"Absolutely. Indeed. Eh? Um, which obligation?"

"The one you've been looking after since last we met."

"Still in the dark, old thing."

"Rugby... ferry... taxi... Elizabeth... vented spleen avoidance."

"Oh, *that* obligation. Of course: and without hesitation. It will be my pleasure."

"Good."

"So, how soon may I fulfil this liability?"

"By close of play tomorrow?" I queried, hopefully.

"Tomorrow? Oh. Er, yes; I should think so. Why not."

"Splendid: couldn't be better. Well, actually, that's not quite true."

"What isn't?"

"Any chance of meeting me off the ferry?"

"With a stiff G and T and a plate of sandwiches perhaps?"

"Only if you insist: and perhaps a packet of crisps for my niece as well."

"Your niece! What? That little pest? What's her name?"

"Mirabella."

"That's the one. Horrible child. Why do you have to bring her?"

"Family commitments."

"You mean your sister's dumped her on you."

"You could say that."

"Then please accept my condolences."

"Thank you."

"So, putting pity proffering to one side, am I to understand that you would like me to carry out some work within your oral cavity?"

"If you wouldn't mind."

"I'm already looking forward to it."

Now, it might be an idea – in case you are feeling a bit bemused about how Duncan and I came to know each other: what with he being many miles and several career links away from me – to explain how we met.

We went to the same school; one of those public schools in the South of England. We both started prep school at the same time; at the same tender age of eight. I expect a lot of you will be thinking that eight is a rather vulnerable time of life to be fledged, but I suspect that if you had a scamp of boy of that age wandering around your house you might have been tempted to hand over the responsibility – even to a complete stranger – and at a younger age: especially if you considered that boy to be a bit bereft in the gorm department.

So ever since then, Duncan and I have managed to keep in touch in one way or another: often, for some strange reason, when one of us requires a good turn and the other adequately fits the bill of provider.

But back to the present, and, after an uneventful drive to Portsmouth, there we were – Mirabella and I – aboard a high-speed catamaran and being made aware that the crossing was going to take about twelve minutes, that we had to sit down all the way over, and that we were not to move from our seats until the vessel was safely moored. Rather like going by plane: and rather a shame it was as well.

I can remember, in what is often referred to as 'the good old days', when the journey from Portsmouth Harbour to Ryde Pier Head was made aboard a real boat. A scattering of seats, an open deck or two and – most importantly for those returning home from work or starting their holidays – a licensed bar. It used to set sail in all sorts of weather, and many was the time that disembarking passengers had to leap from the deck on to the pier; and vice versa. Great fun, it has to be said.

However, in these sanitised, litigious days, the catamarans never seem to make the crossing if there is more than four and a half inches of swell on the water. For safety reasons, so they say. What safety reasons? The craft, as far as I am aware, were built in, and then sailed from, Tasmania. Not quite sure how many miles that is, but a good deal more than the handful across the Solent. Furthermore, and this is just a guess you understand, I think they would have encountered, and successfully negotiated, conditions that significantly surpassed those deemed too challenging for a Solent crossing.

I have a feeling that it is another example of the spreading Health and Safety tentacles at work again. I shudder to think of the number of people who get paid (I refrain from using the expression 'earn' a living) for conducting such interferences. They will make valetudinarians out of us all ere long.

Anyway, we were soon disembarking from the catamaran at the end of Ryde pier, and whilst making our way along the platform towards where the train was standing I became aware of a hissing sound coming from one of the ghastly green wheelie-bin things which were lined up alongside the back of the waiting room. I took a moment to glance about me, in case the hissing was coming from somewhere else. The hissing continued, only now a little more forcefully. I sniffed, anxious to detect if there might have been some kind of a gas problem.

"Psst. William."

I took a couple of rather startled steps in a backwards direction.

"Eh? What?"

"It's me... Duncan."

"What?" I looked about again. "*Duncan*! Where?"

"In the bin."

I am always ready to admit to being a bit slow on the uptake with many things, but I imagine that I would have had to phone several friends, and probably ask the audience as well, before coming up with a reason that would have been anywhere near sensible to explain why an Isle of Wight dentist should have been hiding in a wheelie-bin at the end of Ryde Pier. I moved forward to look inside.

"No – don't," came the voice from within. "Can you see Elizabeth anywhere?"

"Who?"

"Elizabeth. My wife."

"See her where?"

"Anywhere."

I cast another glance around me. "No," I then said, smiling at two teenage girls who were walking towards me.

"Nutter," one of them said, as they passed.

"Oi! Don't you speak to my uncle like that."

"Whah-evarh."

Luckily, I managed to grab hold of Mirabella before she had time to remonstrate further, and was in the process of explaining why when another, loud 'psst' came my way.

"What?" I asked.

"Can you see her?"

"I have already indicated in the negative."

"Are you sure?"

"Of course I'm sure. I think I would have remembered if I had said yes. After all, it was only a few seconds ago."

"No, you addle-brain; are you sure you can't see Elizabeth?"

"Yes. Why?"

"Because I don't think she trusts me."

"About what?" I asked, whilst considering whether or not *I* would trust somebody who felt the urge to hide in a wheelie-bin at the end of Ryde pier: or anywhere else for that matter.

"About the fact that I said I was going to the mainland to see an exhibition of paintings in the thingamajig centre: you know, that place along the front from one of the landing spots. I think it has something to do with Egypt."

"You said you were going to see *Egyptian paintings*! It's small wonder she didn't believe you."

"No, you numbskull; the name of the centre has something to do with Egypt. You know what I'm trying to say… something to do with that sort of… Oh yes, the Pyramid Centre."

"That place with lots of blue glass?"

"That's the one."

"The one near the hovercraft terminal?"

"Yes."

"The one with the swimming pool?"

"Yes, yes, and thrice yes."

"So what has it got to do with why you're hiding in a wheelie-bin?"

At that moment, Duncan chose to stand up; and the old lady walking by thought it was a good opportunity to shriek loudly and then set about him with her parasol.

"Confounded thug," she yelled, administering blows that would have done a man half her age proud.

"Madam," yelled Duncan in return. "I can – *yow* – assure you that I – *ouch* – am not – *eeh* – a thug or any other – *wooh* – form of ne'er-do-well."

It may have been Duncan's accent; it may have been his choice of words; it may even have been the fact that the parasol had broken in half. Whatever the reason, the old lady ceased her physical assault and began expounding her theories on what sort of low-life was usually to be found hiding in rubbish receptacles, that falling on hard times did not give one *carte blanche* to go around scaring vulnerable old women, and that she was sure the Isle of Wight had plenty of drop-in centres for society's unfortunates.

On top of which she thought that I looked as though a jolly good bath wouldn't go amiss, and handed me twenty pence. My apposite riposte was interrupted by the sound of the wheelie-bin falling over as Duncan tried to climb out.

"Righty ho," he said, as he brushed the plethora of rubbish from his shoulders. Then, as if he greeted all his old pals in such a manner, "Phalarope, hello!"

"Strewper, hello yourself!"

"Cómo está, mon ami?"

"Très bien, gracias."

As you may have surmised, Duncan and I like to display our polyglottic talents from time to time. I think Mirabella was rather impressed; certainly if the expression she pulled was any indication: a sort of wide-eyed, stunned mode to her visage, if you know what I mean.

"Salutations now completed," I continued, "perhaps we could kick off with an explanation regarding the dustbin disguise."

"Oh that… ahm… just trying to… er… hide from Elizabeth; that's all."

"Hide from Elizabeth! What on earth for? Some sort of game is it?"

"Would that it were. No, it's just that I… I haven't actually told her that you were going to be in the vicinity."

"Am I in her bad books for something?"

"Somewhat. Do you still remember what happened the last time you were down this way?"

"Naturally."

"Well so does she."

"Ah."

Perhaps I ought to tell you about what happened the last time that Duncan and I got together. I'm sure it had something to do with avoiding a touch of matrimonial disharmony on his part. Something to do with…? Oh what was it? Oh yes, he wanted to get off the Isle of Wight to go and play in a veterans' rugby match, and I had to go down to Portsmouth and help sort out an alibi for him.

Fair enough, you might think; and you would be thoroughly justified in doing so. A fellow has to do what a fellow has to do; even if his beloved is very much against it. Depending, of course, on what the action happens to be. I have always been a fidelity-supporter myself; so I wouldn't have offered my services if some kind of extra-marital shenanigans been on the cards. But to play in a game of rugby? Even if there was the outside chance of picking up an injury… which might mean a while off work… which might mean fewer readies for a certain female to spend in the sales? Well, full steam ahead, I say.

And so it was that a chap, who was looking forward to an afternoon laced with the occasional slurp of ale whilst cheering on an old chum as he ran about a muddy field collecting bruises, made his way by train down to Portsmouth. But it should have been a chap who knew that anything remotely associated with, or organised by, people called Duncan Strewper would be bursting at the seams with drawbacks, glitches, snags and all manner of fly-infested jars of ointment.

I had thought 'providing an alibi' meant that my role was simply to back up Duncan by vouching for the fact that he wasn't where he was when he wasn't where he should have been: or something like that; I think. I find that the more tangled a web is the more likely I am to come unstuck: or is it to get more stuck? Or… You see, even thinking about such things tends to fuddle my grey stuff.

"What's the matter?" Duncan asked when we met at the Portsmouth Harbour railway station. "You look as though you've lost a shilling and found sixpence."

"Well, actually, I have spotted something. Well, not actually 'spotted' something; more a case of noticed that something is missing."

"What?"

"Shouldn't you have a bag of some description?" I pointed out. "Perhaps even a pair of rugby boots?"

"Whatever for?"

"In which to play."

"Play?"

"Rugby."

"Oh good lord…"

"What?"

"I think I left it on the catamaran."

"That wasn't very bright of you."

"Well just don't stand there scoring points: be a good fellow and dash back and get it for me, will you?"

"What!"

"The cat will still be there. It's not due to leave until… until about several minutes from now. You've got plenty of time. But you'll still have to hurry."

"Well why can't you go and get it?"

"Because Elizabeth might be there."

"Where?"

"On the catamaran."

"Why would she be on the catamaran?"

"To make sure that I'm going to where I said I was going."

"Eh?" I could already feel a fog of sorts forming within the spaces available for my cognitive processes. "And what do I say if she sees me?" I gently enquired.

"I'm sure you'll think of something."

I have lost count of the number of times I get talked – actually, 'coerced' would probably be a better description – into doing something that totally goes against the grain of what I had in mind when I got up that morning. It must run into thousands, I expect: maybe even more.

Or perhaps, as my mother used to say, "If I've told you once, I've told you a million times: don't exaggerate."

Whatever the number, it was with mounting trepidation that I trudged back towards the ramp that led down to the jetty. Fortunately, there was no Elizabeth to be seen; and, equally fortunately, I managed to find Duncan's kitbag roughly where he thought he had left it. I suppose that was mainly on account of its contents not having been washed since their last outing, and not because of the honesty of the other travellers. I was only surprised, given the proximity to the sea and the likelihood of someone with a working knowledge of angling passing by, that no-one had purloined the bag with a view to providing his pets with a good-sized fish supper.

I shall decline the chance to provide you with a selection of the comments I received whilst carrying the kitbag back to Duncan: suffice to say that most of them had something to do with haz-mat suits and dirty bombs.

Anyway, Duncan got to play in his match and I got to stand, watch and applaud. How the game has changed since I last played it. What on earth is going on in the line-outs? Players must be nearly six feet off the ground when they catch the ball. Why? What was wrong with having to jump? I don't suppose it will be long before a team employs the use of a member of the Moscow State Circus: perhaps there will also be judges to award marks for artistic merit.

On top of which, so I understand, there are about eighty different possible 'calls' for each line-out. *Eighty!* Back in my day there were three: front, middle and back. I have a feeling that part of the problem with line-outs was that referees were having so much trouble policing what went on that they decided to make just about everything legal. Now where have I heard of that approach before? Probably the same place that I read about the pandemonium that results from employing it.

Anyway, I enjoyed watching Duncan enjoying himself, and was able to sample the local victualler's offerings at the same time. As you may have guessed, by the end of the game I had sampled a bit more than might have been deemed wise; and, as you may have also guessed, by the time that Duncan emerged from the changing-room he had, courtesy of the laden jugs supplied by the generosity of his team's opponents, all but caught up. Then, once the post-match tiffin had been consumed, and all the regulation songs, toasts to the Queen, and goodbyes had been made, we set off on our way back to the railway station.

Now whether it was because we had started singing songs that might have been a border-line choice for a television talent show or because we were walking along as if we didn't know who was supporting whom, we found ourselves having to assure a member of the local constabulary that we were both pillars of society (even though neither Duncan nor I have any connections with Freemasonry, or the temple of King Solomon) whose current states were simply due to an unfortunate reaction between an antihistamine tablet and the small sherry that we had shared earlier.

Our explanations fell upon deaf ears. Well, I say 'deaf', but I have a feeling that those ears were simply full of the cotton wool that was leaking from the skull of Mr Plod. Have I already alluded to the low esteem in which I hold many members of the thin blue line that separates normal members of society from those who dwell within the criminal fraternity? By 'criminal fraternity' I do, of course, include that underclass whose numbers seem to be swelling at an alarming rate.

I'm quite sure you know the people I mean – those with ten children who have to share half a brain between them all, those who think that Life (in the form of taxpayers) owes them a very comfortable living, and those who believe both the EU and the Human Rights Act gives them the entitlement to land on our shores and take advantage of the British hospitality. Just thinking about the types who do that makes my blood start to heat up: well, them and the politicians who seem traitorously keen to let even more in.

Now calm down, William. Breathe slowly. There. Okay.

Where was I? Oh yes: the police. Having said all that, I'm quite sure I do not have the temperament, or ability, to don the uniform and do the job. Indeed, I have a suspicious feeling that I would be spending a great deal of time at Her Majesty's pleasure for some infraction or other as regards the way that I would respond when faced with any of the above mentioned. I would, to use the old expression, probably end up swinging for them.

For those of you who think that means that I would throw a punch at one of them, I shall explain. 'Swinging' for someone meant that you had killed them and were going to be hanged.

But back to the reaction of a certain police constable to the festive frame of mind in which Duncan and I had found ourselves. Was he going to regard us as a pair of wandering *chanteuse* who were doing no harm to anyone – except, possibly, in an auditory sense? Of course not. Was he going to use any common sense and realise that simply asking us to hush up, and then allowing us to continue on our merry way would be the most cordial, and expeditious, way of resolving the state of affairs? Of course not. In fact, was he going to display any sort of intelligence or discretion? By way of an answer, I believe the verbal exchange went as follows –

"I am arresting you under section 5 of the Public Order Act, okay?"

"Okay?" I queried. As an aside, why do some many police, when making an arrest, ask if it's okay? "What do you mean 'okay'?" I went on. "Of course it isn't okay."

"You do not have to say anything – "

"I very much wish that you were the one who didn't have to say anything," interrupted Duncan, as he took over from me; before embracing a nearby lamp-post like an old friend.

"… but it may harm your defence if you do not mention when questioned something – "

"Actually, I'll tell you what I shall mention; because I feel that it needs mentioning; I shall mention that… Oh; I do believe I have forgotten what it was that I was going to mention. How peculiar."

"… that you later rely on in court. Anything you do say will – "

"I remember what it was! I was going to mention that we really do have to be getting along. You see my wife is expecting me back at seven. And in any case…" Duncan then raised an eyebrow in a manner which told me that a certain level of sobriety was rapidly returning to his thought processes; as well as another level – that of mischief! "… unless I am very much mistaken, Section 5 of the Public Order Act involves the use of threatening, abusive or insulting words or behaviour: or even disorderly behaviour."

There was a pause in the proceedings as Constable Dimwit frowned for a moment. Then, cautiously, he continued with "… be taken down and may be given in evidence. Do you understand?"

"I understand that I have not been threatening, or abusive, or insulting. Furthermore," Duncan added, as he slowly looked around, "we are not within the sight or hearing of a person who is likely to be caused harassment, alarm or distress thereby."

"I can still arrest you."

"Only if I continue to do that which you have warned me to stop doing. Am I continuing to do that which you have warned me to stop doing? Actually, come to think of it, have you even warned me at all? About anything?"

"Well, that is…"

"Exactly. Quod erat demonstrandum."

"What?"

"My dear fellow, much as I would love to stand and fritter away the rest of the day exchanging semantics with someone whose intellect would leave the average nematode feeling confident about being engaged in a debate, I really do have to get home and allay any possible fears that my beloved spouse may currently be experiencing concerning my whereabouts and wellbeing."

The silence and accompanying befuddled expression displayed by the rather poor and, I'm sure, unrepresentative, descendant of Robert Peel's contribution to British society meant that Duncan and I felt we were able to continue on our way without further ado.

Naturally enough, the 'ado' bit made an appearance later on: about the same time that Duncan's good lady made an appearance. I can't remember all the details – actually I can't even remember half of them; but I do recall Duncan was using his mobile phone to summon the services of a local taxi firm.

His phone, so he swaggered, was one of those known as a 'Smartphone': one of those capable of doing all manner of various functions. I have since heard terms such as Gingerbread, Jelly Bean and an Ice-cream sandwich (a strange term to ascribe as I would have thought that such a thing would only appeal to a small minority of people, show that the user had poor taste, and only last for a short while).

Obviously the plethora of impressive tasks can only be carried out while the battery lasts. The analogy, I suppose, is a car that can get from 0 to 60 mph in less than five seconds, has a top speed of 180 mph, but only has a 4 pint fuel tank. Can't see the point myself; but there we are. I think I would much prefer a telephone that can make and receive calls and has a battery which allows you to do both for at least eighteen uninterrupted hours.

Anyway, one of the functions on Duncan's phone was being able to locate, and contact, various purveyors of various services: and one of those purveyors was meant to have been a taxi firm. I write *was*, as, generally speaking, a machine is only ever as good as the person operating it; and although Duncan was a dab hand with a high-speed or contra-angle handpiece, he would only ever use either of those when there wasn't even a trace of covalently-bonded hydroxyl groups in his system. Letting him handle a smartphone when he had had a few, wasn't being all that smart.

The call, from what I could hear, went along the lines of…

"I say, can you… yoo-hoo… send a taxi to collect a couple of upright chaps who aren't quite so upright… at the moment? Please."

"Is that you Duncan?"

"Good heavens! How on earth did you know my name? These phones really are awfully clever." Then turning to me, "Aren't they awfully clever, William?"

"Absolutely," I replied, easily impressed with the capabilities of modern technology. "Awfully clever."

"Where are you? And is that William Phalarope with you?"

"Well I'll be a son of a matrix band."

As Duncan studied his phone from several angles, postulating on whether he had used the firm before and that, perhaps, there was some intricate form of voice recognition system at play, I had an epiphany. Another explanation came to me; and whilst it may have involved 'voice recognition', there was nothing 'intricate' about it. You see, I was pretty sure that I recognised the voice on the other end of the telephone.

In fact, I was absolutely sure I recognised the voice; and I was equally sure that Duncan must have pushed a couple of the wrong buttons, and instead of a semi-lucid drawl to the person in charge of taxis, he was delivering a semi-lucid drawl to the person in charge of his matrimonial wellbeing.

By using a few gestures, I tried to get Duncan to end the call before any more damage was done; but he clearly wasn't in the right frame of mind to pay charades.

"What on earth are you doing?" he asked, frowning as though he thought I was trying to explain the process of photosynthesis through the medium of dance. "Can't you see I'm trying to book us a taxi?"

"Yes; but…" I whispered, tapping the third finger on my left hand and then pointing at the phone.

"What? Ring? That's what I'm trying to do. I want to – "

The sound of pennies dropping could probably have been heard several streets away. So, probably, could the sound of the other voice on the phone as its decibel level soared.

"Duncan: would you please tell me what is going on? Now."

"Please? Who is Duncan? Me no Duncan. Me velly nice man flom take-away. You must have long numbah. Shop shut now. So solly. Please call back when open."

Duncan then ended the call and assumed the look of a man who for whom the bell had just tolled: and a very loud toll to boot.

"Was that who I think it was?" he timidly asked.

"I believe it may well have been."

"How long do you think I've got?"

"Until your guts are being used by a hosier?"

"Yes."

I'm not sure why I looked at my watch, but I did. "About an hour or so."

"Oh my." Duncan then went rather quiet as he saw his life pass before his eyes. "I say, William, dear friend," he ventured. "You don't fancy a brief sojourn to the IOW do you? By any chance? All in."

"The only 'all in', Duncan, dear friend, will be the variety of wrestling towards which you, most assuredly, are heading."

Apart from the fact that I had bought a day return for the train, I have always felt that marital imbroglios should stay well within marital confines: as well as the fact that I was confident Duncan would find a way of deflecting the imminent barrage in my direction. And even if he only managed to deflect half the salvos, that would be more than sufficient to completely spoil the rest of my day.

Don't get me wrong, Elizabeth is a very fine woman, and most right-thinking men would be proud to be wedded to her. However, as with most married women, she owns an armoury; and she has two very powerful weapons in that armoury: her voice, and her right arm. I'm sure that tornados have moved across Kansas more quietly than Elizabeth would when she is in one of her indignant moods; and, by the timbre of her voice, I had a feeling that one of those moods was in the offing.

Duncan's face was now going through its entire repertoire of fearful expressions.

"Do you think she's going to kill me?" he asked, looking more than a little pallid.

"If she thinks she can get away with it," I replied, unhelpfully forgetting that I should have been offering solace.

"What should I do?"

Being a bachelor of some years, I was hardly the person to ask for advice in the connubial arena – other than don't do it in the first place – but I had a go anyway.

"Would flowers help?"

"She'll have them made into a wreath."

"Chocolates perhaps?"

"She has a cocoa allergy."

"I know; a nice new vacuum cleaner?"

"You're quite naive about all this wedded strife malarkey, aren't you?"

"Tell her," I then jested, "that you were led astray by a heinous influence; a veritable modern-day Svengali-like emotion. The throes of a last-ditch attempt to hang on to your youth: purely to try and keep young for your darling wife, of course."

Duncan looked thoughtful for a moment. "That's not a bad idea. Yes, I'll blame it all on you."

"What!"

"I'll say you suggested it; as a way of staving off my onrushing middle age."

"So I'll be the one who receives the broadside?"

"Well, yes. But at least you don't have to live with her; and I'll make it sound as though you were only doing what you thought was best for me."

"But I don't like the thought of being tainted with even a few drops of vented spleen."

"I'll make it up to you."

"How?"

"I'm sure you'll think of something."

And so it was that I did think of something; and that brings us nicely to our current whereabouts.

"And who is this... young lady?" Duncan asked, with a cautious expression on his face.

"My niece; Mirabella," I replied.

"Niece? As in your sister's offspring?"

"I believe that is the usual arrangement."

"Goodness," Duncan continued, turning to Mirabella. "You've grown quite a bit since I last saw you."

"Well, it's either that or like you've shrunk," came the rather mordant reply.

I really am at a loss to suggest a place from where this strain of the child's nature originates. "Have you eaten yet?" I then quickly asked Duncan, anxious to stem the potential flow of invective.

"No."

"Good. Neither have I."

"Does that mean that we have the perfect excuse to pop in somewhere and have a swift one?"

"Not before you repair my tooth, it doesn't."

Perhaps it is because I am a trifle old-fashioned, but I have always felt the need to insist that whenever a dentist is keen to perform acts upon the enamelled content of my person that they (be it a he or a she, I am not prejudiced in that way) be of a sobrietous bearing, have the full complement of tactile and visual organs, and not have partaken of anything containing garlic within the previous forty-eight hours.

I have no idea how the patients – or the dentists for that matter – in France manage; but I suppose if you smell of something unpleasant then you are less likely to notice something similar in other people. I am quite sure that one of my ideas of hell would be requiring extensive dental treatment which is to be carried out by someone whose *fetor oris* matched that of an onion seller who had just eaten a bowl of garlic cloves.

While I am thinking along these lines, why is it that the worse someone's breath smells the closer they always want to get to you? You must have met those of whom I write – breath smelling as if hydrogen sulphide was used to flavour their last meal and, oblivious to the fact that your eyes are bloodshot and you have started retching, they still feel the need to come and stand close enough to touch noses. Ghastly people.

Anyway, Duncan seemed to have fulfilled all the necessary criteria, and I was intending to keep him that way.

The drive back to his surgery took twenty minutes and ten minutes after that I was ensconced in a rather fancy chair, and reminiscing of the days when dental chairs were raised by pumping on a foot pedal.

Duncan interrupted my thoughts to speak of the time when, as a dental student, he had to use cord-driven, slow (contra-angle) handpieces, and how many a time the cord would get caught up in the long hair of a student who had leaned forward to see what he (or she) was doing. Of how – when he had come to give his very first injection of local anaesthetic – his hand had shaken so much that the patient had politely enquired if Duncan was in need of an extra sweater. Of how – before he had been let loose on real people – he had to practice on something called a 'Phantom Head'. Of how – before moving into the Tower Block – life in the old Conservation Department had often involved getting in early to 'reserve' a chair with one of the high-speed handpieces.

Highly fascinating stuff for someone who hadn't heard it all before, I can assure you: but for someone being subjected to it for the umpteenth time it was, to put it mildly, bordering on soporific. But I suppose such an occurrence was to be expected.

Poor old Duncan has to find a topic of conversation so many times a day that he is prone – bound maybe – to repeat himself from time to time, to time. After all, how many of us could come up with a different subject for each new patient that comes through the door? As well as remembering which patient it was with whom you had discussed which topic. Not me, that's for sure.

"Did I ever tell you about the time – "

"Yes." I felt the chances were that he had.

"… that I was in the ortho department when a visiting professor of – "

"Yes you have told me; thank you for asking."

"… orthodontics from the States was over for some kind of exchange visit. Or Arthur-darnics, as they call it on the other side of the pond. And there was a young lad of about – "

"Twelve?"

"… twelve, who had mild crowding in both arches; in what we call a – "

"Class two, div one?"

"… Class two, div one. The English consultant asked the American professor what treatment plan he would suggest, and got about ten minutes of how he would use fixed appliances and all sorts of – "

"Extra-oral traction?"

"… extra-oral traction. It did sound rather as though he intended moving every tooth in the poor lad's head about six inches. All probably very *de rigueur* back in the US of A; but in SE1 it did seem rather OTT. And do you know what our man said?"

"Let's take out the four fours and review in six months?"

"Let's take out the four fours and review in six months. You should have seen the look of relief on that lad's face: and the look on the prof's face was priceless."

Before I go any further, I would like to correct any illusion that you may now have as to the extent of my knowledge in the orthodontics arena. I have none. Well, none that I have gained from official tutelage that is. But I am equipped to say that 'four fours' means all four of the fourth tooth along in each of the four quadrants: that is, the first premolars. As for 'extra-oral traction'? I believe that involves the use of pulleys attached outside the mouth with some sort of a headgear contraption. I am uncertain, however, as to whether any part of it has to be bolted to a wall.

So there I was, being totally ignored as Duncan set about repairing my damaged tooth. It was with great relief that I saw, as his hand approached with a syringe full of lignocaine that it wasn't shaking. It was also with great relief that I wasn't going to be subjected to an inferior dental block. New local anaesthetics are, so it turns out, very adept at making their presence felt by simply infiltrating the adjacent bone.

Anyway, further relief was to be gained when Duncan kindly waited until things started to feel numb – a splendid example of an oxymoron, and much along the lines of 'pretty ugly' – before he set to work with his drill. Ten minutes later, and having used a filling material that only required some kind of ultraviolet light shone on it (rather than a couple of hours' wait) to go hard, I was all set to go and enjoy the rest of the day. How dental treatment has changed over the years.

Speaking of which; why, if the bits of removed amalgam fillings have to be disposed of under very strict regulations – that is, not simply rinsed away down a sink or stuck in the bin to be slung on to a land-fill site – are dentists still allowed to shovel the stuff into someone's mouth? Maybe there is a website that can explain it.

"Now then," Duncan continued, as he threw a pair of rubber gloves into the dustbin, "what about that drink?"

"Goob eye-thea," I replied, splurting the mouth rinse towards the bowl.

"And I'm getting hungry," piped up a young voice from the corner. "Can we go for a burger?"

Do you know how it is when you have a vision of a glass of heavenly restorative fixed in your mind's eye and then have it dashed asunder by a suggestion that would take you to the other end of the contentment spectrum? Well that was pretty much what happened at that moment. A burger, indeed! Wouldn't be so bad if said burger was entirely made of Aberdeen's finest Angus: but made from over one hundred different cows, possibly several equine contributors, and heaven only knows how much bread and water and whatever other 'padding' chucked in as well? I don't think so, thank you.

"Woobent ooh arther haf umthing thay-thee?" I then asked.

"What?"

"Woobent ooh – "

"Your uncle," interrupted Duncan, kindly handing me a couple of tissues, "wants to know if you would prefer to eat something that has a bit more taste than polystyrene?"

"Like what?" asked my niece.

"Like… like a fillet mignon."

"No!"

"Even with a yummy-scrummy Béarnaise sauce?"

"Yuk."

"You see, William, my old *ami de coeur*, this girl is barely into double figures; and the sort of thing that you and I would enjoy is probably far too sophisticated for her palate. Having three little bugg-… er… children of my own, I know these about these things."

"Yeah, right; like you know where kids my age are at."

"Where you're *at*? Oh. Um. Well, what would you prefer instead? I know, how about something like a nice, light, Dover sole."

"I want a burger."

"Perhaps a lovely shepherd's pie?"

"No; I want a burger."

"Oh… ah… I know; how about some local sausages and mash? They're awfully good."

"I WANT A BURGER."

I think that this may be a good spot to point out that I have nothing against purveyors of… I'm trying to think of a polite way to describe a standard burger: other than a lump of ground-up cow that has been stuck inside a bun; but I can't. I can, however, easily find a large selection of comments to make about the people they often seem to employ to serve them.

Once again, I shall highlight my huge degree of tolerance towards those whom Nature chose to ignore when it came to handing out the genes responsible for charisma and intelligence: and, strangely enough, those genes that may have helped somewhat in the comeliness department. These poor unfortunates didn't choose to be brought into this world a few neurons short of a hemisphere, or with looks that probably inspired Picasso: but what on earth possesses so many of them to apply for positions that involve coming face to face with other people in places that sell food?

Or, and probably more to the point, what possesses the managers to employ them? Is it because they think that staffing the establishments with people who stick bits of blue adhesive tape on their noses and earlobes would attract more customers? Or perhaps that having unprepossessing staff behind the counter would make the goods on sale seem more appealing? Is it simply a case of hiring people they can pay the least? I know not. Perhaps that is why I have never been tempted to apply for a managerial position in such places. Or any other places, if truth be told.

"Is there nothing I can do to persuade you otherwise?" Duncan tried.

"No."

"Oh."

So there it was: my good friend Duncan and I doing our utmost to persuade Mirabella that partaking of a burger was quite far down on our own lists of 'must dos' for the day, and making no headway whatsoever. Even the offer of a doll did nothing to sway the obduracy of my little ward.

As a keen observer of human beings, I have often found an hour or so in their company to be immensely disheartening. Except on very rare occasions, I seem only to find new depths to which the qualities that separate us from the rest of the animal kingdom have descended.

What hope, I ask myself, does Mankind have when so many of the younger generation cannot string together more than a dozen words without inserting a handful of expletives? And should you ever have to ask one of them to write down a sentence, just make sure that you haven't decided to hold your breath while they try; or that the pencil isn't sharp enough to be used as a weapon. Then, as if that wasn't cause enough to – I think that I shall now get down off my soapbox.

Anyway, we found the nearest burger-bar, went in, grabbed a couple of coffees and whatever it was that Mirabella felt drawn towards. I say 'coffees', but I remain unconvinced. I should stress that I am in no way an expert on the beverage that results from pouring boiling water on the roasted and ground seeds of a certain tropical shrub – I may have made mention of the many difficulties I faced when asking for a cup of the stuff during my stay in San Francisco – but I have a rough idea of what it should and should not taste like.

When it comes to coffee, I have long been an 'instant' man. I do not exude the air of someone well versed in the nuances to be found between the Malabar and the Mocca, and I wouldn't know a Mandheling if a sack-full of it happened to be securely attached to my leg at the time. But I am able to detect if what is in my cup would be better suited to resurfacing sections of the Queen's highway or repairing coracles.

Having said that, I must own up to recently developing a liking for the sort of coffee that comes in a… I think they call it a 'pod'; which is then stuck in a machine that has a water container on the back. Do you know the sort of thing I mean? You switch it on, press a button or two, and then wait as the contraption heats the water and forces it through the 'pod' and into a waiting cup below.

But the coffee I received in the burger-bar? How I kept myself from spitting it across several tables I shall never know. Duncan, however, showed a little less restraint and – along with a couple of brusque enquiries as to what it was that had recently died in his cup – managed to spray the back of the head and jacket of the man sitting at the table opposite.

Now that in itself would have been unfortunate; but the fact that on a sunny day the gentleman would have cast a shadow large enough to prevent a family of four from getting sunstroke was enough to suggest that the three of us would be well advised to make a hasty departure from the eatery: and that was what we chose to do. Well, not so hasty as to prevent Mirabella from grabbing her repast. Duncan and I, however, chose to leave what was left of our infusions exactly where they were.

With the benefit of hindsight, it transpired that the recipient of Duncan's mouthful of coffee had so much trouble getting up from the table that we might well have had time enough to order seconds before the need to concern ourselves about injuries would have arisen.

What I couldn't understand was why a fellow as large as he was, and with the embarrassment of comestibles on the table before him, should have gone to the trouble of ordering a diet cola. I had images of stable-doors and bolting horses coursing through my cortices: I also received some more images concerning those bolting horses and the burgers themselves.

So where were we? Oh yes; running along the pavement, trying to keep up with Mirabella: and I do mean *trying*. Ah, the vitality of the young: the level almost matches their reluctance to use it: and ah, the absurdity. *Si jeunesse savait, si vieillesse pouvait*, as they probably say in uptown Marseilles.

And she wasn't just running. Oh no. It was as if she had decided that particular afternoon would be a splendid time to show the local inhabitants that not only could she outrun two grown men, but that she could do it whilst eating a meal.

"Wise move back there, Duncan," I said, after we had chosen a safe spot to catch our breath and my diction was, at last, returning to normal.

"What was?"

"Beating a hasty retreat."

"Oh, don't mention it."

"Well, I think I should. Especially as it wouldn't have been necessary if you hadn't decided to spit hot coffee substitute all over the back of that large fellow."

"Well how on earth was I to know that the contents of my cup would taste as if they had been filtered through undergarments belonging to a Turkish prosti–"

"Thank you Duncan, for nearly sharing that insight with us. I am quite sure that neither Mirabella nor I would have been the better for knowing it: nor how you happened to come by that information."

"Strange you should ask. I was in Istanbul, back in the – "

"As I said, we have no interest."

"But, Uncle William, I do."

"Well, that's hard lines. Young ladies of a particular disposition should be kept as pure as the driven snow."

"But that's like usually full of sulphur-based chemicals and heavy metal residues."

"Not in my vocabulary it isn't."

"Well it should be. It's like full of sulphur-dioxides and chlorofluorocarbons."

"I don't care."

"Huh!"

Duncan took a quick peek around the corner. "All seems clear," he said, looking one way and then the other. "Back to plan A, I presume."

"Which is?"

"Sensible food."

"Lay on, Macduff."

Did you notice how I used the word 'lay' – instead of 'lead'? So many people when using the quote (from Macbeth) say 'lead': as in "Lead on Macduff". Naturally, they are misquoting. I, however, being the sort of fellow I am, like to get the quotations correct: makes the day seem brighter, you know. *Mot pour mot*, and so forth.

Actually, while I'm on the subject of misquotes, perhaps I could mention one or two more from my list of the usual culprits.

'Chomping' instead of 'Champing' at the bit.

'All that glitters isn't gold' instead of 'Nor all that glisters gold'.

'Money is the root of all evil' instead of 'The love of money is the root of all evil'.

'The proof is in the pudding' instead of 'The proof of the pudding is in the eating'.

Small details, it has to be said, but it does cheer me up when I hear them correctly quoted.

Ten minutes later – and with little missy having since polished off whatever it was she had started – the three of us were taking our places around a table in a corner of a public house. Duncan had assured me that the *fare d'hotel* was above average, and so it turned out to be: you can't beat a good roast, can you? Mind you, the smallest of our number insisted on putting lashings of tomato ketchup all over her potatoes: and how she found room for a second meal, I can only guess at.

This small hiatus in the action might be a good place to let you know that I am not a connoisseur of fine cuisine. Not even close, actually. Whilst I admit to having some gastronomic tendencies – certainly rather than all that fast, processed, pre-digested rubbish that has invaded most of the supermarket shelves – I also have to admit to not being able to tell the difference between a Hollandaise and a Béarnaise sauce. Except that the Hollandaise should really be consumed within twenty minutes; and probably shouldn't have any tarragon in it: I think.

I prefer to forego gamey foods – duck, pheasant, venison, rabbit and so forth – but not because of any matters of taste: it's just that the idea seems a bit off course to me, and I don't think that there is anything 'game' about shooting them.

As for some of the things that certain types shovel into their mouths? Well! What on earth possessed the first… I'm trying to think of a term that sums up people who like to eat things that I wouldn't even want to tread on. I know, I'll call them 'French'. What on earth possessed the first 'French' person to think that an animal which leaves a trail of slime or a sea-shell inhabitant that looks as though it was the result of a violent sneeze would make a nice meal? Or that a small, croaking amphibian had the sort of legs that were just crying out to be made into a lovely *Cuisses de Grenouille à la Provençale*? Most peculiar, I have to say.

Anyway, things at our table were progressing nicely until Mirabella started pulling on my sleeve in a manner designed to attract my attention whilst also causing me to flick bits of mint jelly on to Duncan's shirtfront.

"Yes…?" I said, hoping that my irritation was clear.

"Look… there…"

"Where? What's going – "

Isn't it amazing the way that certain things can shock you enough to render you speechless? As a rule, I am one of those chaps who can usually talk through most things: often, it has to be said, to the utter annoyance of all those around me. I do, however, draw the line whilst at the theatre, or other events to which auditory interference would have a detrimental effect, and whilst working my way through a mouthful of food. I also, strangely enough, find a need to maintain silence when confronted with an object likely to cause me injury: and one such object was stationed outside the window nearest our table. Yes, it was the unpleasantly large gentleman from the burger place.

Whether he had taken all that time to extricate himself from the table I knew not, but I did know that he was looking in through the window of the pub: and there lay another conundrum. Was he trying to find us or was he searching out somewhere to have a quick snack on the way to his next meal? A bit of both, I expect. But whichever reason occupied the prime position, his gaze was certainly heading in our direction.

"Ooh er," was about all I could manage.

"Ooh er indeed," was the sum contribution from Duncan, who had by now established that something was amiss.

The large gentleman moved closer and pressed his face against the glass, his nose spreading out like a lump of plasticine. The three of us immediately decided that there was something interesting under the table, and the waiter chose that moment to approach and ask if everything was alright.

"Quite alright, thank you," I said, peeking out from under the tablecloth.

"Are you sure?"

"Very much so; thank you for asking. By the way, is there a rather disagreeable collection of facial features still pressed up against the window?"

The fact that the waiter then yelped and took a little hop backwards gave a most explicit answer. "Yes. No. He's just moved away," he expounded.

"Phew."

"And now he's going round to the entrance."

"Yipes! Now listen up; you mustn't let him in."

"Why not?"

"Because… er… Duncan?"

"Because," Duncan fabricated. "Because he is a friend of a friend of mine, and I know for a fact that he… has leprosy."

"Leprosy!" the waiter shrieked.

"Yes."

"But that's…"

"Very contagious. Even from a distance."

"Oh my god."

"My sentiments exactly."

"But, surely he needs help."

"Not from us, he doesn't. So would you be kind enough to see him on his way?"

"Shouldn't I call him a doctor?"

"You can call him whatever you ruddy well like; just don't call him over here."

It was about this time that the attention of the others seated in the restaurant was focusing on the conversation that the waiter appeared to be having with a table. Now that by itself would have seemed a tad peculiar, but the fact that the table was answering back added a certain *sui generis* to the event.

Then we heard some rather heavy footsteps heading in our direction. Actually, I think that we might have felt them as well: and we also heard several articles of furniture being hastily pushed to one side and quite a few "What the devil" and "How dare you?" pronouncements being bandied about.

To the unaccustomed people amongst you, such a situation might have seemed a touch daunting. On the one side there was a large, irate fellow ploughing his way towards us, seemingly intent on hammering our heads into our thoraxes; and on the other side there was a solid brick wall.

"*Quid faciendum?*" as they may well have asked down at the forum. Well, as you probably know, the Phalarope clan has an ability to come up with a means of extrication as and when required; and this was one such situation when an escape *velis et remis* was called for.

So, with all my dendrites reaching for the relevant sails and oars, my thinking set sail and the grey matter dug deep into the memory banks and brought to mind a similar situation, when I and a school friend – by the name of Crocker – were in the process of helping ourselves to cake in the masters' common-room in the early hours when we heard some equally heavy-sounding footsteps approaching.

I can already sense a couple of questions about to pass your lips.

"What on earth were you and Crocker doing in the masters' common-room in the early hours?" and "Why were you helping yourselves to cake?"

Well, the 'early hours' was the preferred time of choice, as during the regular hours the masters' common-room was usually full of masters; and even a developing intellect can figure out that a couple of ten-year-olds wandering in and helping themselves to cake would probably attract a lot of undesired attention.

As for the 'cake' part of things… Crocker and I were partial to the occasional slice of the stuff. The usual M.O. was to take it in turns to stay awake in the dormitory until around 2.00 am and then – having put a pair of socks in the pocket of our pyjama trousers – we would slip out of one of the windows, crouch our way across a flat roof, drop down to the ground by hanging off the wall built to hide the pig-swill bins and, using a window that we had earlier left slightly open, gain access to the corridor that went past the door to the masters' common-room.

Once in the corridor, we would brush any detritus from the soles of our slippers, and then put the socks over said slippers so that we wouldn't make a sound as we walked along the polished floors. The door to the common-room was nearly always unlocked, and we would go in and have a look to see what treats were available. Cake was always the preferred bounty; but cheese, of whatever sort, came in a close second.

So, back to the footsteps that were both heavy and approaching. Crocker had been stationed by the door and, after a couple of whispered, and urgent, '*K-Vee*' warnings (from the Latin *caveo*, for beware by the way) and in less than the time it took for the footsteps to reach the door, Crocker and I had put the cake back on the shelf whence it came, wiped clean and replaced the knife, and taken up positions behind the curtains. By the time the door was opened and the light turned on, the common-room contained not a hint of anyone other than a certain Mr Dearle.

I would like to describe the way his eyes narrowed as they scanned the room for errant minors, the way his nostrils quivered as they allowed molecules of scent to pass across olfactory sensors, and the way his right hand clenched and unclenched at the thought of 'whacking' tender buttocks. But I can't. It seemed fairly important that no visual contact was made in case I made some involuntary and, more importantly, audible reaction.

I am trying to remember how long we waited for Mr Dearle to leave – it was probably only thirty seconds, but it would have seemed like hours – before adding on a few more minutes in case he had been dastardly and simply pretended to leave the room. When the coast was deemed to be clear, I stole a quick peek from behind the curtain: so far so good.

Crocker came out from behind his curtain and whispered the question "What if Dearle is waiting outside in the corridor?"

What indeed. Two more minutes passed before Crocker took his place behind the curtain once more and I carefully opened the door to have a look. We had an arrangement that we took it in turns to check around corners and so forth in case a trap had been set: that way, so the theory went, only one of us would ever get caught. In that instance the coast was clear and we were able to hightail it back to the dorm without being discovered.

Unfortunately, the restaurant in which we now found ourselves had no handy curtains and, as Armageddon was nearly upon us, I had to conjure up another ruse: and p.d.q., as the expression goes.

Luckily for all concerned, the rapscallion in our midst came up with a corker of an idea. In a flash, she reached up for the plastic squeezable tomato ketchup bottle on the table and squirted lashings of the stuff across her face. Then, as if auditioning for a place at RADA, she stood up and screamed for all her worth.

"Aaargh. My head. I've cut my head. Oh god, I'm bleeding. Help me. Someone please help me. Aaargh."

With that, all sorts of things started happening. The barmaid screamed, people at the other tables stood up and yelled, the waiter threw his arms in the air, I threw my arms in the air – before realising that the blood was ketchup – and then threw them around Mirabella (taking care, of course, not to get any of the ketchup on me) and bundled her towards the door. Duncan decided that his best course of action would be – after having paused to leave three ten pound notes on the table – to crawl very quickly after us on his hands and knees.

Fortunately, once again, the large fellow was a bit slow off the mark and we were able to make good our escape from the restaurant and hare off up the road.

"Full marks, oh small person," I said, when we were far enough away to slow down to a walk. "That was a splendid diversion you conjured up back there. Jolly well done."

"I got the idea from a joke book I once read."

"Then jolly well done to the joke book."

"There were lots of other jokes. Do you want to hear some of them?"

"Perhaps another time, eh?"

"Huh."

Then, tacitly, a majority decision was made and we headed for Duncan's car and thence to a quiet pub, up a quiet lane, by a quiet stream, on the other side of the island; and were able, finally, to enjoy a quiet, albeit late, lunch.

Duncan eventually drove us back to the ferry and, after a quick reconnoitre to verify the absence of any lurking leviathans, we exchanged 'goodbyes', and made quasi-binding promises to make sure the gap before our next convention would be a small one. With a final wave, we crossed the water back to my car and the drive home. One good thing about all the excitement was that my garrulous companion slept most of the way. I'm not sure the overall technique would win much in the way of approbation as an ideal, or easy, way to get youngsters to sleep; but I can certainly vouch for its efficacy.

Golf with my father.

I received a phone call from my old man this morning. Luckily it was after nine o'clock, and so, like the proverbial lark, I was already awake and the brain cells were fired up and functioning.

I am not one of those chaps who can be expected to think cogently without a good night's sleep; or even before the sun rises: must be something to do with the light, I suppose. Quite how those wallahs in polar climes manage when the nights last for weeks is totally beyond my comprehension. I also understand that the situation gives rise to all sorts of behavioural problems and can disrupt people's lives. Sad, isn't it?

Anyway, there I was, mug of Darjeeling in one hand, having a cursory glance through the paper, and thinking that – apart from all the news about the many global faux pas – all was well with my environs. An altogether splendid feeling, I don't mind admitting: apart from, that is, the mollusc still slumbering in my spare bedroom.

"Good morning," I said, when I answered said call.

"William?"

"I am he."

"It's your father here."

Have I mentioned my father before? A grey-haired old fellow who has a distinguished war record and hates anything to do with Europe? Well, that's who it was on the other end of the telephone.

"Oh."

"*Oh?* Is that a proper way to greet your begetter?"

"I think it is an appropriate way to greet anyone who has taken the trouble to interrupt my morning's ritual."

"Never mind all that: have you looked out of the window yet?"

"Yes, thank you; I did take time to glimpse through the curtains."

"And?"

"And through the window pane as well."

"Buffoon! Did you notice anything?"

"Merely that day had indeed broken. Though, fortunately, not irreparably."

"And did that make you wish to do anything?"

"Yes it did."

"And that was…?"

"And that was to grab my tea and paper and go back to bed."

"On a morning such as this?"

"On a morning such as any. Why?"

"Because, dear boy, the sun is shining and I can hear the call of the Great Outdoors."

"Then, pater old thing, you had better dash off and answer it; and allow me to return to the simple pleasures that I should like to continue enjoying."

"Utterly impossible."

"And, pray, why is that?"

"Because I have accepted an invitation from Dennis to play golf."

"What! When?"

"This afternoon."

"But I thought you couldn't stand the fellow."

"I can't. But it's a splendid day for it: and he has suggested a certain wager."

It might be worth mentioning here that the combined chronological ages of the two gentlemen concerned made a grand total of one hundred and sixty-seven years. Their combined psychological age, however, is closer to twenty-five. The combined total of their physical ages is variable and depends on factors such as the weather, what's on the television, and how much intoxicant has recently crossed the gap twixt cup and lip.

"And what exactly is the ante involved in this flutter?"

"Well, you know how Dennis has coveted my old sextant?"

"Yes…"

My father has a sextant – made by Frodsham & Keen of Liverpool – which he used when embarking on his career in the Merchant Navy (or Merchant Service as some like to call it). Back then there weren't the electronic aids which are available these days, and seafarers had to be able to use the sun and stars, and suchlike. I expect that when we get the sun-storm onslaught that many predict, such skills will be much sought after once again.

"Well, Dennis wants to win it off me."

"And what is he wagering?"

"His prized photograph of him meeting Monty, just before the battle of Alemein."

"Do you want that?"

"Not particularly."

"Then why on earth have you accepted the bet?"

"Because I know how much he wants to keep it; and losing it would make him susceptible to further wagers."

"But what if *you* lose the bet? Aren't you worried about losing your sextant?"

"Impossible. Ha! No chance of that. Have you seen Dennis recently?"

"Not for a while, no."

"Well if his stomach is still like it was last month, then I doubt if Dennis will be able to see the golf ball; never mind hit it," my father added, laughing.

"Oh. But hang on, you haven't played golf for quite a long time."

"Maybe not, but I have been brushing up on it."

"You've been practising?"

"In a way."

"In what way?"

"In the way of watching that video you bought me a while back."

"The Tony Jacklin one?"

"That's the fellow."

"That hardly counts as practice," I pointed out. "And if that is all the 'practice' you've had, then I rather think that constitutes a very good reason for giving this whole idea a miss. Practice indeed!"

"But it's all arranged."

"Well un-arrange it then."

"Too late. In any case, exercise is good for you; and I think I should make every effort to play whilst I still have the ability."

"Don't you think that particular train has already left the station?"

"What! Good lord, no. I'm still as sprightly as I was five years ago."

"And that, I fear, adds another hundredweight on to my side of the scales."

"Don't be so stupid, William."

"Well, you must do as you see fit. Be sure to let me know how you get on."

"Oh, I can do better than that."

"Better?"

"Yes, I can *show* you."

"How? Are you going to take a video of it all?"

"No. You're going to come and watch."

"*Watch*? This afternoon?"

"Yes."

"That would have been wonderful, I must say," I said, casting my nets for a good excuse. To be honest, any excuse would have done. "But, as providence would have it, I have a prior engagement." I was still casting.

"What prior engagement?"

"The one… that… that I arranged with… with Mirabella. Yes, that's the one."

"To do what? I thought you couldn't stand the urchin."

"I… er… That is true, of course; but I feel morally obliged to do my bit when the occasion calls for it." The nets still felt very light.

"And what, exactly, is your 'bit' for today?"

"Ah. That is… um…"

"Well?"

"A… a walk. Yes, that's it. We're going for a stroll into town." *Phew!* My inventiveness never fails to amaze me.

"What town? You live in the middle of the country, for goodness sake. Miles from any town."

"Well, er, that is… true. So… so it'll be quite a long walk."

"Well that's perfect then. You can combine the two. You can do your 'bit' by taking little Miss Conception for a walk with me and Dennis."

"I beg your pardon!"

"Tell me, you addle-pate; are you in the process of recovering from a blow to the head?"

"No."

"Then why are you blithering like an idiot?"

"I… er… that is…" I really must remember to restock my inventiveness inventory.

"I'm waiting."

"Ah…"

"Come on, you vacuous vacillator; give me one good reason why you can't join us."

"I…" Then a jolly good reason sprang into view. "Mirabella is only fourteen years old," I said, once again feeling quite pleased with myself. "Far too young for that sort of thing."

"What utter nonsense. And that's more than enough of your preposterous prevarication. So, come down and collect me at midday. We can have lunch at the club and play in the afternoon."

"Oh."

"And you may carry the clubs."

"Yours?"

"Both sets. You can't expect Dennis to struggle round at his age."

"Can't I?"

"Don't be so damn silly: and don't be late either."

With that, my father replaced his receiver with the all deftness of touch one might expect from someone currently undergoing electro-convulsive therapy. I should make mention at this point – in order to clarify any possible future confusion – that I am not an avid supporter of golf. I tend to think of it as a game whose design is simply to hit a small ball across pastures and then into a small hole. Next, once the ball is in the hole, you have to lift it out again and proceed to hit it across more pastures and into another small hole.

All very peculiar. Mind you, it does have the advantage of being a very good way of keeping a certain type of person off the streets at weekends: and may it ever remain so.

Today, however, is a Wednesday; and that means that there will be an entirely different category of people hacking their way around perfectly decent parts of the countryside. I am not going to cast aspersions, although what else you can do with them I'm not sure, but I should like to make it plain that I feel people who have such a dislike of vegetation should really make every effort to stay indoors. After all, what is the point of going to all the trouble of landscaping certain areas, and then allowing people to wander about, unsupervised, thrashing large chunks out of it with metal sticks? Any further thoughts on the matter were then interrupted by the appearance of a small person.

"Uncle William…"

"Yes…"

"What are we going to do today?"

"Er… How does a walk sound?"

"A *walk*?"

"Yes. You know; fresh air and all that."

"Does it involve *walking*?"

"I believe a clue was in the title. So yes, a walk does involve walking."

"Do we like have to?"

"I am afraid so. Your grandfather has requested that we accompany him."

"For a *walk*?"

Have you ever been in one of those situations where you have the impression that you are speaking English – and plain English at that – but the words that leave your mouth appear, to all around you at any rate, to be a mixture of Yenisian and Na-Dene? Seems to happen to me quite a lot these days. Especially with people who are either three decades older or three decades younger than me. Most peculiar.

"Yes," I affirmed.

"Why?"

"Because he has developed an urge to go and play golf today, and he wants us to accompany him."

"Oh."

"Quite."

"Is there like no way out of it?"

It was another of those unexpected situations: almost serendipitous. I had, at last, found something that my sister's issue and I had in common.

"I am racking the grey matter even as I speak," I replied, thoughtfully.

"Well hurry up about it."

Ah, always the ubiquitous pin to burst a fleeting bubble of pleasurable thoughts.

Two hours later, with nothing of consequence having emerged from my dendrite ensemble efforts, I was to be found pulling up outside the domicile of my parents.

Am I alone, I wonder, in noticing how, over a period of years – usually about seventy – people become less fastidious in matters that would have once occupied several filing-cabinets of concern. Brown marks and cracks in tea cups seem unimportant, kettles full of calcium deposits seem commonplace, and old milk in the fridge is almost obligatory.

I must point out that I do not begrudge people who take the time, and effort, to grow old. Indeed, hats off and a loud round of applause to them all. I just wish that there was some mechanism for letting them know, gently and tactfully of course, that the *fugit* of *tempus* does have a price that inevitably has to be paid. A youthful spring to your mind is so much better when it is accompanied by a corresponding youthful spring to your step. *Mens sana in corpore sano*, and so forth. Yes, I know, easy enough for me to say and perhaps my viewpoint will change with time.

Actually, I am absolutely certain it will. Aging, I suppose, is something that needs to be experienced to properly understand it.

It has sometimes been said – usually by people with whom I have crossed paths – that I have been generously endowed in the tact sphere, and that a career in the overseas diplomatic service would suit me well: and those same people have even gone so far as to suggest that my gift would be best served somewhere in the centre of the African continent.

The more central the better, by all accounts. I can only surmise there must be societies therein that would really benefit from my brand of insight.

It is with my special variety of diplomacy that I have, on many occasions, broached the subject of dementia with my parents. Not jumping in with both feet, you understand; but employing the mantle of a concerned son. I can well remember the sort of conversations we used to have.

"Dad, mon cher vieux chose," I would begin.

"Yes, leech features."

Naturally, I have always enjoyed the repartee and merry badinage that would pass between the two of us. "Have you checked your bag of marbles recently?" I ventured.

"What on earth for?"

"You know; to count them; so to speak."

"Why?"

"To… (and this is where the tact came in)… see if any of them are missing."

"Listen, you dim-witted student of Pythagoras; I could lose half my marbles and still have twice as many as you'll ever possess. Now what is it you want?"

"I'm just showing some concern for your welfare, that's all."

"Really? Then why do I get the feeling you're just worried that I'm thinking about moving to Boeotia? Eh? Are my faculties beginning to wear a bit thin?"

"Good lord, no. I'm merely…"

"Hoping that I don't lose those faculties, have to book myself into an expensive care home, and start spending your inheritance?"

"You are a wag, aren't you?"

Oh, the fun we would have. Indeed, many is the hour we'd spend biffing banter across the net at each other. I would lob a jovial witticism, he would backhand a compliment in return: to and fro they'd go; epigrams and axioms, puns and jibes. How we'd laugh: and he was so keen to quote Shakespeare as well. I'm just trying to think of one of his favourites. Something from 'Two Gentlemen of Verona', I think. Oh yes, when Thurio says "Sir, if you spend word for word with me, I shall make your wit bankrupt."

Further reminiscences were obstructed when the little person next to me then asked, "Golf, you say? And we definitely have to watch?"

"Yes."

"That stupid game with the stupid little ball."

"Indeed."

"At his age?"

"He's not that old."

"What! He's like at least a hundred and ten."

"Eighty-four, actually."

"Same thing. People that age shouldn't be allowed out by themselves."

Now whilst I might agree with the tenet involved, I fear that I would cause affront if I endorsed it in front of my forebears. I do, however, harbour such feelings towards those senior citizens who meander like opium-eaters about our streets. Or, worse still, have a predilection to take to the roads and drive motor vehicles.

Yes, I know that I may well be a little sparrow myself one day; and yes, I know that many of those citizens made extraordinary sacrifices for the maintenance of freedom within our shores – a freedom which, incidentally, certain political entities are hell-bent on handing over to some very sinister people anxious to create a single World Government. Have I inadvertently drifted back to the peril that is *novus ordo seclorum*? Probably: please accept my apologies.

However, to return to the subject of poor/annoying drivers and the examples that really irk me; I shall highlight those on motorways.

1: When you move into the middle lane to allow a driver to join the motorway, and he/she accelerates until he/she is alongside you: and then just stays there.
2: Drivers who overtake by going 1mph faster than you. Especially as you soon need to pull out to get past the car in front.
3: You fall in behind a car that is travelling at a speed that suits you; say 70 mph. Then you notice that the car's speed has dropped to 65

mph, so you decide to overtake: but you have to do 90 mph to do so as the driver begins to accelerate as soon as you start to go past.
4: Drivers who don't use their headlights when conditions demand that they should.
5: Audi and BMW drivers.
6: Lorries that spend five minutes overtaking another lorry.
7. Middle lane squatters.

That's better: it's always nice when you get a gripe out of your system. I try to ration myself to no more than twelve a day; if I can: it doesn't always work out that way though. Sometimes I wish that my personality allowed me to indulge myself limitlessly, as I often let several good gripes go to waste.

Where was I? Oh yes, old people. I know that they have as much right to be driving as I do: but all the same, it can be frightfully infuriating.

"Well, he *is* allowed out on his own," I continued. "Whenever your grandmother says so that is; and today happens to be one of those days."

"Huh!"

"Quite."

"Ah, there you are: and about time too. I thought I told you midday." I looked up to see my father struggling to get a large leather golf-bag through his front door. "And you can come and give me a hand with this," he added.

"As you wish," I said, bursting into action: and then I thought I was going to burst completely when I tried to pick up the club container. "What on earth have you got in here?" I asked. "Lead shot?"

"A small selection of clubs."

"St. Andrews and Wentworth amongst them, by any chance?" My father gave me a look which made it clear that my stabs at levity was not going to be appreciated. So I tried another. "Or perhaps the clubs are simply made of cast-iron."

"Some, it has to be said, are slightly on the hoary side; but they are still functioning."

"And how many have you got altogether?"

"I've no idea: about twenty."

"Twenty! I thought you were only allowed a dozen."

"Who says?"

"Some Royal and Ancient fellows."

"Pah! Dennis and I have always used as many clubs as we wish to."

I then took a quick glance inside the bag, and involuntarily took a quick leap backwards. "When was the last time you looked in here?" I asked.

"Why?"

"Because it's full of cobwebs; and there are things moving about in there as well."

"So?"

"So, I hope you weren't thinking of putting the bag in my car. I don't want to open the door tomorrow and find that half my upholstery has been chewed away and the other half is acting as home to several thousand baby spiders, thank you very much."

"Then we'll take my car, for goodness sake."

"That would definitely be preferable."

"And I'll drive."

"That would definitely not be preferable."

I have a feeling that my reply might have been a touch rapid, and might have been dripping with disapproval regarding the thought that my father was going to drive. For most of my formative years I had been under the illusion that my physical constitution had been constructed from the same material as those paper hats you find in cheap Christmas crackers. Just about every time my father drove I was to be found with my head hanging out of the car window, trying my hardest not to be sick. It was only when I became old enough to notice the correlation between my affliction and who was behind the wheel at the time that I came to realise the reason for my 'mal de voiture' was entirely down to the way that the car was being driven.

You know the sort of thing – accelerating away from everywhere before screeching to a halt somewhere else; steering so that every trip felt as though it was being conducted on narrow country lanes; and, probably worst of all, getting so close to the car in front that you got the impression you were being towed. I often wondered if my father felt the need to check if the driver ahead was suffering from dandruff.

"Even better," he said. "That means I can enjoy a pre-prandial swift one."

To be perfectly honest, I had intended proposing that I took over the driving duties; regardless of whether the liquid refreshments were before, during or after the game. I am not going to imply that my father is not as competent behind the wheel of a motor vehicle as he was, say, thirty years ago – I am going to state it in the most unambiguous way that I can. The man is a menace: and there is no other way of saying it. He is a menace of the first water; and probably the second and third as well.

Not that my father drives too fast these days: quite the opposite in fact. I am all for driving at a speed that is within the legal limits and allows people to enjoy the passing vistas as they travel along the Queen's highways; but I am against those drivers who travel at a speed that would allow their passengers to hop out, collect a bunch of wild flowers, and then hop back in again without adding any time to the journey: and, I have noticed, that is the same feeling being displayed by the drivers of the numerous cars that have inevitably built up behind.

Then, when faced with a straight stretch of road, he suddenly feels the urge to drive as if chased by Vlad Basarab who was carrying several spare impaling stakes.

I am sure that we have all driven behind such drivers. Thankfully, they tend to keep away from inner city roads; but that, unfortunately, means they show up on country roads. They brake for every corner and when faced with oncoming traffic; and then, as mentioned, just as you reach a straight bit where you can overtake, they speed up: as if to demonstrate that they can still drive fast and warrant being allowed to keep their driving licence. Infuriating in the extreme.

Perhaps I should now tell you about his car. I shan't say which make it is – as I doubt the manufacturer would be thrilled to have their name brought into disrepute – and simply describe it as being green, and having all the usual refinements that tend to appear in modern cars.

Whilst I am amongst the first to applaud most additions – such as seat-belts (and Nils Bohlin who invented them, as well as Volvo for not stopping other car makers from using them), side impact bars, ABS and padded dashboards – I am also probably fairly near the front of the line of people wondering why car radios need to have graphic equalisers.

When I'm trundling down the motorway at a respectable speed, and I happen to be listening to the cricket, the Afternoon Play or, heaven forbid, accidentally straying into territory occupied by musicians who could successfully earn a living scaring birds away from arable crops, I really don't give two hoots about whether or not my graphics are equal: or anywhere near it. In fact, in the case of any 'yoof group', I would more than likely be wondering why the record producers had gone to all the trouble of installing recording equipment inside a working abattoir.

I shan't divulge my opinion on 'rap' music; other than to ask why they left off the first letter.

But back to the car. My father has, for some reason best known (and probably best kept) to himself, decided that driving would be more easily conducted by having his seat several notches nearer the steering wheel than might be advised by a chiropractor, and then leaning the seat back at an angle that affords him an uninterrupted view of the inside of the roof.

I have to admit that I could well have been daydreaming when those requiring commonsense were asked to step forward; but I have always assumed that it was fairly important – if not actually paramount – to have a good view of your surroundings when in control of a moving motor vehicle: and to be in a reasonable degree of comfort at the same time.

Father, so it seems, is under the impression that driving is best conducted with his knees wedged on either side of the steering-wheel, and his feet angled in such a way as to be ready should an attack of calf muscle cramps develop. I, however, remain to be convinced.

Anyway, there I was, undecided about whether to put my father's golf bag into the back of his car or simply set fire to it. Whilst I was quite certain that the latter course of action would have won unanimous approval from the W.H.O., I felt a moral obligation to choose the former alternative.

It was then that my gaze fully assimilated the attire in which my father had chosen to cover himself for the afternoon's endeavour. I would like you to imagine, if you can stomach it, an octogenarian dressed in an unpleasant olive-green flat cap, a long-sleeved bri-nylon turquoise shirt, a black-and-gold checked sleeveless sweater, cavalry-twill tartan plus-twos, purple socks and a pair of blue and white golfing shoes that was probably embarrassed to have left the sanctuary of the dark cupboard in which it had been languishing for the past year or two.

Not an appealing sight at the best of times; but when coupled with the thought that I had to accompany it around a golf course, it was enough to make me reach for a *kozuka* and commit as touching an act of *Seppuku* as I could manage. I am more than sure that Mirabella would have leaped at the chance of being my *Kaishaku-nin*.

However, it was a little late in the year for *Hanami,* and my father was already drawing more attention than felt appropriate. So, once all was loaded and I had spent several minutes adjusting the driver's seat to allow me to both see where I was going and not pass out from haemostasis, we set off.

Some twenty minutes – and several derisory comments – later, we were passing a hostelry, known as the Bunker and Divot, which was about a mile away from the course when my father – by yelling "Fore!" and whacking me across the side of the head with a golfing glove – thoughtfully drew my attention to the old black Rover P5B saloon parked outside.

"He's in there," continued the barking noise from father.

"Who is?" I pondered aloud.

"Dennis."

"How do you know?"

"Because, you silly arse, that's his car."

"Oh."

I have more than a passing dislike to a large number of modern cars: especially the smaller ones. It seems as though the manufacturers don't want their product to be noticed: well, not in the shape department anyway. I am quite sure that if the cars – with one or two exceptions, it has to be said – didn't have the make written on the side of them, people would have no idea what they were. Not a problem encountered with the likes of the Morris Minor, Ford Anglia, Triumph Vitesse; to name but a few of the past smaller ones: and I would use up several pages listing the other cars that had no need for the name to be attached to the outside. I'm sure that not only do you know the ones I mean, but that you also have your own favourites.

I shan't comment on the relative merits of the older cars as regards performance or safety – mainly because I'm not qualified to do so – but, as a fellow with an eye that likes to be pleased, it was always a pleasure to look at them; and you knew what they were from over a hundred yards away.

Anyway, back to the impending game. As I said, quite why my father should have chosen to play golf with Dennis is… Well, most peculiar: and quite why he should have chosen to wager his sextant against Dennis's photograph is even more peculiar. But there we are. I guess old age makes the mind do unexpected things; or at least it certainly seems to.

Why else, for goodness sake, would people – mainly those of a female persuasion it must be said – want to colour their hair blue? Or – mainly, but not exclusively, those of a male persuasion – only want to shave parts of their face and leave the rest of it looking like a badly-mown lawn?

Admittedly there are some advantages to be enjoyed with the passage of time. I am occasionally envious of those who show no embarrassment whatsoever about going shopping wearing odd socks – or shoes – and with a tea-cosy stuck on their head. What a liberation it must be to feel no compunction to follow convention; to not care about breaking wind, loudly and in company; to push your way to the front of the queue explaining to all and sundry that you are eighty years old. A truly splendid licence to have; and the sort of thing in which I would like to indulge at my present age. However.

"Come along then," my father said, as I parked alongside Dennis's car.

"Come along what?" I politely enquired.

"Into the hostelry."

"What ever for?"

"For a quick snifter: what else?"

"Can I have a coke? And a packet of crisps? And I need to go to the loo," voiced the third member of our entourage.

"You want a drink before you play?" I asked.

"Naturally."

"But won't that… I don't know. Interfere with your swing… or something?"

"Good lord no. Loosens it up no end. Why do you think Dennis is in here?"

"I have no idea. Does his swing need loosening?"

"What about my coke?"

"I would imagine that if his swing got any looser it would fall off."

"What about my crisps?"

"And there was me thinking that you should never drink and drive."

"I *really* need the loo."

"Oh for heaven's sake."

"Dad, she's only a child."

"And children have no business going into public houses."

"But they're allowed to."

"Since when?"

"Since… ages ago."

"Pah! What's it all coming to? Eh?"

"It's called progress."

"Progress, my eye. It's just wishy-washy-liberal-trendy-dumbdown-hogwash is what it is. Promulgated, no doubt, by some covert organisation determined to eradicate the ethos of this country. They couldn't do it by dropping bombs on us, so they have devised another –"

"Thank you father: as much as I may agree with your sentiments, I think this is neither the time nor the place to debate the matter."

"Pah! It's still wrong."

"Perhaps; but she's still allowed in."

"Pah again."

And so, with a less than palpable air of equanimity, the three of us ventured inside the establishment. My eye soon found Dennis, standing at the bar with a glass of something in the range of 40% in his hand.

Dennis, to give you a picture of the fellow, is in his early eighties, bald as a coot, sports a moustache that – with a squirt of hairspray – could easily be used to keep a Brough Superior in a straight line, and who possesses a glass eye with only one redeeming feature: that it happens to be in the right place. I believe he bought it in a 'souk' whilst on holiday in Marrakesh during the late seventies. To this day nobody knows whether or not it had originally been designed for a camel.

Dennis likes it though, and says it reminds him of North Africa. It's just a pity that it reminds everybody else of Bela Legosi on a bad day. It can be most unnerving when sitting face to face with Dennis at the dinner table, I can tell you. Apart from the fact it is awfully difficult to concentrate on the conversation when faced with fellow who has one eyeball that is several sizes larger than the one next to it; you can never be sure that it isn't going to drop out into the soup tureen.

Actually, now I am on a reminiscence roll, I do recall an occasion when Dennis's eye fell out during a garden buffet one summer. I think it was to celebrate his fortieth wedding anniversary.

"Okay," I hear you say. "That was unfortunate; but not exactly a hanging offence."

Absolutely; and it would have remained in that category: had it not been for the fact that when Dennis came to make his speech, it transpired that instead of putting the glass eye back in the socket, he had managed to jam a pickled onion there instead. The result was to create a wave of nausea that flowed through the assembled guests and sent those of a weaker constitution scurrying for the hedges with napkins pressed to their mouths.

My thoughts were then interrupted by a piercing shriek. Dennis had just turned around and Mirabella had seen the eye for the first time.

"Uncle William," she yelled, grabbing me in a vice-like hold. "That man has something horribly wrong with his face."

"It's just a false eye, that's all. Nothing to worry about," I said, comfortingly.

"It's terrible."

"Well, I don't know about 'terrible'. It's… er… "

"Revolting. Wearing like a patch would be better."

"Charles, old boy," Dennis bellowed.

"Dennis, dear chap."

"All set?"

"Absolutely."

"Time for a tincture?"

"Categorically."

"A pink one?"

"Naturally."

"A pink one?" Mirabella asked, looking at me askance.

"Gin. With Angostura bitters," I knowingly replied.

"And what about you, William?"

"Oh… um… a small scotch, if I may."

"A *small* one?"

"Yes. I'm driving."

"So?"

Perhaps I had better explain this less-than-responsible attitude of Dennis's to the intake of alcohol and then getting behind the wheel of a car. His stance is as a result of having been in charge of a Sherman tank during the Battle of El Alamein and – to use his words – "If I can control one of those whilst being fired at by Jerry, I'm damn sure I can manage to look after my motor vehicle under any circumstances. So buzz off."

I'm not entirely sure that Dennis quite understands the difference between tearing around a desert shooting off 75mm 6lb shells at Panzers and negotiating his way along Acacia Avenue behind the wheel of a car whilst one or two sheets are flapping in the wind. Even if his car were a 1971 Rover!

"I just think it best to maintain the legally required degree of sobriety when driving," I averred. "After all, I don't want to lose my licence: or hit anything; or anybody."

"As you wish. Now what about that small person I saw earlier? Is it with you?"

"Yes."

"Well, where's it gone?"

Mirabella peeked out from behind me.

"Ah, there it is." I felt nails digging into my waist. "Come out here, where I can see you." The nails dug deeper. "Come on. I won't bite."

"How do I know that?" asked the object of Dennis's curiosity.

"What makes you think I would?"

"Because you look like a dog my mother once had to have put down."

"I say; that's not very nice."

"No: and the dog wasn't too happy about it either."

"What! Listen here, you little – "

"Did you say you wanted the loo?" I interrupted.

"Yes."

"Then I think you'd better go and find it."

"Huh."

I expect you know how it is; you set off with a sharply defined objective and then, what with one thing and another, the plans go astray somewhat: and the 'one snifter' soon turned into another… and then another… and another. Not for yours truly, you understand, but for the two recidivists at the centre of my tale. I believe Mirabella was quite happy about the delay, as it meant she was able to fill her face – several times, I might add – with all manner of simple carbohydrates and carbonated drinks; which, apart from hastening the onset of acne, was going to do little else but ensure she was well acquainted with the washroom facilities before we finally left.

Once the two elderly livers had received a good pounding, did their owners abandon the intended match and ask to go home? No they did not. The appetite for the afternoon's conflict had merely been sharpened. And so it was that, with two rather inebriated octogenarians, Mirabella and I squeezed into father's car – Dennis having decided that four large ones might have dulled his reactions a bit more than the law would allow – and we all proceeded to the golf course.

It was, however, agreed that even though the blast of war blew in their ears and they both had every intention of imitating the action of the tiger (I did feel a bit bemused at that point, as I failed to see how crawling about on all fours was going to improve their respective swings – although crawling about on all fours ought to have been as much as they could manage by then), the two old-timers felt that their sinews (along with knees, hips and backbones) were stiffened enough and decided that the wager would be best fought over only three holes: and 'hoorah' to that, said I.

The three holes chosen were the first, second and eighteenth. Not for any reason other than they were the nearest to the car park, the flattest and the easiest: and weren't designed to take either of them further away from the clubhouse than was absolutely necessary.

It was also decided that matters of a prandial nature could wait until after the contest. Which was a pity: as apart from the fact that I was feeling hungry, I thought that some solid gastric-bound material might help steady the pitching and yawing that was likely to arise with the two old galleons as the round progressed.

So it was, with mounting apathy, that I shepherded the two protagonists – or should that be 'antagonists'? – to the awaiting first tee. I don't know if you have ever tried carrying two sets of golf clubs. By which I don't mean two sets of pared down ladies' clubs; I mean two sets of antiquarian clubs that were, as I mentioned earlier, seemingly made from cast iron. If not, then I can tell you that Hercules probably got off lightly. On top of which, as if that were not enough malaise for a chap to bear, I also had to keep an eye on Mirabella.

There we were; two antediluvians, a juvenile delinquent, and a rather resigned-looking fellow whose thoughts were vacillating between his present predicament and taking tea and biscuits in his cottage.

"Heads or tails?" called Dennis, as we reached the tee.

"What coin is it?" asked father.

"Why does that matter?"

"Certain coins fall in certain ways. Especially that old half-crown of yours."

"What! There's nothing wrong with my old half-crown."

"Then how come you only use it when your opponent calls 'tails'? Eh?"

"Stuff and nonsense."

"Uncle William…"

"Yes."

"What's a half-crown?"

A question like that always makes me do three things: feel sorry for present-day children who have a dearth of interesting coins to use, yearn for the days when a fellow's pockets jangled to the sound of tanners, and feel awfully old.

"Apart from the obvious?"

"If, by the 'obvious' you mean that a half-crown is half a crown, I had already sussed that."

"Sussed?"

"Worked out. Der-err."

"Right. Well, it was a coin that was worth two shillings and sixpence," I explained. "That's about twelve and a half new pence."

"That's not much."

"It was back then. One of those could last you all day."

"Well you wouldn't get more than like a tiny bar of chocolate these days."

"Well don't look at me as if it's my fault."

"It's the fault of your generation."

What is it the French have a tendency to say? Oh yes; '*La vérité sort de la bouche des enfants*': or something like that. What I would like to know is who taught all that *véritié* stuff to *les enfants* in the first place; and how did they get them to pay attention while they did so? Then, perhaps more to the point, why did they do it? Pretty much all *les enfants* with whom I have had the misfortune to meet display the social niceties of an amoeba.

Anyway, I had been trundling along in a conversation, happy in the knowledge that I should have had a larger savings account of info than the person with whom I was conversing, when she suddenly produced another chequebook. It is, oddly enough, the sort of thing that happens to me quite a lot: and it is frightfully embarrassing when it does. Especially when said person happens to be a mere slip of a lass.

"One shouldn't... you know... actually... that is..."

"Well?"

"Well... ?"

"Well you belong to the generation of corporate greed that takes pleasure treading on the little man; and to hell with the utilitarian principle. Never mind the repercussions, as long as you can make a quick profit. Eh?"

"Now listen here, oh small person; I'm not sure that the latter half of the twentieth century is the sole province for edacity. Or do I mean cupidity? Both I expect. Anyway, I'm sure a trawl through the history books will reveal that certain types have always had a propensity for fleecing their fellow man."

"Such as…?"

"Well, I think you can include the incident where tables belonging to money-lenders were overturned in a certain temple. I believe that was something to do with extortionate rates of interest. And then there was the Bubble from the South Seas. All things, may I remind you, from yesteryear."

"Maybe; but I bet they were all people of your age."

I had been hoping to bring the score back to deuce; but no, another ace was served up by someone not much bigger than the racket.

Speaking of tennis, whilst on a previous sojourn to the IoW, I booked a court at a local club in order to see if I could muster up enough energy to develop a complaint that might elicit more sympathy than those I normally carry. Tennis elbow always sounds more dashing than tendonitis, don't you think? Gives other people the impression that you spend your leisure hours indulging in pastimes of an active nature. I'm not sure that actually makes sense!

Anyway, on to the court I strode, expecting to find Duncan warming up with his usual enthusiasm: and that, incidentally, normally involves little more than tying up his shoelaces without having to sit down.

Duncan, for reasons into which I shall not presently go – except to say that they involved a rather snooty lady who was trying to hurriedly park a large four-wheel drive vehicle so that her precious (Duncan told her that 'precocious' would have been more accurate) little Jonathon wouldn't be late for his tennis lesson – was still looking for a space in the car park; so I was left to bounce a ball on my racket while I waited.

It was then that a young lad, who was indulging in the same sort of thing on an adjacent court, asked if I might like to have a rally or two whilst I was hanging. I wasn't sure what he thought I was 'hanging', but I agreed to the suggested rally.

"Yes indeed," I replied. "But just make sure that the balls you send in my direction are travelling less than the speed of sound, pass within arm's reach, and don't involve stooping of any kind."

I quickly explained that I had only recently emerged from time spent in an iron lung and any excessive movement might exacerbate an already fragile condition. My attempt at levity was totally ignored; because, I presumed, the instrument to which I had referred meant nothing to a person of his age. Not that I should have attached any jocularity to something invented by Philip Drinker and Louis Agassiz Shaw back in 1927 (although I believe Alexander Graham Bell began the process – but we all know what he did to poor old Antonio Meucci and his telephone) to enable people who had unfortunately lost the ability to breathe to continue to do so. It seems that most of those born after about 1960 have no idea what an iron lung is; or, for that matter, have even heard of polio. How easily we take the good fortune of living in the present day for granted.

"No matter," I replied. "Let us commence."

"Yeah. Hey, what's that you've got?"

"Where?"

"In your hand. Is that a racket?"

"Yes…"

"Is it made of *wood*?"

"Indeed it is. Why?"

"Wow. I've heard of them, but never thought I'd actually get to see a bloke using one."

Do you recall how I mentioned that there are things which can crop up in my day that have a tendency to make it seem that time has flown a bit more than I thought? Well this was another such instance. Blooming cheek of the lad.

In its day, the wooden implement – as endorsed by the likes of a certain Lew Hoad – that I was holding was considered *de rigueur*; and, aside from some bits of fur still attached to the strings, was just the sort of accessory that a chap needed to impress the fairer sex. Currently, however, it appears it's just the sort of thing to draw ribald laughter from all and sundry.

Apparently terms such as Hot Melt Carbon, Throat Bridge and Sweet Spot are very much *la fleur des pois* these days: unfortunately, my racket was more than a touch *démodé*. But there you are.

Does everyone have to endure more and more instances of derision as they get older? Is it one of those rites of passage, like teenage skin complaints, that are seemingly unavoidable? Surely younger people should be envious of their elders; especially when they consider the heartache and the thousand natural shocks that flesh is heir to, for having had the good fortune to get to their current age.

Anyway, to return to the half-crown; father insisted on a different coin being used, called tails and flipped it in the air. Mirabella and I stood and watched as the first toss sent the coin inside Dennis's golf bag, the next one caught father in his right eye, and the third attempt bounced off my foot and disappeared into a rabbit hole.

"Is this something that has to be done every time they play?" asked my bemused niece.

"No, but it – or something very similar – invariably does," I replied, before suggesting that I put my hands behind my back, hold a stone in one of them, and they could have a guess at which one it was. Father guessed correctly, and elected to allow Dennis to drive first.

"Why?" Dennis asked, looking suspiciously.

"Because it's my choice."

"Then you should go first."

"But I don't want to."

"Why not?"

"Because I don't."

"Hmmph. Most peculiar. Are we playing strict rules?"

"Naturally."

"What about 'gimmees'?"

"Only if the ball is no more than three feet from the hole."

"Three feet, eh? Not more? Say… ten?"

"No.," my father asserted. "That would be making a mockery of the game."

"Then how about eight feet?"
"Five."
"Seven?"
"Six."
"Agreed. And what about preferred lies?"
"Permitted if placed within three strides of where the ball is."
"Right."
"Right."

At this juncture, I must iterate that I am not a golfer. I shall readily admit to having played the game, but I think it should only be afforded the same attitude as I adopt when taking a bath: *id est* there to be enjoyed, and nothing more.

I must also point out that, rather like most of the fellows with whom I have played, I do get my money's worth. Not for me the eighty shots or so – which can work out at 25 to 50 pence a swing: oh no, I am usually in the 10 to 15 pence a swing region. And, by virtue of the fact that I tend to hit the ball to the left and to the right with equal ease, I also get to see a lot more of the course and meet many more people than others might ordinarily do.

Admittedly not all of them are aglow with joy to see me – especially if I happen to be playing with a five-iron from the green that they were currently using – but, on the whole, pleasantries are exchanged: along with sound advice on extricating my ball from the types of vegetation that I have a tendency to encounter.

"What about air-shots?" continued Dennis.
"Let's say that the first three per hole won't count."
"Right."
"Right."

Mirabella and I were then treated to thirty seconds worth of buttock muscle callisthenics while Dennis went through his somewhat protracted routine of addressing the ball, twenty seconds of practice back-swings, and then a rather alarming final downward swing that was accompanied by a banshee-type wail. The ball didn't move.

"One," voiced my father.
"One? I never touched it."

"One *air*-shot."
"Oh. Right."
"Right."
The routine was repeated.
"Two."
"I know."
"Just checking."

The third attempt resulted in a respectable contact being made between the head of the driver and the ball; and I was about to comment on the sound it had made when it became apparent that although club-head and ball had made good contact, the elevation of the trajectory of the ball was many degrees below that which would have ensured a round of applause from any nearby spectators.

The net result of this deficiency of altitude was that the ball struck the marker pyramid on the ladies' tee and whizzed back towards Dennis who barely managed to prostrate himself before he would have received a bright yellow object on the temple. I say 'managed' to prostrate himself, but I think he had actually lost his balance and was in the process of toppling over anyway: and very lucky he was too.

Father, on the other hand, had remained upright and vigilant; and with rather a deft lean to one side was able to watch as the ball went on its way to the car park.

"My hole, I believe," he said, haughtily.

"What! Never."

"The only 'never' here is the never in the answer to the question of how long it will take you to find your ball."

"People have played from car parks before. What was that chap's name…? Burly stair-rods or something. He was always playing out of car parks; so I'll do the same."

"Not before it gets dark you won't. As I said; my hole. One up and two to play."

"Harrummpphh!"

The two old codgers then made off in the direction of the second tee, leaving me and Mirabella to carry the clubs. Mirabella then made off in the direction of the second tee, leaving me to carry the clubs.

It was father's turn to play first and, after several wiggles that nearly dislocated both his hips, he managed to send the ball about 120 yards down the fairway. Not the second fairway, you understand, but it was *a* fairway; and the ball was marginally nearer the green than it had been prior to being struck.

Dennis made an improvement from his previous contribution in that he was also nearer the green: and he was able to see where the ball had come to rest. He wasn't able to play it; but at least he knew where it was.

"Preferred lie option being taken," he called through the trees back to where my father was kicking something with the toe of his right shoe.

"You must stay within three strides," came the response.

"Of course." Dennis then quietly said "William…"

"Yes…"

"Be a good fellow and retrieve the pill for me."

"What! How? It's in that pond; which must be at least two feet deep."

"By using this."

Dennis proceeded to take something out of his bag that – after initially looking like a club with a very thick shaft and grip – turned out to be a telescopic pole with a ring on the end. "I think it could be described as an 'iron': and a very useful one it is too," he added.

Having, on previous such outings, seen where the majority of golf balls that Dennis 'clubbed' usually ended up, I had no trouble believing that statement. Needless to say, apart from positioning itself in water that looked as though it hadn't been changed for ages, the ball I had been instructed to salvage had also decided that it would enhance my general *bonheur* by lodging itself between two sunken boughs.

Then, as if Providence thought that my day couldn't possibly get any better, the bank alongside the pond at the closest point to the ball was wet; and slippery; and very soft. Oh what pranks Nature can play when it has a mind to do so.

A little while later, looking as if I was modelling the latest army camouflage outfit, I handed the ball back to Dennis; who had been taking a couple of swigs of some tea-coloured liquid from a plastic bottle in the meantime.

"I think you had better go and check on your father," he said, pointing over my shoulder. "He seems to have developed a nasty, jerky twitch in his right leg."

I looked across; and true, my father, although standing in grass that was halfway up his shins, was doing a pretty good impression of someone practising a one-legged Highland fling. For a moment I wondered if his plus twos had been bought with a clause that stated the wearer was obliged to pay the occasional homage to its tartan roots.

"What about your next choice of club?" I asked, turning my attention back to Dennis. "I don't want to have to keep lugging both sets between you and my father."

"Oh, don't you worry about that. I'll cover the rest of the hole with my trusty six-iron. Hurry along now; and I'll see you at the green."

"And have you decided where you are going to drop the ball?" I further asked, wondering if the paradigm of fair play was still being observed: however tenuously. "I believe I heard that it has to be no more than three strides away from where the ball was."

"Absolutely."

Dennis then took a few paces backwards before launching himself in a geriatric form of the triple jump, collapsing in a heap, and taking a couple of rolls.

"Are you alright?" I tentatively enquired, as he struggled back to his feet.

"Splendid, thank you. Now, that would be about here, I believe," he said dropping the ball in a lawn bowls action. "Yes, that should do nicely."

Knowing that there are occasions when a simple, well-intentioned question can lead to all manner of irate responses, I decided to feign indifference, and took my father's bag of clubs over to him.

"Is everything okay?" I asked, as he made his way through the long grass and on to the fairway.

"Yes, thank you."

"It's just that you seemed to be having a bit of trouble with one of your legs."

"One of my legs?"

"Yes: it looked as though you were having a sudden attack of St Vitus's dance."

"Whose dance?"

"St Vitus. A Christian saint from Sicily; who died around 300 AD. I believe he is the patron saint of epileptics: amongst others."

"Would they be people who learn useless facts?"

"Ha!"

"Ha indeed. So what about him? Did he invent a dance?"

"No; but people who twitch in a particular way are said to have his dance. It's something to do with a neurological condition known as Sydenham's chorea."

"They've named a twitch after a place in south London?" My father looked thoughtful for a moment. Then, "Mind you, I can't say as I blame them."

"No; I meant that you were hopping oddly about on one leg."

My father looked thoughtful for another moment. "Oh that. Probably cramp."

"Oh." I remained unconvinced; and hoped that the expression on my face would encourage my father to come up with a better explanation before Dennis posed a question or two of his own.

Anyway, after another ten minutes filled with groans, yelps, and several other assorted noises normally associated with the lambing season, we all met up again at the edge of the green.

"You made it then," father remarked, looking a bit furtive.

"Naturally," replied Dennis.

"In how many?"

"How many have you had?"

"What difference does that make?"

"I would just like to know. I'm entitled to know you know."

"Oh. I've, er, taken… eight so far."

Mirabella and I exchanged glances, both wondering if our numerate skills had taken a tumble somewhere along the way: or perhaps the Royal and Ancient had changed the rules since I parked the car.

"Eight!" Dennis exclaimed.

"Yes."

"So what was all that kicking in aid of back there?"

"Kicking?"

"Yes. You were thrashing your legs all about."

"Oh, *that* kicking. Ahm… Frogs."

Well, I thought to myself, at least my father was having a go at a reason other than 'cramp': even if it was just as implausible.

"Frogs!" Dennis exclaimed, patently unimpressed.

"Yes. Might have been toads though. Hard to tell. The blighters were all over the place. Very off-putting, I don't mind saying."

"Hmmph."

"Indeed."

"Well I've only taken seven."

Once again, glances were exchanged between Mirabella and me.

"*Seven*! Seven?" my father asked, eyebrows high enough to almost reach his hairline. "Are you quite sure?" Eyebrows having dropped again, and his forehead now furrowed like a ploughed field.

"Absolutely positive."

"So what was all that club waving I noticed?"

"Ahm… Bees."

"Bees? At this time of year?"

"Might have been hornets. Hard to tell."

Had Mirabella and I then closed our eyes we would have been forgiven for thinking that we were standing on the shores of the Galápagos Islands and listening to a brace of aged male sea lions as they vocally competed for any available females. We were treated, maybe 'subjected' might be more accurate, to a stereophonic cacophony of loud 'harrumphs' as the two challengers made it abundantly clear that neither believed the other.

To this day I wish that I had recorded the sound, as I am sure that there must be a market for it; somewhere. Perhaps crowd control?

The two of them then performed an act of pastoral vandalism with their respective nine-irons, and chipped on to the green. Soon after, having taken a couple of putts each, they were both about six feet off the hole.

"Gimmees?" asked Dennis.

"Indeed not, sir."

"But I thought we had agreed."

"When the distance is *less* than six feet."

"But they are: surely?"

"And both players agree."

"I think we can both agree that we are both closer than six feet from the hole. I can get a tape measure, if you insist."

My father did some rapid reasoning. "But that would give you the hole," he said, not looking pleased.

"Good heavens, so it would."

"And that would mean it was all square with one to play."

"Well I never!"

"But that's…"

"My hole. On we go."

If scowling were ever to become an Olympic event, my father would be feted far and wide. Speaking of Olympic events, what ever happened to the concept of *Citius, Altius, Fortius*? I can just imagine how thrilled the Baron de Coubertin would be at the inclusion of the likes of clay-pigeon shooting, tennis and football in the modern games. What on earth is Swifter, Higher and Stronger about those?

Yes, I know the good Baron borrowed that expression from the headmaster of Arcueil College, in Paris; but it does encapsulate the intended spirit of the Games a lot better than a probable modern counterpart of Money, Drugs, and Cheating. How would *Pecunia, Lenimen, Decipio* sound? Snappy; but it might not sell as many tickets!

I shan't elaborate on my feelings towards synchronised swimming or rhythmic gymnastics; other than to say that even writing the words makes me feel a bit nauseous. To my way of thinking, it seems that the modern Olympic Games have little to do with the original values and a lot to do with making money. In other words, incorporate a sport that is popular and you will, therefore, attract the largest (and by that I mean 'paying') crowds.

I often wonder what Dr Brookes would have made of it all.

"Dr Brookes? Who on earth was he?" you might well ask.

Dr William Brookes was the fellow, in a place called Much Wenlock, who thought it would be a rather good idea to rekindle the Olympic Games – as a way of promoting the moral, physical and intellectual improvement of the inhabitants of the town and neighbourhood of Wenlock. So, in 1850, he arranged for it to start up again. I know that most history books will witter on about 1896 and the Baron de Coubertin, but if it hadn't been for Dr Brookes the show wouldn't have got off the ground.

Actually, perhaps a mention should also be made of the lawyer Robert Dover who, in the early 1600s, in the Chipping Campden area, laid the foundations for a revival of the Olympic Games. So a loud 'hurrah' to him as well.

Anyway, to his credit, the Baron de Coubertin did acknowledge Dr Brookes, albeit begrudgingly, in his inaugural speech.

Where was I? Oh yes, the golf. There it was, two down, all square with one to play, and a little under an hour gone. The excitement was bordering on tepid as we all walked over to the eighteenth tee. Well, the other three walked whilst I laboured with the two sets of clubs, and wearing shoes that looked as though they had been used for trail hunting.

Why golf club manufacturers cannot design a club with an adjustable head I shall never know: apart from the fact that the rules say that you are not allowed to adjust any club whilst playing that is. But it would make life so much easier, wouldn't it?

Obviously not for the golf club manufacturers, who need to persuade gullible players that the latest titanium-carbon-fibre-graphite set of clubs is just what is needed to take their play from being that of a hopeful fair-to-middlin' player to being a skint fair-to-middlin' player.

Anyway, the final hole. Dennis had the honour, and treated us all to another selection of his favourite wiggles; and then adjusted the height of his tee about six times before finally steadying himself to drive off. I have to say, quite candidly, that the wait wasn't worth it; and if I had taken the time to work out the energy expended in relation to the distance the ball actually travelled, I would probably have estimated that it might have been in the order of one kilojoule per linear foot travelled. I'm not sure how many ergs that works out as, but quite a few I shouldn't wonder.

Then it was my father's turn; and up he stepped. The eighteenth is a par four on which a player can – on a good day, and with a following wind – expect to reach the green in two. By a 'player', I mean an average club player who can carry the ball – in the desired direction that is – about 200 yards (over a small water hazard thing) with enough momentum to take it down the ensuing slope; and then hit the ball the remaining 150 yards or so on to the green.

I am not sure that my father, even in his halcyon days, could have been described as an average club player. A player who would attack the ball as someone with a machete might set about jungle creepers? Quite possibly. A player about whom Napoleon may well have been speaking when he said '*Du sublime au ridicule il n'y a qu'un pas*'? More than likely. A player for whom breaking 'the 100' was something normally reserved for the first nine holes? Most assuredly. All of those, in fact: but an average club player? I don't think so. Although, there may be many reading for whom the above forms an adequate 'average' description.

So, with the bet at stake and a mounting desire for reminders of *tempi passati*, my father asked me to withdraw from the bag a club he called 'Big Bertha'. I do not believe there was any actual connection to a certain Friedrich Alfred Krupp (or his daughter) – either in appearance or lineage – but he felt that the intended force about to be imparted to the golf ball deserved a club with a titular association to a certain high-angle, heavy calibre, howitzer that was rather popular around 1914.

The club in question had a purple and red leather grip with something to do with 'Original Lacky' inscribed on it; and at the other end there was an odd shaped block of wood with various metal plates screwed on to it (with ordinary wood screws by the look of it) that was attached to the mottled shaft with a range of black thread and white insulating tape.

"Are you sure this is the one you want?" I asked, as I handed it over.

"Certainly. Marvellous club; never lets me down."

"Really?"

"What do you mean by 'really'? What on earth is the matter with you, you numskull? Now keep still while I prepare myself."

If I thought that Dennis had performed a wide range of aerobic manoeuvres at the first tee, it was as nothing compared to the display to which we were all then subjected at the eighteenth. My father did a few knee bends, then scratched his shins a few times (he may actually have been trying to touch his toes, but it was hard to tell and I didn't like to ask), before placing the club behind his neck and proceeding to twist from side to side. The noise that greeted my ears made me look round to see if his bag of clubs had fallen over.

As someone who is still serving his 'Life' apprenticeship – well, that's how I like to think of it; although many might think that being in your fifties would be stretching the 'apprentice' description somewhat – I am not really in a position to pass comment on the antics of those who've been around for a good while longer than I have. Bearing in mind that I have only slightly more gorm than the average *drosophila*, I have observed that those of the eldest generation seem keen to behave in ways which are designed to irritate those in the one below. I am not, I hasten to add, including those who, due to illness or misfortune, have lost the ability to have much of a say in their circumstances.

Apart from the above-mentioned unfortunates, I have often wondered why this phenomenon should exist. Then one day, in a sort of flash – not of the Damascene type, but you know what I mean – it came to me. What better way to placate the loss of a loved-one than to have them become a complete and utter pest during their final stages? The result of which would be that, by the time they decide to hand in their notice, their nearest and dearest will be almost welcoming the day with open arms.

A sweeping generalisation I realise, but there is a kernel of truth in there all the same. My father, so it has seemed for the past five years or more, has embraced the principle with a vigour that quite belies his age. As Dylan Thomas once put it –

'Do not go gentle into that goodnight,
Old age should burn and rave at close of day;
Rage, rage against the dying of the light'.

I never knew that quite so much high dudgeon could be stored in one man: but there we are. I wonder if it's hereditary.

After a couple of minutes of what looked like a *kata* devised by

Leopold von Sacher-Masoch, my father was ready to send the ball greenwards. With all the speed of a slow-motion replay, he took the driver through the backswing, paused at the top, and then, with a yell and a commendable impression of a *Dervish*, he returned the clubface to the ball and smote it a blow with which men half his age would have taken pride.

Now, logically, the ball should have been well on its way by the time father realised that he was unable to halt his follow-through, and had pirouetted off the tee and disappeared from view into the ditch behind him: and so it was. Well on its way, that is. To this day I have still got no idea where 'its way' happened to be; but on it, it most certainly was: and so was something else.

Whilst trying to follow the trajectory of the ball, I was aware that another object was spinning through the air, at right-angles to the direction of the green; and the first notion I decided upon was that it was some kind of carrion bird: and that, apparently, was also the first impression that a passing farmer in the adjacent field drew. For, within a second or two, there was the most enormous blast from two barrels of a shotgun, and the black flying object exploded into a thousand pieces.

That event caused me great puzzlement; as my recollection of the normal response of one of our feathered friends upon receiving a load of buckshot was that they tended to squawk loudly and then drop. There may be a polite folding of the wings, perhaps time for a wish that they had chosen to walk that day instead, and then they plummet. They don't, to my knowledge, perform a complete disintegration.

A moment or two later, my father emerged from his examination of the drainage facilities and began making enquiries as to the current whereabouts of his golf ball. I was about to explain that as being a new mystery which had descended upon Mankind, when I could see that the head of his driver was missing. I expect that a lot of you would have spent many a restless night pondering upon said conundrum, but it only took me about thirty seconds to arrive at the solution.

"This is so cool," piped up the small person on my left. "I had no idea that golf was this much fun. It's never like this on the television."

"Has anyone seen the head of my driver?" asked my father.

"It's over there," replied Dennis, smirking. "And there," he pointed. "And there as well. I believe there may also be another bit yonder. But I have no idea where the ball went. So you'll have to play three."

"What!"

"Strict rules. As we agreed."

"But that was without being fired upon by hostile forces."

"I do not believe there is any such clause in the rule book."

"Well there damn well ought to be. It's like facing the U-Boats all over again."

"Play three, if you don't mind: and know that I shall be counting."

The expression on my father's face bounced between that of a cadaver which had been left out in the rain for a week, and a look that would have made the leaves on all the trees within half a mile respond as if autumn had come early. "My seven-iron please," he growled at me.

I searched for, and finally found, an iron with all manner of legends on the back of the head. No-shock-neck, True Angle Deluxe, Rustless; and it seemed to have been in the care of a certain H.E. Shoesmith at one time. Then, in order to prevent another firearm incident, I gave the head of the club a quick tweak to make sure it stood a better than even chance of remaining attached to the shaft.

"Are you sure you want this club?" I asked, passing it over.

"Of course I'm sure. Marvellous club: never lets me down."

I was sure I had heard that expression somewhere before; so, just to be on the safe side, I saw to it that both Mirabella and I were stationed at a safe distance before my father went to hit the replacement ball. He gave a few wiggles, and then began to brandish the club around his head. A moment later contact was made between ball and club – I wasn't entirely convinced it was precisely as intended – but the spherical white object began its journey to the green.

"And don't forget," said Dennis, still smirking, and striding away with the air of someone for whom the day is just about to get much better. "That was your third shot."

"Pah!"

"Pah-hah!"

We had walked about forty or so yards when my father turned to me.

"Son…"

I know that he and I share a genetic link, and that the man is perfectly entitled to attract my attention by calling me thus; but I always feel an air of foreboding whenever I hear that word from him: and I instinctively know that a request for some variety of favour is about to burst upon the scene.

"There's nothing wrong with that," I hear you say. "After all, if it wasn't for the old fellow, a certain gamete wouldn't have been provided, and a certain morula wouldn't have formed into you."

And so on and so forth: and I quite agree. But I am pretty sure that when Fate stepped in and decided that starting life would be a good wheeze, it didn't envisage that the results of some adult connubial activities would end up owing their creators an inexhaustible number of obligations. Especially when those obligations are invariably accompanied by trouble in one form or another.

"Yes…?" I cautiously replied.

"It's all down to this hole, you know."

"Yes, I do know."

"And if Dennis wins this hole he gets to take my sextant."

"Yes; I know that too."

"And we wouldn't want that to happen, would we?"

"No, I suppose we wouldn't."

"So I have to win, don't I?"

"That would seem to be a logical conclusion. But you're not exactly in pole position, are you?"

"No: and that, dear boy, is where you come in."

I did mention that there would be impending trouble of some sort, didn't I?

"And what do you mean by that?" I asked, fearfully.

"I mean that you are going to devise a dash of the old subterfuge."

"Me! What? How? And, more to the point, when? We're already half-way through the final hole, in case you hadn't noticed."

"Then you had better get your cogs turning, hadn't you."

"But… but… but…"

"For goodness sake, this is no time for silly speedboat impressions."

What was a chap to do? Fewer than 300 yards, and probably no more than three more shots to come up with a plan to let my father at least halve the hole and keep his beloved sextant.

Needless to say, even though I put the entire right side of my brain to work, I was unable to think of a suitable ruse. In fact, such was my preoccupation, that I hadn't even managed to keep score as my father and Dennis hacked their way to the green. I was vaguely aware that the two players had been watching each other like hawks, shouting out as they each took their shots, and yelling other words that seem to oscillate between expletives and 'whoops' of joy or derision.

Fortunately Mirabella had kept an eye on the proceedings and was able to assure me that both men had miscounted by the same amount. I was then asked, by both men, to confirm the state of play, when they were poised over their respective golf balls, putter in hand.

"Going by the information provided by the walking abacus…" Mirabella clasped her hands and shook them to either side of her head, in, I assumed, celebration; and perhaps in case the players might have forgotten who she was. "… Dennis is on the green in eight; and father, remembering that he played three from the tee, is on the green in ten. As father is furthest from the hole he will putt first."

"How much do you think that sextant is worth?" Dennis asked, as my father deliberated how best to play out the hole.

"Financially, a lot more than your photograph: sentimentally, nowhere near as much. Indeed, I really don't envy how you're going to be feeling soon."

"How *I'm* going to be feeling. Ha! You're further from the hole than me and I have two shots in hand. Your sextant is going to look lovely on my trophy shelf."

"What trophy shelf? You haven't got any trophies."

"I had the shelf made especially for today."

"Poppycock. William; mind the flag, if you please."

I gingerly made my way across the green and stood with one hand on the pole, waiting to lift it out of the way should the ball come anywhere near. I had a feeling that I wouldn't need to pay too much attention.

It was obvious that, to stand any chance of halving the hole, my father would need to sink his ball in no more than two putts. His first, therefore, would need to get within a couple of feet of the hole; and as he was currently nearly forty feet away, that was going to require a miracle that would make the one that Moses did at the Red Sea pale into insignificance.

For the first time that afternoon, silence fell, as my father lined up his putt: but it was only for a few seconds.

"Get on with it," Dennis then bellowed. "It'll be dark soon."

My father stepped away from the ball, and gave Dennis a look that he usually reserved for East European mendicants: one with the menace of a flame-thrower and a withering brand of haughty disdain. It is a look well worth practising, I have to say; but I haven't quite mastered it yet. Mine always comes out looking as though I was trying to separate my jaws after the toffee I was chewing had stuck them together.

Father readdressed the ball; made a few wiggles, had a few knee bends, and took a few squints at the hole. His grip tightened, the putter slowly went back, and I felt as though the pleasantness – or otherwise – of the rest of my life depended on what was going to happen next.

I wondered if Dennis would try to break my father's concentration; but I doubted it: because any deviation from the usual was more likely to improve the outcome than just letting the natural order of things prevail.

The putter swung towards the ball, the world seemed to quieten; even the birds hushed their chirruping. Then 'click'; the putter and the ball made contact, and the ball was on its way. I watched, slowly lifting the flag from the hole, as the ball rolled nearer and nearer.

Would it go all the way? It couldn't, could it? It wouldn't, would it? If God was going to produce a sensation, surely there must be more deserving cases: and I couldn't imagine the 18th green of a golf course as being a suitable venue for pilgrims. On top of which, I was quite sure that the club committee would have something to say about having a shrine so close to the clubhouse. They certainly wouldn't want hordes of candle-carriers traipsing all over the place: heaven forbid.

Well, I needn't have worried. The ball didn't go in; but it did, somehow, roll until it came to stop approximately two feet from the hole. Do minor miracles count? Would the Vatican be interested?

If my face held an image of undiluted shock, it would have been as nothing compared to the air of abjection that Dennis was displaying. He looked as though he had just received notification that his house, wife, children, grand-children and dog were about to be repossessed: the poor fellow's demeanour had gone from inflated to deflated as the ball traversed the green. Imagine a car tyre when you take out the valve: only without so much hissing.

My father, on the other hand, seemed to stand straighter and taller, as if waiting for gallantry medals to be pinned to his chest. I had a feeling that there might have been a touch of shock mixed in with all the hubris; or else we would have been treated to a celebratory jig, whilst he whirled his club above his head.

Indeed, all that he manifested was a restrained, albeit with a dash of self-satisfaction, "That'll do."

Dennis now had to get down in three or fewer to win the hole, the competition, and the bet. Maybe my father's muted triumphalism wasn't going to last much longer.

Dennis asked me to keep attending the flag. He then paced the distance to the hole; he scanned the green for any and all undulations; he even noted the way the blades of grass leaned.

I wasn't sure if any of that information was going to be of the slightest use, but I nodded sagely as he muttered his calculations. Finally, and presumably fully aware he had three putts for the hole, he addressed the ball. Thirty-five feet in three putts; a little under twelve feet per putt: but surely, as I couldn't imagine my father even considering the notion of a six-feet 'gimmee' at such a pivotal point, the last one would have to be no more than two feet. So that meant the first two putts would have to share thirty-three feet between them.

As Dennis had been a bank manager for the last fifteen years of his working life, I felt confident that he would have worked that out; and I watched, nervously, as he took his first putt. I can only assume that Dennis didn't have enough time to replace the air he lost when deflating earlier, because the ball travelled no more than five feet. The next putt was going to have to travel twenty-eight feet. The tension mounted; my father was looking a bit more confident; Mirabella was looking a bit more bored.

Another putt, another 'click', and another five feet. Dennis was looking distraught; my father was looking very confident; Mirabella was looking at her mobile phone.

The next shot was hit a good deal more firmly, the ball whizzed on its way, and would have had a lot more promise than the previous two shots were it not for the fact that the ball was in the air. Before I knew it, I had been struck on the shin, and had shrieked with pain: and also before I knew it, the ball dropped on to the grass and rolled into the hole.

It was now the turn of the other two men to shriek: Dennis with jubilation, and my father with desolation.

"My hole, I believe," Dennis crowed. "My sextant, I believe. Bad luck old chap, eh? To the victor the spoils."

"I don't think so," Mirabella interjected, as she ran her finger across the screen of her phone.

"What?" Dennis huffed.

"What?" my father puffed.

"I think you'll find that a player will incur a two-stroke penalty for hitting the flag-stick attendant. With the ball, that is, rather than simply walking over and punching him. At least that's what it says in the rules."

"What!" came the joint exclamation. Although the same word may have been used by both men, I could sense that it was for different reasons.

"It means," Mirabella explained, "that the hole, and therefore the match, is a draw."

So there it was – the match halved, honours evened, and each man allowed to keep his own trophy. It was hard to tell if they were annoyed or relieved. Ten minutes later, and with shoes changed, we all repaired to the bar where I was graciously invited to put my hand in my pocket and stump up for all the requested libations. Isn't life wonderful?

Mirabella and I go to a theme park.

I was, once again, enjoying a mug of tea and looking forward to watching the opening morning of the test match when, with a whoosh that led me to believe the tornado season had not only lost its way but had also decided to start early, my bedroom door burst open. It was thanks to the steady hand that is a predominant characteristic of the Phalarope clan that I managed to prevent my tea from spilling in my lap and causing an injury of a personal nature.

"What are you up to?" I asked, when all parts of my equilibrium had returned to their rightful levels and reminded me that I was, once again, saddled with a house guest.

"Uncle William…?"

"Yes…?"

"It's a lovely day."

Another rather useful characteristic with which I have been endowed is the ability to spot the blindingly obvious. I realise that some people have difficulty when it comes to noticing matters that have come to rest – often with an accompanying band of musicians – right under their noses; but I am not to be counted amongst their number.

With some, I realise, such a location may prove – as a result of the size of their hooter – to be a bit inconvenient. Indeed, plants may have been known to wither in the shadow thus caused; but such is not the case with me. Plus, I knew that – as a result of having noticed the glittering specks of dust that floated like plankton in the golden shaft of light that parted my curtains – it was, in the weather department at any rate, indeed a morning of some merit.

I was going to make a comment on television weather forecasters, but wasn't sure if I really wanted a bout of tachycardia: but I decided to take the risk.

Am I the only person who gets irritated by the way that said forecasters –

Think they are 'celebrities'.

Cannot mention, say, East Anglia without pointing to it. We all know where East Anglia is – we may not want to go there, but we certainly know which part of the country to avoid. Some of us, so I understand, have even had the place deleted from their satnav.

By pointing to, say, East Anglia, they let their left arm tarry across most of South Wales; so that what is destined for that part of the UK is hidden from view. I realise that this is probably because what they forecast is going to be proved wrong and keeping it covered will go some way to help provide a denial later on.

Try to dramatise what they have to say. Such as 'There will be a STRONG northerly wind, and temperatures may Der-ROP below freezing.' Are we excited? No we are not.

I have often felt tempted to do a couple of things. Firstly, spend a year comparing what they predicted with what actually happened, and then working out the percentage of correct forecasts. Secondly, tell them to stick their forecasts where the sun doesn't shine. I fear, however, that suggestion might be a waste of time as they probably wouldn't be able to work out where that was! Perhaps it is just me, but I often get the impression that they couldn't look out the window and describe the weather.

"Weather forecasting is an inexact science," they bleat, by way of mitigation. Don't we just know that! Doesn't stop them from demanding big salaries and millions being spent on propagating that 'inexact' science though, does it?

Is there another occupation – apart from being in Government – where you can get it wrong so often and still go back to your job the following week?

Excuse me while I check my pulse rate. Now, where was I? Oh yes, a lovely day.

"So...?" I ventured, warily, in reply.

"So I thought it would be a wicked idea if we like went to a theme park."

Don't you just love it when youngsters suggest that? "Oh really."

"Yes. So what do you think?"

"I think that 'nefarious' would be a very apt description for such an undertaking."

"It's a different sort of 'wicked'. Der-err. And it'll be like great fun."

"For the dim-witted, I have no doubt. But for the rest of us – and by that I mean those who can, at the very least, read and write – I beg to differ."

"Mum said that you'd keep me amused while I stay here."

Isn't it strange how people, usually young females I have to add, will oscillate between describing their maternal parent as 'Mum', 'Mummy' or 'Mother' depending on whether they wish her to seem caring or not?

"Your mother has probably said a great many things about a great number of things."

"But Uncle William, it's an awesome day; and it would be so lame if we didn't do something with it."

"*Lame?*"

"Yeah. Lame. Uncool. It would be like a waste."

"Not from where I'm sitting it wouldn't."

"Do you mean you'd be happy to spend such a lovely day sitting in a chair, drinking tea and reading a paper?"

"Happy? I think 'euphoric' would be nearer the mark."

"But Uncle William…"

It was about then that I heard the flow of water. Salty water: tears to be exact. I am quite sure that back in the mists of pre-history the female of the species must have noticed that a great deal of benefit was to be gained from switching on their lachrymal glands when confronted with a foreign body in the eyelid region: and subsequently, and probably more importantly for them, when confronted with intransigence from the male of the species. For some reason totally beyond my discernment, Nature saw to it that a lot of men would be suitably influenced. Perhaps the response was designed so as to avoid a lot of applications with heavy blunt instruments to the cranial area.

Whatever the reason, the male side of the Phalarope lineage has always been a bit of a soft touch when it comes to blubbering females.

"Well… that is…" I said, falteringly.

"Can we go? Please? I'll be so good. I promise."

"I really don't think I… "

"You'll be so surprised at how well I'll behave."

"But I would much rather – "

"You'll have the best time."

"It's just that I – "

"Oh *please*."

What is the term that describes being unable to get a word in edgeways when talking to someone? I'm sure that there is a technical term for it. I think the condition may be known as logorrhoea – from the Greek *logos* (word) and *rhoia* (flow). Do women ever suffer from lalophobia? I somehow doubt it.

"Oh," I sighed, before throwing in the towel. "I suppose so."

"Oh, Uncle William, you're the best uncle."

Then, apart from realising that the possibility of a tranquil day was rapidly fading, I had to fend off a fourteen-year-old who was determined to occlude the flow of blood through my carotid arteries with some sort of wrestling hold.

"I say… steady on…"

"But you are, like, *soooo* nice."

"That is as maybe; but I would still like to remain conscious."

"I'll get dressed; and then we can go."

"Go? Now? But… but what about *notre petit dejeuner*?"

"Our breakfast can wait. And anyway, I'm sure we can have something to eat when we get there."

"We can?"

"Yes."

I then felt it necessary to ask the obvious question: especially as my familiarity with theme parks was on the deficient side of irrelevant. "And where might 'there' be?"

"I used my phone to check out what's round here, and there's one that's really close. Well, fairly close. Twenty miles. That's close for round here, isn't it?"

"In this particular year of our Lord, quite possibly."

"That's great then."

With another whirl of eddies, the pocket cyclone departed, and left me feeling that I had just been the victim of a psychological mugging. As I have pointed out on previous occasions, I might not be the brightest star in the firmament – possibly some kind of brown dwarf I expect – but I pride myself on knowing when I have fallen prey to a *coup de maître*. However, as Cicero might have said – possibly whilst showing support for Octavian – *eventus stultorum magister*: and, as one of Nature's prime fools, I strive to learn from events and be on the lookout for any such manoeuvres in the future.

About an hour or so later, and with my gastric environs making their complaints heard above the sound of the car engine, Mirabella and I found a suitable space in the car park adjoining the requested citadel of entertainment. Then, after having bid a sad farewell to the best part of twenty-five pounds sterling, the two of us were granted access.

Despite considerable protestations to the contrary, I insisted on replenishing my energy stores before any expedition was made into the hinterland of hedonism, and made a beeline for the closest refectory: and then rather wished I hadn't. What is it, I wonder, that makes such purveyors of comestibles imagine that such as I would welcome the opportunity to swallow victuals that had been wrapped in what amounted to several square yards of cellophane?

As a rule, I try not to eat anything that bears the legend 'contains meat products'. *Meat Products*? Personally, I should have thought that a pie entitled 'steak' really ought to contain steak. I don't want to read that it contains 'meat products'. I want it to contain 'meat'. Nice chunks of topside; and not chunks of some gruel that may contain a lot of water and bits of unmentionable origin from any variety of species of any number of animals. As for meat products of the 'reconstituted' or 'mechanically recovered' variety? Well, it would appear that everything apart from the moo gets used. Hardly an appetising thought, is it?

A bit of a sage once said that if you wished to maintain a degree of composure, never observe the making of laws or sausages. You really don't want to know what goes into either of them.

As for their 'jam' doughnuts… I had, possibly like the ingénue I am, imagined that there was better than an outside chance of finding some of the aforementioned conserve within the musty confines of what appeared to be a flat sugary tennis ball. But I was to be sadly mistaken. Unless, that is, I just happened to have a microscope about my person at the time.

However, once my appetite had been quelled (or as near as could be), I took several tentative steps into the 'World of Fun'. Oh dear, oh dear. To me, a 'World of Fun' is a world that is filled with fun things; things that bring enjoyment; where pleasure features quite highly on the list of emotions being felt at the time.

What makes people want to see how long they can hang on to their last meal? I may be a tad on the old-fashioned side of things, but I do not consider strapping myself into a seat before being shaken, turned upside-down, subjected to enough G-forces to implode my eyeballs, and all whilst in the company of shrieking retards, as being even close to fun.

From the moment I stepped out from the eatery, I was bombarded with sounds and visions of hordes of people intent on scaring the proverbial out of themselves. Why pay good money to do that? I should have thought that it would have been much simpler to wander about certain parts of certain major cities after dark.

Then, as if the aforementioned wasn't reason enough to stay at home, why do so many of those same people seem incapable of behaving with any sense of decorum? I'm sure that I didn't see a 'Please leave your brain here' tray when I entered; so why do they conduct themselves in a manner best described as appalling? Is there a problem with enjoying yourself and behaving at the same time? Maybe there is for some people. Why has the word Faliraki just popped into my head I wonder?

Further cogitations were curtailed by a firm tug on my right sleeve and a small voice – actually the voice wasn't that small at all – asking (maybe demanding might be closer) that we hurry up and have a go on something that sounded as if it was called 'The Emetic'. I would be lying if I were to say I felt enthusiastic at the prospect.

The contraption she had singled out for our opening feature was a rather large roller-coaster. As you may remember, I am not the world's greatest traveller. In fact, I am not even in the top ninety-five per cent. I have, which can be rather irritating for those in the immediate vicinity, a tendency to part company with partly digested items whenever those little otoliths within my semicircular canals are agitated beyond a certain degree. Which in my case, is a degree of some little magnitude.

There I was, standing next to a mischievous child who intended to take me on a contraption that was designed – if not actually guaranteed – to help people rapidly lose weight in a fairly undignified manner. *Oh good*, I thought. *Just the ticket.*

I have read articles regarding whereabouts you should sit on the collection of carriages in an attempt to find a spot that is either less or more likely to induce an outbreak of reverse peristalsis. Some said that being in the front – although increasing the visual fear aspect – is better because the front of the train travels slower than the rest. Others said that being in the back allows you an extra bit of time to prepare for the next part of the 'thrill'. The bet-hedgers said that the middle portion provides the best (or did they say the worst?) of both worlds.

My own experience has shown that it matters not a jot where I place my gluteus maximus muscles, as I am almost certainly going to part company with whatever happens to be residing inside my stomach at the time. The only variable is the number of people over whom I deposit said contents, and whether I can get away without being assaulted.

The rear carriage is usually the most considerate choice – for obvious reasons. I shan't even begin to describe what happened the time I took a ride in something called a 'Gondola'. I still blanche at the memory.

"Come on, Uncle William. It'll be great fun."

"I'm sure it will: especially if you happen to suffer from bulimia."

"Oh pleeeze."

Is there a specific gene that allows females to flutter their eyelashes at members of the opposite sex? I have tried the procedure on occasions – in order to garner favour – but the only reaction I manage to elicit is a polite enquiry as to whether or not I may have something lodged in my eye.

So it was, with no small degree of trepidation, that I found myself occupying a small compartment on the ride with Mirabella. Apart from the difference in our sizes, the casual observer would have also noticed that I happened to be losing a lot of natural colour from my cheeks, and that the knuckles on both my hands were white with the effort I was exerting in grasping the safety bar.

"Are you excited, Uncle William?"

"Beyond adequate description, dear child."

"Cool."

"If you say so."

"Well, my heart is going like ten to the dozen."

"Why would it be going slower than normal?"

"No; it's going quicker."

"In which case you should have said that it's going eighteen to the dozen."

There was a pause as the logic of my statement burrowed its way in.

"Oh yeah. Yeah! That makes sense. Wow; like everyone I know makes that mistake."

Before I had time to point out all the other mistakes, we began moving. Then, for what seemed like the next three hours – it may have been considerably shorter than that, but I have never really been a good judge of time when fearing that my *medulla oblongata* was in danger of protruding through the back of my neck at any moment – I was subjected to a series of manoeuvres that seemed to defy all the known laws of physics. Gravity, inertia, momentum, reciprocal, centripetal and centrifugal forces all merged into matter that would have had Sir Isaac Newton developing a thorough dislike for all *pseudocarps*; and Albert Einstein would probably have ignored all the general and special theories proffered by his relatives.

Up we went, down we went; even upside-down we went: there may also have been a moment when a touch of inside-out occurred. I cannot be certain. I was, however, fairly sure the experience was not going to be on my list of 'must be repeated' ones. For goodness sake, it would have been so much easier – and quicker – to have simply applied two fingers to the back of my throat.

Finally, with the shrieks of my fellow passengers still ringing in my ears, the contraption jerked to a halt and, with the aid of two attendants, I managed to reach the nearest bench. I have a vague recollection of Mirabella asking if we could go round again: I also have a vague recollection of saying that I would rather shove one of the carriages somewhere that would require me to have it surgically removed at a later date.

I believe a very loud "Huh!" was the reply I received.

Once my balance was restored, the Phalarope spirit compelled me to resume our perambulation around the plethora of activities available; and I saw people willing to subject themselves to all manner of indignities as they were propelled at various speeds in various directions.

I was on the point of mentioning that I really didn't understand how the food stalls managed to make any money (or perhaps they did because people needed to replace the food they had disgorged) when I noticed that Mirabella seemed rather preoccupied: frantic even. I raised my eyebrows in her direction.

"Uncle William," she said, looking about her in a rushed manner.

"Yes."

"I've lost the talisman you gave me."

"The what?"

"The talisman. That good luck charm."

"Oh. Where?"

"I don't know. It might have been on the 'Electic'."

"The *Electic*? Do you mean that up-and-down, vomity thing?"

"Yes. It must have been there. My bad."

"Your what?"

"Bad. My bad. My mistake."

I suddenly had a vision of having to go round again on the wretched thing, and would willingly have paid for half a dozen talisman replacements.

"Don't worry, my dear," I said, trying to play down the dilemma. "I can always buy you another one."

"But I don't want *another* one. I want that one. And anyway, I thought you said that a Chinese mystic gave it to you as he lay on his deathbed."

"Ah… well; yes… that is. That is I'm sure he wouldn't mind if I bought you another one. He was that sort of a mystic, you know. Always willing to be pragmatic: very much so. In fact, I believe he was known as a 'Pragmamystic'."

"I don't care. I want the original."

Do you ever have times when you wished that you hadn't embellished a tale in order to make it seem more interesting? I often do.

To cut a long story short, when I was in San Francisco I bought several key-rings. I'm sure you know the sort of things I mean. They consist of a ring on to which you can slide some keys, a short chain, and a miniature metal facsimile of something to do with wherever it is you are when you buy it. London would have Tower Bridge, Paris the Eiffel Tower, and San Francisco had depictions of the Golden Gate bridge and cable cars: as well as the one that I purchased in China Town. It was designed to show the twelve animals – tiger, dragon, monkey and so on – that the Chinese use to represent a cycle of twelve years; and it's meant to usher in lots of wealth, good luck, friendships and benefactors. Makes you wonder why, if it is so effective, the chap from whom I bought it was still scratching a living hawking the damn things. Anyway.

"Well, okay," I said. "We – that is you – will have to trot back and have a look for it."

"Aren't you coming?"

"Yes; but just not at a trot."

With that, the issue of my sister tore off in the direction whence we had just come; and I followed at a more leisurely pace. Yes, I know I maybe should have shown a bit more concern and have at least tried to 'trot'; but I'm generally more at home with an amble.

When I arrived at the designated spot, it was to find Mirabella remonstrating with another girl of similar age on the path that led to the gate that led to a path that led to a gate where a notice informed people that they only had another fifteen minutes left to wait.

"Hello," I said, ambling up to where the pair was standing.

"Uncle William, this girl has got my talisman."

"No I 'aven't," the other girl snapped back: and rather too coarsely for my liking, if you must know.

"Yes you have," continued Mirabella. "You've got it round your neck. I can see it. Now give it back to me. It's mine."

"DAAADDD..."

It might be that I have sensitive ears, or it might be that my ears are simply acutely tuned to a particular frequency – usually the one used by females I have to add. Whatever the reason, the sound that emanated from that young girl's face was sufficient to send me into a state of near-paralysis, and it turned the heads of everybody within two hundred yards.

It was also sufficient to attract the attention of a rather large fellow who gave the impression of being nearer to the Neanderthal end of things than he was Cro Magnon. Possibly even as far back as Australopithecus if I was going to be really accurate. My initial impression didn't alter when he began to speak.

"Wot is it, Letisha?"

"Waaahhh…"

"Tell me, darlin'… wot's 'appened?"

"It's this girl, dad. She says this neckerless is 'ers. And it ain't. You give it me."

"Yeah? Oh yeah, that's roight. So ooh says I didn't? Eh?"

"She did. An' 'im."

It was at that point the behemoth turned his attention in my direction.

"Are you sayin' it's yours? Eh? Are yer?"

"Well, I do have to declare that it does bear more than a passing resemblance to the one that I gave to my niece."

"A passin' wot?"

I have long been of the opinion that people who struggle to understand speech when it contains words of more than two syllables really ought not to be allowed to venture more than one hundred yards from a given institution: if at all, actually. We – the English – have a wonderful language that, at any one time, boasts far in excess of 800,000 words, as well as their derivatives. I do not expect people to know them all; not even half: but I think that a working knowledge of a tenth of that number would be rather nice. Alas, nowadays most people only use in the region of 400 different words in an average day; and I had a feeling that the troglodyte presently before me would have struggled to surpass forty: and those would almost certainly include the names of his family – which would be quite a large one.

"Resemblance. By which I mean that this talisman looks very much like the one I gave to my niece." I indicated to Mirabella, just in case 'niece' was a term with which Mr Flintstone might have been unfamiliar.

"Tell him it's not, dad. It's mine. It's…" The girl then looked closely at the item in question. "Yeah. It's got my fav'rit animals an' that. A rabbit, an' a… pig… an' a 'orse. Yeah. That's wot."

"The animals are actually those of the Chinese horoscope," I explained. "As was mentioned earlier, it is a talisman."

"A wot?" asked the father.

"A talisman. A lucky charm," I continued.

"Well it ain't. Goh it?"

"As a matter of fact I haven't 'goh' it. Which, when you think about it, is why we are experiencing this altercation."

"Wot? Don't try and get clever wiv me, mate."

"Apart from the fact that I am not your 'mate', by adopting a stance of aggression against anybody who appears to be getting 'clever' with you, you will restrict most of your communicating experiences to items of household furniture and pot plants."

"WOT?"

It was then that I sensed the mercury in the man's 'rage thermometer' was rapidly approaching 212° Fahrenheit: and as said cave-dweller was in the region of six stones heavier and taller than my good self, I decided that a change in tactic would be advisable.

"I feel that this is a good stage in the proceedings to point out that it is probably just as well that the 'neckerless', as your daughter so eloquently put it, is more than likely not the one that belonged to my niece. You see, I can tell that your daughter is much better at acting, and will be much more likely to win the Ebola prize."

The man's forehead then looked as though someone had just used a garden rake on it; and his eyebrows, although not far apart to begin with, now seemed to overlap. "A bowl'a prize? A bowl'a wot? Wot you talkin' abaht?"

I had a strange feeling that however long I spent explaining what the virus was, what it does to the human body, and why you should always keep as far away as possible from it – especially as they now think it can be transmitted by air as well as blood – only about three or four percent of what I said would end up within the grasp range of his severely limited understanding. As it was nearly one o'clock, and would surely be dark before six hours had elapsed, I decided to forego the effort and let somebody else try.

"It is all part of a competition," I went on.

"Wot competition?"

"The owners of this park like to give a prize to the person who has that lucky trinket and can convince them they also have Ebola. I'm sure that your daughter would be really good at doing that." I could tell that I had the man's attention. "So your best chance of winning will be to go over to that tent – can you see the one I mean?" I asked, pointing at the First Aid tent. "If you go in and tell them that your daughter has recently come into contact with someone…" I once again indicated Mirabella, this time in much the same way that a museum curator may have brought an exhibit to the attention of a party of errant schoolchildren. "… who has Ebola. And remember to pronounce 'Ebola'… *E-bowler*… as clearly as you can. I am quite sure the staff in the tent will be only too pleased to give you all the help they can."

"S'pose ah don't wonna do it? Eh?"

"It'll be well worth it. As I said, there's a prize involved. And it's a cash prize."

"A cash prize! Yeah?"

"Oh 'yeah' indeed. And, if your daughter has any lipstick with her, it would greatly improve your chances of getting the prize if she makes dots all over her face. The competition organisers love it to look as real as possible. Maybe if she foams at the mouth a bit and then pretends to pass out." I looked at the girl. "Do you think you can do that?"

"An' I'll get a cash prize if I do?"

"A great big one."

"Then yeah; no probs."

"Well, I hope you win the prize."

With various grunts of confusion ringing in my ears, I grabbed Mirabella by the sleeve and rapidly put distance between us and the source of the clamour.

"Don't forget," I shouted back, "to go to the tent I showed you, and make sure you say you have Ebola; and then lay it on as thick as you can."

"But Uncle William, that *was* my talisman."

"I realise that; and I also realise it is a matter of principle that we rectify the situation. However, I further realise that merely walking up and grabbing it may well have caused one of us – namely me – to spend quite a long time in traction."

"So what are we – you – going to do about it? And why did you tell them I have Ebola? I don't do I?"

"I sincerely hope not; or your mother will be absolutely furious with me. Anyway, I'm going to go and have a cup of tea, and sit back to watch the merriment."

As I may have mentioned before, we Phalaropes are not quite as green as we are cabbage-looking. Quite the opposite, in fact, if you take Great Aunt Bertha's nose as a reference point: and who was an extraordinary lady, if I might take a moment or two to elaborate.

Great Aunt Bertha was married to one of my maternal grandfather's brothers. She was a delightful old lady who seemed, to a young boy like me, to spend an inordinate amount of time sipping tea whilst sitting at the small table near the window of her front room.

Now, the 'seem' part of my story refers to the 'sipping tea' aspect. Yes, she was drinking out of a teacup; yes, she filled the teacup from a teapot; and yes, the liquid that poured out of the spout was brown in colour. But the liquid was, in fact, brown ale; and rumour had it that she used to lace the brown ale with more than a dash of whisky. The ever-beaming smile on her face may well have had more to do with the drink than her naturally cheery disposition.

The demureness, however, used to be marred somewhat when she made the journey back to the nearby Brown's Hotel with a large collection of bottles hidden beneath her baggy cardigan. Clanking loudly whilst walking is often a bit of a giveaway.

Perhaps the most amusing part of the Aunt Bertha story was that concerning her demise. Not, I hasten to add, the fact that she died; but the attending anecdote. The dear old girl died in the days, and in a part of Wales, when the deceased was laid out in the front room for a day or two. In a shroud, and in a coffin; rather than simply plonked down on the floor, I should make clear. Those involved in the procedure then left

Bertha's body, as was the custom, for the night; but when they returned the next morning the body had gone.

As the likes of Burke and Hare were not at large, the disappearance did prove a bit of a puzzler; until someone went upstairs and found Aunt Bertha fast asleep in her bed. It seemed that her passing had been somewhat misdiagnosed. I expect it was down to one of those incidents of catatonic states; and the sort of thing that encouraged people to be buried with a rope attached to a bell which they could pull if they woke up and found that they had been interred prematurely.

People were paid to sit by graves during the night and listen out for the sound of ringing bells. I believe that is where the expression 'doing the graveyard shift' originated. I also believe that it is the origin of the expression when – if you saw someone who looked the double of old so-and-so (deceased) – you said "Oh, you are the dead-ringer of old so-and-so." I know some people think that last expression has more to do with substituting horses in racing, but I prefer the burial version.

I expect that these days people will ask to be buried with their mobile phone. Mind you, if you are, you had better make sure it is on a pay-as-you-go arrangement and also let everybody know that the phone was in your coffin: otherwise it could make for an interesting conversation.

"Hello."
"Is that you Deidre?"
"Yes. Who is this?"
"It's John."
"*John?*"
"Yes."
"John who?"
"John your husband, John."
"But you're dead. We buried you yesterday."
"I know; and that's what I'm calling about. I'm not dead."
"Not dead? So where are you?"
"I'm still in my coffin."
"Does this mean you're calling me from beyond the grave?"
"No; I'm calling you from *inside* the grave."

I suppose that some will probably want to take their tablets with them. I guess it would help while away the hours – reading the papers, sending a few emails and so forth – while you waited to be exhumed. It might be just as well for graveyards to have some sort of booster aerial system set up; as I would imagine that the signal, certainly from six feet under, might be a bit on the weak side.

Anyway, the net result was that when Aunt Bertha next gave the impression that she had shuffled off her mortal coil (about three days later), they re-laid her out in the coffin with a bottle of whisky next to her; figuring that if the bottle hadn't been touched the next morning, there was little chance of her doing another 'Lazarus'.

The old ways are usually the best, I always say.

However, back to the current state of affairs and Mirabella's talisman.

I managed to find a bench that was not only within earshot of the medical tent but which also afforded a good view, and sat down to enjoy a cup of tea whilst I watched the anticipated entertainment. I didn't have long to wait.

The unpleasant gentleman and his daughter entered the tent, practically bursting with ebullience, and set about claiming their anticipated reward.

There were several loud shouts, a couple of screams, two people in St John's Ambulance uniforms came running out of the entrance, another used a knife to cut his way out of the back of the tent, and an overweight woman with an overweight child wobbled out after him. I took a mouthful of my tea. A moment passed, and then the unpleasant gentleman and his daughter emerged, both looking very pale, and he threw a small object into the bushes before running off.

"Mirabella," I said. "I think you may go and collect your talisman."

I expect that you are now waiting for me to tell you all about the rest of our day at the amusement park; if so, I am either going to disappoint you or fill you with relief. Not long after Mirabella retrieved her talisman, a loudspeaker announced that the park was going to be closing earlier than scheduled. Unfortunately it wasn't soon enough to prevent us from going on two more rides.

The first was something that shot us up over a hundred feet at a speed that made my ankles swell, before dropping us at a speed that brought a lump to my throat: and I don't mean that I felt emotional. Well, unless you define 'emotion' as 'feeling'; and I was full of that, that's for sure. You will be pleased, however, to know that I didn't convert the way I was feeling into words.

The second was a ghost train which, although more impressive than the last time I went on one, wasn't even going to come close to staying within my memory's hard drive. The version that remains forever etched in my grey matter took place while I was spending ten days at a Corps Camp during one school summer holiday.

It was down in Cornwall and, on the one rest day that we were allotted, and because the weather was inclement, some of us went to the local funfair; for some fun. We had a go at most of the stalls, without much success I have to add; and then, because it had started to rain, we decided to have a spin on the ghost train.

All was going as expected until the fellow with whom I was sharing a 'cab' – a largish chap called Hamish – decided that it might be a bit of a laugh if he hooked the handle of his umbrella around the neck of one of the skeletons as we passed it. Well, he had either underestimated the robustness of the vertebrae or the strength of his grip on the umbrella, because our cab came off the track: which then caused the cab behind ours to bump into us and stop as well; and the two cabs behind that.

Some friends of ours outside had wondered why all four cabs had gone in and yet none had come back out again. Perhaps the ride was spookier than advertised. Anyway, help soon arrived – in the form of the proprietor and two of his assistants – and questioned our 'I've no idea, we just came off the tracks' version of events when confronted with a skeleton whose neck was bent at an unnatural angle and an equally bent umbrella in Hamish's hands. Needless to say, we were not offered a complimentary ride.

Finally, and with people wondering what the commotion was all about, Mirabella and I returned to my car and wended our weary ways back to my cottage.

Left Hand drive...

In the time that Mirabella had been staying with me, I came to recognise one phrase as being the harbinger of a great deal of anxiety.

"Uncle Williammmm...?"

I expect that there are thousands of loco parenti across the country who shudder even reading that: especially when there is a loitering effect on the final syllable. You instinctively know that the remainder of the question will involve either money or a favour that stands a very good chance of causing you embarrassment of one kind or another.

The other possibility is that the question requires an answer which, by being able to answer it, displays some flaw or another in your character; or by not being able to answer it displays some flaw or another in your education. I have a remarkable predisposition to display flaws of both varieties. Strange really, but there we are.

"Yeh-ess..." I replied, bracing myself for the inevitable discomfiture.

"Why do we drive on the left?"

Well, I certainly hadn't been expecting that. The history and reasons for choosing one side of the road upon which to drive has always been a bit of a favourite subject of mine: and whilst I will freely admit that lots of my opinions on many matters are based on unfettered bias towards all that is good about these sceptred isles and the desirable part of the population that lives herein, the reasons for driving on the left display the most wisdom – on common sense, safety and ergonomic grounds, that is.

For starters; if you look at the choice by purely thinking about control of the current vehicles available, I would rather have my strongest hand on the steering-wheel when I use my other hand to change gear. If you delve back a bit, it was logical – whilst driving your cart – to sit on the right-hand side, or else you stood a better than even chance of removing the eyes of your passengers every time you cracked the whip; which would almost certainly be held in your right hand.

As the roads weren't all that great back then, you would want to be as near the middle as possible when passing other road users; so keeping to the left would allow you to see how close your wheels were when encountering another cart heading in the opposite direction.

If further proof were needed, excavations of a Roman quarry (somewhere near Swindon I believe) showed that the road down into it had deeper ruts on one side than the other – the side used when the wagons were laden and making their way back out: and that side was on the left. Backing up that conclusion is a denarius (a Roman coin circa 50BC to 50AD) that showed two horsemen riding past each other with right shoulder to right shoulder. As the Romans were hardly known for their stupidity, I feel that I can rest my case.

All of which is rather straightforward, and should be fairly simple to implement: unless, of course, you happened to be French and went by the name of Monsieur N. Bonaparte. But then, as he was French, *Res ipsa loquitor*

"But what about the Americans?" you ask.

Ah, the Americans. Well, as they found the need to control their wagons whilst sitting at the rear of them, they decided – initially – to sit on the left and that the right side of the road made more sense. What they were doing sitting at the back is, as with most things American, another matter entirely.

Then they moved the driver to the right side because the ditch was considered a greater menace than the passing wheels, and so they drove on the left for a while. This was continued with many early American motorcars – those before 1910, and many up to 1915 – which had the driver sitting at the front and on the right. I believe it was a fellow by the name of Ford who, with his 1908 Model T, popularised the left-hand driving position; and the rest followed.

Having said that, there is still one place in the USA where you drive on the left (out of convenience) – I believe that it is part of the I5 in the Grape Vine mountain pass – and, for reasons of safety, in parts of the US Virgin Islands. Oddly enough, there is one piece of road in the UK where you have to drive on the right! The road approaching the Savoy hotel from the Strand: for reasons of not having cars that are dropping off people at the Savoy Theatre from blocking the entrance to the hotel.

"So there you have it," I replied, feeling that I had put forward a pretty good case for the defence.

"You do know your stuff, don't you?"

I expect that most of you will have spotted the beginnings of a trap that was being carefully laid. I, however, strolled into it without suspecting anything. Is there, I ask, a facet to the education of women that is known only to those of a female construction? Perhaps an extra-curricular lesson to which those possessing both X and Y chromosomes are not privy?

"I like to think that I have a grasp of certain matters," I replied, with a bit of a swagger. Yes, if mind-reading had been within my cerebral inventory I would have picked up on the opening gambit that was pinging around inside the cranial confines of my niece. But it wasn't; and I didn't.

"You know so much."

"Steady on, diminutive kinsperson."

"No, I mean it. And you have like a great way of explaining things."

"Well, that is… I suppose so. Yes."

It is not often compliments get passed in my direction; so I do have an, albeit slightly shaky, excuse for the intellectual myopia I was displaying.

"You would make a really great teacher."

"Well, I did once consider a career in the pedagogue profession."

Right up to the time that I realised I would probably only last a week before I introduced some malefactor to the back of my hand. In the days of my education – which, admittedly, were very closely based on the 'Flashman' era – pupils understood that they were at school in order to learn, and teachers both earned and received respect.

Lately, it seems that school is just a place where children spend time during the daylight hours: unless, of course, playing hookey seems more attractive, and any evidence of discipline seems to have disappeared along with the truants. I just couldn't imagine any of the boys at school with me ever assaulting one of the teachers. They may, possibly, have pinned a pejorative note on the back of his gown; but then they wouldn't have remained a pupil long enough to enjoy the bragging rights.

The current state of affairs is utterly preposterous, and I think we all know with whom the blame lies. Surely, if the object is to close the gap between the standard of private and state education, wouldn't it be better to do that by enhancing the standard of state schools and not by hampering that of private schools? Future generations will read about what was happening at this time and wonder how those in charge ever got to be in charge. A splendid example of *Quam parva sapienta mundus regitur*.

When I bear in mind that the above expression was first penned in Roman times, over 2000 years ago, I do wonder how Mankind is still around. With how little wisdom the world is governed: and as true today as it was back then

"I'm sure you could manage to teach anybody anything," she continued.

"I have to admit that, if I were given a pupil with a larger than average amount of grey matter, I could probably impart a decent helping of know-how."

"By being a really good teacher."

"Absolutely."

"Someone who would be capable of passing on knowledge."

"Indeed."

"Someone who would be willing to give people the benefit of his experience."

"Undeniably."

"Someone who would be willing to give me a driving lesson."

"Undoubtedly. I wou— Just a minute! A driving lesson? You aren't old enough."

"We could do it on private land."

"I don't have any."

"There's a very large beach near your cottage."

"But that is open to the general public; and others of a sundry nature. I believe the army likes to show off the occasional bit of ordnance there as well."

"We'd be okay between high and low water. And the army puts up flags when they're firing."

"You seem to be rather clued up on all this."

"I checked it on the Net."

I am all for people extending their range of knowledge and so forth, and I am all in favour of that thing called the Internet: well, up to a point that is. There is – so I have been told, you understand – a lot of stuff on there normally only available to people above a certain height. Material that really ought to remain on top shelves and not make its way into the readily accessible domains of the computer buff: especially the younger ones. But I am not going to comment on the subject.

Where was I? Oh yes, the Internet. Good source of information, as long as the people who put it there were correct in the first place: and you happen to reside in a country that doesn't censor what you can access. Thinking about it, if you write a letter to a newspaper, how can you be sure that the person who is doing the vetting (for salacious language and so forth) doesn't hold diametrically opposite views to those you hold? I would imagine that would substantially reduce the chance of your letter making the pages. A case of *quis custodiet ipsos custodies?* But then who guards the guards who guard the guards?

"Is that so?" I continued.

"Yes."

"And did you also check to see where you were going to find someone who would let you loose in their car?"

"I didn't have to."

"No? Why not?"

"Because I can use your car."

"What! My car! But that's... "

"Ideal."

"Ideal! I should think it was the absolute opposite, if you must know. Drive my car. Ha! The very thought of it!"

"Well, I think I could."

"Well, I *know* you couldn't."

"Why couldn't I?"

"Because, as I have already mentioned, you are too young; and too short, and you have no insurance: and... and I won't let you."

"But Uncle William, I'd be really careful."

"The subject isn't up for debate, my dear. You are not going to drive my car, and that is an end to the matter."

"Huh."

"Huh indeed."

There was a pause during which some adults might have backed down at the sight of a fourteen-year-old child giving an impression that her dog had just died and could she have a new puppy. Had it been regarding such a matter I have no doubt that my resolve may well have vacillated a touch. But when it comes to drawing lines under things regarding the combination of pubescents and motor vehicles, I use a pen with a very broad nib and indelible ink: particularly if it happens to be my motor vehicle that is under discussion.

On top of which, when speaking of criminals and cars, I do get agitated whenever I watch one of those television programmes about road crime. Why, when some delinquent gets arrested for stealing a car and then driving like a lunatic, does he only get cautioned or sentenced to a few hours of community work? Why not lock him up for a couple of years of hard labour? Admittedly such a punishment will give the felon a bit more incentive to get away from his pursuers: but surely, with all the technology now available, the police should be able to apprehend them regardless. If not at the time, then once all the relevant data have been collated and verified. Personally, I should like to see the use of heat-seeking missiles to bring a chase to a rapid conclusion. However.

Furthermore, what is the point of giving someone a few points on their licence when they don't actually have one? Then, to mention another stupid thing the courts do, when the malefactor is found to be driving without insurance, they fine him about £200. Why not fine him the full cost of what the insurance would have been, and then add the £200 on top for good measure? If he says he hasn't got the money to pay the fine, then take the car, the ubiquitous plasma television/satellite dish/games console/smart-phone, and anything else he has that can be sold. It's no wonder some people have so little regard for law and order.

Would I like to see stocks reintroduced? Absolutely. Maybe after a few hours of having rotten fruit thrown at them and the accompanying public humiliation they might pause to consider the consequences of any future felonious actions. Maybe.

I was thinking of mentioning some more of the asinine decisions made by some of the judges in our courts, but I don't think my cardio-vascular system could take it.

Anyway, my car remained road-worthy: but my exposure to the combination of juveniles and driving was still in line for another bout.

You may recall I mentioned that I once tried to play a video game by the name of Tomb Raider; and how, without the assistance of several pages of cheats and 'walkthroughs', I would have been unable to get the heroine of the saga to do any more than park her car. Well, I have since discovered that there are four or five subsequent versions of it – there may even be six by now – and each one has become more sophisticated than the one before.

Imagine my delight when Mirabella told me that she had brought the newest version – both of the game and the console on which it was played. 'Hooray' I thought; really looking forward to wasting many more frustrating hours at some stage in the future. But there was better to come: she had brought it with her. I fair wept with joy.

In less time than I was able to point out that my television was broken, that I had repetitive strain injury in all my joints, and that a phial of the Bubonic plague had just broken on the lounge carpet, the little blighter had set the whole thing up and was rushing through the opening credits.

My discomfort was assuaged slightly when I realised that Ms Croft was nowhere to be seen, and a gentleman of Scottish descent was inviting people to drive a rally car around various circuits.

"Uncle William, would you like to watch as I take a car for a spin round an international rally circuit?"

"When?"

"Right now."

"With you driving?"

"Of course."

"Haven't we already had this conversation?"

"I don't mean in real life: I mean in virtual reality."

"At the risk of sounding as if Nature decided that, as by way of compensation for my somewhat agreeable features, it would intermittently rearrange my grey matter with an egg-whisk, I should be very grateful if you would explain, in terms that one such as I might understand, what on earth it is you are talking about."

"I mean that I can take you on a spin along a rally course without ever leaving this room."

"Still just beyond the reach of my cognitive processes, I'm afraid."

"This console allows me to drive a car along a rally course. It works the same as a computer: and everything is done from inside."

"Of course it is: silly me."

"It's like the Lara Croft games; only instead of taking her round an obstacle course, you take a car round a rally course. But the graphics are like much better now. It's really cool. And you can like choose all sorts of weather conditions. Even snow."

Whilst I was still in the process of trying to look as though I was keeping up, madam had pressed a few more buttons and was pointing out that she was now behind the wheel of a blue rally car: some sort of Mitsubishi I believe. It transpired that the person in control of the box of tricks was able to choose from a selection of rally cars; and then change the suspension, tyres, steering, and the type of gearbox as well. Factors which, I hasten to add, are not normally on my list of priorities whenever I set off to collect my weekly comestibles.

My 'car history' doesn't make for particularly exciting reading: unless, that is, you count the Jaguar S-type (1968) and a Daimler Double-Six (1976) that I once owned. The Jaguar, my first car as it happens, was a 3·8 manual with overdrive that always attracted attention as it went past. Not sure if that was because of the iffy exhaust or because onlookers couldn't work out why someone of my tender years was driving a car that demanded the owner wore a tweed jacket. As for the Daimler? Well that was black and chrome with tinted windows, and was so quiet that I needed to look at the rev-counter to see if the engine was running.

These days, however, I drive an oldish diesel Skoda Octavia. Not exactly a head-turner, I have to admit; but any car that does over 60 mpg gets my vote.

Speaking of which, can someone explain to me why successive governments, after they keep whinging on about how they want to stop us using too much fossil fuels, then go and make diesel more expensive? If keeping down the amount of fuel used is truthfully their main priority, then surely they should make diesel cheaper than petrol in order to make us buy cars with diesel engines and, therefore, use less fuel. Or am I missing something? Is diesel more expensive than petrol because we are using less of it and therefore the Government raises less revenue? Am I ever likely to meet a politician who tells the truth? Ha!

As to what is going to happen to the fiasco regarding the vehicle excise duty, I have no idea. Other than the probability that if 90% of drivers buy a car with zero duty, then the remaining 10% of drivers will have to make up the shortfall. I have a feeling that they are going to object somewhat if it costs £75,000 to tax their car for a year. I wonder why the expression *Quam parva sapienta mundus regitur* has just popped into my head. Once again!

Anyway, with the use of an accompanying steering wheel and set of pedals, Mirabella proceeded to show me the capabilities under her control. After a preliminary gunning of the engine, she propelled the aforementioned car along lanes that, due to the hazardous drifting of snow, I thought should have been cordoned off by the local constabulary.

As you know, I enjoy foreign climes; but I'm not all that partial to the actual relocation process: especially if I am making the trip within the confines of a small motor vehicle. Unless, of course, I am the one behind the steering wheel. Oh yes, put me in charge of a jalopy and I shall happily negotiate the Queen's highways until I have emptied the contents of the fuel tank several times over. If, however, I am to play a supporting role in the peregrination, then I shall rapidly lose my enthusiasm for the venture; and it will be the contents of my gastric regions that will have been emptied several times over: and over quite a lot of the car's interior.

And that is pretty much the way I was feeling as I watched the television screen. You see, one of the drawbacks about making the graphics very life-like is that the response elicited from me will also be very life-like. So, whilst *ma petite mouffette* whizzed around with the sort of gusto normally reserved for the likes of Colin McRae and Hannu Mikkola, I had to hold a cushion in front of my face.

Whilst such a display of pusillanimity was acceptable when, as a six year-old, I had occasion to watch William Hartnell prepare to do battle with Daleks, it was less than becoming for a gentleman of my years when confronted with nothing more than a simulated car race. However, the Phalarope brain roared into action and, by way of an explanation, I said that I was merely checking the intricate weave on the cushion material as I found the pattern fascinating. I think I got away with it.

Then I was invited to take the controls and have a bash at completing the course in as fast a time as I could manage; and I was positioned at the starting gate of the rally course. I was given a brief tour of the controls, a choice of viewpoints, and a "Go, go, go," to point out that the stage had started.

With a glint of determination – it could have been dread – in my eye, off I went. Off with the handbrake, off from the starting platform, and very shortly thereafter, off the course. All of which, bearing in mind it was my first attempt at simulated car racing, would have been understandable: and, in certain sections of society, may have given rise to some gentle ribaldry. What went a long way to remove any sympathy that I may have harvested from any onlookers was the manner in which I yelled "Aaaargghhh" and put my arms in front of my face in order to shield myself during the crash.

Apparently, such histrionics are frowned upon and tend to bring forth comments such as might not be suitable to print on these pages. I, however, was spared any such profanities; but I was subjected to as voluble a guffaw as I might have expected from one who was watching a Monsieur Houlot film whilst liberally helping themselves to whiffs of Nitrous Oxide.

After that one moment of imprudence, I managed to circumnavigate the course without further mishap: albeit in a time that it would have taken a one-legged man on a penny-farthing. And may I say that I actually rather enjoyed it: it really is quite amazing what those computer wizards are capable of producing.

Not only was I able to experience what it might be like to drive a high-performance car around a rally course, even if in a rather sedate and leisurely fashion, but I was then able to watch an action-replay of what television viewers – or actual on-site spectators – would have seen at the time. Absolutely astonishing. Not my performance, you understand, as I should imagine that those who chose to watch it on the television would have yearned for a commercial break, and those at the course would have requested a refund from the organisers.

Having expressed how impressed I was with the technology, I was then informed that a new version of the equipment was due out in the very near future that would put the current one so far into the gloom that it would only be of interest to collectors of antiquaries. The new one, I was reliably informed, was going to be over ten times as powerful and bring realism to a new level.

I wasn't sure that was going to persuade me to buy one. Being more realistic would surely involve having the machine squirt water at you when travelling through a puddle; and possibly some device to shower you with broken glass whenever the windscreen went west. As to what might occur should you have the misfortune to drive into a tree I didn't care to contemplate. Would someone materialise and hit you with a length of 4 x 4?

I sometimes wonder if children were happier in the days when they only had a hoop and a stick to play with: I wouldn't be at all surprised. You can probably figure out my response when I was informed that some of the driving video games involve having to first steal a car and then shoot at people as you went from A to B. Am I missing something here? Are we all heading towards a societal and intellectual form of meltdown? *Solus narrabo* as they probably used to say in Roman times. We shall see.

Me and Mt. Blanc.

"Uncle William…"

"Yes."

"Do you remember the day we climbed Mount Snowdon?"

"Yes, thank you; and I'm very likely to do so for some considerable time to come. Why do you ask?"

"I was wondering…"

Despite my advancing years, and knowing that something I should do my utmost to avoid is rapidly approaching, I do seem to stumble headlong into it all the same. Females and pauses in their speech are to be circumvented at every opportunity and, much in the same way as smoke detectors, houses should be fitted with some kind of alarm.

"Yeh-ess…" I foolishly invited.

"Have you ever wanted to go higher?"

"Higher? What do you mean by 'higher'?"

"You know, like up a higher mountain. Like a proper mountain."

"A *proper* mountain? I was under the impression that Snowdon was a proper mountain. It was certainly 'proper' enough for Lord Hunt to have used to train his team for the first – proven that is – summit climb of Mount Everest."

I still have a soft spot for George Mallory and Andrew Irvine, and their climb on the north side of Everest. I know sceptics are quick to point out that they didn't have the use of any ladders; but since the likes of Oscar Cadiach (1985), Theo Fritsche (2001), Conrad Anker and Leo Houlding (2007) have shown that Second Step is possible without using one, and that when Mallory's body was found he didn't have the picture of his wife with him, my sentiments have leaned towards him having got to the top. I suppose I shall have to wait until incontrovertible proof is found; but it won't stop me romanticising about it in the meantime.

"I know that, Uncle William; but wouldn't you like to have a go at one that people rate?"

"What do you mean by 'rate'?"

"I was reading on the Internet that there is like a list of the highest mountain in each of the seven continents; and people go and climb each one."

"Good for them."

"Wouldn't you like to have a go at doing that?"

"No, I wouldn't; but thank you for asking."

"Why wouldn't you like to have a go at it?"

"Because I'm too old to even start thinking about doing such a thing. It would take me years."

"Then what about just doing one of them? That would be so cool."

"I think 'cool' would be understating it. Do you have any idea how cold it gets at the top of really high mountains? And do you have any idea how much preparation is involved? You can't just turn up, pay up and go up, you know. There are all sorts of things that have to be arranged. Such as getting all the correct gear, and acclimatising. It's all very involved."

"So what? I reckon you could manage it."

"Well I don't."

"Well I do."

"Well bad luck."

There was then another of those pauses, during which, once again, I ought to have known that a fresh tack was being implemented.

"In fact I *know* you could. I have faith in you."

"You have faith in me? Do you?"

"Yes."

"Really?"

"Oh yeah, Uncle William. You've got that special 'something'."

"Do you honestly think so?"

"I really know so."

"Oh."

The more perceptive amongst you will probably have spotted the moment that the Phalarope guard slipped. What is it about females that lets them know the most direct route to a man's soft underbelly? Are they given extra tuition at school about massaging the male ego? Do finishing schools specialise in the subject? Thirty seconds before, I had absolutely no desire to subject my body to the rigours associated with scaling heights. Then, as if given a prod by Pan (it may have been Tmolus, I couldn't tell), I was suddenly feeling the need to don crampons and head for the 'death zone'.

Anyway, before I had time to fully consider what I was saying, I had agreed to have a go at one of the seven highest continental peaks. Very soon after that, as sense began to filter through my grey matter, I felt a bit faint. *To have a go at one of the seven highest continental peaks!* Oh for heaven's sake.

"Which one do you want to try?" asked the cause of my predicament. "Which continent?"

"Oh, um: maybe the closest one. How about Europe. That's quite close."

"Okay."

I was trying to think of which mountain that was, and praying that it would be the lowest of the seven: and the easiest. Mont Blanc popped into my head. The Alps: nothing over 15 or 16 thousand feet: surely. Then that height sank in. *Fifteen thousand feet!* Nearly five times higher than Snowdon. Oh dear goodness.

"Perhaps," I started back-pedalling. "Perhaps I was a bit rash. Perhaps I could just have a go at one of the other Alpine peaks. A smaller one: a much smaller one, that is."

"But Uncle William; you promised. You… promised."

"Did I? Are you quite sure? I don't recall making such a commitment."

"Well I do. And you wouldn't want to break a promise, would you? That wouldn't be a very good example to set an impressionable young girl, would it?"

"*Impressionable*! Since when have you been impressionable? I doubt –"

I was then interrupted by several sobs, and the sight of Mirabella covering her eyes and shaking her shoulders.

"Now, steady on," I continued. "I think there's been a bit of a misunderstanding. I don't think I actually *promised* anything. I'm pretty sure that I merely – "

"Boo-hoo, boo… hoo."

"I'm sure it was just a suggestion. You know, more of a – "

"BOO-HOO…"

"Hang on a second. That's a bit of an over-reaction to a simple mix-up, don't you think?"

"Just you wait 'til I tell mummy. Then see what she thinks."

Realising that telling her mother might give rise to the sort of over-reaction that would make the first over-reaction pale into insignificance, I hurriedly donned my *chapeau diplomatique*.

"Oh I don't think there's any need for that. I'm sure we can straighten out this confusion, between us."

"Does that mean you're going to keep your word and do it?"

"When I said 'straighten out this confusion', what I actually meant was for us to sit down and think about how to realign what might have been misconstrued."

"In other words, you still intend to break your promise."

What was I to do? Accept the challenge and suffer whatever the mountain had to throw at me; or decline and suffer whatever might get thrown at me from an even colder region? Tricky.

I yielded. "Oh, alright then."

"You're going to do it? You're going to like climb the highest mountain in Europe?"

"It would, er, seem that way. I suppose."

There are times – many, if you must know – when I wish I had the capacity to completely ignore people: or, even better, get them to completely ignore me. Life would be so much simpler if you never had to interact with others. Wave at them from a distance, or drop them a line from time to time; but never to actually get close enough to converse.

It was only a little while later that what I had agreed to do began to sink in. Is there a procedure for getting yourself committed to some type of institution? The sort of place that will let you stay until the current vicissitudes have blown away. *Mont Blanc*! Dear oh dear.

A quick squiz in my old atlas showed me that the peak is pretty close to a place called Chamonix; and that, unfortunately, is in France. Can't be helped, I suppose. The next question was how would I get there, and thence find my way to the summit? As some of you may have gathered, I am not the most perspicacious of individuals upon whom you might happen during the course of an average day; but I was able to work out that a certain amount of travelling would be required. I also realised, that having arrived at said location, I was going to need some kind of 'hands-on' assistance to help get me up to the pointy bit.

Under most circumstances, that is the place at which dreams such as this would normally grind to an ignominious halt. It is also the place at which the words of one Robert Browning often intrude into my consciousness – 'Ah, but a man's reach should exceed his grasp, or what's a heaven for.'

Actually, I also rather like the sentiment expressed by Benjamin Elijah Mays

when he wrote that one of the greatest tragedies in Life is not failing to achieve your dreams; it is not having any dreams in the first place. Well, for once, the Phalarope resolve decided to start dreaming and poke its head above the parapet and resolve any immediate impediments.

With more than a little help from Mirabella – as my aptitude with the internet still hadn't advanced much beyond the minimum required – I was able to find a firm that specialised in such endeavours. I was advised that as well as the three days that would be required to carry out the Mont Blanc undertaking, I ought to first consider spending a week completing the 'Alpine Introduction' course that was held in nearby Switzerland. Something to do with familiarising myself with glacier travel, crevasse rescue, route finding and navigation, and techniques involving ropes, ice-axes and crampons.

It was about then that I felt my incisors had overestimated the chewing capacity of my molars. What had, initially, seemed to be only a reasonable bit outside my regular environs, was rapidly turning into something that was an enormous bit outside them. Indeed, it was something that would, in all likelihood, require quite a lot of effort on my part.

Anyway, amongst the ensuing haze, I agreed to whatever was deemed necessary; and was told that I would soon receive details about the intended project. I remember having to go and find a quiet corner in which to lie down so that I might allow the merry-go-round inside my head to slow down and come to a halt.

As promised, the details duly arrived a few days later. What had I let myself in for? The brochure contained many images of climbers in all manner of situations – most of which, I have to say, looked quite splendid. The situations that is, rather than the climbers themselves.

Although having said that, I did notice a shapely female with whom I would gladly have spent time in some romantic cabin or other. Other photographs, however, showed one or two people that I would have been quite happy to donate a kidney in order to avoid.

Yet more of the photographs in the brochure showed people in all manner of precipitous circumstances. I have to ask, why does anybody in their right mind feel the urge to hack their way up an ice wall? What possible joy is there to be derived from hanging above a huge drop by little more than what appears to be a pair of claw hammers? Maybe I answered my own question: the bit where I asked about people in their right mind.

It was then I remembered seeing climbers making their way up the face of El Capitan when I was in Yosemite. People who, presumably, would have seemed perfectly normal if they happened to be sitting opposite you on a bus; and yet, for some unfathomable reason, they felt a compulsion to spend a couple of days stuck to a sheer cliff face two thousand feet above the rest of us.

I also recalled doffing my hat in admiration, and giving thanks on two counts. One, that there were those who had the mettle to embark upon such endeavours; and two, that I was not amongst their number.

When you come to think about it, I suppose we should all be grateful for such plucky individuals. Without them, we would probably still be living in caves; having been too fearful to venture out any further than to do a bit of quick foraging. We might all be vegetarians. What a ghastly thought.

Speaking of vegetarians, I didn't know – until recently, that is – that the term 'vegetarian' has nothing to do with vegetables. Indeed not: it derives from the Latin word *Vegetus*, which means lively or sprightly. The Romans had noticed that those who didn't eat any meat were a lot more lively or sprightly than those who did. Whether that was because those who ate meat tended to eat a lot of the stuff – and probably consumed vast quantities of wine to go with it – and were, therefore, less likely to be found indulging in pastimes of a lively or sprightly nature; or because there was something in vegetables that made people more active is not for me to decide. If pressed, however, I would choose the former explanation.

Now where was I? Oh yes; cavemen who ventured beyond their caves, and why they did so. I know that feeling hungry makes people do more than when they are just feeling bored; but I'm sure that feeling frightened trumps all the other emotions.

Hark back to the first fellows who, after seeing a white flash from the grey nebulous things floating in the sky – often accompanied by a very loud rumble – which hit a tree and caused it to go very bright and crackle a lot, decided that the heat generated might be worth using to their advantage.

Did they stop to worry about health and safety issues? Did they think 'Ooh, I might hurt myself'? No, they did not: they strove to find a way to reproduce it and then harness the results. Without, obviously, setting fire to themselves and everything they owned. I would imagine that a bit of 'trial and error' was involved in their initial attempts; but they stuck at it until they had, if not actually conquered it, managed to reach an understanding and form a symbiotic relationship.

Yes, for the pedants amongst you, I know that symbiosis involves two living organisms; but fire, I think, often seems as though it is alive.

Anyway, and shelving further cogitations, a perusal of the received literature assured me that climbing up sheer faces was not on the agenda for my intended goal. I think the sense of relief I experienced might have been felt by anyone within half a mile.

Further scrutiny showed me the sort of equipment I would need to get before leaving these shores. It transpired that I was going to require rigid leather boots, a breathable waterproof jacket, breathable waterproof trousers which had full-length side zips, all manner of base layer clothing, gaiters, socks, gloves, hat, a 45 litre rucksack, head torch… And so the list went on: and on.

What the list failed to mention was the cost of all those items. Probably just as well, actually; as I came close to having a cardiac incident when I eventually found out.

Yes, I could have got the items more cheaply from one of the lower-echelon outdoor shops; but, so I was reliably informed, the worse place to find out why the items were cheaper would be halfway up a mountain, in a blizzard, in the dark.

* * *

A few months later, I was in a shop in Betws-y-Coed, purchasing several of the aforementioned items. I had decided that a quick shimmy up Snowdon in wintery conditions might be in order; and that while I was in the area, I should make some inroads into getting all the required bits and pieces.

And that was when the first shock of the weekend hove into view. You see, even when making an effort to keep a tight hold of Prudence's hand, the bill total progressed with leaps and bounds in the direction of £600.

I expect that there are several amongst you who are nodding sagely and pointing out that hostile environments require the best equipment, and that the best equipment comes with a price. But all the same – £200 for a jacket? Anyway, you will be pleased to know that I weaved quality with cost to get the best value, coughed up the necessary sponduliks with a refreshing degree of alacrity, and strode out of the shop with my head held high.

You might also be interested to know that as soon I was a respectable distance from the premises, I hurried back to my car and wept quietly for half an hour.

I spent that night in one of the local hostelries, trying on the assortment of clothing and equipment that I had purchased. Despite battling waves of nausea as images of £20 notes floated away before my eyes, I managed to don the aforementioned apparel and, with scrutinising glances in the available mirrors, I strode around my room.

I have to admit that I did cut a quite dashing figure, and I was able to imagine myself approaching the summit of Mont Blanc. Further images of my, previously mentioned, heroes came bounding into view; and I almost felt a tap on my shoulder as George Mallory wandered past. Stirring stuff aplenty, I have to say. Then, whilst still enjoying visions of derring-dos, I carefully packed away my new acquisitions. No sense in getting them creased before the time, eh?

At 8.30 the following morning, I was togged up in my usual cold-weather gear, and champing at the bit to start going up Snowdon: and sweating rather a lot, if truth be told. Perhaps it is only me, but regardless of how cold it is, by the time I have got into my ascribed outfit I am dripping with perspiration. Then, no matter how graceful and accomplished I try to appear, I often end up falling backwards into the boot of my car when sitting on the lip and pulling on my footwear: or one of the sleeves of my coat takes on a life of its own, and decides to play hide-and-seek with my arm.

Such incidents would be embarrassing enough if I were the only occupant of the car park; but Lady Luck always deems it necessary that a coach-load of eagle-eyed people, usually of the female variety, and invariably armed with cameras and smart phones, arrives at the moment when I finally lose my balance, and patience, and wish that mountains had never been invented. This particular occasion proved to be no exception. Unless, that is, you count the fact that as I toppled into the boot I grabbed for the nearest thing to help steady myself.

Unfortunately for me, but not for the myriad of onlookers, the nearest thing happened to be the strap on the inside of the boot lid. I imagine the picture that has just entered your heads is that of a hapless Englishman in the process of being eaten by the back of his car: and so it was.

The more I pulled on the strap, the harder the lid of the boot crashed against my legs; the harder the boot of the lid crashed against my legs, the more I shouted; the more I shouted, the louder the onlookers laughed; the louder the onlookers laughed, the more I tried to extricate myself. I don't think there is any necessity to elaborate further.

I shall, however, finish by saying that it was more than a minute before a passing Samaritan came to my aid. A gentleman in the employ of the Park Warden organisation, as it happens, who felt that if the situation were allowed to continue for much longer, I might lose both my feet: and there was a risk that one of the onlookers might end up by cracking a rib or giving themselves a hernia through their strenuous laughter; and the emergency services were stretched enough as it was.

Once I had managed to right myself, and salvage what little dignity I had left, I began to make my way up the familiar Pyg trail: and very soon I was puffing like an old steam locomotive. It gets me every time, so I shouldn't sound surprised: you see, for some reason or another, the first half-mile always seems to highlight my shortcomings.

I can hear all you sagacious types drawing in your venerable breath in preparation to lecture about second winds, diaphragm control and temperature equilibria: but I would like to save you the trouble of issuing forth on the subject. I already know! And may I tell you what else I know? Knowing about it doesn't make a jot of difference to me: not one iota.

For some reason or another, Providence deemed it necessary to provide me with a physiology whose higher and lower centres only communicate with each other when they have little else to do. The grey matter lurking within the confines of my skull is well aware that setting off with a stride pattern that any passing RSM would applaud is likely to produce enough heat to broil several good-sized halibut should I have felt the inclination to stuff them about my person: as well as causing my face to go red enough to create confusion for car drivers passing on the nearest road.

But Nature does not stop there: oh no. My higher centres are also aware that ardent striding is likely to confuse my diaphragm into thinking that its hours are numbered, and thus encourage my adrenal medullae to pump out enough Epinephrine to enable me to flee or fight anything I found threatening.

This amount also has a tendency to remove the blood from my skin, dilate my pupils until it seems that my irises have disappeared altogether, and cause all movement within my intestinal tract to cease. The battle between my sympathetic and parasympathetic systems rings its stern alarums loudly within my ears, as I stagger to the nearest flat rock in order that I might tarry awhile.

Honestly, I ask you; what kind of design allows for one set of chemicals to make you go red and another one to make you blanch like a full moon to both leap into action at the same time? It's enough to make a fellow want to burn all the tomes on the subjects of Evolution and Creationism.

I was later to learn that, in cold weather, it is usually best to begin your hike/climb whilst feeling a bit on the chilly side. Obviously, in case you twist an ankle and have to wait a while for rescue, you need to pack a few spare items as well.

So it was, as usual, that I reached the point where Llyn Llydaw comes into view before the battle raging within the precincts of my epidermis was back under control. It was also, coincidentally, at that point I was beginning to wish that I had packed my new crampons. From the car park I had not been able to fully appreciate the extent of the snow: and even if I had, I would not have been able to judge the degree to which ice had formed beneath its surface.

Had Professor Stanley Unwin been present I am sure he would have said something like "Deep joy, happy days." I am equally sure that I would have replied with an expression that, whilst finding great favour amongst spectators in most football stadia, would have proven to be a tad too robust for these pages.

As I mentioned earlier, I am not someone with a penchant for fairground rides. Indeed, not for me the thrill of being turned upside down, inside out, or whichever other way the designers felt the need to have me experience. I have long since passed the age when the exuberance and bravado of youth overrides my innate instinct for self-preservation. If I were to use the Latin quotation '*Animus et Prudentia*' (the one about using courage and discretion), I would have to admit that these days my 'prudentia' far outweighs my 'animus'.

Perhaps I am alone in my feelings. Although, would not a person of adequate intelligence feel a touch of anxiety when his hitherto unyielding contact with terra firma had been replaced with one of a distinctly more untrustworthy nature? *Videlicet*, one where your hindquarters introduce themselves to the ground with a greater speed and frequency than that you would ordinarily appreciate.

I must confess that, despite the vast experience I have amassed in the area of falling on my fundament, I have never managed to acquire the art of doing so with any sense of decorum.

Not for William Phalarope the ability to repose with the grace of a falling feather; gently swaying from side to side as it lays its downy structure upon the patiently waiting surface of Mother Earth. No: picture if you can, something more akin to a large sack of carrots being thrown out of the back of a passing lorry, accompanied by a very loud "Whooo", and you would be getting close to appreciating the elegance with which I usually perform the procedure.

Mind you, having said a few unkind things about the ice and its ability to make me look as if my sense of coordination had seen better days, I would like to say a few words on behalf of water's solid state. It was exquisite: as much an *objet d'art* as it was an impediment to my progress.

Boulders had stalactites like fingers belonging to glass hands that gripped them; hanging as if waiting for me to play a tune upon them. The rising peak of Snowdon, proud against the sky, seemed to be wearing a cloak of ermine. Streams of water that normally played like happy children amongst the rocks, as they weaved their way down to the waiting lake below, were now motionless; sparkling, encased beneath layers of harsh, and yet protective, ice. It was indeed a wondrous sight to behold; and a special place that only shows itself to those who dare to enter.

It was at that point, however, while my thoughts and my camera were focused on the magnificence of my surroundings, that Destiny decided it was a good time for me to re-test the robustness of the seat of my trousers.

A slope that had felt no steeper than ten degrees on the way up, suddenly took on a declivitous nature, seemingly acquiring the properties of one nearer seventy; and I found myself, on my backside, haring off in a downward direction. I expect most of you will now have your heads filled with all sorts of images involving falls of three or four hundred feet before meeting an untimely, and very messy, end upon a jagged rock below. Funnily enough, those were the same ones I had when I began sliding: unnerving to say the least.

Perhaps I should have been yelling for help; perhaps I should have offered a quick prayer to whichever deity was on duty that morning; perhaps, even, I should have simply closed my eyes and crossed my fingers. But for some reason, I found myself continuing to take photographs. I expect that it must have seemed jolly odd to the couple I passed; although probably not quite as odd as the fact that I took the time to say a polite "Good morning" to them as I went by.

Fortunately, Destiny did not want to test my trousers to their limit; and I came to a stop before I managed to pick up any real speed. It was real enough for me, I have to say; and for a while it seemed as though I had inadvertently entered a Luge competition. Not a sanctioned one you understand, but a bare-knuckle equivalent. One so unratified, in fact, that competitors didn't even get to sit on a Luge. Anyway, the upshot was that I traversed about sixty feet in a fraction of the time that it had taken me to cover it in the first place; and I managed to get five very blurry photographs of my slide.

Regardless, I proverbially picked myself up, dusted myself down, and gave a cheery wave to the onlookers to signify that, apart from some slight bruising to my rump, and slightly more to my pride, I was fit and well and ready to resume my ascent: and so I did.

About an hour later, and after several more rounds of introducing soft parts of my anatomy to hard parts of Snowdon, I arrived at the top. Once again, I know that the purists amongst you will be voicing thoughts concerning the fact that Snowdon really isn't all that high and that anyone with even a modicum of common sense and a functioning diaphragm should be able to make it to the top.

But once again, and in defence of all those who have been in the position that I found myself, I will retort by saying that everything is always relative. To those who have conquered Aconcagua on a bad day, Snowdon is, I am quite sure, fairly small beer.

However, for those of us to whom Snowdon is three and a half thousand feet of hard slog – even on a good day – then reaching the top on a day when Zeus decided that a liberal sprinkling of white stuff was in order is not to be sniffed at. By 'white stuff' and 'sniffed at' I do not wish to attract the attentions of Her Majesty's Constabulary; and would like to make it very clear that I was not alluding to any crystalline white powder derivative of a certain South American plant.

The one drawback of going up at that time of year – well, at least the one that seemed most relevant at the time – was that the café at the summit was closed. Hardly surprising, I suppose, when you weigh up the projected financial returns at the till against the cost of running the staff up there: all the same, a small respite from the elements in the company of a freshly-made cup of tea and a sticky bun would have been most welcome.

But 'Hey ho' I thought as, with an expression of determined stoicism, I turned and headed back towards the buttress stone and the descent. After, that is, a few minutes of shelter by crouching behind a stone wall to allow the consumption of a mug of coffee and something that consisted of congealed muesli – which tasted a bit better than it looked, I have to say; and probably replaced quite a few of the expended calories.

I did try to fathom all that stuff about carbohydrates – whether they be of a simple or a complex nature – and their subsequent oxidation and what not; but it all went way over my head. As soon as I came across matters to do with the storage and breakdown of glycogen in muscle tissue, a substance known as adenosine triphosphate, and some things called mitochondria, I'm afraid to say that the Phalarope brain staged a walkout. Probably just as well.

I have no doubt some of you will have spotted along the way that I'm not the sharpest knife in the drawer – prone to the occasional *faux pas* and so forth – and that I'm often keen to take refuge behind the expression *vitiis nemo sine nascitur* (which states that no one is born without faults) but I do try not to commit blunders that would have Charon doubting he has enough time for a quick sandwich before his next passenger comes along.

Alas, there are others who, either as a result of a blow to the head or some kind of congenital defect, feel that death shall have no dominion, and that not even a scintilla of common sense is required when negotiating steep rocky slopes which are covered in snow and ice. What is it, I ask, that entices people who, for all I know, hold down a perfectly sensible method of paying for Life's essentials, into suddenly behaving as if they were auditioning for roles in a reality TV remake of 'One flew over the cuckoo's nest'?

I – and several others who had also probably read treatises on matters concerning gravity and frictionless surfaces, to say nothing of hypothermia – watched as certain individuals made their way up in outfits that would have been more appropriate on a Mediterranean beach. Sensible was not the word that immediately sprang to mind, I have to say: and, as if they wanted to leave no doubt that there was not even a spoonful of functioning grey stuff inside their respective craniums, they had also thought it would be a good idea to bring along their children as well.

I'm sure I have mentioned Proverbs on a prior occasion, but it warrants repeating; and it was the reason that I declined to offer any advice. 'Advise a wise man and he will thank you; advise a fool and he will pour scorn upon you'. Although adequately dressed for most things that the inclement elements might have felt inclined to chuck in my direction, I felt that a deluge of disparagement from the ignorami involved would certainly have spoilt my day.

What is that German expression which shows you cannot legislate for idiocy? Is it '*Mit der Dummheit kämpfen Götter selbst vergebens*'? Against stupidity, even the Gods contend in vain: and how true that is.

Just about the only glimmer of rudimentary sense being displayed was that they had, at least, chosen to go up on the Llanberis Path. Still not advisable, but not as inadvisable as using any other route. Why can't people such as they make their life-threatening mistakes before they have children?

It is at such times that I worry about what the future holds for those minors unlucky enough to have resulted from some nuptial naughtiness between adults who are under the impression that inanity is a virtue. Probably more of the same, I shouldn't wonder.

Fortunately for all concerned, it became apparent – before any permanent damage resulted – that making it all the way to the summit was not going to be achieved; and several *volte-face* manoeuvres were undertaken.

Anyway, I made my own way back down to the car park and, once I had removed all evidence of my labours, was able to enjoy the pleasures of a mug of tea and a plate laden with an 'all-day' breakfast.

It was whilst gently masticating a mouthful of fried egg and sausage that my mind began to conjure up images of Mont Blanc and my forthcoming endeavour. Was I going to be fit enough for a climb that was between four and five times higher than Snowdon? Would I have problems with the altitude? Would my newly acquired equipment be as good as the salesman said it would be? Would I have to share a room with a Frenchman?

Thinking of such weighty matters reminded me that I hadn't arranged my flight, or parking for my car whilst I was away; and, once back at my domicile, I got started.

Well, what a to-do! You would have imagined – well, I did – that all you had to do was pick up a telephone and give the airline a tinkle: well, you would have been wrong. Despite a plethora of airlines, finding one that would fly from a nearby airport to Geneva on the day I wanted and at a time that did not involve resetting my alarm-clock was a good deal more laborious than I had anticipated. Yes, there was a plane that went on the Saturday; but it arrived an hour after the last train from Geneva to Sion and was about £100 more expensive than the plane on the Friday. Yes, there was a plane that flew on the desired day, at the desired time, to the desired airport; but it flew from Glasgow!

I was, however, soon to discover that by flying out on the Friday I would be able to stay overnight in an hotel in Geneva – with breakfast thrown in – easily manage to catch a train to take me all the way to Sion the following day, and still be over £50 in front. Needless to say, the Phalarope cognitive powers very quickly came to a decision about which course of action to take; and the appropriate reservations were duly made.

A couple more phone calls elicited that the train from Geneva to Sion would take around two and a half hours, and I then had to take a bus from Sion to Arolla where I would be met, at a particular hotel, by one of the representatives from the company running the trip.

It was, therefore, with a tranquil mind that I crept under my duck-down that night: all was well within my centres of concern. By the next morning, however, several other aspects of the trip had managed to barge their way to the front of my thoughts and had decided that then would be a jolly good time to start nagging away at me. Foreign currency was one.

Call me old-fashioned, but I have always preferred the feel of proper currency between my fingers. Gives me a sense of well-being, and what not: unless, of course, you happen to notice a pair of burly ne'er-do-wells lurking in the vicinity. But have you noticed the way that banks and governments are increasingly encouraging us to use credit cards – especially those that you simply have to wave in front of a scanner? As for the way that those same agencies are quietly pushing us towards a 'cash-less' society...

I would ask all those who think how 'convenient' such a set-up would be to carefully consider just how much control over how and where you spend your hard-earned money would end up under somebody else's management. You wouldn't be able to buy anything without some government department knowing all about it; and should that government department decide to stop you buying what you want, all it has to do is decline authorisation for your card. A bit worrying if you ask me.

Anyway, the day of my departure arrived – the Friday before the Saturday, if you recall – and, shortly after breakfast, I was making my way to Bristol airport. I had arranged for my car to be kept under 'secure parking' whilst I was away, and so my first call was with a firm that not only promised to make sure that my mode of transport would be well looked after during my sojourn, but that they would also convey me to the airport in time to catch my flight. How considerate, I thought: a couple of examples of a *sine qua non*, if ever there was one. I don't suppose they would get much business if they proclaimed that not only did clients stand a good chance of missing their flights, but that their cars would probably get vandalised while they were rebooking.

Have I mentioned the weight of my boots? The ones that I had purchased for use on the mountain? The ones that seemed, if you substituted Sterling for avoirdupois, to weigh about as much as they cost? Well, if I haven't, then perhaps now would be a good time.

The chap in the shop said that I needed a pair of good quality 'winter' boots; because even the best 'three-four' season boots wouldn't offer the support, warmth or protection that would be required to cope with the sort of weather and terrain that I was likely to encounter on Alpine slopes.

Before I had the chance to point out that I was rather hoping to steer clear of the sort of conditions to which he was alluding, he began rattling on about all manner of things concerning lateral stability, flex zones, mid-sole support and crampon compatibility. That was all confusing enough for a fellow with my intellectual boundaries; but when he started on something called a 'Rolling advanced sole concept' my eyes glazed over to such an extent that he asked me if I would like to sit down and could he get me a glass of water.

The upshot was that I parted with the required remuneration, and left the shop with a very natty pair of mountaineering boots: and it is to that same pair that I now refer; and specifically the weight. What the vendor had forgotten to mention when extolling the virtues of said boots was the fact that they would take up about half my luggage weight allowance. Not an insurmountable problem if I was only going to be spending a couple of days over there; but as my trip was scheduled to last about ten days, I felt that more than one change of garments would probably be required.

It was about then that I heard my grey matter start up. Why not put the boots in my carry-on? Airlines very seldom weigh that. They do occasionally raise an eyebrow if your carry-on looks as though it is causing the wheels on a trolley to buckle; but if you give the impression that little more than a couple of books and a spare pair of socks are contained within, then, apart from an X-ray, scant attention is usually paid. On top of which, I like to think that my 'profile' is hardly one to arouse any suspicions regarding nefarious intentions. It may arouse apprehension regarding my behavioural anomalies in the tolerance department towards most of the other people on the flight; but that would be highly unlikely to cause any danger. Apart from, possibly, some psychological effect it may have on those closest to me. Anyway.

'Right', I thought, 'bung them in the carry-on'. Ha! It was a nice idea in theory; but, unfortunately, not so in practice. I managed to get one of the boots inside, but not both. I tried all sorts of angles; I tried employing the sort of skill required to solve one of those 'cube' things (not that I have that skill, you understand, just that I had a stab at what I thought it might be), and I even tried sneaking up on the carry-on when I thought it wasn't looking: but all to no avail. What was a fellow to do?

Then, just as visions of having to post the boots to the required destination began hovering before my eyes, I fell upon a possible solution. What if I was to wear them? Brilliant, eh?

Unfortunately, up until that point the only time I had worn the boots was when I had wandered about within the confines of my cottage – in an attempt to see if there were any areas of potential chafing and so forth – and that hardly prepared me for the rigours of wearing said footwear under 'hostile' conditions. To be perfectly honest, it hadn't even come close. Had the boots been intended for casual wear around the home, then I was more than adequately primed. Had the boots been designed for supporting my feet whilst watching the television, or even answering the telephone, then I was most assuredly in a position to vouch for their efficacy.

I can hear the cogs of your cerebral centres lining up in preparation to quote a certain Robert Burns. Yes, my scheme did 'gang aft a-gley.' It ganged in quite a big way, if you must know; and the problem manifested itself within minutes of arriving at Bristol Airport. Oh, by the way, I didn't try driving in them: even the modicum of intelligence that I possess was sufficient to have spotted the perils involved with that.

I shall, if you don't mind, take a couple of moments to mention drivers who feel it is fine to drive in such as high heels and flip-flops. What are they thinking about? That is if, in fact, they are thinking. Isn't there something in the Highway Code that says you should wear appropriate footwear? If not, then there jolly well should be. I have even seen someone who was barefoot get out from behind the wheel; in the summer; when feet get sweaty and slippery. Utter madness.

Furthermore, my advice to anyone involved in a vehicular 'bump' is to take photographic evidence of whatever the person in the other car had on their feet: as well as whether or not they were wearing glasses. Not that the wearing of glasses is an indication of an inability to drive well; but if it later transpires that the other driver has an eyesight problem, you will be able to point out that they weren't wearing glasses. Small wonder that 'dash-cams' are becoming so popular!

Mind you, I did read something the other day that made me wonder what sort of people are entrusted to look after us. Somebody driving a car was so short-sighted that he couldn't read a number plate from more than eight feet away, and killed a pedestrian as a result of driving without glasses. His excuse was that he hadn't worn his glasses for more than a year because he couldn't find them. What did the court do? It gave him a few hours of community service! Had it been down to me, the man would have been locked up for not less than ten years. Okay, rant over.

Back to my boots, and the fun that I was about to have in them. You see, what I did not anticipate, when deciding on my plan, was the entertainment value to be gained from trying to walk down a flight of stairs whilst wearing the boots. When I say 'entertainment', I mean solely from the point of view of the people who were near by whilst I was engaged in the aforementioned manoeuvre.

The problem arose because the boots were about half an inch longer than they seemed when looking down at them. Not a huge amount, it has to be said; and had that half inch been positioned forward of my toes there would have been little inconvenience caused. My misfortune came to pass from the fact that the additional span was located at the heel end.

Hindsight was to show that additional shoe material at the front causes an impediment going up steps, and at the back when coming down. Both are a nuisance; but should you stumble on the way up a flight of stairs, you have the opportunity to put out a hand and gain support from a tread within easy reach. The same, however, cannot be said when you are going down a flight of stairs.

Imagine me making my way down the first flight and, when intending to plant my right foot firmly on the next step down, I do little more than catch my heel on the same step upon which my left foot was resting. The effect was to cause me to overbalance, and then lose the control and proprioceptive awareness of both my feet. Next, I tottered further forwards, grabbed hold of the railing with my left hand, and rotated in an anti-clockwise direction – this was positively encouraged by the rucksack upon my back, by the way – before losing my balance completely and staggering all the way to the bottom of the stairs.

If you had asked me before I embarked upon my pirouette display what sort of response I might have expected from the gathered onlookers, I would have hazarded guesses ranging from anxious concern to a mild round of spontaneous applause. What I had not anticipated (and really should have done knowing the burgeoning tendency of certain sections of society to display it) was the complete apathy that my near-fatal (as I am sure it must have looked – it certainly felt that way) tumble aroused.

Not one person stepped forward to enquire about my wellbeing. Not one, I say. I like to think that had I been one of the witnesses I would have, at the very least, stepped forward to assist the unfortunate back to his feet. But there we are; such is the direction in which our levels of compassion are headed. Or maybe it was just an isolated occasion: maybe it was simply the cross-section of those present at the time. I do hope so.

Anyway, I settled myself, and sallied forth to find the appropriate checking-in desk and the anticipated brouhaha. Twenty kilograms was my allowance – as far as the main case was concerned – and I was fairly confident that I was abiding within those limits. I say *fairly* confident, as the figure at which I had arrived was obtained by standing on my bathroom scales, both with and without the case, and then calculating the difference.

I expect that those amongst you who have tried the same technique will already know the pitfalls. Firstly, when you are holding a large case it is rather difficult to see what the scales are reading without holding that case to one side: secondly, when you are holding the case to one side you run the risk of getting a false reading because your centre of gravity is no longer where it should be: and thirdly, there is the possibility of dislocating your shoulder and/or tearing through several layers of deltoid, latissimus dorsi and infraspinatus muscles.

Well, I must have been fairly accurate, as my case sailed through without causing any complaints from the efficient young lady on the other side of the desk. My sigh of relief was somewhat curtailed, however, when she then smiled and asked to see my carry-on. You see, for this particular trip, I had chosen to use the rucksack that I hoped to employ on the mountains.

"So what?" I hear you enquire. "Rucksacks are allowed."

Well, yes: and as a rule, there is usually no problem.

What was causing a certain amount of apprehension in my camp was the fact that the rucksack was a 45-litre one; and that is, I had presumed, normally considered to be a mite bigger than the normal variety used as hand luggage. I had seen a sign, near the queue for the desk, which read that a bag would be allowed as a carry-on if it could comfortably fit into the box situated immediately below the sign. I did wonder what constitutes 'comfortably'. Does it mean without the bag feeling any discomfort, or does it mean without having to get the fattest person you can find to come over and sit on it?

As my personal experience of bags went as far as not knowing any with feelings, I opted for the second explanation and had a trial run. I managed to get the rucksack to fit into the receptacle; but I cannot say that the bag, had it been able to, might not have uttered something resembling an 'Ooh'. I decided not to tell an outright lie in response when I was asked "Does your bag comfortably fit into the box?", and simply chose to raise the rucksack with one arm in a manner designed to give the impression that the act would be ridiculously easy.

The young lady seemed suitably convinced, smiled again, and proceeded to deal with the next passenger: and that was fortunate, as it meant that I was able to move away and find a quiet spot to massage some life back into my shoulder.

The rest of the time spent waiting for my flight passed without incident, and fifty minutes later I was walking across to the plane.

"Just a moment," some of you are now remembering. "Didn't you once say that you made a habit of arriving several hours before take-off in order to procure a seat that had sufficient leg-room to avoid requiring the services of either a chiropractor or a phlebotomist?"

As a general rule that would be true; and in the case of a long-haul flight absolutely essential. However, the plane I was about to catch belonged to one of those 'budget airlines' – not one that may charge you to use the toilet – and I felt that the exercise would be both fruitless and unnecessary as the flight was only going to be a little over an hour.

On top of which, I had been informed that although boarding was done on a first-come-first-served basis, the seats with space in front were always allocated to people with infants: and as it was mid July, there was likely to be more than enough of those to take up the best ones. I boarded the plane and sought a vacant place.

My initial thought of 'Oh god no' when I saw that the only one available was the middle of three seats was quickly dissipated when, having sat down I found that I had more leg-room than anticipated; and, after a couple of minutes, it became apparent that the gentleman on my left intended to go to sleep before take-off and the lady to my right had her face buried in a book.

It was with a relieved demeanour that the airborne section of my trip got underway; and, in a very short space of time, we were landing in Geneva. Twenty minutes later, and without any discernable sort of check, I was heading towards the taxi rank and thence, after a short bout of mispronunciation, to the hotel.

I shan't bore you with the formalities of my time at the reception desk, other than to say that printouts of receipts from the Internet were the order of the day.

After unpacking and a quick wash, I ventured out into the Geneva air; and made my way down to the lake that accompanies the city, and the wide promenade that is attached to its edge: and may I say how absolutely splendid it looked. All around was a mixture of yachts, cyclists, water-skiers, strollers, gulls, people reading whilst sat on benches; and braces of sweethearts, oblivious to their surroundings, as they whispered mellifluously of love which alters not when it alteration finds or bends with the remover to remove.

Such billing and cooing is always charming to behold; but for ever puts me in mind of a salutary ditty I once heard –

'By the time you swear you're his,

All shivering and sighing,

And he vows that his love is infinite, undying;

Lady, make a note of this; one of you is lying.'

One always hopes to the contrary, of course; and wishes all participants the very best of futures. Good relationships seem so hard to find these days; and even harder to maintain.

I also noticed one or two individuals who had decided that the best way to spend the late afternoon was to finish a bottle of cheap sherry, and then go to sleep on a patch of grass, wearing clothes that hadn't been washed – or possibly even changed – for several weeks. *Chacun à son goût*, as they probably say in those parts of Switzerland that use the French language.

What did come as a complete surprise was the number of people who smoked. Not just the odd person, you understand, or even one in five; but it seemed just about everybody. It was quite extraordinary. Almost as if the culture of Geneva had somehow managed to sidestep any information about the drawbacks of inhaling smoky carcinogens into your lungs. It seemed that everywhere I went there were people who had burning leaves in their mouth.

At one point I even considered asking a policeman if I would be liable to a fine if I didn't join in. Forget all that you may have read about clean Swiss air and the invigorating effect it will have upon your constitution, and nip down to bookies to make a wager on becoming a victim of passive smoking if you live in Geneva. Hopefully things have changed since I was there, or it was simply that there was a tobacco-lovers convention going on.

Anyway, putting thoughts of impending pleurisy to one side, I wandered around until I came across a purveyor of victuals that, having some Dickensian connotation to its name, looked likely to provide a ploughman's and a pint; and went in.

For those of you who have travelled and made use of eateries across our planet, it will come as no surprise to know that the barman hailed from Parramatta and thought that Englishmen were a form of diuretic. I shan't start on what he thought was going to happen in the upcoming Ashes series, except to say that he knew of a much better place from which to 'draw' stumps.

He was, however, gracious enough to serve me with a very decent club sandwich and a pint of bitter. He was also, strangely, gracious enough not to totally ignore me when I asked if he had enjoyed the events of November 2003, and muttered something about the fact that referee was a South African. You will be impressed to learn that I restrained myself from saying that it was that reason that nearly stopped the English team from winning. The combination of those two nations certainly cost us the next Rugby World Cup final.

So there I was, enjoying my evening meal, watching, bizarrely, some English county cricket on one of the large television screens that were dotted around the walls, whilst trying not to inhale too much of the pall of smoke that hung in the air.

"Well," I hear you begin, "the sooner they adopt the ban of smoking in places that serve food the better."

A very good idea: but I suppose, being the tolerant chap that I am, I tend to pin my colours to the mast that has the 'I always have the choice of eating somewhere else' flag run up it. Perhaps we could have some sort of colour-coded scheme that allows prospective patrons to choose beforehand if they wish to run the risk of contracting lung cancer or heart disease while they eat.

How about an azure flag for restaurants that forbid smoking, and an old mechanics rag for those that don't? Or maybe displaying a specimen jar containing a section of a nice pink lung at one place and a jar that has a section of lung which is black and dripping tar at another. Or do you think that might put people off their meals?

Whatever your choice, I decided to stay and finish my meal; and, before leaving, asked about the possibility of watching the third Lions' test against the All Blacks the following morning.

"Are you serious, mate?" the barman enquired, looking for all the world as if I had just asked him to help me perform self-trepanation.

"Indeed," I replied. "Why? Is there a problem?"

"No; no problem. Not for the boys in black anyway. Are you sure you want to watch your blokes get another hammering?"

Perhaps I should point out – for those who have less than a passing interest in the game involving an ovoid ball – that the Lions' team had already played two tests against the New Zealand team and had been on the losing end on both occasions: and by quite substantial margins. Time, space and good manners prevent me from criticising the referees; but I shall just mention that ignoring blatant offside infringements, forward passes, scrum-feeding, lazy runners, lying on the ball and crooked throw-ins may have hindered our boys somewhat.

Yes, the All Blacks are often a good team; but watching them nearly always leaves a bad taste in my mouth.

"My dear chap," I said, drawing myself up to accentuate the fact that I stood at least six inches taller than the antipodean. "I am not a fair-weather fan and, unless the team behaves like footballers, I will always be found offering my support."

"In that case mate, the game starts at 9.00 tomorrow morning."

After expressing my appreciation, I wandered off back to my hotel. I checked at reception, found that breakfast was served between 7.00 and 9.00, and reasoned that should allow me plenty of time to eat, pack, and get back to the pub in time for the game.

In actuality, it allowed me more than enough time. The reason being that I did not savour my breakfast as much as I had wished: and that was for two reasons. One was that there are only so many croissants that a chap can manage (what I wouldn't have given for a full English); and secondly, was the number of Korean businessmen occupying some of the surrounding tables.

I do not, as a rule, have much against Koreans; and I am not going to use this opportunity to make known my feelings towards having man's best friend served up as the Sunday roast: but I object to them (or anybody else for that matter) when they employ appalling table manners and chain smoke at the same time.

Call me old-fashioned by all means, but I do insist on good manners at the table. I really cannot abide those who, for example, hold their knife like a pen, scoop up peas on their fork, or keep their forearms on the table whilst doing the above and have to lean forwards in order to get the food to their mouth. If they happen to be smoking in between courses as well, then I tend to spend as brief a time as possible in their vicinity.

I really think that public eating places should have some sort of 'manners patrol' in operation. You know the sort of thing; someone who walks around, checking that the patrons are negotiating their meals with sufficient decorum. If not, perhaps the application of a cricket bat across the back of the head might help rectify the situation.

Anyway, the upshot of it was that my breakfast was consumed with haste and I was sitting at a table in the pub with a cup of coffee about thirty minutes before the game was due to start.

Although, that isn't strictly accurate. When I wrote 'cup' of coffee, what I actually meant was 'thimble'. What is it about those Continental types that makes them serve coffee in a cup that would barely fit over the end of your thumb? And if that wasn't bad enough, they have to make the coffee so strong that you need a knife and fork to get through it. Why, I ask myself, don't they put the contents of the small cup into a bigger cup and then add some more hot water? Is there a shortage of sensible sized cups over there? Or is it simply a joke they like to play on visiting British people? Or did I simply not notice that the 'Espresso' is the only way that coffee is served?

Whilst on the subject of coffee, I have noticed that the practice of 'al fresco' cafés has started to creep in on my side of the English Channel. There seems to be an increasing number of coffee bars that have tables and seats outside on the pavement. Have the people who thought we'd all enjoy sitting out there never experienced the British weather?

Anyway, back to the rugby. I mentioned that I had found a vacant table and had sat down to enjoy the match whilst chewing my coffee. Well, that state of affairs didn't last very long as, in the last few minutes before the game started, eight other people came and sat at my table; and seven of them were from that brace of islands to the East of Australia.

What about the eighth fellow? He was from South Africa; so no help there.

Honestly! What was I to do? Not only had the quietness of my corner evaporated, so had my corner. Did I move? Absolutely not. I have to admit that, only for a moment you understand, I had considered trying out my Kiwi accent; but decided that it might be better not to as I would probably have ended up sounding as though I had just got off the plane from Reykjavik.

As it turned out, it was just as well I didn't try subterfuge as, apparently, I look like an Englishman and my cover would have been blown: at least so the rather large gentleman on my right told me. It seems that the way I was holding my coffee cup and the fact that I had a copy of the Daily Telegraph under my arm were a bit of a giveaway. I suppose I should be grateful that not all English qualities are synonymous with loutish behaviour whilst abroad.

Sad to report, the Lions lost the third test and I had to say "Well done," to all and sundry whilst enduring a barrage of thinly veiled swipes at all British sporting endeavours. I like to think that their ribaldry was in good humour, just as I like to think that they accepted my response of "Just wait until England play the All Blacks in November and we beat them just as we did the last time we met," in the same vein. Time will tell.

And so on I went to the next stage of my trip: the train ride to Sion.

* * *

Ticket duly bought, I made my way to the appropriate platform and awaited the train. I tarried for an hour, nearly caught the wrong train – twice – before climbing aboard my penultimate mode of transport for the weekend.

I found a window seat and settled down to spend the journey plugged into my opera recordings. I can certainly recommend a train trip along the shore of Lake Geneva whilst Placido belts out the likes of 'Che Gelida Manina'. A truly delightful combination, and no mistake.

I arrived at Sion at the exact time forecast, and then spent an hour waiting for the coach that was to take me up the valley to Arolla. The hotel was situated at the top end of said valley, and the road used to get there was either very steep in places or furiously weaved from side to side; and I would be lying if I said that I felt on top of my game by the time I reached my destination. As my experience of Swiss hotels is somewhat limited, I cannot pass any meaningful judgement on its standard, but I will say that it fitted the bill more than adequately and I would have no hesitation in returning.

I was told at reception which room I had been allocated, and that the fellow with whom I was to share was already up there. The room was number 40, and I, as I would have done in any other hotel, assumed that it was on the fourth floor. So up the stairs I trudged. Unfortunately, when I arrived on the fourth floor – after a great deal of suitcase lugging I might add, and at an altitude noticeably above sea level – I found the rooms on that floor went from 61 – 80.

'That's odd' I remember thinking. I also remember thinking one or two other things as well – mainly to do with the fact that I had expended a great deal of precious energy in getting up there and would have to expend some more going down again – but propriety prevents me from mentioning them.

Whilst going back down to the third floor, I noted that the rooms thereon went from 41 – 60, and hazarded a guess that room 40 might well be on the second floor: and so it was: and right at the far end of the corridor.

"You seem as though you're going to mention another problem," you posit.

Well, yes; and that showed up after I knocked on the door and entered room 40. Now, bearing in mind that I had unnecessarily traipsed up two floors with a heavy case, and was still feeling a wee bit whoozy after the convolutions of the bus trip, my immediate reaction upon being greeted by a fellow who said –

"Allo; ma nam is Dah-veed, and I arm your rum-mate."

– was probably not quite what he had been expecting. Unless, of course, people in his part of the world normally hop backwards a couple of steps and appear to have spontaneously developed trismus.

Have I mentioned my rather low tolerance levels towards those of a French persuasion? Quite possibly, I expect. However, in the interests of *entente cordiale* and all that, I refrained from launching into a tirade of my thoughts on the CAP and the garlic-sucking types who appear to extol such institutionalised corruption. No, you will be gratified to hear that, having recovered my composure and blaming my bizarre reaction on the altitude, I extended my hand for shaking and introduced myself.

Dah-veed, just when I thought it couldn't get any worse, was a lawyer! Oh, happy days. Anyway, he was in his mid-thirties, single, a bit of an old hand at Alpinism, and, fortunately for both of us, spoke pretty good English.

Yes, I know I should really make an effort to speak another language;

and believe me, I have tried. Unfortunately my brain, for some reason best known to itself, is one of those that has no end of trouble with assimilating foreign tongues. It just can't cope: much in the same way that it can't cope with music scores, legal contracts and circuit diagrams.

I can manage 'please' and 'thank you' in French, German and Spanish; which, I suppose, are two important words to have in one's vocabulary: and I have crossed paths with quite a few amongst those in the UK who haven't yet mastered them in their own language; never mind anybody else's. But when it comes to holding a meaningful conversation on, say, Jean Paul Sartre's rendering of existentialism, you might just as well ask me to juggle soot.

But back to Dah-veed. After a few minutes of unpacking and exchanging potted versions of our respective reasons for being there, it was decided that we ought to head downstairs and say hello to the rest of our group. As you may have gathered, I am not the most social human being who has ever walked this planet, and I doubt if that is ever likely to change: and this trip would turn out to reinforce that state of affairs.

It wasn't that the others were in any way unpleasant people, but I soon got the feeling that their focus of conversation was pretty well restricted to what they did for a living. I did try to steer the topics in more stimulating directions, but in next to no time, spreadsheets and targets were back again. Another example of if you take away a person's job they disappear?

Maybe my sense of ennui had a silver lining; as it made me leave the ensemble earlier than might otherwise have been the case, and I missed the other seeming focus of their time on this planet – alcohol.

So it was that when I awoke the next morning I found my head was clear and that nobody was playing football inside it. Breakfast was the usual continental mixture of cereal, coffee and croissants; and I experienced another major yearn for a full English: and afterwards we assembled outside the hotel for a kit check.

One of the drawbacks to being a 'first-timer' is that you have no real idea of what to put in your rucksack. Yes, you recognise the need for the necessities of course: and therefore you have to find room for waterproofs, axe, crampons, water bottle, helmet, gloves, goggles, gaiters, food snacks, sun hat, sun cream, blister kit, harness, karabiners, prussic ropes, and a spare sweater: but it is only after your third or fourth trip up a mountain that you work out what is really required.

To say that my rucksack felt as if someone had popped in a bag of cement when I wasn't looking would be a bit of an understatement: it felt more as if I had the sand, water and the mixer as well. To this day I have no idea how the straps didn't break, or how I was able to do more than slowly sink into the ground under the weight.

Another benefit that is to be derived from doing a few sorties is that you discover exactly which bits of your clothing live up to their billing – windproof, waterproof, and breathable – and for how long into the trip those characteristics are still functioning. Unfortunately, it is usually only at those times when the properties are put to the test that you discover whether or not they actually work: and then, of course, it is impossible to do anything about it. Rather as the only time you find out that your roof leaks is when it rains: and I was about to make that discovery with the one item that I had picked up fairly cheaply.

I thought that you could buy an all-singing, all-dancing fleece for £20. Ha! I was later to find out, when wearing it for the first time under active conditions, that all it really did was to keep absorbing moisture (and getting heavier as a result). When I came to take it off it resembled a towel that had been left on the bathroom floor. Bad enough on its own; but when you realise that unless you can find a way of drying it you're going to have to put it back on again the next time you go out, the mountains start to lose quite a bit of their appeal.

Anyway, feeling enough butterflies inside me to keep a keen lepidopterist happy for days, I boarded the minibus that was to take us for our first trip into the mountains and the object of the day's training – namely, glaciers.

We set off and spent the next thirty minutes going down one valley and up another on roads that were quite obviously envious of the reputation enjoyed by Lombard Street in San Francisco – steep, and wanting to squeeze as many bends into as short a distance as possible.

That combination would be all well and good for those who enjoy 'extreme' fairground rides; but for someone who sometimes feels a bit green about the gills on escalators it does not come recommended as the ideal way to start your day.

I was, needless to say, very pleased when the minibus arrived at our destination: and that was when an unexpected surprise turned up. Would I be correct in thinking that the word 'unexpected' was superfluous there? Yes, I think I was: a surprise is, by definition, unexpected. Anyway, I had always been under the impression that glaciers were to be found in rather cold places. Something to do with them being formed out of ice, and not really the sort of place that you would expect to be on the warm side. However, one of the first things to come along and tap me on the awareness shoulder was just how hot the place could be.

There I was, with woolly hat, thick gloves and scarf, and the ambient air temperature was hovering somewhere between 70 and 80 degrees Fahrenheit. I also noticed an unpleasant sneer on the face of one of our guides who, for some unfathomable reason, had obviously taken a bit of a dislike to me and had made no mention earlier that I might have been a bit overdressed for the day's objective.

After taking off a few redundant items of clothing and packing them into my already overflowing rucksack, I swung the rucksack on to my back. This, as it turned out, was a bit of a silly thing to do as the rucksack now weighed more than a morbidly obese teenager; and, adhering to some of the laws that govern the conservation of momentum, it proceeded to throw me off balance and into the nearest bush.

It took the efforts of two of my companions to first extricate me from my predicament, and then to extricate some rather sharp thorny things from about my person. I've called them sharp thorny things as – because roses are said to have prickles rather than thorns – I wasn't sure what the correct term was. Regardless, they were very sharp and very thorny. Then, once my equilibrium was restored, we set off towards the glacier.

Have I mentioned the fact that everybody in our party was at least 15 years younger than me? Well, if I haven't, I shall now. Everybody in our party was at least fifteen years younger than me. Now, whilst an extra two decades on the surface of this planet might well endow someone with more wisdom and wherewithal, it does precious little as far as enabling that same someone to keep up with the sort of walking pace with which those blighters shot off.

As my attention had been a bit distracted by my unscheduled excursion into the bush, allied with the fact that I don't have 20-20 hearing, I must have missed the starting pistol. Don't get me wrong; I am all in favour of a brisk walk from time to time; but as a rule I prefer to walk at my own pace, on the flat or a slightly downward slope, and without two cubic yards of mountaineering equipment strapped to my back. In next to no time, the others had practically disappeared from view. On reflection, there was no 'practically' about it – they *had* disappeared from view.

I can recall wondering if perhaps it was some sort of initiation to which the oldest of the group is subjected. Three possible outcomes then came to mind. Perhaps my companions would all spring out from behind bushes a few hundred yards or so up the trail and yell "Surprise!" Perhaps I was going to collapse and die of exposure. Finally, perhaps I ought to plod on and hope for the best.

About a mile and a half later I discovered the others and was introduced to a routine that was going to play a recurring part of my Alpine experience – The rest of the group dashes ahead leaving me behind, they pause to have a rest and a bite to eat, I catch up, whereupon they gather their things and push off again. I thought that the practice was pretty poor show, if you must know; but I resolved to gamely struggle on.

After another couple of miles of this uphill fun and games – it could well have been more, I know that it certainly felt like it – we arrived at the lower edge of the glacier: and there I had another surprise. I had always imagined that – as well as being very cold – glaciers were in something of a pristine condition. You know, all white and shiny: but not a bit of it; unless that one was the exception that proved a rule of some kind. It was absolutely filthy!

It looked as though the glacier had stopped off at every house on the way down and collected all their refuse. Which, I suppose, in a way it had: but all the same. Another surprise was how hard it was – rather like walking on concrete: only very slippery. I tell you what though, those crampons certainly proved their worth. I didn't take the opportunity to prove it, but I should imagine that trying to make progress on a sloping glacier would have been nigh on impossible without them.

I'll tell you another thing that surprised me. I had been under the impression that water flowing out of a glacier was just the sort of thing to swig down when you were thirsty – cold, clear, and guaranteed to make a fellow feel that life might be worth struggling on with for a bit longer: but that wasn't to be the case. The appealing blue-grey colour that I thought was due to the coldness is actually due to all the bits of grit and whatnot being carried along; and the only feeling that you are likely to get having imbibed a pint would be an overwhelming desire to avail yourself of the nearest toilet facilities.

So, on we trudged. The hares at the front and poor old me keeping up the rear: until we got somewhere near the top of the thing; whereupon our guides split us up into groups of three and embarked on showing us the ins and outs of negotiating the various obstacles that you are likely to encounter on a glacier.

We were made to go up steep bits, we were made to go down steep bits; we were even made to go across steep bits. We were also shown how to use our ice-axes to hew out steps. I don't think my guide was terribly amused when he saw that I had cleaved out a step large enough to resemble an armchair: especially when I then sat down on it for a bit of a breather.

"What you are doing?" he asked in a manner that I felt was a bit too brusque.

"Giving my main-frame a bit of time off," I replied, taking advantage of the respite to enjoy a bit more of the view than I had hitherto.

"What?"

"I'm having a rest."

"This is not time for rest!"

As I didn't think that was the ideal occasion to point out the mistakes the chap had made with his sentence construction, I merely said "I beg to differ. I think it's an absolutely perfect opportunity for a rest. Why don't you come and join me?"

"Excuse me?"

"Come and take the weight off your feet. Sit and enjoy the view."

"We have not time for this. We have lot much more to do."

Call it a sort of sixth sense if you like, but I could feel that all was not well with the Swiss *joie de vivre* at that moment; and if I tarried any longer the glacier was likely to melt at a faster rate than Nature had intended. It even seemed that in the short time the guide had been standing there, the heat emanating from his boots had caused him to sink an inch or two into the surface of the ice.

The rest of the glacial experience passed without incident: apart from being roped together whilst going over narrow crevasses. Now I know that a certain amount of roping together is sensible – in case one of the party happens to drop into a bit of a hole, and the others can get together and tug him back out again – but feel I ought to point out that having the rope kept taut and constantly parallel with your waist means that everybody has to keep moving at the same speed: or else the sort of thing that happened to my group could happen to any group.

"So what did happen to your group?"

I am, by nature, a fairly cautious person; and I like to slow down to have a good look when I find myself approaching a gap in the ground. You know what I mean: you stop to check how wide the gap is and whether or not you need a bit of a run-up to get over it. The other two, one fore and one aft of me, were the sort that just keeps trundling forwards and trusts to good fortune that they'll make it over.

Can you imagine what happens when the first fellow bounds over and the second fellow stops? Yes, that's right; either the second fellow is pulled forwards and has to jump, ready or not, or the first fellow is halted mid-crossing. Luckily for me, I was a bit heavier than the gazelle-like chap in front and his progress came to something of an abrupt halt. And so it was that my group was the first to have a go at retrieving someone from a crevasse. Fortunately the abyss wasn't all that deep and, even more so, it wasn't me who fell in.

The look on the face of the chap as he came back into view wasn't what could best be described as friendly, and it did go a long way to explain some things that happened a couple of days later.

We then headed back to our rendezvous with the minibus: everyone else gambolling along like spring lambs whilst I struggled with boots that were beginning to feel like concrete blocks. What is the opposite to a spring lamb? Apart from a Sunday roast that is! Autumnal mutton? Anyway.

The trip back to the hotel was pretty much like the trip away from it, and I can't say that I felt all that great when we got back. Motion sickness at altitude is not something I could recommend. However, I rallied and made my way back to my room for a bath and some recovery time: and that was when I found a blister on my right heel about the size of a thumb-nail.

I can't put all of the blame on the boot; although, obviously, it was the source of the abrasion. No, I must admit that I might not have secured the boot tightly enough in the first place: and, as they probably say hereabouts, it only takes a little bit of movement to cause a whole lot of chafing.

Anyway, there seemed no point in bemoaning my lot: primarily because it wasn't going to do any good; and also because nobody else would have cared. Not as a result of any animus as such in my direction, you understand; but mainly as I think most of them were also suffering as a result of new or ill-secured boots.

So, the first day was over and nobody was unable to continue. Supper that evening was a decent spread – I will say that the hotel kitchen staff certainly knew how to knock up a passable plateful of provisions – and, with the help of the day's efforts and a couple of beers, most people slept like proverbial logs.

The next morning, once breakfast was consumed and ablutions completed, we all gathered on the patio for an equipment check before we set off for that day's adventure – a trek of about five miles with a climb of about 3000 feet – which would take us up to a hut on a hill and our first night at real altitude.

Off we went: but only for about 400 yards, where we had a stop at the local grocers to grab some food and suchlike for the day. I knew what I wanted to eat on the trip, but I also knew that I wouldn't be able to carry it all: so, as I didn't think I would be able to cajole one of the others into helping out, I settled for a small box of those cereal bars that promise to provide you with a good proportion of the calorific intake required to keep an average male adult on the preferred side of moribund.

I found the box soon enough; and that was shortly before I found the queue for the check-out. A reasonable assumption told me that five or six people shouldn't take that long to get through and I would have a moment or two to put my feet up before we pushed off again. Well, those five or six people might just as well have been fifty or sixty. Each one of them wanted – "Three slices of ham, 3 more of cheese, a tomato, a baguette – no, not that one, the one next to it. Oh, could I have another slice of ham? And a small cucumber; and have you got any of those little pats of butter? No, I don't mind waiting while you open a new carton."

Well, I can assure you, that *I* minded waiting. It was very inconsiderate of them, I have to say; and that was compounded by the way that they had all made inroads into the next stage of the trek by the time I came out of the shop. Having the slowest person being the last to start didn't make much sense to me. I would have thought it better to let those of a slower inclination set off first: but nobody asked me, so there we are.

If I had been under the impression that the previous day's exertions were more than sufficient, the next four hours saw to it that my yardstick had to be moved somewhat. We went up, and then along, up again, across a stream, up, along, up and yet more up. Naturally, I was well astern; and, like the day before, every time I reached the place where the others were having a bit of a bite and a breather, they upped sticks and pushed off.

But, as I was soon to discover, there was to be one big difference between the two days. The days were similar in that the path was steep, I was tiring, and the hike seemed interminable: but, as if all that wasn't hard enough on a fellow who was still a bit of a newcomer to the joys of mountains, the dissimilarity was that as we were going quite a bit higher, so noticeably lower became the available amount of the life-sustaining element that occupies the eighth berth in the periodic table.

There I was, getting more and more exhausted, needing more and more oxygen, but having less and less of it to breathe; which didn't seem entirely fair to me. I'm quite sure that had I been in charge of the atmospheric arrangements, I would have seen to it that some sort of reward awaited those who dared venture above the clouds. Or perhaps it was the Olympus occupants' way of saying "Oi, mortals, keep off our territory."

Makes sense, I suppose, as I ponder further. When you have found a rather nice spot, you really don't want the hoi polloi turning up in their droves every time the sun comes out, do you?

Musings to one side, I trudged onwards; and upwards. Another hour passed, and the guide then pointed out our day's destination. I squinted; and in the distance I saw, perched on the edge of a rather steep bit, what was to be our refuge for the night.

"Not far to go," he said. I thought I detected more than a dash of insincerity in his tone. "Shouldn't take too long," he continued. I then knew I had.

'Not far' to me means – certainly when you take into consideration my overall state of discontentment – a distance of about 400 yards: 800 yards tops. I would not, even if I had been standing too close to someone with a peculiarly-shaped cigarette stuck in his mouth, have considered two miles to have fallen into the category of 'not far'. Especially not had those same three and a half thousand yards been going in an upwardly sloping fashion.

Thinking back, I suppose I really should have been expecting that sort of thing: after all, mountains do have a tendency to be high structures. Anyway, I endured more purgatory before finally arriving at the building. I expect the sharpest among you will have spotted that I haven't described the plethora of vistas that were simply crying out to be described; and, for those with room for a couplet or two, to open up and wax lyrical: but my attentions were rather focused on keeping my lungs within the confines of my pleural cavity.

Anyway, I had arrived. The quarters were constructed in a mixture of local stone and timber, with a steeply-sloping roof, some rather nice red shutters on the windows, and arranged inside into a selection of rooms designated for use when either sleeping or eating. I expect that I should have noticed more, but I wasn't really concentrating too much on the finer details while I looked around for my companions.

I soon found them, and was then shown to where I was to be sleeping that night. I had been under the impression, when the brochure stated 'bunk beds', that it had meant bunk beds. How silly of me. What 'bunk beds' means in the Alps is often just a shelf. So, instead of being in a room with a selection of one-up-one-down type things, I found myself staring at two shelves with lines of 2'6" mattresses (all touching the ones on either side I might add) and being told that mine was on the top shelf, two from the far end.

Rapture would not have accurately described my feelings at the time; but, being the stoic that I am, I took the news with good grace and set about putting my rucksack somewhere out of the way. After a cup of something resembling tea, I joined the others for a bit of a lesson in map reading and knot tying; whilst experiencing the type of nausea often associated with hanging around at more than 9000 feet above sea-level for the first time.

I have now forgotten what all the knots were; but seem to recall names such as Clove Hitch, Figure of Eight, Alpine Butterfly Bend, Cow Hitch, and another called a Prussik. All very interesting I have to say; and, apart from the aforementioned nausea, helped to pass an hour or so.

I forget exactly what it was we had to eat that afternoon – partly because I don't think my taste-buds were in full swing and partly because I don't think my memory banks were fully open for business either. But there you have it. Then, after a quick stroll around to see if I could find any spare oxygen, I decided to go and have a bit of a lie down on my shelf.

On the way, I was told, by that guide fellow – you know, the one who thought that a struggling Englishman was fair game – that we would be leaving the hut at five o'clock the following morning.

"Five o'clock!" I exclaimed.

"Yes. Maybe earlier."

"What! Why?"

"Because we don't want to be on the slopes when sun is at the hottest."

"Speak for yourself, matey; but in an area where there is an awful lot of cold white stuff everywhere, I should have thought that warmth from any sector would be appreciated."

"It does not work like that. We need to be off the snow before it become too soft. So we leave at five."

And with that the fellow left: probably to do some late afternoon jogging, I remember thinking. Five o'clock, indeed. Still somewhat shaken by the news, I climbed aboard the sill and hoped to get a few minutes of shuteye.

Was my plan accomplished? Would I get the precious respite I so desired as I put my head on the pillow? The answer was quickly provided by the pillow itself. True, on the outside, it looked like a pillow; true, when I manoeuvred it into a suitable position I hadn't noticed anything unusual about it; and true, my cognitive processes were probably a bit below par, and so I have only myself to blame that the problem did not become apparent until my right ear had made contact.

You see, instead of filling the pillowcase with handfuls of feathers, the proprietors had seemingly decided that using conkers would be a splendid alternative. Presumably for eating, if they ever got stranded up there for any length of time. Needless to say, my desire, and ability, for a quick zizz rapidly evaporated.

A few moments later I went outside to have a wander, admire the views and acquaint myself with the general layout of the place. Well, to be specific, the location of the bathroom facilities. Did I say 'bathroom'? How silly of me. What I meant was a tap and three garden sheds perched on the edge of a precipice.

I jest not when I say thus. Imagine, if you will – actually, if you *can* might be more apposite – something akin to the sort of thing in which you would stow your garden spade. Further imagine opening the door and finding a bench with a toilet seat attached to it; then picture lifting the seat and finding yourself peering down into the valley below. Hardly the sort of thing to help you relax, I have to say. I shan't enthral you with a description of the accompanying fetors; except to say that you really wouldn't thank me if I did.

To describe the arrangement as primitive would be an insult to those many tribes that can be found deep within the Amazonian whereabouts. In fact, if I did so, I have no doubt that should a member of the Korubu tribe ever encounter such facilities they would be voicing their complaints in no uncertain terms. They were appalling, and likely to evoke the sort of memories that your subconscious deliberately bins at the earliest opportunity.

Enough on the subject.

Was I through with getting surprises? Not a bit of it. One thing I can vouch for, should you ever find yourself in the same sort of surroundings, is that the place is practically awash with surprises; and my next one was served up with the evening meal. Being on the top of a mountain, and with no cable-car in sight, means that deliveries cannot be easily made; and as a helicopter was the preferred mode of transport, items of cargo are priced by weight. The net result was that drinking water was about £4·00 for a couple of pints.

A further surprise? The bread wasn't what I could really describe as fresh; but probably a lot fresher than if I had carried it up there. The main course of the meal was meat and vegetables – not sure what the meat was, but I didn't notice any 'OK Corral' branding on it: nor, fortunately, a collar!

When it came to sleep time, I did feel a bit of sympathy for the two girls in our party – having to share a shelf with ten men. Mind you, on reflection, would I have been upset at having to share a shelf with ten women? Quite possibly, if they had resembled the men: and the brochure should have mentioned, and heavily underlined, that you must ensure you pack earplugs.

I have shared sleeping quarters – nine years at boarding school spring to mind – with those who feel that the dark hours are somehow enhanced by adding the sounds of a building site to the prevailing ambience; and they proceed to treat the others to their entire repertoire of naso-pharyngeal reverberations. I have even heard what sounded like excerpts from a Noel Coward play, and a rather wheezy opening to Beethoven's Pastoral Symphony played through the obstructed airways of an asthmatic. What I had not expected was a very convincing impression of the mating call of a lonely blue whale as it scoured the oceans in search of a suitable partner. It was almost as if the poor mammal was on the mattress next to mine.

Quite extraordinary, and certainly worthy of a prolonged round of applause had I been treated to it at a variety hall theatre. Hearing it, however, whilst trying to stock up my sleep account merely elicited another desire to find a cricket bat and execute a standard cover drive to the chin of the perpetrator.

Sleep eventually came, and the rest of the night, what was left of it, passed unnoticed. The next morning, at about half-past four, I was woken and told that breakfast was being served. Normally at that time, my tank of *bon hommie* is pretty much hovering around empty, and people would be best advised to approach me with caution: or, at the very least, be wearing running shoes.

As I may well have mentioned, my idea of breakfast is a glass of orange juice and a small bowl of porridge to start with. Then a decent-sized plate of crispy bacon, fried eggs (softish in the centre and slightly burnt at the edges; or, as our American cousins may request, 'over easy'), some mushrooms (that have been fried in butter), a couple of reputable pork sausages, and all served on two slices of wholemeal toast. I like to complete the repast with a couple more rounds of toast, some orange marmalade, and all washed down with a pot of tea.

What I am not too keen on is a bowl of muesli that quite obviously had warm milk poured on it at least thirty minutes prior to my arrival, bread that had, equally obviously, arrived a fortnight earlier, conserves that had more in common with the sort of jelly one might serve at a children's party, and a hot beverage that was either very poor coffee or passable onion soup.

You will be delighted to know that, as I remembered my whereabouts were high above sea level, I refrained from passing any acerbic remarks whilst at the table; and I consigned the comestibles to my gastric regions as rapidly as I could, in order that they didn't dwell upon my tongue long enough for my taste buds to start making complaints.

Then, ten minutes later, we were on our way.

I made it my duty to set off before the others, and led the way for at least 300 yards: coincidentally, right up to the point that the path started steepening beyond the angle that I found to be tolerable. Thereafter it was up, up and more up; and I fell further, further and further behind.

What can I tell you about my feelings when I eventually arrived at the intended summit? Quite a lot actually, but I doubt if several paragraphs of 'Wow' would make for very interesting reading. However, I shall briefly try to convey the mixture of pleasure, awe and humility that suddenly surged through the Phalarope corporeal confines.

The pleasure was, fairly justifiably, at the thought that there wasn't anywhere else nearby that was higher than where I was standing; and that my guide could no longer pass comments about how he had seen goats – even after the inhabitants of the Spanish village of Manganeses de la Polvorosa had chucked them from their church belfry – walking with more energy than I had shown.

The awe made sure that I was sufficiently aware of the grandeur of the vista that lay before me. Yes, I know that I wasn't standing on the top of Everest; and yes, I know that local schoolchildren probably made the trip to the top many times before their tenth birthday: but I was looking through the eyes of someone for whom this was the first time he had, on foot, been anywhere near as high. Added to which was the fact that I could clearly see both the Matterhorn and Mont Blanc; which is something that doesn't happen when standing on the top of Snowdon.

Another of the differences I noticed was just how far below the clouds were, and how many pointy bits of rock poked up through them: all of which amounted to an astonishing sight for me.

What was the third thing I mentioned? Oh yes, humility. I felt a need to doff my hat to the architect; and the fact that someone had plonked a metal cross on the top seemed most appropriate, I have to say. What was it Descartes said? Something about there must be a God, as there are things on this planet that are so wonderful that only a God could have created them. I guess a mountain top seems a good place to give thanks.

Anyway, after about twenty minutes for contemplation and a bite to eat, we headed back down again. To simply return to the hut? No; our esteemed guide had decided that some time spent familiarising ourselves with a few mountain rescue techniques would be very much in order. You know the sort of thing – how to react if someone you're roped to falls into a crevasse. Apparently the earlier example didn't count, as the crevasse in question was neither wide nor deep enough.

I have to say that my first reaction if the person to whom I was roped fell into a 'suitable' crevasse would rather depend on the dimensions of that person. Should they happen to tip the scales at anything exceeding my own weight, my first reaction would almost certainly be to topple forwards and follow them into the aforementioned hole. Perhaps 'reaction' was the wrong word: perhaps it was an inescapable application of Newton's first law.

I was about to point out this rather salient fact to the guide – whose name was Paul, by the way – when I was told to forget about saying anything clever and just pay attention to what he had to say.

There then followed a demonstration of how to construct an anchor with an ice-axe, a sling, a harness, and a Prussik rope. Well, at least how one of the remaining two fellows on the rope was to do it whilst the other dug in his heels and tried to prevent the poor unfortunate at the front from descending any further. I wanted to ask what would happen if there were only two people in the party, but Paul sensed my imminent enquiry and shot a look that told me such a dilemma would be dealt with at the appropriate time.

So it was that I and another chap made an anchor and, with the aid of a pulley rigged up from a couple of karabiners, hauled the third member of our party from within the crevasse. Then, after the second fellow had a go, it was soon my turn to be the focus of the rescue.

I don't know if you have ever had the opportunity to tie yourself to a rope and jump into a crevasse – whilst hoping that those on the other end of the rope have enough grunt to prevent you from disappearing for good – but I really cannot recommend it highly enough. Actually, that's not quite true: I really cannot recommend it at all.

The reasons, I was soon to remember, for beginning any climb at some ungodly hour in the morning have little to do with wanting to make sure that you are off the mountain before it gets dark and more to do with wanting to get off the mountain before the sun gets too high and begins melting the surface of the snow and ice. Apparently it makes progress a good deal harder and much more precarious. It also, as I soon discovered, turns the edge of a crevasse into something of a waterfall. Not in itself an unpleasant sight; unless, of course, you happen to be dangling on the end of a rope underneath it.

Whatever you may have read about how invigorating a cold shower can be, taking one whilst languishing on the end of a rope that is less than half an inch in diameter does not have the desired effect. I have never been the sort of person for whom icy water cascading down the inside of my collar has done anything other than make me wish that I were somewhere else – preferably in a comfortable chair with a cup of tea. Add to which joys the thought of being certain that those to whom your wellbeing has been, albeit temporarily, entrusted have decided there is sufficient time to have a drink and a biscuit before getting round to extricating you from your predicament, and you have a situation that I am sure was never mentioned in the advertising blurb.

Fortunately, in much the same way that is said of all good things, my anxiety was short-lived and I soon found myself being dragged back up again. A cause for celebration? Possibly; had it occurred earlier on in the day – you know, when the ice was in a firm condition. However, when you are lying face down, when the surface six inches of the ice resembles the sort of slush that you find at the roadside a day or two after the gritting lorries have passed, and when your companions feel it necessary to haul you up with the sort of jerky movements normally displayed by those with a neurological dysfunction, you will understand my irritation.

After a moment or two to make sure that everything that should have been attached to my torso was still attached, I stood up in time to watch the others set off back down the slope. I didn't immediately follow, as I like to sit down whilst I do a couple of extra checks before springing back into action. My guide, true to form, didn't give a blue raspberry about my levels of felicity and made some remark about wanting to show me a new way of playing the Alpenhorn. I made a mental note that I would not turn down an opportunity to *accorde ma flute*, as they might say in a certain neighbouring country.

So there I was, up a mountain, bedraggled and rather wishing that

I was relaxing in a hot bath. I needn't have worried though, as my good friend George Mallory came to my rescue by popping into my head and reminding me that I was of true British stock. So, with little more than a shrug of my shoulders, I donned my rucksack and headed back to the hut; where I enjoyed a rather nice omelette and a can of beer before starting the rest of the descent.

Three and a half hours later I entered the hotel, waved cheerily at the receptionist and, skilfully hiding the fact that my knees felt as though they had undergone bilateral meniscectomies performed by a rather bad-tempered wildebeest, I made my way up to my room and a well-deserved lie-down.

The next day was scheduled as a rest day. Psshaw! When I think of a rest day I conjure up images of a day of, well, rest. Rather like, as they say, what is written on the tin. I think of an extra hour in bed, being brought a cup of restorative and asked how I would like my eggs done. Then, after having replenished the energy reserves with all manner of simple and complex carbohydrates, perhaps a gentle stroll to get a paper which I can peruse at leisure whilst reclining under the shady bough of a willow tree. The images, even after a thorough examination, do not include an early, scant, continental breakfast followed by an hour's walk to a rock face up which I am then expected to shimmy.

Do you recall my comment when I saw people climbing up the sheer face of El Capitan in Yosemite – that I was glad there are people who feel compelled to attempt such undertakings whilst equally glad that I wasn't one of them? Well, then you can probably imagine my sentiments when I was told that I was expected to put on a helmet and harness, attach myself to a length of string, and climb up.

"What!" I remember saying.

"Go on; it is most easy," the guide, Paul, stressed.

"No it isn't," I replied, "as I can assure you that there are no arachnid genes lurking within my chromosomal make-up."

"What?"

"I do not possess eight legs; and on the last occasion I looked, I didn't notice any spinnerets on the under-surface of my abdomen from which I could exude a viscous fluid that hardens on exposure to air."

"What?"

"I do not spend my leisure hours under the guise of Spiderman."

"I did not say you did."

"Your implication deemed otherwise."

"My *implication*! What implication?"

"The one that expected me to go up that," I said, pointing to the rock face. "It's damn near vertical."

"But that is the whole point."

"The whole point of what?"

"The point of... It is a challenge."

"Well, challenge me to something else: something that I'm more likely to be able to achieve. Such as playing snooker with my eyes closed and getting a break of 147." Yes, I know that the maximum possible break is 155, but I didn't think there was enough of my life left to explain that to him.

"In other words, you are saying you are not going to do this."

"Those are the exact words."

"Oh."

I should like to point out that my reluctance wasn't due to any lack of fortitude on my part – even though the guide quite obviously thought so, and was already trying to construct a way of imparting this concept to the others – but to the fact that in order to be a rock climber of any note you need to be endowed in several ways that Nature had clearly decided would not suit me.

Firstly, you need to have fingers that are no more than three inches long; secondly, you should not weigh more than nine stones; thirdly, you must have feet about a size eight; and fourthly, possess arms that are the same length as your legs. As you may have gathered, I did not join any of the queues when they were handing out those qualities; preferring instead to stand in the one in which common sense and structural ratios that acknowledged *phi* were being dispensed.

"Well, you probably could not do it anyhow."

"I beg your pardon."

"You obviously have not got what it takes to do this."

It had taken a bit longer than I thought it might have, and the riposte would hardly grace the covers of a book entitled 'The best Rejoinders of Our Time', but at least the poor fellow had a go.

"My dear chap," I said, putting on one of my haughtiest haughty looks. "Are you familiar with the term 'prudence'?"

"Prudence? What is 'prudence'?"

"It is the act of showing care and thought for the future."

Perhaps I was being a bit too insensate, and perhaps I shouldn't have expected him to have had an exemplary command of the English language. In any case, I was hardly in a position to rebuke him as my command of French – or any other language for that matter – didn't entitle me to criticise. I tried to wave my hand in a placatory manner, but I don't think it had the desired effect.

"So, are you going to climb up there?"

"No."

"Why?"

"Because, thanks to the advice that I was given – by you, incidentally – before I left the hotel, I am currently wearing a pair of heavy hiking boots. Now, unless I am very much mistaken, a more unsuitable form of foot attire for the task you have suggested, with the possible exception of flippers or clogs, I cannot imagine."

I knew by the awkward expression on his face that I was occupying the higher ground; but, as much as my baser instincts were compelling me, I declined the opportunity to apply Sodium Chloride to his wounds and simply volunteered my services to help belay another of our number.

I forget what the fellow's name was – possibly Mark, though it could have been Rob – but I was highly impressed with the way he seemed to run up the rock. Almost too fast for me to keep up with the belaying: quite astonishing. I suppose, going back to sometime in the misty bits of Man's history, such an ability would have been quite an advantage; and those who possessed it would have been only too keen to pass it on to future generations. I have a suspicion that my ancestors must have found another way of eluding danger and had probably set off on a more convenient route several hours beforehand.

Anyway, I have to admit that, whilst watching some of the others ascend like they had been born to, I did feel as though I was possibly missing out on something that I might have enjoyed. Not enough, I hasten to add, to warrant entrusting my wellbeing to the adhesiveness of my fingers; but enough to having a bash at ascending another rock face with the aid of a rope and two Prussik loops.

I expect you've seen the sort of thing I mean – one loop is attached to your harness and the other to a strap thing into which you put one of your feet. The idea is that you slide each loop up the main rope in turn, alternating the weight between your harness and your foot as you ascend. Quite a handy routine if you find yourself dangling on the end of a rope, so I'm told.

Well, it turned out to be something – about the only thing, actually – that I was able to handle without appearing as if I had signed up for the wrong course: you know, finding myself doing taekwondo instead of table-tennis. The only slight flaw in being able to ascend the rope with relative ease was that when I stopped to take a look at the others I found myself a jolly sight higher off the ground than I had thought. Rather unnerving, I don't mind admitting; especially as I wasn't even halfway up.

I shan't bore you with the details of how I got to the top and scrambled over the lip to reach the relative safety of the ledge above – not because it was actually boring, but just in case you are the type of person who, to use a German expression (just about the only one that we have in the English language, by the way), enjoys a large helping of *Schadenfreude*. Actually, I think we also use *doppelganger*: and there are probably some others as well.

I don't know what it is in my makeup that, when close to the edge of a drop, makes me want to go and lean over it: almost as if some unseen thread pulls me closer. I cannot, for one moment, imagine that there was any advantage to be had in having the trait and that, as a general rule, those who possessed it tended to perish before they reached the age of maturity. Fortunately, I was aware of it and made sure that my first action on reaching the top was to securely attach myself to something that would act as a brake to counteract the rather stupid compulsion.

So there I was, attached to a sling that was attached to a karabiner that was attached to a rope that was anchored to a bolt in the rock; sitting at the top of an overhanging rock face and wondering what on earth I was doing up there and, more importantly, how on earth I was going to get back down again.

The answer to the first question is destined to remain in the ether, but the answer to the second question was provided by Mark; or was it Rob? Joy of joys; my return to ground level was going to be achieved by way of a procedure known as abseiling. 'Hurray', I remember thinking. 'What a lovely way to round off the exercise'.

I then had to grab hold of another rope, lean out backwards over the drop and, by using a belay device and a series of hops, drop back down to the ground.

By dint of the fact that I am typing this without the aid of something attached to my forehead you may assume that I made it down in one piece. I would like to now regale you with an account of how I managed the feat with the sort of aplomb usually associated with those to whom such acts are second nature. I would like to, as I said; but as I had my eyes shut most of the way, and made the descent very slowly and feeling as if my life could end at any moment, I think that it would be rather unjustified.

Fortunately, my time in Switzerland came to an end before I was able to do any lasting damage to anything other than my pride; and the next phase of my Alpine spree was spent in a minibus that went to Chamonix.

I am not one to extol the virtues of very much that is of a European nature, but I could not leave my stay in Arolla without saying how much I enjoyed it. Admittedly my judgment wasn't based on a surfeit of familiarity as I didn't do much in the way of interacting with many of the locals, or try my hand at conversing in their tongue.

Apart from, that is, when I tried to explain to the lady in the post office that I wished to buy some stamps so that, upon my return to the UK, I could send some photographs (of me on a mountain) printed as postcards back to the hotel and they would then be sent from there – using the Swiss stamps – back to the UK. This was so the recipients would think that I had bought the postcards in one of the local shops, and would wonder what the dickens I was doing on them.

I did get the feeling that perhaps I hadn't explained myself coherently enough as the aforementioned lady gave me a look that seemed to suggest that I wasn't the round shilling, and she passed me some literature extolling the benefits of joining the Foreign Legion.

The trip from our hotel to Chamonix was, despite the plethora of bends, rather a pleasant one; and it took about a couple of hours for us to arrive at our destination. There was to be a change of room companions for all of us – apart from the four that had decided against doing the Mont Blanc extension – and my new roommate was a chap called Phil.

I know that I have already mentioned that most of the group was little more than half my age; and then, as if I needed more confirmation that quite a lot of water had flowed under my particular bridge, I was to receive it in two further deliveries.

I had decided not to apply a razor to my face whilst on my trip: not for any reasons allied to the possibility of French women finding designer stubble attractive (some might mention that a surfeit of facial hair has always been desired by French women, but I am far too polite to venture down that road), but rather to make my load lighter and, as a by-product, to give people the impression that I was, indeed, a man of the mountains.

What, however, I had not foreseen was the fact that a good deal more grey hair had appeared since the last time I had foregone shaving. Rather than the rugged look for which I had hoped, children were approaching me and telling me what they wanted for Christmas: blooming cheek.

The second, and probably the more damaging, reminder was that I found the receptionist – a lady with long black hair – to be rather attractive.

"So what? Finding a woman attractive shouldn't make you feel old," you say.

Ordinarily not; but how about when all the other males in my group said that they didn't find her attractive because, as they put it, she was 'well past it'? Things like that can be a touch demoralising, don't you know.

Where was I? Oh yes, Phil, my new roommate, and our new room.

True, the room was bigger than the one I had to share in the previous hotel; true, it had an equally nice view as the previous facility; true, it also had an en-suite bathroom: and that was where the problem lay – in the bathroom.

Don't get me wrong; I am always grateful for an en-suite bathroom, as I do have something of a dislike for sharing one with a load of people about whom I have no knowledge. Did that sentence seem pleonastic? If so, please accept my apologies and its replacement. I dislike having to share a bathroom with people I don't know. Not for me the redolence of previous occupants who may have overdone the curry the night before. Oh no; I much prefer to be secure in the knowledge that, whilst not always reminding me of fields of hyacinths, the bathroom is not going to kindle images of… Well, such as that extraordinary arrangement I encountered up at the hut.

Something else that I have a tendency to insist upon is being able to use the bathroom without having to get from one part to another on my hands and knees. You see, the room we were given was up in the roof area, and the bathroom was on one side; and that meant the ceiling sloped from about one foot above the door-frame to about one foot above the floor.

All very well if you happen to have a wedge-shaped head and a spinal deformity. I shall resist describing how much fun it was trying to have a shower if you wanted to wet more than the lower half of your body: and as for spending a penny… Let me just say that it required holding the dormer-window open with my head and standing on one leg at the same time.

Minor inconveniences aside, all was auguring well for a bash at Mont Blanc. Well, apart from when our guides turned up later that evening and announced that a bit of a storm was forecast for the area and we were going to have to modify our intended route up the mountain. I'm sure I crossed my fingers at that point, and made a quiet request to the deity overseeing my interests for that part of the trip that the amended route would involve a bit of a ride in a cable-car. Well, perhaps more than just a 'bit'.

My application was received; and the following morning we did, indeed, hop on a cable-car – I believe it was called the Telepherique de L'Aiguille du Midi – that whizzed us up to the top of the Aiguille du Midi: and that is when some unforeseen drawbacks decided to show themselves.

I have, as you know, a predisposition to feeling light-headed when my immediate environment is in motion: well, the Telepherique produced one such occasion. Imagine being inside a glass cage – about 10 feet by 15 – that is full of people, and suspended above the ground by a wire cable, shooting up the side of a mountain.

I must not give the impression that there was any immediate danger – as regards problems with cables snapping or low-flying aircraft – or concerns about the operator having just got back from a liquid lunch: it was more of a sense of queasiness arising from the fact that the container was continually performing 'pitch and yaw' manoeuvres that did little to mollify my gastric regions. I had to delve deep within the Phalarope reserves in order to control my desire to lie down on the floor and cover my eyes; and my discomfort was not helped by having the entire assemblage go "Whoo-hoo" every time we passed one of the supporting pylons, whereupon the oscillatory actions were accentuated.

The other matter that did little to improve my day was the number and the total lack of social refinement displayed by those who hailed from certain parts of the Far East. I shan't give the exact location; other than to say the whereabouts lie between the Yellow Sea and the Pacific Ocean: and that they may well have been related to my breakfast companions back in Geneva.

Perhaps it is a talent handed down from parent to child; perhaps there is simply something in the British psyche that enables us to form an orderly queue: even if we are on our own. Whatever the reason, it seems to be an art form that is peculiar to most of the indigenous population of the British Isles. Maybe we could set up a company which exports it to those parts of the globe that exhibit a dearth of such social graces. Having written that, I believe that the Japanese are quite good at it as well.

The numbers of the aforementioned malefactors I can do nothing about, and I am sure that the Chamonix populace was more than willing to put up with their transgressions long enough to divest them of any spare currency they might have had. I cannot, however, accept the disgraceful manner in which they pushed and shoved their respective ways – totally oblivious to the fact that other people had taken the trouble to wait their turn – to the front of any queue that happened to be in the vicinity. It was almost as though they sought out a line of people in order to barge their way to the front.

Such a technique, I am more than happy to acknowledge, might work very well when boarding a rush-hour train in their own country; but in the neighbourhood of those who have a modicum of understanding when it comes to social etiquette, it really does become more than a little unacceptable. You will, I hope, excuse me when I confess to having been a little less than vigilant when worrying about the positioning of my rucksack (bearing in mind that it had an ice-axe strapped to the outside) whilst negotiating my way through the hordes of those diminutive individuals. As the locals might well have said in those parts, "Chacun pour soi".

Anyway, I followed the others up a flight or two of stairs, out on to a platform, and was rewarded with – bearing in mind the swarms of Orientals – the most magnificent view. Admittedly my opportunity to admire it was somewhat curtailed by my guide reminding me that I had to get my harness and crampons on 'tout suite', and make my way across a footbridge and then along a dark tunnel in the rock.

At this point I was filled with a bit more than my fair share of trepidation, as I had already seen the arête down which we were about to make our way. I must also say that had my fairy godmother appeared and granted me a wish, it might have been that the next time I opened my eyes I would find myself several thousand feet below where I was currently standing: in one of the rather nice bars in the centre of Chamonix to be precise. I may even have clicked my heels together and settled for Kansas.

However, that was not to be; and I followed the others further, with, for some reason, visions of lemmings trundling through my mind; and soon found myself standing on a ledge with a gate that allowed access to the arête.

Yes, I know that lemmings don't throw themselves off cliffs, and that the misconception came about as a result of a certain film maker – Walt Disney I believe, but I cannot be sure – scaring a bunch of them into running in a direction they hadn't intended: but you will, I hope, conjure up the image all the same.

I would be lying if I said that my joy was unconfined; and I would be lying if I said that my joy was only slightly constrained. I would, however, be serving out veracity in great big dollops if I said that my joy had been squashed into a container the size of an ant's knapsack.

Picture two playing cards leaning against each other, and then increase the size of the cards until they are about 2000 feet high; sprinkle them liberally with snow, and then set out to walk along the 18-inch-wide bit on the top of them. Oh, and don't forget that the ridge slopes downwards, and that you have to stop from time to time to let other people – making their way up the slope – get past you.

I managed to make my way along said arête without falling off – or causing anybody else to do so – but I have to confess to paying little regard to the views available on either side; and spent the whole exercise concentrating on an area in front of me that measured about 18 inches wide by five feet long. It was only when I noticed the slope had flattened out that I realised my ordeal had come to an end.

The next part of our day's itinerary involved about half a mile in a downward direction curving round to the right, followed by three or four hundred yards uphill to the hut that was to be our accommodation for the night.

As huts go, and certainly by comparison to the other one we stayed in, this hut was quite acceptable: or perhaps I was just getting acclimatised to more than the altitude. I can, however, unequivocally state that the toilet facilities were a jolly sight more in keeping with normal arrangements: in other words, they were flushable and didn't expose your nether regions to an entire valley.

The 'acceptability' of the hut then became important– actually, perhaps I have been doing these 'huts' a bit of a disservice as they are really more than huts. Is there a term to describe something that is between a hut and a chalet? A chaulet? Anyway, the standard of the domicile was fortunate as, unbeknownst to me at that time, I was going to be spending the best part of 36 hours in it.

Do you recall the impending storm that I mentioned earlier? Well, it arrived that afternoon: and with quite a bang. Some of the other groups of climbers had earlier gone to have a go at Mont Blanc du Tacul, but had to dash back before the tempest reached them: and just as well, too. Thunder, lightning, hailstones the size of gob-stoppers, snow, winds over 60 mph, and visibility down to little more than a few yards. All very exciting I have to say; and all the better when enjoyed from within the chaulet.

There were several individuals that I had been able to make out in the valley below, who had chosen to spend the night down there in tents. I can only assume that it was from choice, and not because they couldn't see our chaulet – called The Cosmiques, by the way. The considered consensus of opinion amongst the onlookers was that those below us were training for something, possibly some kind of a Polar expedition, and that a night under canvas would help them prepare for whatever it was that lay ahead.

Anyway, the obvious storm aside, there was another one brewing: inside my head. It would seem that altitude sickness can take several hours to make you aware of its presence. I was fine when I arrived at the hut, but about halfway through the evening meal I began to feel a bit below par. By the end of the meal it felt as though the chaulet had mysteriously slipped out to sea; and a very rough sea at that. By the time I turned in for the night I felt as though I was suffering from a bad hangover and travel-sickness at the same time. To say that I wasn't the life and soul of the group would be a superfluous dash of litotes. In fact, 'Absolutely bloody awful' was the expression I used when a colleague asked how I was feeling.

My visions of conquering Mont Blanc were evaporating like a puddle of ethyl chloride on a hot and windy day: altitude sickness at 3,600 metres doesn't augur well if the target is 4,800 metres. I know that hope springs eternal and all that, but this particular brand of hope appeared to have had its quadriceps tendons severed.

To cut short a long, and not very interesting story, any attempt I may have harboured to reach the summit of Mont Blanc had to be called off; and all I could manage was to wish the others good luck as they set off at some ungodly hour the next morning. I was still in a fragile state when they returned eight hours later having – due to some more inclement weather – only managed to get halfway between Mont Blanc du Tacul and Mont Maudit: a spot known as Col Maudit. I say 'only', but I am sure that any of you in the know will recognise that getting to that particular place is to be applauded.

So the trip wasn't the resounding success that I had wished for, and there wasn't much I could do about it. I simply had to console myself with at least being able to get back to the cable-car station at the top of Aiguille du Midi the following morning and managing to reach an altitude of about 3800 metres in the process.

Incidentally, going back up that arête was slightly less daunting than going down it. Slopes, to me at any rate, seem less steep when going up them than when going down: hardly surprising, I suppose, as my eyes are nearer the ground when I'm facing uphill.

Twenty minutes after reaching Aiguille du Midi, and another 'oscillating' cable-car ride later, I was in a restaurant, tucking into a meal of steak and chips and a large beer; whilst experiencing a mixture of gratitude to be back down and disappointment not to have accomplished the principal task.

Actually, as well as those sentiments, I was also a bit apprehensive at having to break the news to Mirabella. You never know how young girls are going to handle disappointment: well, at least *I* never know. Would she burst into tears? Would she be inconsolable? Would she never want to see or speak to me again? Would she – That was the point where I stopped being concerned. Not the 'tears' bit, you understand; I mean the part about not wanting to see or speak to me again. Maybe the trip wasn't going to be such a failure after all.

Unfortunately, as well as having little or no idea about how the mind of an adolescent girl works, I had also misjudged the competency of the thing.

"Don't worry about it, Uncle William," she said, with a concern-causing degree of indifference when I broke the news of my failure to her. "It really doesn't matter."

"Why ever not?" I asked. "I thought you would be upset: or at least something close."

"I would have been, but I discovered a new fact while you were away."

"Eh?"

"I was talking to a friend – telling them what you were up to; ha, ha! – when I found out. I tried to let you know, but the phone signal wasn't strong enough to reach you. Something to do with an electrical storm."

That bit made sense: but the reason for her lack of concern about the outcome of my endeavours…? "Still no wiser, I'm afraid," I said.

"Well, it seems that Mont Blanc was only a practice run. It isn't the highest mountain in Europe after all."

"No? But I thought…"

"It's the highest mountain in *Western* Europe; but not the highest mountain in *all* of Europe."

"Isn't it? Then what is?"

"Mount Elbrus."

"Where's that?"

"In the Caucasus Mountains."

"Oh."

"Mont Blanc is 15,770 feet high. Elbrus is 18,510 feet. Much higher."

Is there a word for the way you feel when your relief at having overcome one obstacle is nullified when you find yourself confronted with another one that is twice the size? Similar, I imagine, to when you have successfully navigated your canoe through some white-water rapids and then find yourself about to go over a huge waterfall.

"Uncle William, is everything all right?"

"Hmm?"

"You've gone a bit pale."

"Have I?"

"Yes. Well, like more than a *bit* pale, actually."

"Oh."

"Are you sure you're okay?"

"Oh yes; yes. It's probably just my body's way of expressing the joy that I'm feeling inside right now. About three thousand feet higher, you say?"

"Very nearly. Isn't it exciting?"

"Practically uncontainable."

I can't be entirely certain, you understand, but I think I spent the rest of that day curled up in a dark corner with a blanket over my head: and my jovial persona remained under wraps for several days after that as well. Reading about Mt Elbrus did very little, nothing actually, to restore my status quo ante shock.

Mount Elbrus

At 5642 metres – or 18,510 feet – Elbrus, an inactive volcano, stands quite a bit higher than Mont Blanc. It is, as *ma petite bête noire* said, situated in the Caucasus mountains – roughly halfway between the Black and Caspian seas – and therefore qualifies as being in Europe. It is actually comprised of two peaks, and from a distance looks like a very large woman lying on her back; and the west peak is about 60 feet higher than the east peak. Depending on which version you read, and whether or not you consider both peaks to count, it was either first climbed by a local fellow back in 1829, or by a team in 1874.

Anyway, Little Miss *Leiden* had deemed it necessary for her uncle to make a complete arse of himself. It wasn't enough that he failed to reach the top of the highest mountain in Western Europe: oh no; she now wanted him to look equally inept on the highest mountain in the whole of Europe.

Do please excuse me: I'm not sure why I chose to refer to myself in the third person – by using different personal pronouns (both objective and subjective, that is) – in the above paragraph. Perhaps my mind still feels a shudder when I think back. Perhaps I should get a T-shirt with the words *Cogito Ergo Sum Doleo* printed on it. I wonder if Descartes ever felt that way?

Finding myself pulled between wanting to find an effective excuse to walk away from it all and not wanting to sully my British heritage, I decided that the best course of action would be to pick up the gauntlet – even if it was a very heavy one. And so it came to be that I embarked upon what was probably going to be the most asinine venture I had ever undertaken. Apart from the Alcatraz swim, that is: and probably one or two others that have presently slipped my memory.

With the aid of the internet, I started to do some research. From examining the relevant photographs, the slopes looked gentle enough (although I was later to discover that between 15 and 30 people die on it each year – more than on Everest!), and the various companies running trips to it described the climb as being a Grade 2A; which, bearing in mind that the grades go up to something like 6E, didn't strike me as being too far outside my capabilities. Needless to say, I was later to write my own classification table.

To return to the 'various companies'; what I actually meant was the one company that was still running trips there. It appeared that the Foreign Office advice was to stay well clear of the area because of the threat from the likes of Chechen extremists. Now, am I the sort of person who heeds advice from the Foreign Office; or any other government department for that matter? Especially given my understanding of their track records? Hardly!

The region is pretty close to the border with Georgia; and if the size and physical inclinations of the forwards in the Georgian rugby team is anything to go by, I rather doubt I would be able to offer much in the way of resistance should some of their number wish to cause any added inconvenience on the predicted four hour journey from the Mineralnye Vodi airport to the hotel in the Upper Baksan Valley.

Book the trip I did; and at 9.00 a.m. on a Saturday in June I entered Terminal 1 at Heathrow airport. At this point I must hark back to something I mentioned a while ago about my attitude to suitcases on wheels and the way that I thought such things were for those whose hobbies might well have included basket-weaving and train-spotting. Well, guess what? After trying to carry my case with all the climbing gear required for a two-week trip, I decided that wheels might be a good thing.

I did, however, draw some solace from the fact that my case hadn't entered the realm of an extending handle. It was one of those kit-bag types that has a soft handle at one end, a shoulder strap and carry handles, and a pair of wheels that was designed to hide away within the material of the bag itself. A small distinction, it has to be said; but one that allowed me to hold my head a little higher than might otherwise, if you'll pardon the pun, have been the case.

Another facet of my persona which should not have escaped you is that I am not the greatest enthusiast of airports or their proffered mode of transport. They are hot, crowded places that delight in keeping you waiting in queues with people you would happily cross a busy road, blindfolded, at rush-hour to dodge. After that, they then insist that you – certainly for someone with my vertical dimension – spend several hours with your legs wedged into a space designed for nothing larger than a loaf of bread. Sometimes I think I should have been born in the era when ocean liners were the principal way of getting between continents: well, apart from the fact that I often succumb to a large helping of 'mal de mer'. On top of which, I'm not sure how well a ten day boat journey would have fitted into a two week annual holiday. Perhaps that's how the Cruise Industry got started.

Anyway, with all the necessary passport and security checks out of the way, I found my seat on the airplane. As I had forgotten to ask for an aisle or bulkhead seat – actually, I'm not sure if I had forgotten or just didn't bother as the check-in staff seldom appear to give a whatnot about the comfort of their passengers – I was on the apprehensive side of happy about my allocation: and my fears were well-founded.

"Hang on," I hear some of you saying. "Couldn't you have chosen your seat on-line?"

Yes, I suppose I could have: if my 'on-line' skills had been up to it; which they weren't, so I couldn't; and I didn't. The net result was that, once again, I had been given the middle of three seats and, because the row was immediately forward of one of the doors, the seat's ability to recline had been deactivated. The seat in front of mine, naturally, had received no such attention, and I am quite sure that its occupant was conducting some research into how far back he could make the thing go before it broke.

I ask you, how long is it going to take before the check-in staff are given instructions on how to allocate seats in accordance with the height of the passengers? Probably too long to be of any benefit in my lifetime, I expect. Mind you, I have read that some airlines are preventing their seats from leaning back – at least on short-haul flights – so maybe things are moving in the right direction. Apart from the weight variance, that is! The flight lasted about four hours, and the runway at Moscow airport didn't feel as smooth as the one at Heathrow; but very much smoother than the runway at the next airport on the agenda.

We, the group that is, didn't really meet up until we had negotiated Russian customs and made our separate ways to where a small coach was waiting to take us to our hotel. The drive in to Moscow took about fifty minutes, along a very straight, very crowded, four lane road; flanked by grey, twenty-storey blocks of flats.

It all brought back some memories of my last trip there – back in the mid 1960s – when my mother, my sister and I flew in from Delhi. As a youngster, I had marvelled at the size of the plane (a TU 114 as I recall) and the way that the pilot had to have two attempts at landing the thing. All good fun to me, but a situation that motivated a lot of spontaneous praying from the other passengers. It was also the weekend that a British spy – I think his name was Gerald Brooke – was arrested; and we were followed by men in trench-coats everywhere we went. There were armed guards all over the hotel, even in the lifts, and we couldn't so much as blink without receiving suspicious looks from them.

"Never mind your reminiscences; what about the group? Were they a band of intrepid adventurers?" you ask.

Well, it was rather hard to tell at first glance: or even after a second one. They seemed okay – even though one of them was a Canadian – but I decided to defer judgement until later. Always wise, don't you know. Although, I should add that as well as a Canadian, three of them were from Lancashire (hardly an auspicious start), three were from Essex (even less promising), and one was from Northampton.

Having cast those aspersions, I ought to add that I doubt if my accent, or demeanour, caused any of them to throw their hands up in the air and praise the Lord for His beneficence. Ah well, *nil desperandum*; after all, I wasn't there to make friends.

I expect a travel brochure would now start to enlighten you about the various treats that Moscow has to offer and the best ways of discovering them. Well, as time was not exactly in great supply, and it took ages for our reservations to be acknowledged by the hotel computing system, we only had enough time to go for a short stroll in order to find somewhere to eat and have a drink: which we duly did.

The eatery was about six hundred yards away and looked like the sort of establishment that is readily found in many parts of many cities. I ordered a plate of something that contained strips of meat and a pile of chips, and accompanied it with a bottle of local beer.

There was some football championship on the television at the time and, amidst quite a lot of drunken cheering (Russia happened to be playing that evening), I tucked in: I am pleased to say, the food wasn't that bad.

What was, however, was that soon after finishing my meal, a Russian fellow – who had quite obviously been at the Vodka – staggered over to our table and gave the impression that he would like to join us. Bearing in mind that the collective knowledge of the Russian language at our table amounted to Smirnoff, Nostrovia, Perestroika and Glasnost, we didn't think that we ought to encourage the man to sit down.

Furthermore, although it might have appeared as though he was offering us the chance to partake of what was left in the bottle he was clutching (which could have been aviation fuel for all we knew) it might well have finished up with us being asked to go back to his place and meet his sisters.

Whilst I am sure that there are some who would have leapt at that opportunity, those seated at our table were otherwise inclined. Guided by common sense, I credited them; and not because they simply didn't want to attract any opprobrium from their fellow diners.

Fortunately, before things might have become awkward, one of the football teams scored and the fellow rushed away to have a closer look at the television; and we were able to make a surreptitious, and probably judicious, withdrawal.

We made our way back to the hotel; and that was when a feature that was to repeat itself on many occasions first surfaced. Rather like those on my Alpine experience, the group walked very quickly: almost as if being the first to get back to the hotel was a competition. I, as you know, have a pace that suits me, and I like to stick to it.

Of course, if I happen to be on an athletics track and I hear a gun being fired close by, I shall make every effort to reach the finishing tape before the others: unless it happens to be more than 440 yards away. Anything over one lap of the track and I would quickly submit. Not by dint of lacking moral fibre; but more by reason of physique. I am simply the wrong shape and weight for middle or long-distance running. If the event involves a sprint, a jump or a throw, then I'm your man: if the event involves several laps of the track and a lot of sweating, then you will be best advised to seek representation from another quarter.

That competitive feature of the group was going to raise its ugly features several times before the flight back to the UK; and especially so on the slopes: and an absolute bloody nuisance it would prove to be, if truth be told. Well, certainly to me: or perhaps I was the 'bloody nuisance'. What, I ask, is the point of rushing to get to the next camp? If, like me, you take your time, then there is every likelihood that the tents will be up and tea will be waiting on the table by the time you arrive. I just cannot see what is to be gained by marching on ahead of all the equipment.

The rest of the evening passed without incident, and the next morning we returned to Moscow Airport and thence to Mineralnye Vodi (Mineral Waters). On the plane I sat next to a woman who spoke no English, but who was astute enough to recognise my discomfort when the fellow in front leaned his seat back; and she spoke to him (in Russian) and made him move forwards again. I was only able to express my gratitude by offering her an 'extra-strong' peppermint.

The rest of the flight could well have been described as 'interesting'. I got the impression that the fellow at the controls was an ex-MIG pilot who, since the official cessation of East/West hostilities, had to seek employment elsewhere. The landing, although very bumpy, was made without injury. The airport was small, the lounge like a bus stop, and there were hordes of taxi-drivers crowded around the door to the parking lot. We had been forewarned that we would be assailed by drivers plying for trade, and that their cars would be in a less-than-roadworthy state and nigh on assuredly without any form of insurance. We had not been warned that said drivers would have few teeth, display little evidence of personal hygiene, and make us feel as though we had just stumbled into a documentary about the Russian Mafia.

We were hurriedly shepherded to a pre-booked minivan and set off on the next phase of our journey. I'm not sure, but I think the vehicle ran on LPG: it was certainly something that smelled a bit gassy. Might have been fish. Can you stuff fish into a fuel-tank? Would you have to de-scale them first?

Was that the only blip on the trip we had to make through volatile territory? Of course not. Although we weren't inconvenienced by armed gangs, the chap behind the wheel of the van drove as though he was tired of his lot, and had recently discovered that suicide by hitting oncoming traffic was quite an effective way of heading off for the next life. I, naturally, begged to differ; and was on the verge of pointing that out to the fellow when I was told that such a *laisser-aller* style of driving was pretty much par for the course: and that, when compared to other drivers who might have been hired, the present incumbent was actually being rather careful. If that comment had been meant to assuage my anxieties it fell quite a distance short of its intended target. However.

Some three and a half hours later, and with a peculiar potato cake offering from the driver to interrupt the trip, we arrived at the Upper Baksan Valley and the hotel that was to be our base for the duration. My initial thoughts that the place looked better than expected were tempered somewhat when I noticed that certain sections of the building still had scaffolding in place; and that the scaffolding was wooden. Still, you can't criticise them for wanting to improve things.

But, I soon reminded myself, we hadn't gone there for the hotel: we had a loftier purpose in mind, and the next morning it all got under way.

The brochure, with the itinerary, I received had clearly stated that the first day was to have been a 'leisurely sightseeing day and would be taken at a very relaxed pace'. What they meant was that it would be a long, exhausting hike on a very dusty track before having to scramble up some steep, shale-strewn slopes to reach the snow.

I realise there are many people who wouldn't have minded the inaccuracy and would simply, and literally, have taken it in their stride: but for a fellow like me it came as a bit of a shock. To say that I was less than a bundle of delight when I got back to the hotel would be another fine example of the use of litotes. However, apart from making my feelings very clear to the guide, I kept them to myself: well, and the person with whom I was sharing a room; and possibly one or two of the others at the dining table that evening.

And that was where the next surprise was to make itself evident. When I get back from a day in the hills, having expended something in the region of 3000 to 4000 calories I expect – especially when I have paid handsomely for the privilege – to replace that calorie deficit with a comparable number of new ones. I do not expect to have a small plate with a small helping of pickled red cabbage plonked in front of me. Small wonder that I had seen so few of the locals with a happy look on their face.

I am hardly an expert on the calorific content of comestibles; but even I was aware that pickled red cabbage was not going to go far in achieving parity on the incoming versus outgoing calorie balance sheet.

I know there is a saying which mentions that when in Rome, one should do as the Romans do: but I am sure that there is also one which mentions that a licensed victualler should really do all he can to make sure his paying patrons are sufficiently provided with victuals. Maybe something is lost during the translation into Russian.

With the exception of one or two of the hardier types amongst us, I think I would speak for the others when I say that a plate of egg and chips would have gone down with far more approval than the range of local fare to which we were being subjected.

I also think that we might even have got more smiles out of the young girl who served us; who – even though she did have a touch of the old Hapsberg affliction about her – had a delightful smile on the rare occasions when she did so.

* * *

Day 3 saw us heading off to make camp at the foot of a peak called Andirchi (some 3800m high); and we were to take our sleeping bags and mats in our rucksacks, with a view to leaving them in a tent up there. The start of the climb was up a slope that looked and, more importantly, felt nearly vertical. As expected, I was soon left trailing behind everybody else as we progressed; and frequently lost sight of them all.

Camp – in the way of one tent, that is – was established and we left the aforementioned equipment inside it before, after a bite to eat and assurances that nobody was likely to make off with anything in the meantime, we made our way back down again. Some ways, of course, were 'made' a lot faster than mine was. I'm not sure what it is in my physiology that decides I shall not feel very comfortable about scrambling downhill over rocks, and inevitably give onlookers the impression there is something amiss in my proprioceptive centres. Probably something to do with my balance not being as good as it used to be: but whatever the reason, 'as sure-footed as a mountain goat' is not a phrase that is often used to describe me. By 'often', of course, I mean 'ever'.

So, having descended and been driven back to the hotel – in another van that used LPG as its fuel (and smelled as though it was full of it) – we enjoyed some more red cabbage, went out to a nearby eatery to have several plates of chips, and retired knowing that we had to climb back up to the camp site again the following day.

It was about this time that I started to query the sense of such an exercise when, for a few roubles, I could catch a cable-car up to the lower slopes of Elbrus and get some acclimatisation by walking to the café thing and having a cup of coffee and a sticky bun. The British guide said that doing so would probably mess up the insurance policy used by the tour company; and why should I be allowed to get out of spending two nights in a tent, on rocks, on a cold mountainside, along with the others? I, unsurprisingly, was immediately able to think of three very good reasons why I might be excused. But, in the *ad captandum* mode for which I am renowned, I capitulated and agreed to remain with the group: I couldn't tell if the British guide was pleased or not.

I did, however, play the infirmity card and pointed out that if the group wanted the rest of the tents erected before darkness set in, it might be advisable to let me carry some of the lighter things that needed to be taken up the mountain. The paper serviettes and a packet of biscuits, for instance. Nothing like keeping the group's spirits buoyant, I always say.

Several hours, and another struggle up the steep slopes later, the tents were duly erected: and with little help from me. Probably for the best, I thought, as I had absolutely no idea what to put where and, had I been asked to assist, we would probably have ended up with a structure able to do little more than collect rain water. But I did help to smooth out the designated spot for one of the tents; and I made sure that the serviettes and biscuits were put somewhere safe.

Then, as if to emphasise the wisdom of keeping me away from the tent erection process, once they were in place, the heavens opened and a rather cold precipitation began to fall. Have you ever tried to unpack a sleeping mat and sleeping bag inside a tent that was meant to sleep two people whilst three people were inside the tent doing the same thing? I can only suppose that whoever decided that a tent would be adequate for three people was probably under five feet tall and in need of several good meals. Honestly, I practically had to go back outside in order to turn round.

As for the comfort afforded by my sleeping mat… I am quite sure that it was perfectly capable of doing the job for which it had been designed, but the collection of small, and rather sharp, stones lurking beneath it did its utmost to ensure that I was able empathise with some of those mystic Indian fakirs. My sleeping bag, I was pleased to discover, lived up to its billing.

When the rain stopped, we had a supper of bread and noodle soup – into which the British guide had accidentally dropped the entire supply of pepper – and sat and watched as the early evening mist began to envelop us. Then, as if a higher power thought that wasn't spectacular enough, we were treated to a visit by a herd of inquisitive chamois and the rumbling sound of a nearby avalanche. Moments such as that seem to reach inside me and tweak my senses in a way that few others can. Life really does have some special occasions, doesn't it? I can vouch that five or six hours of slogging up a steep hill are heavily outweighed by even a few minutes of the best that Nature has to offer. Suitably tweaked, I settled down for the night.

Our mission for the next day was to climb the mountain that overlooked us – the aforementioned Andirchi (3800m) – as another part of the acclimatisation process. The brochure had stated that Andirchi was going to be an easy rock scramble, and I began to wonder if the brochure compiler had been anywhere near the place or was aware of a phenomenon known as 'weather'. Okay, it wasn't too hard; but it was completely covered in snow.

Actually, thinking back, perhaps being covered in snow made the climb a bit easier for me; as I'm not all that keen, or adept, on clambering over uneven rocks: especially, as I said, when going back down again. Maybe it had been a blessing in disguise. The previous year, apparently, there had been no snow; but for us the snow line had come down past the spot where we were camping.

Three and a half hours later I arrived at the summit. Everybody else had got there before me, probably having used half as much energy, and had started tucking into their respective lunches. I say 'lunches', but I really mean a cheese sandwich that looked as if it had been rejected by one of the British railway companies, and a selection of small bars of chocolate. I declined the sandwich, but I did try a few of the chocolate bars.

My reluctance to avail myself of all the provisions on offer was to have predictable consequences later in the week. But for goodness sake, how much wisdom/perception does it take to notice that all is not well with certain members of the team as regards their nutritional requirements? Admittedly, I probably have different tastes from most other people – especially those to be found going up the side of a mountain. But a simple, and polite, enquiry would have confirmed what should have been fairly obvious; and thus allowed the situation to be rectified in next to no time. Perhaps it was my fault for not being more vociferous about my needs.

While we were sitting at the top of Andirchi, and able to see the adjacent mountains, it was decided that, as the snow was unstable, we would give the nearby Krumrichi (4200m) a miss and replace it with an extra exercise on the lower slopes of Elbrus. It was also at the top that we got a pretty good view of Elbrus. Wow! I remember thinking. I also remember thinking 'I have to go up *that?*'

We then set off back down again, and about an hour later than the others, I got back to our camp. After another supper that fell woefully short of what I had wanted, we settled down for another night in the tent. My next memory began with being awoken, at 5 00 the next morning, by someone informing us that there was a spectacular 'inversion' to be seen outside.

Up to that point I had no idea what an 'inversion' was and, thinking that one of our number had misplaced a few of his marbles and decided to stand on his head, I reluctantly stumbled out of the tent to see what was happening. An 'inversion', it soon transpired, is short for 'cloud inversion', and it is when the clouds decide to assemble below you and fill up the valleys. Not the wispy, cotton-wool type of clouds you see wandering by in a lonely fashion, floating on high o'er vales and hills; but more as if they were a solid mass, like a duvet. With the early sun adding a touch of gold leaf to the mountains opposite, and a full moon lingering shyly above them, it was indeed a memorable sight. Made me reflect that Nature has an order to it, and it had certainly been well worth getting up at that hour to see.

After breakfast – and I use that term with no accuracy whatsoever – of something that was called porridge, but what I would have referred to as a handful of dried oats and desiccated apple shavings dropped into a bowl of tepid water, we packed up the tents and made our way back down the mountain.

I say 'we' packed up the tents, but of course I really mean the others; as I had been told to set off beforehand in order to keep the overall time to a minimum. That tactic got my vote on two counts. Firstly, I would have been of little or no use to the procedure of packing up; and secondly, it meant that I was excused from carrying anything heavier than that with which I was already struggling. Mind you, I still managed to get down to the bottom in last place.

We then had another gas-ridden ride back to the hotel, another meal of meagre merit, and another walk to forage for some much needed calories. After breakfast the next morning, we assembled for the main purpose of the trip – our climb up Mount Elbrus.

A check was carried out to make sure that we all had what we were likely to need, and then we made our way over to the cable-car station and, with a further trip on a very rickety and unstable chair-lift, we arrived at the 'Barrels'.

"The what?"

The Barrels (circa 3800m), also known as 'Bochky' or 'Karabashi', were sleeping compartments that consisted of, essentially, barrels. Not, obviously, the sort of things in which coopers might show a passing interest; but as in the back of a lorry used for transporting petrol, which had then been converted into accommodation.

Each 'barrel' was divided into three sections: one taking half of the structure and making a sleeping area for four beds; and the other half was split into a sleeping area for two more beds and an entrance area with a door from the outside.

I write 'beds', but I mean only insomuch as they weren't, say, baths or dining-room tables. Each was just about long enough to accommodate me, and roughly three feet across. There was also a selection of blankets and something else that might, at one time, have been a pillow: but you would have been ill-advised to come into direct contact with any of them.

Still, as the ever-tolerant Phalarope persona was swift to point out, it was going to be a jolly sight more comfortable than the floor of a tent; and that an absence of stones beneath me had to be a step in the right direction.

My companions in the section were three others from our group – the fellow from Northampton, the Canadian, and the British guide.

Have I mentioned that the guide had taken a bit of a dislike to me? For some reason or another, the chap seemed hell-bent on making my visit as unpleasant as possible. Thinking back to the animus displayed by the Alpine guide, I began to wonder if it was perhaps a trait that comes about from spending time at altitude: I mean to say, it couldn't possibly be as a result of being confronted with such as me. Could it?

I know I have that sign on my back which reads 'Please Annoy', and I am also aware of the consummate ease with which I can sometimes appear aloof to others; but all the same. Do people in their mid-twenties not understand that people twice their age have a tendency to know more and to do things in a different way and at a different pace?

One of the examples was soon shown when we set off for that morning's exercise, and came about because of the manner in which I went up the slopes in the snow. The British guide walked with one foot in front of the other – and I mean directly in front of the other – as if he were walking along a four-inch beam. As a rule, I prefer to walk with my feet as if they were on two separate beams – one alongside the other: and I preferred to walk with slightly shorter strides than the guide did. Those of you who have trudged up a snowy incline in someone else's footsteps will know that trying to match their stride pattern can be more tiring than using your own.

Fair enough if the footsteps have been formed in ice and can act as steps; but not so fair enough if the snow is soft. Rather like runners on a track each having their own cadence: different stride lengths and different stride frequencies. Fairly obvious, I would have thought. The British guide, however, said that I should use his footsteps; and a small contretemps was in the making.

Anyway, I ignored him and stuck to my own pattern; and we carried on up to the Pruitt 11 hut (4200m). There we had a bit of a rest and something to eat, and then came back down again; and spent that night in the Barrels.

The next morning didn't get off to a great start as the British guide slept through his alarm and castigated me for not waking him. I decided that calling him an impudent oaf might not improve the day, so I put my vitriol back in the cupboard. After a reasonable breakfast, we made our way back up to the Pruitt 11 hut and waited for a snow-cat to bring our sleeping bags and rucksacks.

We had a short rest, and then went on up to the Pastukhov rocks (around 4800m). These, by the way, were named after a Russian army topographer who, because his body wouldn't acclimatise, only managed to go that high. I had hoped, that as we went higher, the desire within our group to compete would wane somewhat; but not a bit of it: they all went as fast as they could. To this day I still haven't been able to work out what made them rush as they did. Mind you, I am sure that there are some who will want to point out that perhaps their seeming haste was nothing more than a manifestation of the disparity in our relative speeds of ascent.

Whatever the explanation, I, unsurprisingly, lagged behind the others and struggled to get up there: and when I did, it was very windy and gave me an indication of just how cold it was likely to be even higher up. Freezing!

One of the group, by virtue of suffering an awful headache, had started showing signs of altitude problems – thought to be early cerebral oedema – and was quite rightly advised to give the following day's summit attempt a miss. Rather a shame actually; especially as he was one of the nicer members of the group. I did find myself wondering if the problem might have arisen because, as he was also one of the fitter members, he had gone too high too quickly. Maybe my slowness had an advantage to it; maybe I should have pretended that I was doing it on purpose. I somehow doubted that the others would have been convinced: especially when they could see the effort that I was making to 'deliberately' go slowly!

Speaking of high altitude oedema, why do they call it HAPE and HACE? Surely, if you are sticking to the correct spelling, it should be HAPO and HACO. Maybe they chose the first pair because the second pair probably sounds like the Marx brothers who didn't make the cut. Whilst I'm on the subject of the Marx brothers, did you know that Zeppo Marx helped design the clamps that held the bomb that the Enola Gay dropped on Hiroshima?

The meal that evening managed to have a touch of the 'Last Supper' about it. Given the way that I was feeling, I would probably have betrayed some of them for thirty pieces of silver. Actually, I think I would have done it for half that.

Sleep didn't come easily that night; which was a pity, as we were woken early for a 3.00am breakfast. Then, after a final equipment check, we climbed on to a snow-cat for a lift of about 200m in altitude. May I say that the lift was most welcome? "It was most welcome." It probably cut out a good hour's trudge up the slope, and, as if to make the undertaking more exciting, we were accompanied by an electrical storm in the near distance.

There was a lot of sheet lightning over the mountains, and it made for the most spectacular backdrop accompaniment as we disembarked and began moving on foot. A few of the others had said that using the snow-cat was cheating and that we should really have walked all the way. I pointed out that we had already used a cable-car and a chair lift to get to the Barrels.

"Oh yeah," had been the response. Perhaps it was the early hour that had dulled their senses. Perhaps.

We climbed… and climbed… and then climbed some more. I should like to eloquently describe the surrounding views, and the sense of awe and isolation that flooded my being as we made our way up the mountain; but it was dark and I had withdrawn into that same being.

"Eh?" I hear you say. "What are you talking about?"

Trudging along in a dark, windy, and cold environment makes your mind play games with itself. Well, it was certainly having that effect on me. At any one moment, while one third of my brain was checking to see where I was and where I was heading; another third was imagining that I was on a beach, beating out a slow rhythm on a drum that exactly matched my footsteps and my breathing. The remaining third felt as though it was scouring my essence and discovering new areas that I never knew existed. It seems that the human mind is a lot bigger than you imagine. Does that make any sense?

Then, its approach hitherto unnoticed, the dawn arrived, and we all stopped for a swig of whatever liquid we were carrying: and, as my hands were beginning to feel a bit cold, I put on a pair of liners to go with my mittens. We now saw that we had reached what was known as the 'Traverse'.

I had been expecting a fairly level section which would have afforded me the opportunity to let my energy reserves assemble themselves in readiness for the 'Saddle' and then the final steep slopes. Was it fairly level? I certainly didn't think so; but perhaps it was when compared to some of the slopes we had completed up to that point. However, even a five degree slope at 5000 metres is a bit of a slog: and on we slogged.

The others, as usual, soon began to leave me behind; and I found myself gasping for air, almost as if I were trying to suck it in through a drinking-straw. On I went, slowly, looking from side to side in case there were any complimentary packets of sympathy waiting for me: you know, to be handed out rather in the way that water bottles are dispensed when running a marathon. Needless to say, there weren't any; or none that I noticed. Trudge, trudge, and trudge I went, for what felt like several hours – but was probably less than two – before reaching the 'Sedlowina Saddle'.

The others had been there for about ten minutes, had enjoyed a welcome rest and some refreshments, and were just about to push off for the final ascent. I looked up to see where they were headed, and felt a bit dismayed. If I had thought that the route thus far had been hard, it all quickly paled into insignificance. Yes, I know that those of you who have conquered the likes of Muztag Ata and Cho Oyu will be thinking 'What a wuss', and other such besmirching opinions. But come on, I'm not George Mallory and I didn't have unlimited energy or antifreeze coursing through my veins.

Anyway, in next to no time – or certainly not enough time to feel that I had properly rested – the remaining three of us (a chap called John, the guide and me) left our rucksacks at the 'Saddle' and began going up the steep, final 350 vertical metres of ascent.

One of the features of going up slopes at altitude I have noticed is that I like to choose a suitable rhythm and then stick to it. My steps synchronise with my breathing, and the procedure becomes, if not actually a subconscious one, then certainly one where my innate bodily mechanisms take control. What I have also noticed is that if someone or something breaks up that rhythm, the process becomes a lot harder. Even stopping to have a drink upsets the pattern: which is obvious, I suppose, as you can't breathe and drink at the same time.

Anyway, the rhythm was constantly being broken by the British guide who kept stopping to talk to climbers who were on their way down, and asking them how it was up at the summit. Not in the least bit helpful, I have to say; and I began to wonder if he didn't want me to get to the top.

We eventually reached the end of the steep part, had to pause while John threw up a lot of brown-coloured liquid, before turning to our left and heading for the summit. Whilst I can say that I wasn't feeling ill, I would be lying if I claimed to have been in the rudest of rude; and I have a feeling that my ability to keep moving owed more to bloody-mindedness than fitness and strength.

We, mainly me that is, struggled on and finally reached the summit: and what a strange collection of feelings that evoked. All the things I had planned on doing – such as taking lots of photographs and reciting from Shakespeare's Henry V – slipped my mind. I had read about how altitude does funny things to one's ordered reasoning; and guess what? It's true!

Whether that is because sentiments such as elation and exhaustion are competing for attention, I shall never know: but imagine being drunk and extremely tired whilst taking, and passing, your finals. You want to celebrate; but you're not sure if you might throw up and fall over at the same time. Fortunately, my list reappeared and, whilst reciting that bit about 'we few, we happy few, we band of brothers', I managed to pictorially record the event. I also remembered asking myself about what possible joy was there to be derived from such as hacking your way up an ice wall: well, at that moment, I began to get some idea.

I had thought that standing on an Alpine peak was a Damascene moment, but that feeling was tiny compared to what I felt at the top of Elbrus. It was so much higher than anything else around that the height felt exaggerated, and absolutely stunning. The horizon, in every direction, looked about a hundred miles away: which it probably was! Well, apart from the Eastern Elbrus peak, that is. I could see people still making their way up, bent over, and struggling for breath. But there was no sense of gloating on my part as I had felt the same – probably a lot worse actually – not long before.

I then had the hymn 'Nearer my God to Thee' playing through my mind. I realise that the reason could have simply been a matter of propinquity, but I didn't think that was the case. I'm sure that if I had been of a musical bent I would have started composing a hymn of my own. Something moving and tuneful; and one that a congregation would want to belt out with gusto.

Handel's Messiah also made a brief appearance; closely followed by Mario Lanza singing Panis Angelicus. I was later to speculate about what sort of auditory offering some of the other major religions would have provided; and I couldn't think of anything I would have enjoyed listening to. I guess that those who are of a Christian persuasion have a lot for which to be thankful.

The British guide, being unnecessarily churlish, didn't want to let me stay up there for long. I said that five more minutes wouldn't make any difference; then, as if to prove my point, I did take another five minutes: and it didn't make any difference.

After a final, and awe-filled, look around, we headed back down again; wary that more accidents happen when descending mountains than ascending them. And, as if anxious to prove it, about two-thirds of the way back, I began to feel rather weak. Actually, I felt *very* weak: I had little or no energy whatsoever.

I had to keep stopping every two hundred yards or so to let my mitochondria recharge: or whatever it is they do. Rather in the same way that if you leave a struggling car battery for a couple of minutes it seems to reinvigorate itself. Something to do with converting ADP to ATP and back again: or is it the other way round? The mitochondria, that is; rather than the car battery. I believe that glucose has to be converted into something called Pyruvate which enters the mitochondria and is converted into Acetyl something which takes part in a process known as Kreb's cycle. All very complicated, and all way above my levels of comprehension.

But the bottom line is that glucose is needed; and glucose was something that I was quite obviously lacking. The lesson learned, I suppose, was that any future excursion of that nature was going to have to be accompanied by a rucksack full of carbohydrates; and, preferably, carried by someone else.

Actually, the lesson learned might have been that I should never again allow myself to be cajoled into doing anything similar.

Anyway, a very kind Russian fellow – by the name of Anatoly – appeared and gave me some tea to drink. At least I think it was tea; but I wasn't really sure: it seemed to have a lot of bits in it and tasted quite fruity. He also asked if I would like to listen to his MP3 player while we continued on down. I stuck one of the ear-phones in, but the noise I heard did little to energise me. Some sort of heavy-metal band; and not the sort of thing I had in mind, I must say. I did, however, later get Anatoly's address and, by way of a firm on the internet who translated an accompanying letter for me, send him a CD of La Boheme.

With mist enveloping us, we eventually made it back to the Pruitt 11 hut, where I was met with a warm handshake from our local guide, Eugene, who seemed very relieved to see me. Probably not half as relieved as I was to see him, though. I was also very pleased to see a seat where I could take the weight off my feet and let my worn out mitochondria reinvigorate themselves at their leisure.

That evening was spent having yet another meal that fell short of wonderful. I know that we were quite a way from the nearest supermarket, and I know that people with epicurean talents seldom apply for employment in mountain huts; but I did think that they might have got in a supply of powdered mash potato and/or spaghetti. Boiling water was all that would have been needed to make a meal with more calories than a bowl of soup and a few slices of cheese.

That night, I had been expecting to enjoy a good sleep, but I didn't. No, not because my mind was wracked with reliving the previous day's labours; but because I was getting quite a lot of discomfort in my right eye. I initially put it down to a foreign body, and tried flushing the eye with saline solution every hour or so; but without any real improvement.

The next morning, after breakfast, we made our way back down to the Barrels. To say that the day had dawned cold and icy would be putting it mildly; and all the others, British guide included, shot off before I had even got my crampons on. Then, as if to add insult to injury, because by now I had removed one of my contact lenses, I was having to make my way down the slopes using just one focusing eye. I was also being reminded that with only one effective eye you do lose rather a lot of your sense of perspective; and all the snow and mist made for a rather slow, and timid, descent.

I eventually got back to the Barrels and found the British guide waiting for me at the start of the path that led down to the cable-car. Pity, I thought; as it had been my intention to take the chair-lift. I said as much and, after a poorly disguised scowl from the guide, I was allowed to do so.

I had wanted to enjoy the views on the ride, but for some reason (exhaustion and the fact that I could hardly keep my eyes open I shouldn't wonder) it took all my resolve not to fall asleep on the chair-lift as it descended. And believe you me, taking into account the height above the ground and the very flimsy safety rail, falling asleep would not have been a sensible option: especially when the chair arrived at the bottom. I imagine that the guide – who had scampered down on foot in the meantime (using my poles I might add) – would have been less than pleased (possibly not surprised though) had I remained in the chair and gone all the way back up again.

I was later to reason that, because my goggles had only been category 2, I was suffering from a mild form of snow-blindness. I explained my condition to the British guide later that day and I was invited to pick something from the box of medical supplies. Very helpful, I thought at the time; especially as I could hardly see and was sure that the brochure had mentioned that the guide would have had some sort of medical training.

The next morning, after a breakfast that I wasn't given enough time to start – never mind finish – we took a van back to the airport and then flew to Moscow.

That afternoon, after we had checked into our respective rooms, the group decided on a short tour of Moscow. Have you ever travelled around Moscow whilst hardly able to keep your eyes open? If not, then you will have to take my word that it is not very easy, or particularly worthwhile: especially when your group appears to want to do it in as short a time as possible. The competitive aspect, so it seemed, was still alive and well.

The underground system was something to behold – speaking, of course, as someone who spends as little time as he can possibly manage using public transport. I really do sympathise with all those, regardless of which country they live in, who have to use it to get to and from their daily grind. The thought of squashing up against all manner of people in a container that would have animal rights activists railing, in order to spend eight or more hours doing something that you didn't like with people you couldn't stand, for less remuneration than a premiership footballer gets paid in five minutes makes me feel quite nauseous.

And then a thought crossed my mind. Yes, I know, that probably didn't take very long – but anyway. Why do people bemoan the fact that a premiership footballer can command £70,000 to £150,000 or more a week, and then keep paying between £40 and £150 to go and watch a match? As well as buying all the associated strips and other paraphernalia. Am I alone in wondering what would happen if everybody refused to pay more than between £10 and £30 for a ticket? How long would the clubs hold out? How long would it take before the price of tickets fell to a level that made sense and the players got paid what they're really worth? What could a person do with the extra £1000 or so they would have in their pocket? Would it help the economy in general? Ah well.

Anyway, musings aside for the moment, Moscow was splendid. Well, at least the bits that I managed to see. Although, I suppose, it was pretty much like most other capital cities. I did, however, get the chance to show off my, albeit limited, knowledge of former USSR presidents – there were three men sitting on chairs at one end of the Red Square whom I recognised as resembling Brezhnev, Lenin and Khrushchev. Unfortunately, it also meant I got the chance to show off the fact that I was old enough to have recognised them.

On the flight back to the UK, I sat next to an attractive woman who was flying to Heathrow to meet her fiancée. It transpired that she was trading her life in Russia for one in Surbiton. Not sure I would have made that swap, but there we are. Mind you, I didn't know exactly what she was leaving behind. It might have been something that made Surbiton and, presumably, if I may indulge in a spot of type-casting, the likely sort of chap who orders a bride off the internet, seem like a step upwards. In her defence, I should add that she didn't seem entirely thrilled at the prospect. Life, eh!

It was nice to land back in the UK, and going through customs didn't present any problems – apart from the fact that, thanks to my facial hair and loss of weight, I didn't look much like my passport photograph: but I have to say that I was a bit disappointed with the greeting committee: or lack of it! I suppose that I must have been expecting a band to welcome me back, and scores of people saying "Well done". But there was nothing. Nobody, obviously, was aware of what we had managed; nor, I suspect, would have cared very much had they known.

I'd like to think that I would have raised a hand to acknowledge another's accomplishments if I was aware of same; and there, I suppose, is the rub. How do you know what others have been doing? I imagine that every year there must be thousands of people whose endeavours would merit a good deal more approbation than mine who pass through Heathrow unrecognised. So hats off to them, one and all; whoever they are.

Still, there might be one person who was going to be impressed: possibly, anyway; unless she had since discovered that Elbrus had been pushed into second place because of some recent boundary or tectonic plate changes. When that thought came sauntering into my centres of reasoning I could feel sweat coming through the skin of my back as if I were being squeezed like a wet sponge. The drive back to Dilettante Cottage was made with my concentration oscillating between the M4 and the prospect of having to take on another peak. They wouldn't have altered anything while I was away, would they?

Twenty years ago I wouldn't have harboured such a thought: but these days, with the meddlesome Eurocrats and their duplicitous antics, I can never be sure of what might happen when my back is turned. However, I made it safely to my abode; and there, inexplicably, was my niece.

"Uncle William, I am so proud of you," she said, running over, throwing her arms around me and giving me a hug.

"Steady on," I replied; even though I did feel my chest puffing out slightly. True, climbing Elbrus wasn't the same as climbing Everest; but I suppose it entitled me to a dash of crowing. "That's very kind of you to say so."

"What you did was seriously cool – pun intended – and I've told all my friends about it. You're quite the star of my social network."

"Am I?"

"The best ever."

"Oh!"

"A real inspiration."

"Goodness!"

"In fact, I'd quite like to do something similar myself."

"You haven't told your mother, have you?"

"Not yet, no."

Two emotions suddenly coursed through my system. Relief, as that meant I was spared the inevitable haranguing; and concern, as it also meant that I was likely to be seeing more of the little termagant: and then a mystery manifested itself before me.

"Just a wee question, if I may."

"Yes."

"Not because I'm not delighted to see you again… But, um, how come you are hereabouts?"

"Mum said that as we had had so much fun the last time I came to stay, she would be more than happy to let me welcome you back… and stay for a day or two to help with your unpacking… and recovery."

A few months ago I would have set a new world record for looking askance, and made an acerbic comment at the same time; but, for some reason, I very nearly smiled.

"I'll just bet she did," was my reply; the tone being ironically facetious: if there is such a description. If there isn't, I'm sure the astute amongst you will know what I mean. "And where is she presently?" I hesitantly enquired, wary of the several possibilities.

"Oh don't worry; she's nowhere near here… or ill."

"Good. That is regarding the 'ill' part, you understand."

"I understand exactly what you meant."

I then began to wonder if mind-reading was an inherited capacity.

"Will she be…?"

"Turning up? In two days. She's staying with some friends in Pembrokeshire at the moment."

"Oh. That's nice. I expect."

* * *

Anyhow, despite the alterations that I would have made to the overall running of the trip, I managed to survive; and was very pleased that I got to the top of Elbrus, and extremely pleased to have got back down again: in one piece. My eye behaved a bit strangely for a couple of weeks; and, once the discomfort disappeared, I noticed something a bit odd – my eyesight, for the next fortnight, was much improved. Once the cornea healed, however, it went back to normal. Some sort of 'natural' laser treatment, I suppose.

The only lasting drawback of the trip, if you can call it so, is that I think I'm now feeling the urge to climb again: only higher. Life's a funny old business, isn't it?